「劉毅董事長英語班」歡迎您！

I. **特別歡迎：** 總裁、董事長、校長、系主任、教授、英文專業老師等，社會賢達菁英。

II. **上課時間：** 每週六上午10:00～12:00
由劉毅老師親自主持，八週一期，循環上課。

III. **收費標準：** 每八週一期，收費8,000元新台幣，八週全勤，頒發全勤獎金2,000元。表現良好，可升為顧問，黃榮松博士已成為本班顧問，不僅免費上課，還賺到獎金11萬元，朝著年薪千萬前進。王宣雯同學升為班長，去年一年已經賺到1,000萬元以上。

IV. **供應美食：** 每次上完課後，提供每位同學1,500元餐費，享用私廚吳昌林董事長精美食，一般市面上吃不一面交流，能結交志同

U0085009

V. 上課目標1：

讓每個董事長都能中英雙語，出口成章。每次會餐時可以自由發言，比賽看看哪一位能中英雙語，句句金句，說得最好。例如，你能說出下面九句，就能成為比賽的冠軍了！

Life is beautiful. 人生很美。
Life is sweet. 人生很甜。
Life is precious. 人生珍貴。

Life is a blessing. 活著幸福。
Health is a blessing. 健康幸福。
Count your blessings. 感恩所有。

Live happy. 活得開心。
Die happy. 死得安樂。
Live your life with no regrets. 生而無憾。

在「劉毅董事長英語班」，我們不僅學說「完美英語」，也學說優美的中文。Knowledge is power.（知識就是力量。）人人羨慕，無往不利。同時也潛移默化，使自己身、心、靈提升，一石多鳥。英文好，中文棒，身體健康，事業成功。

VI. 上課目標2：

團結就是力量。（Union is strength.）劉毅老師親自領軍，協助你創業成功。吳昌林同學，在本班樓下開Turn Right餐廳，同學們捧場，已經成功。每一位董事長都是領導者，背後有一群人，認識一位，就等於認識百位以上。我們現在推出「完美英語神杯」，有一千組，每個成本100元新台幣，同學可以賣到500元。任何產品只要沒有中間剝削和差價，有好的人脈，人人可以致富。

Make it big. 飛黃騰達。
Hit it big. 一炮而紅。
Make big bucks. 要發大財。

完美英語神杯

我們分享的是正能量，不僅是在賺錢，還能協助別人。我們的產品，有靈氣、有靈魂，會自動傳播。**把握這個寶貴的機會，和劉毅老師一起傳播正能量，中英雙語，句句金句，人生非常精彩。**

> *Make a move.* 採取行動。
> *Make history.* 創造歷史。
> *Make life amazing.* 精彩人生。

　　劉毅老師上課50多年，一生最大的願望，就是讓大家喜歡說英文。說「完美英語」是最好的方法。

Ⅶ. 上課地點： 台北市許昌街17號6樓（壽德大樓，捷運台北車站M8出口1分鐘）Tel：(02)2389-5212

創新就是世界第一

在比賽中，想要世界第一幾乎不可能。但是，發明、創新，就是第一。我發明的「完美英語」，我自己喜歡說，更喜歡教，像是變魔術一樣。

Make magic. 製作魔法。
Make magic happen. 魔法成真。
Make dreams happen. 夢想成真。

我提倡「使用」中英雙語，句句金句，一旦說成習慣，天天進步，人生變得更美。

Just do it. 做就對了。
Go for it. 拼命去做。
Make it happen. 立刻去做。

但是，發明新東西往往不被人接受。美國人常常說下面三句話，勸人不要害怕失敗，甚至要擁抱失敗。

Fail fast. 快點失敗。
Fail often. 失敗連連。
Fail forward. 百折不撓。

失敗愈早（Fail early.），失敗愈快，失敗愈多，愈快成功，失敗等於前進。Don't worry about failure. Worry about missed chances. 別擔心失敗，要擔心沒有把握機會。大家有沒有注意到，我失敗了無數次，但是，我依舊充滿夢想！

Keep hoping. 保持希望。
Look forward. 展望未來。
Expect good. 期待美好。

這三句話，英文美，中文更美！　　　　**完美英語神杯**

「英文二字經」的重要

　　我學英文學了五十多年，現在還在學，發現一個祕訣，就是「英文不要學，要使用。」今天又發現一個祕訣，那就是要使用「英文二字經」。兩個字一句話，任何人都會，改變全世界人類學英文的方法，就兩個字就好了，何必講那麼多個字，句子太複雜、太長，大家都不會講，兩個字改變一切。例如：中國人說：「做好人，做好事，說好話。」這個成功的祕訣，外國人也有：

> *Be good*.（做好人。）
> *Do good*.（做好事。）
> *Say good*.（說好話。）

又引申為外國人常說的三句話：

> Do good.（做好事。）
> Do right.（做對事。）
> Do well.（做得好。）

這三句話可加長為：

> Keep doing good.（持續做好事。）
> Keep doing right.（持續做對事。）
> Keep doing well.（持續做得好。）

所以不要學文法，只要背短句就好了。

> *Do it*.（去做吧。）→ Just do it.（做就對了。）
> Do it now.（現在就做。）
> *Do enough*.（做得夠。）→ Do what is necessary.
> （做必須做的事。）
> *Do more*.（做更多。）→ Do more than expected.
> （做得比預期的多。）

英文句子越短越好，以兩個字為核心，再衍生成其他的句子。如：*Do good*.（做好事；做得好。）可說成：Do good things.（做好事。）*Do right*.（做對事。）可說成：Do the right things.（要做對的事。）*Do great*.（做得好。）也可說成：Keep doing great.（要持續表現良好。）Do a great job.（要做得很好。）

　　全世界的人學英文都學錯了，大家都沒有學好英文，就是因為沒有使用英文，沒有使用正確的英文，正確的英文，是從「兩個字」開始，不要講七、八個字，句子分析了半天，沒有人會。為什麼寫文章容易錯？因為方法錯了，不應該背單字，應該要背句子，一個句子可能會錯，三個句子絕對不會錯。

　　為什麼我寫英文和說英文都那麼有信心？因為我知道我說的和寫的每句話都是正確的，而且又短，聽起來很震撼人心。例如：

　　　　Do wonderfully.（要做得棒。）
　　　　Keep doing wonderfully.（要持續做得很棒。）
　　　　Do a wonderful job.（要做得很棒。）

　　　　Do magnificently.（要做得讚。）
　　　　Keep doing magnificently.（要持續做得讚。）
　　　　Do a magnificent job.（要做得讚。）

結論就是，第一，學英文一定要使用。第二，要先從學兩個字一句話開始。兩個字連小孩都學得會，而且我們要先學每天都可以用得到的句子。要在哪裡使用？網路上就可以用。所以這個方法就是，先學「英文二字經」，這兩個字一句話絕對不會錯，就可以了。

　　去掉文法，不要想文法，只想句子。我研究文法，研究了一輩子，浪費時間。我學英文 50 多年，教英文 50 多年，我現在告訴你，我的方法就是「背短句」，短句的最高境界，就是兩個字一句話，簡單易學。我們走捷徑，學「英文二字經」，海闊天空。

怎麼會想出「英文二字經」？

　　我教了 50 多年的書，每天都在收集「金句」，爲了在課業上激勵人心。有一次，跟美籍老師 Edward McGuire 聊了一整天，到最後，他說：

> ***Money comes.*** 錢會賺到。
> ***Money goes.*** 錢會花掉。
> ***But friendship is always there.***
> 但友誼長存。

我馬上給他 1,000 元台幣鼓勵。這三句話讓我高興了一整天，因爲是最佳的教材。一般口說的「金句」，書本上找不到。學英文，要先從學說「金句」開始。

　　一般心靈雞湯的中外書籍，往往是一大篇文章中，才一兩句金句，而且句子又臭又長。我們改成簡單易懂，最簡單的是「一個字一句話」，所以我們出版了「英文一字經」，以「高中常用 7000 字」爲藍本，學生背完之後，單字增加又會說英文。

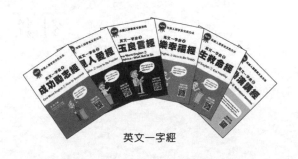

英文一字經

我們接著出版「英文三字經」，三個字一句話，這本書讓老師教得快樂，因為能夠教學相長，身心靈同時提升。老師熱情教書，學生自然上課有精神，因為大家在「使用」英文，看了有感覺，說了有感覺，就是在「使用」。英文唯有「使用」，才記得牢。

英文三字經

我們收集了全世界所有「兩個字」的心靈雞湯，更容易學，說出來更簡潔有力。例如：

> *Never stop*.　永不停止。
> *Never quit*.　永不放棄。
> *Never surrender*.　　永不投降。

你背 stop, quit, surrender 還不如背這三句話，可以脫口而出，能鼓勵別人，又能激勵自己。言以簡潔為貴，只說一句，不夠熱情，一次說三句，能讓別人更明白你的意思。

劉毅

CONTENTS · 目 錄

📖 BOOK 1

目錄

BOOK 2

目
錄

目錄

BOOK 3

目錄

目
錄

📖 BOOK 5

目錄

● PART 3 ⇨ Short Phrases for a Good Life

BOOK 1 / PART 1

Keys to a Good Life
美好人生的祕訣

PART 1・Unit 1~9
英文錄音QR碼

UNIT 1

Dreams 夢想

Dream big.
夢想要大。

Dream bigger.
夢要很大。

Dream beautifully.
夢要很美。

** dream〔drim〕*n.* 夢；夢想　*v.* 做夢；夢想
　　big〔bɪg〕*adv.* 大量地；大大地；懷著雄心
　　dream big 有遠大的夢想
　　beautifully〔ˈbjutəfəlɪ〕*adv.* 美麗地；
　　　　出色地；完美地

Chase dreams.

追求夢想。

Chase passions.

追求愛好。

Chase happiness.

追求幸福。

** chase〔tʃes〕*v.* 追逐；追求

　　dream〔drim〕*n.* 夢；夢想

　　passion〔'pæʃən〕*n.* 熱情；愛好

　　happiness〔'hæpɪnɪs〕*n.* 快樂；幸福

Aim higher.

目標更高。

Aspire higher.

渴望更高。

Shoot higher.

志向更高。

** aim〔em〕v. 瞄準

high〔haɪ〕 adj. 高的　adv. 高；向高處

aim high 向高處瞄準，引申為「胸懷
　大志；志向遠大」。

aspire〔ə'spaɪr〕v. 渴望；嚮往；胸懷大志

shoot〔ʃut〕v. 射擊

shoot higher 目標更遠大

【Unit 1 背景説明】

Dream big.　要有遠大的夢想。(= *Dream big dreams*. = *Have big dreams*.) 也可説成：
Have big ambitions. (要有雄心壯志。)
When dreaming, don't hold back. (當你在夢想時，不要有所保留。)

Dream bigger.　要有更遠大的夢想。(= *Dream bigger dreams*.) 也可説成：Be more ambitious. (要更有抱負。)

Dream beautifully.　要有美麗的夢想。
(= *Dream beautiful dreams*. = *Have beautiful dreams*.) 也可説成：Be courageous when you think about your future. (當你考慮未來時，要勇敢。)

Chase dreams. (追求夢想。) 也可説成：
Chase your dreams. (追求你的夢想。)
(= *Pursue your dreams*.) Pursue what you want. (要追求你想要的。)

Chase passions. (追求愛好。) 也可説成：
Chase your passions. (追求你的愛好。)
Pursue the things you are passionate about.
(追求你熱愛的東西。)

BOOK 1・PART 1

Chase happiness. 追求快樂。(= *Pursue happiness.*) 也可說成：Chase the happiness you want. (追求你想要的快樂。) Do what you need to do to be happy. (做能使你快樂必須做的事。)

Aim higher. (要有更遠大的志向。) 也可說成：Aim higher than before. (要有比以前更遠大的志向。) Aim for more. (要渴望得到更多。)

Aspire higher. (要渴望更高。) 也可說成：Aspire to more. (要渴望得到更多。) Aspire to higher goals. (要渴望達成更高的目標。)

Shoot higher. 向更高的地方射擊，引申為「目標更遠大。」也可說成：Shoot higher than before. (要比以前目標更遠大。) Shoot for more. (要想得到更多。) Set your sights high. (目標要訂得高。)

UNIT 2

Living Well 過得好

Live fully.

過得充實。

Live passionately.

熱愛生活。

Live wholeheartedly.

全心生活。

** live〔lɪv〕*v.* 生活；活著；過…的生活
fully〔ˈfulɪ〕*adv.* 充分地
passionately〔ˈpæʃənɪtlɪ〕*adv.* 熱情地
wholeheartedly〔ˈholˈhɑrtɪdlɪ〕*adv.* 全心
全意地；真摯地

Live gracefully.
優雅生活。

Live gratefully.
感激生活。

Live generously.
大方生活。

** live〔lɪv〕*v.* 生活;活著;過…的生活
gracefully〔'gresfəlɪ〕*adv.* 優雅地
gratefully〔'gretfəlɪ〕*adv.* 感激地
generously〔'dʒɛnərəslɪ〕*adv.* 慷慨地;
　　大方地

Embrace life.

擁抱生活。

Cherish life.

珍惜生命。

Celebrate life.

慶祝生命。

** embrace〔ɪmˋbres〕v. 擁抱；欣然
    接受；利用

    life〔laɪf〕n. 生活；人生；生命

    cherish〔ˋtʃɛrɪʃ〕v. 珍惜

    celebrate〔ˋsɛləˌbret〕v. 慶祝；讚頌

【Unit 2 背景說明】

Live fully. 要充實地過生活。(= *Live your life fully.* = *Live a full life.*) 也可說成：Live life to the fullest. (要盡情地過生活。) Get the most out of life. (要盡情享受生活。) Delight in life. (要樂在生活。) Enjoy yourself. (要感到愉快。)

Live passionately. 要熱情地過生活。(= *Live your life passionately.* = *Live your life with passion.*)

Live wholeheartedly. 要全心全意地過生活。(= *Live your life wholeheartedly.*) 也可說成：Live a full life. (要過充實的生活。) Live enthusiastically. (要充滿熱忱地過生活。)

Live gracefully. 要優雅地生活。(= *Live your life gracefully.*) 也可說成：Be elegant throughout your life. (一生都要很優雅。) Be charming every day. (每天都要很迷人。)

Live gratefully. 要充滿感激地生活。(= *Live your life gratefully.*) 也可說成：Be thankful throughout your life. (要一生都充滿感激。) Be thankful every day. (要每天都心存感謝。)

Live generously. 要慷慨地生活。(= *Live your
life generously*.) 也可說成：Be generous
throughout your life. (要一生都很慷慨。)
Be charitable every day. (要每天都慈善。)
Be kind every day. (要每天都善良。)

Embrace life. 要擁抱生活。(= *Embrace your
life*.) 也可說成：Relish life. (要品味生活。)
Live a full life. (要過充實的生活。) Live
wholeheartedly. (要全心全意地生活。)

Cherish life. 珍惜生命。(= *Treasure life*.
= *Value life*. = *Appreciate life*.) 也可說成：
Cherish your life. (要珍惜你的生命。)
(= *Treasure your life*. = *Value your life*.
= *Appreciate your life*.)

Celebrate life. 慶祝生命；讚頌生命。
(= *Celebrate your life*.) 也可說成：Appreciate
life. (重視生命。) Treasure life. (珍惜生命。)
Live a full life. (過充實的生活。)

BOOK 1・PART 1

UNIT 3

Courage 勇氣

Be brave.

勇敢一點。

Stay brave.

保持勇敢。

Explore bravely.

勇敢探索。

** courage〔ˈkɝɪdʒ〕 *n.* 勇氣
brave〔brev〕 *adj.* 勇敢的
stay〔ste〕 *v.* 保持
explore〔ɪkˈsplor〕 *v.* 探索；探險
bravely〔ˈbrevlɪ〕 *adv.* 勇敢地

Take chances.

勇於冒險。

Take risks.

冒險一試。

Risk everything.

孤注一擲。

** chance〔tʃæns〕*n.* 機會
take chances 冒險
risk〔rɪsk〕*n.* 風險；危險　*v.* 冒…的危險
take risks 冒險（= *take chances*）
risk everything 孤注一擲；賭上一切；
　奮不顧身

Stand tall.

抬頭挺胸。

Stand firm.

堅定立場。

Never retreat.

永不退縮。

** stand〔stænd〕*v.* 站立；站著；處於(某種狀態)

tall〔tɔl〕*adj.* 高的；高大的 *adv.* 趾高氣

昂地；昂然

stand tall 昂然挺立；昂首闊步；自信滿滿

firm〔fɜm〕*adj.* 穩固的；堅定的

never〔'nɛvɚ〕*adv.* 絕不

retreat〔rɪ'trit〕*v.* 撤退；退縮

【**Unit 3** 背景説明】

Be brave. 要勇敢。(= *Be courageous.* = *Be daring.*) 也可説成：Be brave no matter what. (無論如何都要勇敢。) Be confident. (要有自信。)

Stay brave. 保持勇敢。(= *Remain courageous.* = *Remain daring.*) 也可説成：Stay brave no matter what. (無論如何都要保持勇敢。) Remain confident. (要保持自信。)

Explore bravely. (要勇敢地探索。) 也可説成：Explore new things bravely. (要勇敢地探索新事物。) Seek out new experiences bravely. (要勇敢地尋找新的經驗。) (= *Seek out new experiences courageously.*)

Take chances. 要冒險。(= ***Take risks.***) 也可説成：Be willing to take chances. (要願意冒險。) (= *Be willing to take risks.*) Don't always play it safe. (不要總是謹慎行事。)

Risk everything. 要冒著失去一切的風險；要
孤注一擲；要賭上一切。(= *Put everything
on the line*.) 也可説成：Be willing to risk
everything. (要願意孤注一擲；要願意賭上
一切。)

Stand tall. (要昂然挺立；要抬頭挺胸；要充滿
自信。) 也可説成：Stand tall no matter
what. (無論如何都要抬頭挺胸。) Be proud.
(要驕傲。) Be brave. (要勇敢。)

Stand firm. (要堅定不移。) 也可説成：Stand
firm no matter what. (無論如何都要堅定不
移。) Be firm. (要堅定。) Stand your
ground. (要堅持立場。)

Never retreat. 絕不退縮。(= *Never back
down*.) 也可説成：Never ever retreat. (絕對
不能退縮。) Never give up. (絕不放棄。)
Never give in. (絕不屈服。)

UNIT 4

Optimism 樂觀

Stay positive.

保持積極。

Stay optimistic.

保持樂觀。

Stay upbeat.

保持開朗。

** optimism〔'ɑptə‚mɪzəm〕*n.* 樂觀
stay〔ste〕*v.* 保持
positive〔'pɑzətɪv〕*adj.* 正面的；積極的；樂觀的
optimistic〔‚ɑptə'mɪstɪk〕*adj.* 樂觀的
upbeat〔'ʌp‚bit, ʌp'bit〕*adj.* 樂觀的（= *positive*
  = *optimistic*）

BOOK 1・PART 1

Keep hoping.

保持希望。

Look forward.

展望未來。

Expect good.

期待美好。

** ***keep + V-ing*** 持續…

hope〔hop〕*v.* 希望；盼望

forward〔'fɔrwəd〕*adv.* 向前；向將來

look forward 向前看；放眼未來

expect〔ɪk'spɛkt〕*v.* 期待

good〔gʊd〕*n.* 好事

Find joy.

尋找喜悅。

Find light.

尋找光明。

Pursue cheer.

追求快樂。

** find〔faɪnd〕*v.* 尋找；找到
joy〔dʒɔɪ〕*n.* 喜悅；高興；快樂
light〔laɪt〕*n.* 光；光亮；光輝
pursue〔pəˈsu〕*v.* 追求
cheer〔tʃɪr〕*n.* 歡呼；歡樂；快樂；愉快；
　高興　*v.* 歡呼

【**Unit 4 背景説明**】

Stay positive. 要保持樂觀。(= *Stay optimistic.* = *Stay upbeat.*) 也可説成：Remain optimistic. (要保持樂觀。) (= *Remain positive.* = *Remain upbeat.*) Remain hopeful. (要一直充滿希望。) Remain confident. (要保持自信。) Remain cheerful. (要保持愉快。) Always stay positive. (要永遠保持樂觀。) (= *Always stay optimistic.* = *Always stay upbeat.*)

Keep hoping. 要持續抱持希望。(= *Keep on hoping.*) 也可説成：Never give up hope. (絕不放棄希望。) Stay positive. (要保持樂觀。)

Look forward. 要向前看；要放眼未來。(= *Look ahead.* = *Look to the future.* = *Think about the future.*) 也可説成：Continue to look forward. (要持續展望未來。)

Expect good. 要期待好事。(= *Expect good things*.) 是慣用句，也可説成：Expect good things to happen. (要期待好事發生。) Assume good things will happen. (要認爲好事會發生。)

Find joy. (要找到快樂。) 也可説成：Find joy in life. (要找到生活中的快樂。) Find something that brings you joy. (要找到能帶給你快樂的事物。) Find something that makes you happy. (要找到會使你快樂的事物。)

Find light. 要找到光明。(= *Find light in life*.)；要找到快樂。(= *Find happiness*.) 也可説成：Choose to be optimistic. (要選擇樂觀。)

Pursue cheer. 要追求快樂。(= *Pursue happiness*.) 也可説成：Pursue cheer all your life. (要終生追求快樂。)

UNIT 5

Change 改變

Change happens.

必然會改變。

Change improves.

改變能進步。

Change empowers.

改變獲能量。

** change〔tʃendʒ〕*n. v.* 改變

happen〔ˋhæpən〕*v.* 發生

improve〔ɪmˋpruv〕*v.* 改善；進步

empower〔ɪmˋpauɚ〕*v.* 給人權力；給人力量

Change inspires.

改變激勵人心。

Change motivates.

改變激發動力。

Change rejuvenates.

改變恢復活力。

** change〔tʃendʒ〕*n.* 改變
　inspire〔ɪnˈspaɪr〕*v.* 激勵；給予靈感
　motivate〔ˈmotəˌvet〕*v.* 激勵
　rejuvenate〔rɪˈdʒuvəˌnet〕*v.* 使返老還童；
　　使年輕；使恢復活力

Embrace change.

擁抱改變。

Embrace progress.

擁抱進步。

Embrace innovation.

擁抱創新。

** embrace〔ɪmˈbres〕*v.* 擁抱；欣然接受
change〔tʃendʒ〕*n.* 改變
progress〔ˈprɑgrɛs〕*n.* 進步
innovation〔ˌɪnəˈveʃən〕*n.* 創新

【**Unit 5 背景説明**】

Change happens. 改變一定會發生。(= *Change always happens*.) 也可説成:Change is inevitable. (改變是無法避免的。) Everything changes. (一切都會改變。)

Change improves. (改變能改善情況。) 也可説成:Change improves everything. (改變能改善一切。) Change makes things better. (改變能使情況變得更好。)

Change empowers. 改變能使人有力量。(= *Change empowers people*.) 也可説成:Change makes you more powerful. (改變使你更有力量。) Change makes you more capable. (改變使你更有能力。)

Change inspires. 改變能激勵人心。(= *Change inspires people*.) 也可説成:New things are inspiring. (新的事物能激勵人心。) (= *New things are motivating*.) New things are exciting. (新的事物令人興奮。)

Change motivates.　改變能激勵人心。(= *Change motivates people.*)也可說成：Change encourages people.(改變能鼓勵人們。)

Change rejuvenates.　改變能使人恢復活力。(= *Change rejuvenates people.* = *Change restores one's energy.*)也可說成：New things energize us.(新的事物使我們充滿活力。)(= *New things are energizing.*)

Embrace change.　要擁抱改變；要欣然接受改變。(= *Always embrace change.*)也可說成：Welcome change.(要樂於接受改變。)Welcome new things.(要樂於接受新事物。)

Embrace progress.　要擁抱進步；要樂於接受進步。(= *Always embrace progress.*)也可說成：Welcome progress.(要樂於接受進步。)(= *Welcome advancements.*)Welcome change.(要樂於接受改變。)

Embrace innovation.　要擁抱創新；要樂於接受創新。(= *Always embrace innovation.*)也可說成：Welcome innovation.(要樂於接受創新。)Welcome new things.(要樂於接受新事物。)

UNIT 6

Kindness 善良

Be kind.
友善待人。

Be gentle.
溫和待人。

Be considerate.
體貼他人。

** kindness〔'kaɪndnɪs〕*n.* 親切；仁慈；善意
kind〔kaɪnd〕*adj.* 親切的；仁慈的
gentle〔'dʒɛntḷ〕*adj.* 溫和的；溫柔的
considerate〔kən'sɪdərɪt〕*adj.* 體貼的
　(= *thoughtful*)

Speak kindly.

要說好話。

Speak softly.

語氣溫和。

Speak compassionately.

有同情心。

** speak〔spik〕*v.* 說話
　kindly〔'kaɪndlɪ〕*adv.* 親切地；仁慈地；
　　友好地
　softly〔'sɔftlɪ〕*adj.* 溫柔地；輕柔地
　compassionately〔kəm'pæʃənɪtlɪ〕*adv.*
　　同情地；富有同情心地

Spread joy.

散播喜悅。

Spread happiness.

散播快樂。

Spread goodwill.

傳遞善意。

BOOK 1・PART 1

** spread〔sprɛd〕*v.* 散播；傳播
joy〔dʒɔɪ〕*n.* 喜悅；高興；快樂
happiness〔'hæpɪnɪs〕*n.* 快樂；幸福
goodwill〔'gʊd'wɪl〕*n.* 善意；友好

【Unit 6 背景説明】

Be kind. 要親切。(= *Be nice.*) 也可説成：
Always be kind. (一定要親切。) Be
compassionate. (要有同情心。)

Be gentle. 要溫柔。(= *Be tender.*) 也可説成：
Always be gentle. (一定要溫柔。)

Be considerate. 要體貼。(= *Be thoughtful.*)
也可説成：Always be considerate. (一定
要體貼。) Be caring. (要關心別人。)

Speak kindly. 要說好話。(= *Say kind things.*)
也可説成：Always speak kindly. (一定要
說好話。) Speak tenderly. (說話要溫柔。)

Speak softly. (說話的語氣要溫和。) 也可説
成：Always speak softly. (說話的語氣一定
要溫和。) Use a soft voice. (要用輕柔的聲
音說話。)

Speak compassionately. 說話要有同情心。

（＝ *Say compassionate things.*）也可説成：

Be compassionate.（要有同情心。）

Always speak compassionately.（說話一

定要有同情心。）

Spread joy.（散播喜悦。）也可説成：Spread

joy everywhere.（到處散播喜悦。）Share

happiness.（要分享快樂。）Make people

happy.（要讓大家快樂。）

Spread happiness.（散播快樂。）也可説成：

Spread happiness everywhere.（到處散播

快樂。）Make others happy.（要讓別人快

樂。）

Spread goodwill. 散播善意。（＝ *Spread*

kindness.）也可説成：Spread goodwill

everywhere.（到處散播善意。）Spread

generosity.（散播慷慨。）

BOOK 1・PART 1

UNIT 7

Advancement 進步

Keep going.
持續前進。

Keep running.
持續奔跑。

Keep moving.
持續前行。

** advancement〔əd'vænsmənt〕*n.* 進步
keep + V-ing 持續…
go〔go〕*v.* 行走；移動；進行
keep going 持續前進
run〔rʌn〕*v.* 跑；進行
move〔muv〕*v.* 移動；前進

Keep pushing.

持續努力。

Keep fighting.

持續奮鬥。

Keep striving.

不斷努力。

** **keep + V-ing** 持續…
  push〔puʃ〕 *v.* 推進；擠出（路）前進；
    努力爭取；用力向前
  fight〔faɪt〕 *v.* 打仗；打架；搏鬥；奮鬥
  strive〔straɪv〕 *v.* 努力

Stay unstoppable.

不可阻擋。

Stay unshakable.

堅定不移。

Stay unbeatable.

保持無敵。

** stay〔ste〕*v.* 保持

　unstoppable〔ʌn'stɑpəbl̩〕*adj.* 擋不住的；
　　不可阻擋的

　unshakable〔ʌn'ʃekəbl̩〕*adj.* 不可動搖的；
　　堅定不移的

　unbeatable〔ʌn'bitəbl̩〕*adj.* 無法戰勝的；
　　不能超越的

【Unit 7 背景説明】

Keep going. 持續前進。(= *Keep on going.*)
也可説成：Continue. (要繼續。)

Keep running. 持續奔跑。(= *Keep on running.*) 也可説成：Keep going. (持續前進。)

Keep moving. 持續前進。(= *Keep on moving.*) 也可説成：Don't stop. (不要停止。)

Keep pushing. 持續推進，奮力向前，也就是「持續努力。」(= *Keep on pushing.* = *Keep striving.*) 也可説成：Keep advancing. (持續前進。) Press on. (奮勇前進。)

Keep fighting. 持續奮鬥。(= *Keep on fighting.*) 也可説成：Keep trying. (持續努力。)

Keep striving. 持續努力。(= *Keep on striving.*) 也可説成：Keep trying. (持續努力。) Don't give up. (不要放棄。)

Stay unstoppable.（要一直不可阻擋。）也可說成：Stay unstoppable no matter what.（無論如何都要一直不可阻擋。）Don't stop.（不要停止。）Don't let anyone stop you.（不要讓任何人阻擋你。）

Stay unshakable.（要堅定不移。）也可說成：Stay unshakable no matter what.（無論如何都要堅定不移。）Remain strong.（要保持堅強。）Remain firm.（要保持堅定。）Remain steadfast.（要堅定不移。）

Stay unbeatable.（要讓人無法戰勝。）也可說成：Stay unbeatable no matter what.（無論如何都要讓人無法戰勝。）Win.（要獲勝。）Keep winning.（要持續獲勝。）

UNIT 8

Resilience 韌性

Keep advancing.

持續進步。

Keep progressing.

不斷進步。

Keep growing.

持續成長。

** resilience〔rɪˋzɪlɪəns〕*n.* 恢復力；韌性

　　keep + *V-ing* 持續…

　　advance〔ədˋvæns〕*v.* 前進；進步

　　progress〔prəˋgrɛs〕*v.* 前進；進步

　　grow〔gro〕*v.* 成長

Never stop.

永不停止。

Never quit.

永不放棄。

Never surrender.

永不投降。

BOOK 1 • PART 1

** never〔ˈnɛvɚ〕*adv.* 絕不
stop〔stɑp〕*v.* 停止
quit〔kwɪt〕*v.* 停止；放棄
surrender〔səˈrɛndɚ〕*v.* 投降

Always learn.

不斷學習。

Always improve.

不斷改進。

Always innovate.

不斷創新。

** always〔'ɔlwez〕*adv.* 總是；一直
learn〔lɜn〕*v.* 學習
improve〔ɪm'pruv〕*v.* 改善；進步
innovate〔'ɪnə,vet〕*v.* 創新

BOOK 1・PART 1

【**Unit 8 背景説明**】

Keep advancing. 要持續進步。(= *Keep on advancing.* = *Keep moving ahead.*)

Keep progressing. 要持續進步。(= *Keep on progressing.*) 也可説成：Keep moving forward. (要持續前進。)

Keep growing. 要持續成長。(= *Keep on growing.*) 也可説成：Keep developing. (要持續發展。) (= *Keep evolving.*) Keep improving. (持續進步。)

Never stop. (絕不停止。) 也可説成：Never ever stop. (絕對不能停止。) Never stop no matter what. (無論如何都絕不停止。)

Never quit. (絕不放棄。) 也可説成：Never ever quit. (絕對不能放棄。) Never quit no matter what. (無論如何都絕不放棄。) Don't give up. (不要放棄。)

Never surrender.（絕不投降。）也可說成：
Never ever surrender.（絕對不能投降。）
Never surrender no matter what.（無論如何
都絕不投降。）Don't give in.（不要屈服。）
Keep going.（要持續前進。）

Always learn. 要不斷學習。(= *Keep
learning.*）也可說成：Always learn new
things.（要不斷學習新事物。）Never stop
learning.（絕不停止學習。）

Always improve.（要不斷改進。）也可說成：
Always improve yourself.（要不斷改進自
己。）Keep getting better.（要持續變得更
好。）

Always innovate.（要不斷創新。）也可說成：
Be innovative.（要創新。）Be creative.
（要有創造力。）Create new things.（創造
新的事物。）Keep changing.（要持續改
變。）

BOOK 1・PART 1

UNIT 9

Serenity 平靜

Be calm.

要冷靜。

Be relaxed.

要放鬆。

Be easy-going.

要悠哉。

** serenity〔sə'rɛnətɪ〕n.（心的）平靜；寧靜
calm〔kɑm〕adj. 冷靜的
relaxed〔rɪ'lækst〕adj. 放鬆的；輕鬆自在的
easy-going〔ˌizɪ'goɪŋ〕adj. 不慌不忙的；
悠閒的；脾氣隨和的

Keep cool.

保持冷靜。

Keep chill.

保持輕鬆。

Keep peaceful.

保持平靜。

** keep〔kip〕*v.* 保持

cool〔kul〕*adj.* 冷靜的

chill〔tʃɪl〕*adj.* 寒冷的；令人放鬆的；冷靜的；
　從容的

peaceful〔'pisfəl〕*adj.* 和平的；平靜的

Stay controlled.

保持自制。

Stay composed.

保持沉著。

Stay collected.

保持鎮定。

** stay〔ste〕*v.* 保持

controlled〔kən'trold〕*adj.* 克制的;受控的;
自制的

composed〔kəm'pozd〕*adj.* 鎮靜的;沉著的;
平靜的【compose〔kəm'poz〕*v.* 組成;使鎮靜】

collected〔kə'lɛktɪd〕*adj.* 收集成冊的;鎮定的;
冷靜的;泰然自若的【collect〔kə'lɛkt〕*v.* 收集;
使鎮定】

【Unit 9 背景説明】

Be calm. (要冷靜。) 也可説成：Always be calm. (一定要冷靜。) Be calm no matter what. (無論如何都要冷靜。) Be coolheaded. (頭腦要冷靜。) Be composed. (要鎮靜。)

Be relaxed. (要放輕鬆。) 也可説成：Always be relaxed. (一定要放輕鬆。) Be relaxed no matter what. (無論如何都要放輕鬆。)

Be easy-going. (要悠哉；要不慌不忙。) 也可説成：Always be easy-going. (一定要悠悠哉哉。) Be easy-going no matter what. (無論如何都要悠悠哉哉。)

Keep cool. (要保持冷靜。) 也可説成：Always be cool. (一定要保持冷靜。) Be cool no matter what. (無論如何都要保持冷靜。) Stay calm. (要保持冷靜。) Stay coolheaded. (要保持頭腦冷靜。) Stay poised. (要泰然自若。)

BOOK 1・PART 1

Keep chill. (要保持冷靜。) 也可説成：Stay calm. (要保持冷靜。) Stay unworried. (不要擔心。) Stay patient. (要保持耐心。)

Keep peaceful. (要保持平靜。) 也可説成：Always remain peaceful. (一定要保持平靜。) Be peaceful no matter what. (無論如何都要平靜。) Stay calm. (要保持冷靜。)

Stay controlled. (要保持自制力。) 也可説成：Always stay controlled. (一定要保持自制力。) Stay controlled no matter what. (無論如何都要保持自制力。) Remain restrained. (要克制自己。) Stay under control. (要受到控制。)

Stay composed. (要保持鎮靜。) 也可説成：Always stay composed. (一定要保持鎮靜。) Stay composed no matter what. (無論如何都要保持鎮靜。) Remain cool. (要保持冷靜。)

Stay collected. (要保持鎮定。) 也可説成：Always stay collected. (一定要保持鎮定。) Stay collected no matter what. (無論如何都要保持鎮定。) Remain calm. (要保持冷靜。)

PART 1 總整理

PART 1・Unit 1~9
中英文錄音QR碼

Unit 1

Dream big. 夢想要大。
Dream bigger.
夢要很大。
Dream beautifully.
夢要很美。

Chase dreams.
追求夢想。
Chase passions.
追求愛好。
Chase happiness.
追求幸福。

Aim higher. 目標更高。
Aspire higher.
渴望更高。
Shoot higher. 志向更高。

Unit 2

Live fully. 過得充實。
Live passionately.
熱愛生活。
Live wholeheartedly.
全心生活。

Live gracefully. 優雅生活。
Live gratefully. 感激生活。
Live generously.
大方生活。

Embrace life. 擁抱生活。
Cherish life. 珍惜生命。
Celebrate life. 慶祝生命。

Unit 3

Be brave. 勇敢一點。
Stay brave. 保持勇敢。
Explore bravely.
勇敢探索。

Take chances. 勇於冒險。
Take risks. 冒險一試。
Risk everything.
孤注一擲。

Stand tall. 抬頭挺胸。
Stand firm. 堅定立場。
Never retreat.
永不退縮。

Unit 4

Stay positive. 保持積極。
Stay optimistic. 保持樂觀。
Stay upbeat. 保持開朗。

Keep hoping. 保持希望。
Look forward. 展望未來。
Expect good. 期待美好。

Find joy. 尋找喜悅。
Find light. 尋找光明。
Pursue cheer. 追求快樂。

Unit 5

Change happens.
必然會改變。
Change improves.
改變能進步。
Change empowers.
改變獲能量。

Change inspires.
改變激勵人心。
Change motivates.
改變激發動力。
Change rejuvenates.
改變恢復活力。

Embrace change.
擁抱改變。
Embrace progress.
擁抱進步。
Embrace innovation.
擁抱創新。

Unit 6

Be kind. 友善待人。
Be gentle. 溫和待人。
Be considerate.
體貼他人。

Speak kindly.
要說好話。
Speak softly.
語氣溫和。
Speak compassionately.
有同情心。

Spread joy.
散播喜悅。
Spread happiness.
散播快樂。
Spread goodwill.
傳遞善意。

Unit 7

Keep going. 持續前進。
Keep running. 持續奔跑。
Keep moving. 持續前行。

Keep pushing.
持續努力。
Keep fighting.
持續奮鬥。
Keep striving.
不斷努力。

Stay unstoppable.
不可阻擋。
Stay unshakable.
堅定不移。
Stay unbeatable.
保持無敵。

Unit 8

Keep advancing.
持續進步。
Keep progressing.
不斷進步。
Keep growing.
持續成長。

Never stop. 永不停止。
Never quit. 永不放棄。
Never surrender.
永不投降。

Always learn. 不斷學習。
Always improve.
不斷改進。
Always innovate.
不斷創新。

Unit 9

Be calm. 要冷靜。
Be relaxed. 要放鬆。
Be easy-going. 要悠哉。

Keep cool. 保持冷靜。
Keep chill. 保持輕鬆。
Keep peaceful.
保持平靜。

Stay controlled.
保持自制。
Stay composed.
保持沈著。
Stay collected.
保持鎮定。

BOOK 1 PART 2

How to Live Longer
如何長生不老

PART 2・Unit 1~9
英文錄音QR碼

UNIT 1

The Importance of a Healthy Diet 健康飲食的重要

Eat well.

吃得健康。

Eat colorfully.

吃得多彩。

Embrace variety.

吃得多樣。

** healthy〔ˈhɛlθɪ〕*adj.* 健康的

diet〔ˈdaɪət〕*n.* 飲食　　well〔wɛl〕*adv.* 很好地

colorfully〔ˈkʌləˌfəlɪ〕*adv.* 多色彩地

embrace〔ɪmˈbres〕*v.* 擁抱；欣然接受

variety〔vəˈraɪətɪ〕*n.* 多樣性

Eat slowly.

慢慢地吃。

Savor slowly.

慢慢品味。

Chew slowly.

細嚼慢嚥。

** slowly〔'slolɪ〕*adv.* 慢慢地

　　savor〔'sevɚ〕*v.*（慢慢地）品嚐；

　　（細細地）體會

　　chew〔tʃu〕*v.* 嚼

Avoid excess.

避免過量。

Control portions.

控制份量。

Hunger cures.

飢餓治病。

** avoid〔əˋvɔɪd〕v. 避免

excess〔ɪkˋsɛs〕n. 過量；過度

control〔kənˋtrol〕v. 控制

portion〔ˋporʃən〕n. 部份；（食物的）一人份

hunger〔ˋhʌŋgɚ〕n. 飢餓

cure〔kjʊr〕v. 治療；治癒

【Unit 1 背景說明】

Eat well.（要吃得好。）也可說成：Eat good food.（要吃好的食物。）Eat healthy food.（要吃健康的食物。）

Eat colorfully. 要多色彩地吃，也就是「要吃各種顏色的食物。」(*= Eat food of many colors. = Eat foods with a variety of colors.*)也可說成：Eat a rainbow.（要吃多種顏色的食物。）

Embrace variety. 要擁抱多樣性，在此引申為「要吃各式各樣的食物。」(*= Eat a variety of food.*)也可說成：Be enthusiastic about eating a variety of food.（要熱衷於吃各式各樣的食物。）Don't eat the same thing all the time.（不要一直吃同樣的食物。）

Eat slowly. 要慢慢地吃。(*= Take your time when eating.*)也可說成：Don't eat too fast.（不要吃得太快。）

Savor slowly. （要慢慢地品嚐。）也可說成：
Savor your food.（要慢慢地品嚐你的食物。）
Appreciate every bite.（要重視每一口食物。）

Chew slowly. （要慢慢地嚼。）也可說成：Eat
slowly.（要慢慢地吃。）Chew your food
thoroughly.（要徹底地咀嚼你的食物。）

Avoid excess. （避免過量。）也可說成：
Don't eat too much.（不要吃太多。）Don't
eat more than you need.（不要吃超過你所需
要的。）

Control portions. （要控制份量。）也可說
成：Don't eat too much.（不要吃太多。）
（= *Don't overeat.*）

Hunger cures. 飢餓能治病。（= *Hunger
heals.*）也可說成：Some believe that
hunger cures.（有些人相信飢餓能治病。）
I believe that hunger cures.（我相信飢餓
能治病。）Staying a little bit hungry can
help cure disease.（保持一點飢餓感，有助
於治療疾病。）

UNIT 2

The Importance of Sleep
睡眠的重要

Sleep well.
好好睡覺。

Sleep deeply.
深度入眠。

Limit naps.
限制午睡。

** sleep〔slip〕*v. n.* 睡覺
well〔wɛl〕*adv.* 很好地
deeply〔'diplɪ〕*adv.* 深深地；徹底地
sleep deeply 熟睡　　limit〔'lɪmɪt〕*v.* 限制
nap〔næp〕*n.* 小睡；午睡

Stretch gently.

輕輕拉筋。

Extend softly.

輕柔伸展。

Breathe deeply.

做深呼吸。

** stretch 〔 strɛtʃ 〕 *v.* 伸展；伸展身體
gently 〔'dʒɛntlɪ 〕 *adv.* 溫和地；輕輕地
extend 〔 ɪk'stɛnd 〕 *v.* 延伸；伸展
softly 〔'sɔftlɪ 〕 *adv.* 輕柔地
breathe 〔 brið 〕 *v.* 呼吸
deeply 〔'diplɪ 〕 *adv.* 深深地

Warm bath.

泡熱水澡。

Warm socks.

穿襪暖腳。

Comfortable pajamas.

舒適睡衣。

** warm 〔 wɔrm 〕 *adj.* 溫暖的
bath 〔 bæθ 〕 *n.* 洗澡；泡澡；洗澡水
socks 〔 sɑks 〕 *n. pl.* 短襪
comfortable 〔 ˈkʌmfɚtəbḷ 〕 *adj.* 舒服的；
　舒適的
pajamas 〔 pəˈdʒæməz 〕 *n. pl.* 睡衣褲

【**Unit 2 背景説明**】

Sleep well. 要睡得好。(= *Have a good sleep.*)

Sleep deeply. (要熟睡。) 也可説成：Sleep soundly. (要睡得很熟。) (= *Sleep like a baby. = Sleep like the dead.*)

Limit naps. (要限制午睡。) 也可説成：Don't take too many naps. (不要睡太多午覺。) If you limit naps, you can sleep well at night. (如果你限制午睡，晚上就可以睡得好。) Don't take long naps. (午覺不要睡太久。) (= *Take short naps. = Don't nap too long.*)

Stretch gently. (輕輕地伸展身體。) 也可説成：*Extend softly.* (輕柔地伸展身體。) Stretch your muscles. (要伸展你的肌肉。) Stretch carefully. (要小心地伸展身體。)

Breathe deeply. 要深呼吸。(= *Take deep breaths.*)

Stretching gently and breathing deeply before bed can help you sleep. (睡前輕輕拉筋並做深呼吸，能幫助你入睡。)

Warm bath. (溫暖的洗澡水。) 也可説成：Comfortable bathwater. (舒適的洗澡水。)

Warm socks. (溫暖的短襪。) 也可説成：Cozy socks. (溫暖而舒適的短襪。)

Comfortable pajamas. 舒適的睡衣。
(= *Cozy pajamas*. = *Cozy PJs*.)

Taking a warm bath and putting on warm socks before bed will help you sleep. (睡前洗熱水澡並穿上溫暖的短襪，能幫助你入睡。)

UNIT 3

The Importance of Being Active
運動的重要

Exercise daily.
每天運動。

Move daily.
每天活動。

Walk daily.
每天散步。

** active〔'æktɪv〕*adj.* 活動的；活躍的
  exercise〔'ɛksə͵saɪz〕*v. n.* 運動
  daily〔'delɪ〕*adv.* 每天（*= every day*）
  move〔muv〕*v.* 動；移動
  walk〔wɔk〕*v.* 走路；散步

BOOK 1・PART 2

Stay active.

保持活躍。

Stay lively.

保持活力。

Stay energetic.

保持精力。

** stay〔ste〕*v.* 保持
active〔'æktɪv〕*adj.* 活動的；活躍的
lively〔'laɪvlɪ〕*adj.* 活潑的；充滿活力的
energetic〔ˌɛnɚ'dʒɛtɪk〕*adj.* 充滿活力的；
精力充沛的

Stay dynamic.

動個不停。

Stay involved.

活動滿滿。

Stay engaged.

參與滿滿。

** stay〔ste〕*v.* 保持

dynamic〔daɪ'næmɪk〕*adj.* 動的；

充滿活力的

involved〔ɪn'vɑlvd〕*adj.* 投入的；參與的

engaged〔ɪn'gedʒd〕*adj.* 從事的；忙碌的

【**Unit 3 背景説明**】

Exercise daily. 要每天運動。(= *Do exercise every day.*) 也可説成：Get some exercise every day. (每天都要做些運動。) Make exercise a daily habit. (要使運動成為每天的習慣。)

Move daily. 要每天活動。(= *Move every day.*) 也可説成：Stay active. (要動個不停。) Get regular exercise. (要規律運動。) Don't be sedentary. (不要坐著不動。)

Walk daily. 要每天走路。(= *Walk every day.*) 也可説成：Take a walk every day. (要每天散步。) Make walking a daily habit. (要使走路成為每天的習慣。)

Stay active. 要保持活動；要動個不停。(= *Keep active.* = *Always be active.*) 也可説成：Keep moving. (要持續活動。) Stay on the go. (要一直活動。)

Stay lively. 要一直充滿活力。(= *Always be lively.*) 也可説成：Remain energetic.(要保持活力。)

Stay energetic. 要一直充滿活力。(= *Always be energetic.*) 也可説成：Remain vigorous. (要一直很有活力。)

Stay dynamic. (要持續活動。) 也可説成：Always be active.(要一直活動。) Always be lively.(要一直很有活力。)

Stay involved. 要一直參與活動。(= *Always be involved.*) 也可説成：Stay involved in activities.(要持續參與活動。) Remain engaged.(要保持忙碌。) Remain active. (要保持活躍。)

Stay engaged. 要一直參與活動。(= *Always be engaged.*) 也可説成：Stay engaged in activities.(要持續參與活動。) Stay involved.(要持續參與。) Stay active. (要保持活躍。)

BOOK 1・PART 2

UNIT 4

The Importance of Hydration
補充水分的重要

Drink water.
要多喝水。

Sip water.
小口喝水。

Sip often.
時常喝水。

** **importance** 〔 ɪmˈpɔrtn̩s 〕 *n.* 重要性
hydration 〔 haɪˈdreʃən 〕 *n.* 補充水分
sip 〔 sɪp 〕 *v.* 啜飲;小口喝
often 〔ˈɔfən 〕 *adv.* 常常

Thirst hurts.

口渴有害。

Fluids benefit.

喝水有益。

Hydration matters.

喝水重要。

** thirst〔θɝst〕*n.* 口渴
  hurt〔hɝt〕*v.* 有害
  fluid〔'fluɪd〕*n.* 液體;流體
  benefit〔'bɛnəfɪt〕*v.* 有益;有好處
  hydration〔haɪ'dreʃən〕*n.* 補充水分
  matter〔'mætɚ〕*v.* 重要
    (＝ *count*)

Hydrate well.

要常喝水。

Hydrate regularly.

經常喝水。

Stay hydrated.

保持水分。

** hydrate〔ˈhaɪdret〕v.（身體）補充水分
well〔wɛl〕adv. 很好地；充分地
regularly〔ˈrɛgjələlɪ〕adv. 定期地；經常地
stay〔ste〕v. 保持
hydrated〔ˈhaɪdretɪd〕adj. 攝取足夠水分的
stay hydrated 保持水分

【Unit 4 背景説明】

Drink water.（要喝水。）也可説成：Have some water.（要喝一些水。）

Sip water. 要小口地喝水。(= *Take small drinks of water.*) 也可説成：Take a little water.（要喝一些水。）Drink water slowly.（要慢慢地喝水。）

Sip often.（要常常小口地喝水。）也可説成：Drink a little water frequently.（要經常喝一些水。）

Thirst hurts. 口渴有害。(= *Being thirsty is harmful.* = *Getting thirsty is harmful.*)

Fluids benefit. 液體有益。(= *Fluids are beneficial.* = *Liquids are beneficial.*)

Hydration matters. 補充水分很重要。(= *Hydration is important.*) 也可説成：Drinking water is important.（喝水很重要。）You must stay hydrated.（你必須保持水分。）

BOOK 1・PART 2

Hydrate well.（要好好地補充水分。）也可說成：Drink enough fluids.（要喝足夠的液體。）Drink a lot of fluids.（要喝很多的液體。）

Hydrate regularly.（要經常補充水分。）也可說成：Drink fluids regularly.（要經常喝液體。）Drink fluids often.（要常喝液體。）

Stay hydrated.（要保持水分。）也可說成：Drink enough fluids.（要喝足夠的液體。）Don't get dehydrated.（不要脫水。）

UNIT 5

The Importance of Nature
大自然的重要

Stay outside.
待在外面。

Stay outdoors.
待在戶外。

Be out-of-doors.
戶外活動。

** nature〔'netʃɚ〕*n.* 大自然
　　stay〔ste〕*v.* 停留
　　outside〔'aut'saɪd〕*adv.* 在外面；在戶外
　　outdoors〔'aut'dorz〕*adv.* 在戶外；在野外
　　out-of-doors〔'autəv'dorz〕*adv.* 在戶外
　　　(= *outdoors*)

BOOK 1・PART 2

Embrace nature.

擁抱自然。

Embrace adventure.

勇於冒險。

Embrace sunlight.

熱愛陽光。

** embrace〔ɪm'bres〕v. 擁抱；欣然接受
nature〔'netʃɚ〕n. 大自然
adventure〔əd'vɛntʃɚ〕n. 冒險
sunlight〔'sʌn,laɪt〕n. 陽光

Improve sleep.

改善睡眠。

Improve breathing.

改善呼吸。

Strengthen immunity.

增強免疫。

** improve〔ɪmˈpruv〕v. 改善

　　sleep〔slip〕v. 睡覺　n. 睡眠

　　breathe〔brið〕v. 呼吸

　　strengthen〔ˈstrɛŋθən〕v. 加強

　　immunity〔ɪˈmjunətɪ〕n. 免疫力

【Unit 5 背景説明】

Stay outside.（要待在外面。）也可説成：
Spend a lot of time outside.（要長時間待
在外面。）Always be outdoors.（一定要
在戶外。）

Stay outdoors. 要待在戶外。(= *Remain
outdoors*.）也可説成：Always be outside.
（一定要在外面。）

Be out-of-doors.（要在戶外。）也可説成：
Always be outdoors.（一定要在戶外。）

Embrace nature.（要擁抱大自然。）也可説
成：Appreciate nature.（要欣賞大自然。）

Embrace adventure.（要擁抱冒險。）也可説
成：Welcome adventure.（要樂於接受冒
險。）Welcome exciting activities.（要樂
於接受刺激的活動。）Welcome new things.
（要樂於接受新事物。）

Embrace sunlight.（要擁抱陽光。）也可説
成：Appreciate sunlight.（要欣賞陽光。）
(= *Appreciate sunshine*.) Welcome sunlight.
（要樂於接受陽光。）(= *Welcome sunshine*.)

Improve sleep.（改善睡眠。）也可説成：
Sleep better.（睡得更好。）

Improve breathing.（改善呼吸。）也可説
成：Breathe better.（更順暢地呼吸。）

Strengthen immunity. 增強免疫力。
(= *Improve immunity*.) 也可説成：
Improve your immune system.（改善你的
免疫系統。）Make your immune system
stronger.（使你的免疫系統更強大。）

UNIT 6

The Importance of Friends
朋友的重要

Make friends.

結交朋友。

Support friends.

支持朋友。

Foster friendships.

培養友情。

** importance〔ɪm'pɔrtn̩s〕*n.* 重要性
make friends 交朋友
support〔sə'port〕*v.* 支持
foster〔'fɑstɚ, 'fɔstɚ〕*v.* 養育；培養
friendship〔'frɛndʃɪp〕*n.* 友誼

Share laughter.

分享歡笑。

Share passions.

分享熱情。

Share experiences.

分享經驗。

** share〔ʃɛr〕v. 分享
laughter〔'læftɚ〕n. 笑
passion〔'pæʃən〕n. 熱情；愛好
experience〔ɪk'spɪrɪəns〕n. 經驗

Enjoy company.

樂在交際。

Enjoy mingling.

樂在往來。

Enjoy socializing.

樂在社交。

** enjoy〔ɪn'dʒɔɪ〕 v. 享受；喜歡
company〔'kʌmpənɪ〕 n. 公司；同伴；
朋友；交際；交往
mingle〔'mɪŋg!〕 v. 混合；交往；交際
socialize〔'soʃə,laɪz〕 v. 交際；參加
社交活動

【Unit 6 背景説明】

Make friends.（要交朋友。）也可説成：
Establish new friendships.（要建立新的友誼。）Develop new friendships.（要培養新的友誼。）

Support friends.（要支持朋友。）也可説成：
Help your friends.（要幫助你的朋友。）Be loyal to your friends.（要對你的朋友忠實。）

Foster friendships. 要培養友誼。(= *Cultivate friendships*. = *Develop friendships*.) 也可説成：Make new friends.（要結交新朋友。）
Pay attention to your friendships.（要注意你的友誼。）

Share laughter. 要分享歡笑，也就是「要一起笑。」也可説成：Laugh with others.（要和別人一起笑。）

Share passions.（要分享熱情；要分享愛好。）
也可説成：Tell others what you are passionate about.（要告訴別人你熱愛什麼。）

BOOK 1・PART 2

Share experiences. (要分享經驗。) 也可説成：Tell people about your experiences. (要告訴別人你的經驗。) Tell others about what you have done. (要告訴別人你做了什麼事。) Do things with other people. (要和別人一起做事。)

Enjoy company. (要喜歡有人陪伴；要喜歡交際。) 也可説成：***Enjoy mingling***. (要喜歡和人來往。) ***Enjoy socializing***. (要喜歡交際；要喜歡參加社交活動。) Take pleasure in being with others. (要喜歡和別人在一起。) Have fun being with other people. (和別人在一起要玩得很愉快。)

UNIT 7

The Importance of Social Activities 社交活動的重要

Socialize often.

要常社交。

Socialize regularly.

定期社交。

Socialize genuinely.

眞誠社交。

** social〔'soʃəl〕*adj.* 社交的
　activity〔æk'tɪvətɪ〕*n.* 活動
　socialize〔'soʃə,laɪz〕*v.* 交際；參加社交活動
　often〔'ɔfən〕*adv.* 常常
　regularly〔'rɛgjələlɪ〕*adv.* 定期地
　genuinely〔'dʒɛnjʊɪnlɪ〕*adv.* 眞正地；眞誠地

Attend parties.

參加派對。

Attend gatherings.

參加聚會。

Attend meetups.

和人見面。

** attend〔əˈtɛnd〕*v.* 參加（= *go to*）
　　party〔ˈpɑrtɪ〕*n.* 派對
　　gathering〔ˈgæðərɪŋ〕*n.* 聚會
　　meetup〔ˈmitˌʌp〕*n.* 見面；聚會；小聚
　　　（= *gathering*）【*meet up* 相聚；會面】

Make connections.

建立人脈。

Connect deeply.

深度交往。

Stay connected.

保持聯繫。

** connection〔kəˋnɛkʃən〕*n.* 關連；關係；
　（*pl.*）人脈
connect〔kəˋnɛkt〕*v.* 連結；建立關係
deeply〔ˋdiplɪ〕*adv.* 深深地
stay〔ste〕*v.* 保持
connected〔kəˋnɛktɪd〕*adj.* 有關連的；
　有連絡的

BOOK 1・PART 2

【Unit 7 背景説明】

Socialize often.（要常常交際。）也可説成：*Socialize regularly.*（要定期參加社交活動。）Get together with others frequently.（要經常和別人聚在一起。）

Socialize genuinely. 要真誠地參加社交活動。
(= *Socialize sincerely.*)

Attend parties. 要參加派對。(= *Go to parties.*) 也可説成：*Attend gatherings.*（要參加聚會。）(= *Go to gatherings.*) *Attend meetups.*（要和別人相聚。）
(= *Go to meetups.*)

Make connections. 要創造關係，也就是「要培養關係；要建立人脈。」(= *Develop relationships.* = *Establish relationships.*)

Connect deeply. 要有很深的連結，也就是「要培養很深的關係。」(= *Develop deep relationships.* = *Establish deep relationships.*) 也可説成：Establish meaningful relationships.（要建立有意義的關係。）

Stay connected. 要保持連結，也就是「要保持連絡。」(= *Stay in touch.*)；「要維持關係。」
(= *Maintain your relationships.*)

UNIT 8

The Importance of a Smile
笑容的重要

Keep smiling.
保持笑容。

Keep shining.
保持閃耀。

Smile daily.
每天都笑。

** smile〔smaɪl〕*n. v.* 微笑;笑
keep + V-ing 一直…;持續…
shine〔ʃaɪn〕*v.* 發光;閃耀;出眾;出色
daily〔'delɪ〕*adv.* 每天 (= *every day*)

Smiles comfort.

笑容撫慰人心。

Smiles connect.

笑容建立關係。

Create joy.

笑容創造快樂。

** smile〔smaɪl〕*n. v.* 微笑；笑

   comfort〔ˈkʌmfɚt〕*v.* 安慰

   connect〔kəˈnɛkt〕*v.* 連結；建立關係

   create〔krɪˈet〕*v.* 創造

   joy〔dʒɔɪ〕*n.* 快樂；喜悅；高興

Always grin.

時刻大笑。

Grin brightly.

燦爛大笑。

Embrace grins.

欣然大笑。

** always〔ˋɔlwɛz〕*adv.* 總是；一直

grin〔grɪn〕*v. n.* 露齒而笑；

咧嘴大笑

brightly〔ˋbraɪtlɪ〕*adv.* 明亮地；快活地；

開朗地；歡樂地

embrace〔ɪmˋbrɛs〕*v.* 擁抱；欣然接受

【Unit 8 背景說明】

Keep smiling.（要一直微笑。）也可説成：
Always smile.（要總是微笑。）Never stop
smiling.（絕不停止微笑。）Be positive.
（要樂觀。）

Keep shining. 要持續發光發亮。(＝*Beam.*
＝*Glow.* ＝*Remain radiant.*）也可説成：
Always be positive.（要一直樂觀。）

Smile daily. 要每天微笑。(＝*Smile every
day.* ＝*Make smiling part of your day.*）也
可説成：Always smile.（要總是微笑。）

Smiles comfort. 微笑能給人安慰。(＝*Smiles
can comfort people.*）也可説成：A smile
makes people feel better.（微笑能使人感覺
更好。）

Smiles connect. 微笑能連結；微笑能建立關
係。(＝*Smiles make connections.*）也可説
成：Smiles bring people together.（微笑
使人更加和睦。）

Create joy.（要創造快樂。）也可説成：Make others happy.（要使別人快樂。）(= *Make people happy*.)

Always grin. 要總是露齒而笑。(= *Always smile broadly*.) 也可説成：Always smile.（要一直微笑。）Always have a smile on your face.（臉上要總是掛著微笑。）Keep smiling.（要持續微笑。）

Grin brightly.（要開朗地露齒而笑。）也可説成：Smile widely.（要露出大大的微笑。）(= *Smile broadly*.)

Embrace grins. 要擁抱露齒而笑，引申爲「要欣然接受露齒而笑。」也可説成：Appreciate smiles.（要重視微笑。）Welcome smiles.（要樂於接受微笑。）Grin all the time.（要一直露齒而笑。）Grin often.（要常常露齒而笑。）

UNIT 9

The Importance of Rest
休息的重要

Relax daily.
每天放鬆。

Relax deeply.
深度放鬆。

Release tension.
釋放壓力。

** rest〔rɛst〕*n.* 休息
relax〔rɪ'læks〕*v.* 放鬆
daily〔'delɪ〕*adv.* 每天
deeply〔'diplɪ〕*adv.* 深深地
release〔rɪ'lis〕*v.* 釋放
tension〔'tɛnʃən〕*n.* 緊張；焦慮

Seek peace.

尋求平靜。

Seek quiet.

尋求寧靜。

Seek stillness.

尋找安詳。

** seek〔sik〕*v.* 尋求；尋找（= *look for*）
  peace〔pis〕*n.* 和平；平靜
  quiet〔'kwaɪət〕*n.* 寧靜；內心的平靜；安寧
    adj. 安靜的
  stillness〔'stɪlnɪs〕*n.* 寧靜；寂靜
    【still〔stɪl〕*adj.* 安靜的；平靜的】

Slow down.

放慢腳步。

Simplify life.

簡化生活。

Live mindfully.

用心生活。

** ***slow down*** 減低速度；放慢；放鬆

simplify〔'sɪmplə,faɪ〕*v.* 簡化

life〔laɪf〕*n.* 生活；生命；人生

live〔lɪv〕*v.* 生存；活著；生活

mindfully〔'maɪndfəlɪ〕*adv.* 謹慎地；
注意地；留意地；用心地

【**Unit 9 背景説明**】

Relax daily. (每天放鬆。) 也可説成：

Take it easy every day. (要每天放輕鬆。)

Set aside some time to relax every day.

(每天都要撥出一些時間放鬆。) Take

some time for yourself every

day. (每天都要留一些時間給

自己。)

Relax deeply. (深度放鬆。) 也可説成：

Relax completely. (要完全放鬆。)

Relieve tension. (消除緊張。)

Get a good rest. (好好休息。)

Release tension. (釋放緊張。) 也可説成：

Get rid of your stress. (擺脱你的壓力。)

Relax. (放輕鬆。)

Seek peace. 尋求平靜。(= *Look for peace.*
= *Look for quiet.* = *Look for calm.* = *Look for*
tranquility.)

BOOK 1．PART 2

Seek quiet. 尋求寧靜。(= *Look for quiet.*
= *Look for peace.* = *Look for serenity.* = *Look*
for tranquility.) 也可說成：Look for calm.
（尋求平靜。）

Seek stillness. 尋求寧靜。(= *Look for stillness.*
= *Look for serenity.* = *Look for peace.* = *Look*
for quiet.)

Slow down. （要減慢速度。）也可說成：Don't
go so fast. （不要這麼快。）Don't do things
so fast. （做事情不要這麼快。）

Simplify life. （要簡化生活。）也可說成：
Streamline your life. （要使生活更有效率。）
Get down to basics. （要反璞歸眞。）

Live mindfully. 要有意識地生活，也就是「要
用心生活；要活在當下。」(= *Live in the*
present.) 也可說成：Live in a conscious
way. （要用心生活。）Be aware of the
things you do. （要知道你正在做什麼事。）
(= *Be thoughtful about the things you do.*)

PART 2 總整理

PART 2・Unit 1~9
中英文錄音QR碼

Unit 1

Eat well. 吃得健康。
Eat colorfully.
吃得多彩。
Embrace variety.
吃得多樣。

Eat slowly. 慢慢地吃。
Savor slowly. 慢慢品味。
Chew slowly. 細嚼慢嚥。

Avoid excess. 避免過量。
Control portions.
控制份量。
Hunger cures. 飢餓治病。

Unit 2

Sleep well. 好好睡覺。
Sleep deeply. 深度入眠。
Limit naps. 限制午睡。

Stretch gently. 輕輕拉筋。
Extend softly. 輕柔伸展。
Breathe deeply. 做深呼吸。

Warm bath. 泡熱水澡。
Warm socks. 穿襪暖腳。
Comfortable pajamas.
舒適睡衣。

Unit 3

Exercise daily. 每天運動。
Move daily. 每天活動。
Walk daily. 每天散步。

Stay active. 保持活躍。
Stay lively. 保持活力。
Stay energetic. 保持精力。

Stay dynamic. 動個不停。
Stay involved. 活動滿滿。
Stay engaged. 參與滿滿。

Unit 4

Drink water. 要多喝水。
Sip water. 小口喝水。
Sip often. 時常喝水。

BOOK 1・PART 2

Thirst hurts.
口渴有害。
Fluids benefit.
喝水有益。
Hydration matters.
喝水重要。

Hydrate well. 要常喝水。
Hydrate regularly.
經常喝水。
Stay hydrated.
保持水分。

Unit 5

Stay outside.
待在外面。
Stay outdoors.
待在戶外。
Be out-of-doors.
戶外活動。

Embrace nature.
擁抱自然。
Embrace adventure.
勇於冒險。
Embrace sunlight.
熱愛陽光。

Improve sleep.
改善睡眠。
Improve breathing.
改善呼吸。
Strengthen immunity.
增強免疫。

Unit 6

Make friends. 結交朋友。
Support friends.
支持朋友。
Foster friendships.
培養友情。

Share laughter.
分享歡笑。
Share passions.
分享熱情。
Share experiences.
分享經驗。

Enjoy company.
樂在交際。
Enjoy mingling.
樂在往來。
Enjoy socializing.
樂在社交。

Unit 7

Socialize often.
要常社交。
Socialize regularly.
定期社交。
Socialize genuinely.
真誠社交。

Attend parties.
參加派對。
Attend gatherings.
參加聚會。
Attend meetups.
和人見面。

Make connections.
建立人脈。
Connect deeply.
深度交往。
Stay connected.
保持聯繫。

Unit 8

Keep smiling. 保持笑容。
Keep shining. 保持閃耀。
Smile daily. 每天都笑。

Smiles comfort.
笑容撫慰人心。
Smiles connect.
笑容建立關係。
Create joy.
笑容創造快樂。

Always grin. 時刻大笑。
Grin brightly. 燦爛大笑。
Embrace grins.
欣然大笑。

Unit 9

Relax daily. 每天放鬆。
Relax deeply. 深度放鬆。
Release tension.
釋放壓力。

Seek peace. 尋求平靜。
Seek quiet. 尋求寧靜。
Seek stillness. 尋找安詳。

Slow down. 放慢腳步。
Simplify life. 簡化生活。
Live mindfully.
用心生活。

BOOK 1・PART 2

BOOK 1 **PART 3**

How to Be a Good Person
如何成為一個好人

PART 3・Unit 1~9
英文錄音QR碼

BOOK 1 · PART 3

UNIT 1

Believe in Love 相信愛的力量

Love wins.

愛能勝出。

Love conquers.

愛能征服。

Love prevails.

愛能戰勝。

** ***believe in*** 相信；信任
love〔lʌv〕*n.* 愛
win〔wɪn〕*v.* 贏；獲勝；成功
conquer〔'kɑŋkɚ〕*v.* 征服
prevail〔prɪ'vel〕*v.* 佔優勢；獲勝

Love achieves.

愛能達成。

Love overcomes.

愛能克服。

Love succeeds.

愛能成功。

** love〔lʌv〕*n.* 愛
achieve〔ə'tʃiv〕*v.* 達成;達成目標
overcome〔,ovə'kʌm〕*v.* 克服
succeed〔sək'sid〕*v.* 成功

Choose love.

要選擇愛。

Embrace love.

擁抱真愛。

Spread love.

散播真愛。

** choose〔tʃuz〕*v.* 選擇

love〔lʌv〕*n.* 愛

embrace〔ɪmˈbres〕*v.* 擁抱；欣然接受

spread〔sprɛd〕*v.* 散播

【Unit 1 背景説明】

Love wins.（愛能獲勝。）也可説成：*Love conquers*.（愛能征服。）*Love prevails*.（愛能勝利。）Love triumphs.（愛能獲勝。）

Love achieves.（愛能達成目標。）也可説成：Love triumphs.（愛能獲勝。）Love always wins.（愛總是能獲勝。）

Love overcomes.（愛能克服一切。）也可説成：Love conquers.（愛能征服一切。）

Love succeeds.（愛能成功。）也可説成：Love wins.（愛能獲勝。）

Choose love.　要選擇愛。(= *Opt for love*.)也可説成：Choose the person you love.（要選擇你愛的人。）Choose love over everything else.（選擇愛，勝過一切。）

Embrace love.（要擁抱愛。）也可説成：Welcome love.（要樂於接受愛。）

Spread love.（要散播愛。）也可説成：Share your love.（要分享你的愛。）Express your love.（要表達你的愛。）

BOOK 1 · PART 3

UNIT 2

Just Be Happy 只要快樂

Happiness first.
快樂第一。

Stay joyful.
保持快樂。

Remain cheerful.
保持愉快。

** happiness〔'hæpɪnɪs〕*n.* 快樂；幸福
  first〔fɝst〕*adv.* 第一   stay〔ste〕*v.* 保持
  joyful〔'dʒɔɪfəl〕*adj.* 快樂的
  remain〔rɪ'men〕*v.* 保持
  cheerful〔'tʃɪrfəl〕*adj.* 愉快的

Happiness wins.

快樂會勝。

Happiness rules.

快樂主宰。

Happiness heals.

快樂療癒。

** happiness〔'hæpɪnɪs〕*n.* 快樂；幸福

win〔wɪn〕*v.* 贏；獲勝；成功

rule〔rul〕*v.* 統治；支配；佔上風；
居首要地位

heal〔hil〕*v.* 治癒

Prioritize happiness.

快樂優先。

Prioritize joy.

喜悅優先。

Prioritize cheer.

愉快優先。

** prioritize〔praɪˈɔrəˌtaɪz〕*v.* 給予優先權；
    優先考慮
  happiness〔ˈhæpɪnɪs〕*n.* 快樂；幸福
  joy〔dʒɔɪ〕*n.* 高興；喜悅；快樂
  cheer〔tʃɪr〕*n.* 歡呼；歡樂；
    愉快；高興 *v.* 歡呼

【Unit 2 背景說明】

Happiness first.（快樂第一。）是慣用句。
也可說成：Put happiness first.（要把快樂
放在第一位。）Prioritize happiness.（快樂
優先。）Happiness is most important.（快
樂最重要。）

Stay joyful.（要保持快樂。）也可說成：
Remain cheerful.（要保持愉快。）Remain
happy.（要保持快樂。）

Happiness wins. 快樂獲勝。(＝*Happiness
triumphs.*＝*Happiness prevails.*)

Happiness rules.（快樂佔上風；快樂最重要。）
也可說成：Happiness conquers.（快樂征服
一切。）Happiness is the most important
thing.（快樂是最重要的。）

Happiness heals.（快樂能療癒。）也可說成：
Happiness is curative.（快樂能治病。）
Happiness can make you feel better.（快樂

能使你感覺更好。）Happiness can help you overcome past trauma.（快樂能幫助你克服過去的創傷。）

Prioritize happiness.（要優先考慮快樂。）也可說成：Put happiness first.（要把快樂放在第一位。）Focus on happiness.（要專注於快樂。）

Prioritize joy.（要優先考慮喜悅。）也可說成：Put joy first.（要把喜悅放在第一位。）Place the greatest importance on joy.（要最重視喜悅。）

Prioritize cheer.（要優先考慮愉快。）也可說成：Put cheer first.（要把愉快放在第一位。）Place the greatest importance on merriment.（要最重視歡樂。）Place the greatest importance on happiness.（要最重視快樂。）Place the greatest importance on joy.（要最重視喜悅。）Place the greatest importance on pleasure.（要最重視樂趣。）

UNIT 3

Guard Your Health 守護健康

Health matters.
健康重要。

Fitness dominates.
健康至上。

Well-being counts.
幸福重要。

** guard〔gɑrd〕*v.* 看守;保衛
   health〔hɛlθ〕*n.* 健康
   matter〔'mætɚ〕*v.* 重要
   fitness〔'fɪtnɪs〕*n.* 健康(= *health*)
   dominate〔'dɑmə,net〕*v.* 支配;居首要地位;
   佔優勢
   well-being〔'wɛl'biɪŋ〕*n.* 幸福;安康
   count〔kaʊnt〕*v.* 重要(= *matter*)

Stay well.

保持健康。

Stay healthy.

維持健康。

Stay fit.

持續健康。

** stay〔ste〕*v.* 保持

well〔wɛl〕*adj.* 健康的

healthy〔'hɛlθɪ〕*adj.* 健康的

fit〔fɪt〕*adj.* 健康的（ *= well = healthy*

= in shape = in good shape ）

Prevent illness.

預防疾病。

Avoid disease.

避免疾病。

Deter sickness.

阻止生病。

** prevent〔prɪˈvɛnt〕*v.* 預防

illness〔ˈɪlnɪs〕*n.* 疾病

avoid〔əˈvɔɪd〕*v.* 避免

disease〔dɪˈziz〕*n.* 疾病

deter〔dɪˈtɝ〕*v.* 阻止；阻礙

sickness〔ˈsɪknɪs〕*n.* 疾病；生病

【Unit 3 背景說明】

Health matters. 健康很重要。(= *Health is important.*)

Fitness dominates. 健康支配一切；健康居首要地位；健康至上。(= *Fitness rules.*) 也可說成：Fitness first. (健康第一。) Fitness wins. (健康勝過一切。)

Well-being counts. 幸福很重要；健康很重要。(= *Well-being is important.*) 也可說成：Good health is important. (良好的健康很重要。)

Stay well. 保持健康。(= ***Stay healthy.*** = ***Stay fit.***) 也可說成：Stay in good shape. (要維持健康。)

Prevent illness. 要預防疾病。(= *Avoid sickness.*) 也可說成：Take action to avoid getting sick. (要採取行動避免生病。)

Avoid disease. 要避免疾病。(= *Stay away from illness.* = *Stay away from sickness.*)

Deter sickness. 要防止生病。(= *Thwart sickness.*) 也可說成：Prevent sickness. (要預防生病。)

UNIT 4

Be a Good Listener 要善於傾聽

Always listen.
時刻傾聽。

Listen well.
善於傾聽。

Listening helps.
傾聽有用。

** listener (ˈlɪsn̩ɚ) *n.* 傾聽者
always (ˈɔlwez) *adv.* 總是；一直
listen (ˈlɪsn̩) *v.* 傾聽；注意聽
well (wɛl) *adv.* 好好地
listening (ˈlɪsn̩ɪŋ) *n.* 傾聽
help (hɛlp) *v.* 有用；有幫助

Share thoughts.

分享想法。

Share feelings.

分享感受。

Talking helps.

聊天有益。

** share〔ʃɛr〕*v.* 分享
thought〔θɔt〕*n.* 思想；想法
feelings〔'filɪŋz〕*n. pl.* 感覺；感情
talking〔'tɔkɪŋ〕*n.* 談話
help〔hɛlp〕*v.* 有用；有幫助

Be genuine.
必須眞實。

Be sincere.
必須眞誠。

Connect honestly.
坦誠交往。

** genuine〔ˈdʒɛnjʊɪn〕*adj.* 眞的；眞誠的
sincere〔sɪnˈsɪr〕*adj.* 眞誠的
connect〔kəˈnɛkt〕*v.* 連結；建立關係
honestly〔ˈɑnɪstlɪ〕*adv.* 誠實地

【Unit 4 背景説明】

Always listen.（一定要傾聽。）也可説成：*Listen well.*（要好好傾聽。）Always pay attention to what people are saying.（一定要注意聽別人在說什麼。）

Listening helps.（傾聽有用。）也可説成：Listening is beneficial.（傾聽有益。）

Share thoughts.（要分享想法。）也可説成：Share what you are thinking.（要分享你正在想什麼。）Express what you are thinking.（要表達你的想法。）

Share feelings.（要分享感受。）也可説成：Share what you are feeling.（要分享你有什麼感受。）Express what you are feeling.（要表達你的感受。）

Talking helps.（談話有用。）也可説成：Talking is beneficial.（談話是有益的。）

Be genuine. 要眞實。(= *Be real.* = *Be authentic.*)

Be sincere. 要眞誠。(= *Be genuine.*)

Connect honestly.（要誠實地與人建立關係；要坦誠地與人來往。）也可説成：Make sincere connections.（要建立眞誠的關係。）Be sincere when making connections.（要眞誠地建立關係。）

UNIT 5

Always Be Grateful
總是心存感激

Be thankful.

要存感謝。

Be grateful.

要懂感激。

Be appreciative.

要會感恩。

** always〔ˈɔlwez〕*adv.* 總是；一直
thankful〔ˈθæŋkfəl〕*adj.* 感謝的
grateful〔ˈgretfəl〕*adj.* 感激的
appreciative〔əˈpriʃɪˌetɪv〕*adj.* 感激的

Express thanks.

表達感謝。

Express gratitude.

表達感激。

Express appreciation.

銘感五內。

** express〔ɪk'sprɛs〕*v.* 表達
thanks〔θæŋks〕*n. pl.* 感謝
gratitude〔'grætə,tjud〕*n.* 感激
appreciation〔ə,priʃɪ'eʃən〕*n.* 感激

Count blessings.

珍惜幸福。

Recognize blessings.

感知幸福。

Feel blessed.

感到幸福。

** count〔kaʊnt〕*v.* 數；算
  blessing〔'blɛsɪŋ〕*n.* 幸福；幸運的事
  recognize〔'rɛkəɡ͵naɪz〕*v.* 承認；認可
  feel〔fil〕*v.* 覺得；感到
  blessed〔'blɛsɪd〕*adj.* 幸福的；幸運的

【Unit 5 背景説明】

Be thankful.（要感謝。）也可説成：*Be grateful.*
（要感激。）（= *Be appreciative.*）Be full of
gratitude.（要充滿感激。）Be thankful for what
you have.（要對你所擁有的心存感激。）（= *Be
grateful for what you have.* = *Be appreciative of
what you have.*）Be thankful for what others
do for you.（要對別人為你做的心存感激。）
（= *Be grateful for what others do for you.* = *Be
appreciative of what others do for you.*）

Express thanks.（要表達感謝。）也可説成：
Express gratitude.（要表達感激。）（= *Express
appreciation.*）Show your thanks.（要表示你
的感謝。）Show your gratitude.（要表示你的
感激。）（= *Show your appreciation.*）

Count blessings. 要數一數幸運的事，也就是
「要知道自己有多幸福。」（= *Recognize
blessings.*）也可説成：Be thankful for what
you have.（要對你所擁有的心存感激。）
（= *Be grateful for what you have.*
= *Be appreciative of what you have.*）

Feel blessed.（要覺得幸福。）也可説成：Feel
lucky.（要覺得幸運。）Know how blessed you
are.（要知道你有多幸福。）Know how lucky
you are.（要知道你有多幸運。）

UNIT 6

How to Show Gratitude
如何表示感激

Always say: 一定要說:

Many thanks.
非常感謝。

Deepest thanks.
深深感謝。

Wholehearted thanks.
衷心感謝。

** show〔ʃo〕*v.* 表示
　gratitude〔'grætə,tjud〕*n.* 感激
　thanks〔θæŋks〕*n. pl.* 感謝
　deep〔dip〕*adj.* 深的
　wholehearted〔'hol'hɑrtɪd〕*adj.* 全心全
　　意的;眞摯的

Forever grateful.

永遠感激。

Incredibly grateful.

非常感激。

Eternally grateful.

感激不盡。

** forever〔fəˈɛvə〕*adv.* 永遠
  grateful〔ˈgretfəl〕*adj.* 感激的
  incredibly〔ɪnˈkrɛdəblɪ〕*adv.* 令人難以
    置信地；很；極為
  eternally〔ɪˈtɜnlɪ〕*adv.* 永恆地；永遠地

Much obliged.

非常感激。

Much appreciated.

萬分感謝。

Much gratitude.

不勝感激。

** much〔mʌtʃ〕*adj.* 很多的　*adv.* 非常

obliged〔ə'blaɪdʒd〕*adj.* 感激的

appreciate〔ə'priʃɪˌet〕*v.* 感激；
　重視；欣賞

gratitude〔'grætəˌtjud〕*n.* 感激

【Unit 6 背景説明】

Many thanks.（非常感謝。）也可説成：*Deepest thanks.*（深深感謝。）*Wholehearted thanks.*（衷心感謝。）Thanks a lot.（非常感謝。）Thanks a million.（萬分感謝。）Thanks a bunch.（非常感謝。）

Forever grateful.（永遠感激。）也可説成：I'm forever grateful.（我永遠感激。）

Incredibly grateful.（非常感激。）也可説成：I'm incredibly grateful.（我非常感激。）

Eternally grateful.（永遠感激。）也可説成：I'm eternally grateful.（我感激不盡。）

grateful 也可用 thankful（感謝的）來代替。

Much obliged.（非常感激。）也可説成：I'm incredibly obliged.（我非常感激。）I'm incredibly indebted to you.（我非常感謝你。）

Much appreciated.（非常感激。）源自 It's much appreciated. 這件事被非常感激，也就是「非常感激。」

Much gratitude. 很多的感激，也就是「非常感激。」也可説成：I'm full of gratitude.（我充滿感激。）I'm very grateful.（我非常感激。）

UNIT 7

Shower Others with Praise
儘量稱讚別人

Compliment friends.
誇獎朋友。

Compliment colleagues.
誇獎同事。

Compliment strangers.
誇獎生人。

** shower〔ˈʃaʊɚ〕v. 大量地給予
praise〔prez〕n. 稱讚
compliment〔ˈkɑmpləˌmɛnt〕v. 稱讚
colleague〔ˈkɑlig〕n. 同事（＝*co-worker*）
stranger〔ˈstrendʒɚ〕n. 陌生人

Praise peers.

表揚同儕。

Flatter neighbors.

誇獎鄰居。

Commend acquaintances.

稱讚熟人。

** praise〔prez〕*v. n.* 稱讚

　　peer〔pɪr〕*n.* 同儕;同輩

　　flatter〔'flætɚ〕*v.* 奉承;誇獎

　　neighbor〔'nebɚ〕*n.* 鄰居

　　commend〔kə'mɛnd〕*v.* 稱讚 (= *praise*
　　　= *compliment*)

　　acquaintance〔ə'kwentəns〕*n.* 認識的人

Boost spirits.

提振精神。

Elevate moods.

提升情緒。

Lift morale.

鼓舞士氣。

** boost〔bust〕*v.* 提高；振奮；振作

   spirit〔'spɪrɪt〕*n.* 精神

   elevate〔'ɛlə,vet〕*v.* 提升

   mood〔mud〕*n.* 心情

   lift〔lɪft〕*v.* 提高；使振奮；振作

   morale〔mə'ral,mə'ræl,mo'ræl〕*n.*

    士氣；鬥志

【**Unit 7 背景説明**】

Compliment friends.　要稱讚朋友。(= *Praise the people in your friend group.*)

Compliment colleagues.　要稱讚同事。(= *Praise co-workers.*)

Compliment strangers.（要稱讚陌生人。）也可説成：Praise people you don't know.（要稱讚你不認識的人。）

Praise peers.（要稱讚同儕；要稱讚同輩。）也可説成：Compliment your co-workers.（要稱讚你的同事。）Compliment your companions.（要稱讚你的同伴。）

Flatter neighbors.（要誇獎鄰居。）也可説成：Praise the people who live near you.（要稱讚住在你附近的人。）

Commend acquaintances.　要稱讚認識的人。(= *Speak well of people you know.*)

Boost spirits.（提振精神。）也可説成：*Elevate moods*.（提振心情。）*Lift morale*.（鼓舞士氣。）Cheer people up.（讓大家振作精神；讓大家高興起來。）

UNIT 8

How to Give Compliments
如何稱讚

You can say: 你可以說：

Nice work!
做得不錯！

Great work!
做得好讚！

Impressive work!
印象深刻！

** compliment〔'kɑmpləmənt〕*n.* 稱讚
nice〔naɪs〕*adj.* 好的
work〔wɝk〕*n.* 工作；工作成果
great〔gret〕*adj.* 很棒的
impressive〔ɪm'prɛsɪv〕*adj.* 令人印象深刻的

Amazing job!
做得太棒！

Fantastic job!
做得極佳！

Excellent job!
出類拔萃！

** amazing〔əˈmezɪŋ〕*adj.* 令人驚喜的；
很棒的
job〔dʒɑb〕*n.* 工作
fantastic〔fænˈtæstɪk〕*adj.* 很棒的
excellent〔ˈɛksḷənt〕*adj.* 優秀的

Well done!
做得很好！

You rock!
你太棒了！

You're incredible!
你太傑出！

** well〔wɛl〕*adv.* 很好地
   well done 做得好
   rock〔rɑk〕*v.* 搖晃；演奏搖滾樂；
      眞棒；極具震撼力　*n.* 岩石
   incredible〔ɪnˈkrɛdəbḷ〕*adj.* 令人難以
      置信的；令人驚訝的

【**Unit 8 背景説明**】

Nice work!（做得不錯！）也可説成：***Great work!***（做得很棒！）***Impressive work!***（令人印象深刻！）Good job!（做得好！）Well done!（做得好！）

除了 Good job!（做得好！）之外，還可以説這五句，表示「做得太好了！」

Amazing job! 做得眞棒！（= ***Fantastic job!*** = ***Excellent job!*** = Wonderful job! = Great job!）

Well done!（做得好！）也可説成：You've done the job well!（你把這個工作做得很好！）

You rock! 你太棒了！（= *You're great!* = *You're amazing!* = *You're wonderful!*）

You're incredible! 你令人難以置信！；你太棒了！（= *You're awesome!* = *You're amazing!*）

UNIT 9

Be Humble 要謙虛

Don't brag.

不要吹噓。

Don't boast.

不要自誇。

Stay humble.

保持謙虛。

** brag〔bræg〕v. 自誇；吹牛

boast〔bost〕v. 自誇；吹噓

stay〔ste〕v. 保持

humble〔'hʌmbl̩〕adj. 謙虛的 (= *modest*)

Don't gloat.

不要得意。

Don't exaggerate.

不要誇大。

Stay modest.

保持謙虛。

** gloat〔glot〕*v.* 沾沾自喜；幸災樂禍
exaggerate〔ɪg'zædʒəˌret〕*v.* 誇大
stay〔ste〕*v.* 保持
modest〔'mɑdɪst〕*adj.* 謙虛的 (= *humble*)

Pride hurts.

驕傲害己。

Modesty benefits.

謙卑有益。

Display humility.

展現謙虛。

** pride〔praɪd〕*n.* 驕傲

　hurt〔hɜt〕*v.* 有害

　modesty〔'madəstɪ〕*n.* 謙虛

　benefit〔'bɛnəfɪt〕*v.* 獲利;受益

　display〔dɪ'sple〕*v.* 展示;顯露;表現

　humility〔hju'mɪlətɪ〕*n.* 謙虛

【**Unit 9** 背景説明】

Don't brag.（不要吹牛。）也可説成：***Don't boast***.
（不要自誇。）Don't blow your own horn.（不要
自吹自擂。）

Stay humble.（要保持謙虛。）也可説成：Be
modest.（要謙虛。）

Don't gloat.（不要得意；不要沾沾自喜。）也可説
成：Don't crow.（不要自鳴得意。）

Don't exaggerate.（不要誇大。）也可説成：Don't
overstate.（不要誇張。）

Stay modest.（要保持謙虛。）也可説成：Be
humble.（要謙虛。）

Pride hurts.（驕傲有害。）也可説成：Being too
proud will harm you.（太驕傲會傷害你。）Being
too proud will affect you negatively.（太驕傲會
對你有負面的影響。）

Modesty benefits.（謙虛有益。）也可説成：Humility
is an advantage.（謙虛是優點。）Humility will
help you.（謙虛會幫助你。）
這兩句話源自諺語：Pride hurts, modesty benefits.
（滿招損，謙受益。）

Display humility.　要展現謙虛。(= *Show humility*.)
也可説成：Be humble.（要謙虛。）(= *Be modest*.)

PART 3 總整理

PART 3 · Unit 1~9
中英文**錄音QR碼**

Unit 1

Love wins. 愛能勝出。
Love conquers. 愛能征服。
Love prevails. 愛能戰勝。

Love achieves. 愛能達成。
Love overcomes. 愛能克服。
Love succeeds. 愛能成功。

Choose love. 要選擇愛。
Embrace love. 擁抱真愛。
Spread love. 散播真愛。

Unit 2

Happiness first.
快樂第一。
Stay joyful. 保持快樂。
Remain cheerful.
保持愉快。

Happiness wins.
快樂會勝。
Happiness rules.
快樂主宰。
Happiness heals.
快樂療癒。

Prioritize happiness.
快樂優先。
Prioritize joy. 喜悅優先。
Prioritize cheer.
愉快優先。

Unit 3

Health matters.
健康重要。
Fitness dominates.
健康至上。
Well-being counts.
幸福重要。

Stay well. 保持健康。
Stay healthy. 維持健康。
Stay fit. 持續健康。

Prevent illness.
預防疾病。
Avoid disease.
避免疾病。
Deter sickness.
阻止生病。

BOOK 1 · PART 3

Unit 4

Always listen.　時刻傾聽。
Listen well.　善於傾聽。
Listening helps.　傾聽有用。

Share thoughts.　分享想法。
Share feelings.　分享感受。
Talking helps.　聊天有益。

Be genuine.　必須真實。
Be sincere.　必須真誠。
Connect honestly.
坦誠交往。

Unit 5

Be thankful.　要存感謝。
Be grateful.　要懂感激。
Be appreciative.
要會感恩。

Express thanks.
表達感謝。
Express gratitude.
表達感激。
Express appreciation.
銘感五內。

Count blessings.
珍惜幸福。
Recognize blessings.
感知幸福。
Feel blessed.　感到幸福。

Unit 6

Always say:　一定要說：
Many thanks.　非常感謝。
Deepest thanks.
深深感謝。
Wholehearted thanks.
衷心感謝。

Forever grateful.
永遠感激。
Incredibly grateful.
非常感激。
Eternally grateful.
感激不盡。

Much obliged.　非常感激。
Much appreciated.
萬分感謝。
Much gratitude.
不勝感激。

Unit 7

Compliment friends.
誇獎朋友。
Compliment colleagues.
誇獎同事。
Compliment strangers.
誇獎生人。

Praise peers. 表揚同僑。
Flatter neighbors.
誇獎鄰居。
Commend acquaintances.
稱讚熟人。

Boost spirits. 提振精神。
Elevate moods.
提升情緒。
Lift morale. 鼓舞士氣。

Unit 8

You can say: 你可以說：
Nice work! 做得不錯！
Great work! 做得好讚！
Impressive work!
印象深刻！

Amazing job!
做得太棒！
Fantastic job!
做得極佳！
Excellent job!
出類拔萃！

Well done! 做得很好！
You rock! 你太棒了！
You're incredible!
你太傑出！

Unit 9

Don't brag. 不要吹噓。
Don't boast. 不要自誇。
Stay humble. 保持謙虛。

Don't gloat. 不要得意。
Don't exaggerate.
不要誇大。
Stay modest. 保持謙虛。

Pride hurts. 驕傲害己。
Modesty benefits.
謙卑有益。
Display humility.
展現謙虛。

BOOK 2 / PART 1

How to Get What You Want

如何得到你想要的

PART 1・Unit 1~9
英文錄音QR碼

UNIT 1

Take Action 採取行動

Act now.
現在行動。

Act swiftly.
立刻行動。

Act promptly.
馬上行動。

** action〔'ækʃən〕 *n.* 行動
 take action 採取行動　　act〔ækt〕 *v.* 行動
 now〔naʊ〕 *adv.* 現在;立刻;馬上
 swiftly〔'swɪftlɪ〕 *adv.* 迅速地;立即地
 promptly〔'prɑmptlɪ〕 *adv.* 迅速地;立刻;馬上

Act boldly.

大膽行動。

Act courageously.

勇敢行動。

Act cautiously.

謹慎行事。

** act〔ækt〕*v.* 行動

boldly〔'boldlɪ〕*adv.* 大膽地;勇敢地

courageously〔kə'redʒəslɪ〕*adv.* 勇敢地;
有勇氣地

cautiously〔'kɔʃəslɪ〕*adv.* 小心地;謹慎地

Act kindly.

行為友善。

Act humbly.

舉止謙卑。

Act wisely.

明智行事。

** act〔ækt〕v. 行為；舉止；表現；採取行動
  kindly〔ˈkaɪndlɪ〕adv. 親切地；和善地
  humbly〔ˈhʌmblɪ〕adv. 謙虛地
  wisely〔ˈwaɪzlɪ〕adv. 聰明地；明智地

【Unit 1 背景説明】

Act now.（現在就行動。）也可説成：Do it now.（現在就做。）Take action.（採取行動。）

Act swiftly. 快速行動。(= *Act quickly*.) 也可説成：Do it right now.（現在就做。）Do it as soon as possible.（要儘快去做。）

Act promptly.（馬上行動。）也可説成：Take action right away.（立刻行動。）Take action as soon as possible.（儘快行動。）

Act boldly.（大膽地行動。）也可説成：Take bold action.（要採取大膽的行動。）Act courageously.（要勇敢地行動。）(= *Act daringly*. = *Act bravely*.) Act fearlessly.（要毫無畏懼地行動。）

Act courageously. 勇敢地行動。(= *Act bravely*.) 也可説成：Act without fear.（要毫無畏懼地行動。）Act confidently.（要有信心地行動。）

BOOK 2 · PART 1

Act cautiously. 要謹愼行事。(=*Act warily*.
=*Act carefully*.) 也可説成：Act
thoughtfully.（要深思熟慮地行動。）

Act kindly. 行爲友善。(=*Do things kindly*.)
也可説成：Be kind.（要善良。）Be
compassionate.（要有同情心。）Do things
compassionately.（做事情要有同情心。）

Act humbly.（舉止謙虚。）也可説成：
Behave modestly.（行爲舉止要謙虚。）
Act respectfully.（行爲要恭敬。）
Do things modestly.（做事要謙虚。）
Be modest.（要謙虚。）

Act wisely.（明智行事。）也可説成：
Do things wisely.（要聰明地做事。）
Do things sensibly.（要明智地做事。）
Be sensible.（要明智。）Be shrewd.
（要精明。）

UNIT 2

Follow Your Dreams 追求你的夢想

Dream boldly.
大膽做夢。

Dream daringly.
勇於做夢。

Dream fearlessly.
不懼做夢。

** follow〔'falo〕*v.* 追隨;追逐;追求
dream〔drim〕*n.* 夢;夢想 *v.* 做夢;夢想
boldly〔'boldlɪ〕*adv.* 大膽地;勇敢地
daringly〔'dɛrɪŋlɪ〕*adv.* 勇敢地;大膽地
fearlessly〔'fɪrlɪslɪ〕*adv.* 無畏地;大膽地

Dream courageously.

敢於做夢。

Dream ambitiously.

雄心做夢。

Dream passionately.

熱情做夢。

** dream〔drim〕v. 做夢;夢想

courageously〔kə'redʒəslɪ〕adv. 勇敢地;
有勇氣地

ambitiously〔æm'bɪʃəslɪ〕adv. 有抱負地;
志向遠大地;雄心勃勃地

passionately〔'pæʃənɪtlɪ〕adv. 熱情地

Dream wildly.

瘋狂做夢。

Dream creatively.

夢想創意。

Dream persistently.

堅持夢想。

** dream〔drim〕v. 做夢；夢想

　wildly〔'waɪldlɪ〕adv. 狂野地；瘋狂地

　creatively〔krɪ'etɪvlɪ〕adv. 有創造力地；
　　有創意地

　persistently〔pə'sɪstəntlɪ〕adv. 持續地；
　　堅持不懈地

BOOK 2・PART 1

【**Unit 2 背景説明**】

Dream boldly.（要大膽地做夢。）也可説成：
Have bold dreams.（要有大膽的夢想。）
Have lofty dreams.（要有崇高的夢想。）

Dream daringly.（要勇敢地做夢。）也可説
成：Have ambitious dreams.（要有遠大的
夢想。）Have extraordinary dreams.（要有
非凡的夢想。）

Dream fearlessly.（要毫不畏懼地做夢。）也
可説成：Pursue your dreams with courage.
（要勇敢地追求你的夢想。）Don't hesitate
in pursuit of your dreams.（要毫不猶豫地追
求你的夢想。）

Dream courageously.（要勇敢地做夢。）也
可説成：Be courageous in pursuit of your
dreams.（要勇於追求你的夢想。）Be bold
in pursuit of your dreams.（要大膽追求你的
夢想。）

Dream ambitiously.（要志向遠大地做夢。）也
可説成：Have ambitious dreams.（要有遠大

的夢想。）Have grand dreams.（要有宏偉的夢想。）Have extraordinary dreams.（要有非凡的夢想。）

Dream passionately.（要熱情地做夢。）也可說成：Go all out in pursuit of your dreams.（要竭盡全力追求你的夢想。）

Dream wildly.（要瘋狂地做夢。）也可說成：Don't restrict yourself when dreaming.（不要限制你的夢想。）Have bold dreams.（要有大膽的夢想。）Have ambitious dreams.（要有遠大的夢想。）

Dream creatively.（夢想要有創意。）也可說成：Have innovative dreams.（夢想要創新。）Have imaginative dreams.（夢想要富有想像力。）

Dream persistently.　要持續夢想。(= *Keep dreaming.*) 也可說成：Don't stop dreaming.（不要停止夢想。）Never stop dreaming.（絕不停止夢想。）

UNIT 3

Be Forgiving 要寬容

Forgive now.

現在原諒。

Forgive yourself.

原諒自己。

Forgive others.

原諒別人。

** forgiving〔fəˈɡɪvɪŋ〕*adj.* 寬容的
forgive〔fəˈɡɪv〕*v.* 原諒
now〔naʊ〕*adv.* 現在；立刻；馬上
yourself〔jʊrˈsɛlf〕*pron.* 你自己
others〔ˈʌðəz〕*pron.* 別人

Forgive quickly.
馬上原諒。

Forgive genuinely.
眞心原諒。

Forgive unconditionally.
寬恕一切。

** forgive〔fə'gɪv〕*v.* 原諒
　 quickly〔'kwɪklɪ〕*adv.* 快地
　 genuinely〔'dʒɛnjuɪnlɪ〕*adv.* 眞誠地
　 unconditionally〔ˌʌnkən'dɪʃənḷɪ〕*adv.*
　　 無條件地

Forgive fully.

完全原諒。

Forgive completely.

全然原諒。

Forgive wholeheartedly.

全心原諒。

** forgive〔fə'gɪv〕*v.* 原諒

　　fully〔'fulɪ〕*adv.* 完全地

　　completely〔kəm'plitlɪ〕*adv.* 完全地

　　wholeheartedly〔,hol'hartɪdlɪ〕*adv.*

　　　全心全意地

【**Unit 3 背景説明**】

Forgive now.（現在就原諒。）也可説成：It's time to forgive.（是該原諒的時候了。）

Forgive yourself. 原諒自己。(= *Pardon yourself*.) 要忘記自己所犯的錯誤。也可説成：Don't be too hard on yourself.（不要對你自己太嚴厲。）

Forgive others. 原諒別人。(= *Pardon other people*.) 也可説成：Don't hold grudges.（不要懷恨在心。）

Forgive quickly.（很快地原諒。）也可説成：Forgive right away.（馬上原諒。）Pardon others immediately.（立刻原諒別人。）

Forgive genuinely.（眞心地原諒。）也可説成：Really forgive others.（要眞的原諒別人。）

Forgive unconditionally.（無條件地原諒。）也可説成：Forgive absolutely.（完全地原諒。）

Forgive fully. 完全原諒。(= *Forgive completely*. = *Forgive absolutely*.)

Forgive wholeheartedly.（全心全意地原諒。）也可説成：Forgive sincerely.（眞誠地原諒。）Forgive unconditionally.（無條件地原諒。）

UNIT 4

Keep Learning 持續學習

Learn actively.
主動學習。

Learn proactively.
積極學習。

Learn constantly.
持續學習。

** ***keep + V-ing*** 持續…
learn〔lɜn〕*v.* 學習
actively〔'æktɪvlɪ〕*adv.* 主動地；積極地
proactively〔pro'æktɪvlɪ〕*adv.* 主動地；積極地
constantly〔'kɑnstəntlɪ〕*adv.* 不斷地

Learn quickly.

快點學習。

Learn eagerly.

渴望學習。

Learn passionately.

熱衷學習。

** learn〔lɜn〕v. 學習
　quickly〔ˈkwɪklɪ〕adv. 快地
　eagerly〔ˈigəlɪ〕adv. 熱切地;渴望地
　passionately〔ˈpæʃənɪtlɪ〕adv. 熱情地

Learn wisely.

聰明學習。

Learn purposefully.

學有目標。

Learn intentionally.

學有志向。

** learn〔lɝn〕*v.* 學習
wisely〔'waɪzlɪ〕*adv.* 明智地；聰明地
purposefully〔'pɝpəsfəlɪ〕*adv.* 有目的地；
　故意地
intentionally〔ɪn'tɛnʃənḷɪ〕*adv.* 有意地；故意地

【**Unit 4 背景説明**】

Learn actively.（主動地學習；積極地學習。）
也可説成：Be a diligent learner.（要勤勉地
學習。）Be an earnest learner.（要認眞地學
習。）

Learn proactively.（主動地學習。）也可説
成：Learn things before you need to learn
them.（在你必須學習某些事物之前，就去學
習。）

Learn constantly.（不斷地學習。）也可説
成：Learn all the time.（要一直學習。）
Never stop learning.（絕不停止學習。）

Learn quickly.　快速學習。(= *Learn fast*.)

Learn eagerly.（渴望學習。）也可説成：
Learn passionately.（充滿熱情地學習。）
Learn enthusiastically.（充滿熱忱地學習。）

Learn wisely.（聰明地學習。）也可説成：
Choose what you learn carefully.（小心
選擇你學習的東西。）

Learn purposefully.　有目的地學習。
(= *Learn with purpose*.) 也可説成：*Learn
intentionally*.（有意圖地學習。）(= *Learn
with intention*.)

UNIT 5

Give Freely 要慷慨地給

Give thanks.

給與感謝。

Give praise.

給與讚美。

Give joy.

給與快樂。

** freely〔'frilɪ〕*adv.* 自由地;慷慨地;大方地

give〔gɪv〕*v.* 給與

thanks〔θæŋks〕*n. pl.* 感謝　　*give thanks* 致謝

praise〔prez〕*n.* 稱讚

joy〔dʒɔɪ〕*n.* 喜悅;高興;快樂

Give time.

給點時間。

Give love.

給點愛心。

Give respect.

給點尊重。

** give 〔 gɪv 〕 v. 給與
 time 〔 taɪm 〕 n. 時間
 love 〔 lʌv 〕 n. 愛
 respect 〔 rɪ'spɛkt 〕 n. 尊敬；尊重

Give support.

給與支持。

Give help.

給與幫助。

Give hope.

給與希望。

** give〔gɪv〕*v.* 給與
support〔sə'port〕*n.* 支持
help〔hɛlp〕*n.* 幫助；幫忙
hope〔hop〕*n.* 希望

【**Unit 5 背景説明**】

Give thanks.（給人感謝；向人致謝。）
也可説成：Be thankful.（要充滿感謝。）
Express your gratitude.（表達你的感激。）

Give praise.（給人稱讚。）也可説成：Be
complimentary.（要稱讚別人。）

Give joy.（給人快樂。）也可説成：Make
others happy.（要使別人快樂。）

Give time.（給人時間。）也可説成：Be
generous with your time.（要大方付出你
的時間。）

Give love.（給人眞愛。）也可説成：Express
your love.（表達你的愛。）Show your
love.（表現你的愛。）

Give respect.（給人尊重。）也可説成：Show
respect to others.（要對別人表示尊敬。）Be
respectful.（要尊敬別人。）

Give support.（給人支持。）也可説成：Be
supportive.（要支持別人。）

Give help. 給人幫助。(= *Lend a hand.* = *Help
out.*)也可説成：Be helpful.（要樂於助人。）

Give hope.（給人希望。）也可説成：Be
encouraging.（要鼓勵別人。）

BOOK 2・PART 1

UNIT 6

Let Love into Your Life
讓愛走進你的生命

Love deeply.
深深地愛。

Love truly.
真心地愛。

Love genuinely.
真誠地愛。

** love〔lʌv〕*n. v.* 愛
deeply〔'diplɪ〕*adv.* 深深地
truly〔'trulɪ〕*adv.* 真實地；真誠地
genuinely〔'dʒɛnjʊɪnlɪ〕*adv.* 真誠地

Love kindly.

仁慈地愛。

Love completely.

完全地愛。

Love wholeheartedly.

全心地愛。

** love〔lʌv〕*v.* 愛

kindly〔'kaɪndlɪ〕*adv.* 親切地；仁慈地；
　和善地

completely〔kəm'plitlɪ〕*adv.* 完全地

wholeheartedly〔͵hol'hɑrtɪdlɪ〕*adv.* 全心
　全意地

Love endlessly.

永遠地愛。

Love relentlessly.

持續地愛。

Love eternally.

永恆地愛。

** love〔lʌv〕 *v.* 愛
endlessly〔ˋɛndlɪslɪ〕 *adv.* 無止盡地；不斷地
relentlessly〔rɪˋlɛntlɪslɪ〕 *adv.* 不間斷地；持續地
eternally〔ɪˋtɝnḷɪ〕 *adv.* 永恆地；永遠地

【**Unit 6 背景説明**】

Love deeply. 深深地愛。(= *Love profoundly*.)
也可説成：Love wholeheartedly. (全心全
意地愛。)

Love truly. (眞心地愛。) 也可説成：*Love
genuinely*. (眞誠地愛。) Be sincere when
you love someone. (當你愛別人時，要眞誠。)

Love kindly. (仁慈地愛。) 也可説成：Show
your love in a compassionate way. (要以充
滿同情心的方式展現你的愛。)

Love completely. (完全地愛；徹底地愛。)
也可説成：*Love wholeheartedly*. (全心全
意地愛。) Love sincerely. (眞誠地愛。)
Love unreservedly. (毫無保留地愛。)

Love endlessly. (無止盡地愛。) 也可説成：
Love forever. (永遠地愛。)

Love relentlessly. (不間斷地愛；持續地愛。)
也可説成：Love unceasingly. (不停地愛。)

Love eternally. 永恆地愛；永遠地愛。
(= *Love forever*. = *Love endlessly*.)

UNIT 7

Share What You Have
分享你的一切

Share blessings.
分享幸福。

Share wealth.
分享財富。

Share resources.
分享資源。

** share〔ʃɛr〕v. 分享
　　blessing〔'blɛsɪŋ〕n. 幸福；幸運的事
　　wealth〔wɛlθ〕n. 財富
　　resource〔rɪ'sors, -sɔrs〕n. 資源

Share wisdom.
分享智慧。

Share knowledge.
分享知識。

Share dreams.
分享夢想。

** share〔ʃɛr〕*v.* 分享
   wisdom〔'wɪzdəm〕*n.* 智慧
   knowledge〔'nɑlɪdʒ〕*n.* 知識
   dream〔drim〕*n.* 夢；夢想

Share joy.

分享喜悅。

Share happiness.

分享快樂。

Share love.

分享真愛。

** share〔ʃɛr〕*v.* 分享
joy〔dʒɔɪ〕*n.* 喜悅；高興；快樂
happiness〔'hæpɪnɪs〕*n.* 快樂；幸福
love〔lʌv〕*n.* 愛

【Unit 7 背景説明】

Share blessings.（分享幸福。）也可説成：
Share wealth.（分享財富。）*Share resources*.（分享資源。）Be generous with what you have.（要對於你所擁有的東西很大方。）

Share wisdom.（分享智慧。）也可説成：
Give advice.（提供建議。）

Share knowledge. 分享知識。(= *Share what you know*.) 也可説成：Tell others what you know.（告訴別人你知道的事。）

Share dreams.（分享夢想。）也可説成：Tell others about your dreams.（告訴別人你的夢想。）Tell others about what you want.（告訴別人你想要什麼。）Tell others what you want to do.（告訴別人你想要做什麼。）

Share joy.（分享喜悅。）也可説成：*Share happiness*.（分享快樂。）Spread happiness.（散播快樂。）Tell others what has made you happy.（告訴別人什麼使你快樂。）Share good news.（分享好消息。）

Share love.（分享愛。）也可説成：Express your love.（表達你的愛。）Be loving.（要充滿愛。）

UNIT 8

Think Before You Speak
三思而後言

Speak truthfully.
要說實話。

Speak honestly.
要誠實說。

Speak genuinely.
要真誠說。

** speak〔spik〕*v.* 說；說話
truthfully〔'truθfəlɪ〕*adv.* 誠實地；真實地；
    講真話地   honestly〔'ɑnɪstlɪ〕*adv.* 誠實地
genuinely〔'dʒɛnjʊɪnlɪ〕*adv.* 真誠地

Speak politely.

禮貌地說。

Speak courteously.

客氣地說。

Speak humbly.

謙卑地說。

** speak〔spik〕v. 說；說話

politely〔pəˈlaɪtlɪ〕adv. 有禮貌地

courteously〔ˈkɜtɪəslɪ〕adv. 有禮貌地
(= *politely*)

humbly〔ˈhʌmblɪ〕adv. 謙虛地；謙卑地；
低聲下氣地

Speak wisely.

智慧地說。

Speak gently.

溫和地說。

Speak thoughtfully.

體貼地說。

** speak〔spik〕*v.* 說;說話
　wisely〔'waɪzlɪ〕*adv.* 明智地;聰明地
　gently〔'dʒɛntlɪ〕*adv.* 溫和地
　thoughtfully〔'θɔtfəlɪ〕*adv.* 體貼地;
　　深思熟慮地

【Unit 8 背景説明】

Speak truthfully. 要說實話。(= *Tell the truth.*)
也可説成：***Speak honestly.*** (要誠實地說。)

Speak genuinely. (要眞誠地說。) 也可説成：
Tell the truth. (要說實話。) Be sincere. (要
眞誠。) (= *Be genuine.*)

Speak politely. 要有禮貌地說。(= ***Speak***
courteously. = *Speak civilly.*) 也可説成：
Speak respectfully. (要恭敬地說。)

Speak humbly. 要謙虛地說。(= *Speak*
modestly.) 也可説成：Speak respectfully.
(要恭敬地說。) Don't brag. (不要吹牛。)
Don't boast. (不要誇耀。)

Speak wisely. (要有智慧地說。) 也可説成：
Be careful about what you say. (要小心說
話。) Say wise things. (說話要聰明。)

Speak gently. (要溫和地說。) 也可説成：
Say kind things. (要說些好話。) Speak
compassionately. (說話要有同情心。)

Speak thoughtfully. (體貼地說；深思熟慮地
說。) 也可説成：Think before you speak.
(說話之前要先思考。) Speak carefully. (要
小心地說。)

UNIT 9

Be a Good Worker 勤奮地工作

Work hard.
努力工作。

Work smart.
聰明工作。

Work intelligently.
明智工作。

** worker〔ˈwɝkɚ〕*n.* 工作者
　hard〔hɑrd〕*adv.* 努力地
　smart〔smɑrt〕*adj.* 聰明的　*adv.* 聰明地
　intelligently〔ɪnˈtɛlədʒəntlɪ〕*adv.* 聰明地；
　　有才智地；理解力強地

Work diligently.

辛勤工作。

Work efficiently.

有效工作。

Work tirelessly.

不倦工作。

** diligently〔'dɪlədʒəntlɪ〕*adv.* 勤勉地
efficiently〔ə'fɪʃəntlɪ, ɪ-〕*adv.* 有效率地
tirelessly〔'taɪrlɪslɪ〕*adv.* 孜孜不倦地；
不知疲倦地

Work passionately.

熱情工作。

Work earnestly.

認眞工作。

Work enthusiastically.

熱忱工作。

** passionately〔ˈpæʃənɪtlɪ〕 *adv.* 熱情地
　earnestly〔ˈɜnɪstlɪ〕 *adv.* 認眞地
　enthusiastically〔ɪnˌθjuzɪˈæstɪklɪ〕 *adv.*
　　熱心地；充滿熱忱地

【**Unit 9 背景説明**】

Work hard.（要努力工作。）也可説成：
Make great effort.（要非常努力。）

Work smart. 要聰明地工作。（= *Work
intelligently*.）也可説成：Do your work
in an efficient way.（要有效率地工作。）

Work diligently. 要勤勉地工作。（= *Work
industriously*.）也可説成：Work
energetically.（要充滿活力地工作。）

Work efficiently.（要有效率地工作。）也可説
成：Work well.（要好好地工作。）Work
skillfully.（要有技巧地工作。）

Work tirelessly.（要不知疲倦地工作。）也可
説成：Work steadily.（要持續地工作。）
Work consistently.（要始終如一地工作。）
Work ceaselessly.（要不停地工作。）

Work passionately.（要充滿熱情地工作。）也
可説成：*Work earnestly*.（要認真地工作。）
Work enthusiastically.（要充滿熱忱地工作。）
（= *Do your work with enthusiasm*.）Put your
all into your work.（要盡全力工作。）

PART 1‧Unit 1~9
中英文錄音QR碼

PART 1 總整理

Unit 1

Act now. 現在行動。
Act swiftly. 立刻行動。
Act promptly. 馬上行動。

Act boldly. 大膽行動。
Act courageously.
勇敢行動。
Act cautiously.
謹慎行事。

Act kindly. 行為友善。
Act humbly. 舉止謙卑。
Act wisely. 明智行事。

Unit 2

Dream boldly.
大膽做夢。
Dream daringly.
勇於做夢。
Dream fearlessly.
不懼做夢。

Dream courageously.
敢於做夢。
Dream ambitiously.
雄心做夢。
Dream passionately.
熱情做夢。

Dream wildly. 瘋狂做夢。
Dream creatively. 夢想創意。
Dream persistently.
堅持夢想。

Unit 3

Forgive now. 現在原諒。
Forgive yourself. 原諒自己。
Forgive others. 原諒別人。

Forgive quickly. 馬上原諒。
Forgive genuinely.
真心原諒。
Forgive unconditionally.
寬恕一切。

Forgive fully. 完全原諒。
Forgive completely.
全然原諒。
Forgive wholeheartedly.
全心原諒。

Unit 4

Learn actively.
主動學習。
Learn proactively.
積極學習。
Learn constantly.
持續學習。

Learn quickly.
快點學習。
Learn eagerly.
渴望學習。
Learn passionately.
熱衷學習。

Learn wisely.
聰明學習。
Learn purposefully.
學有目標。
Learn intentionally.
學有志向。

Unit 5

Give thanks. 給與感謝。
Give praise. 給與讚美。
Give joy. 給與快樂。

Give time. 給點時間。
Give love. 給點愛心。
Give respect. 給點尊重。

Give support. 給與支持。
Give help. 給與幫助。
Give hope. 給與希望。

Unit 6

Love deeply. 深深地愛。
Love truly. 真心地愛。
Love genuinely. 真誠地愛。

Love kindly. 仁慈地愛。
Love completely. 完全地愛。
Love wholeheartedly.
全心地愛。

Love endlessly. 永遠地愛。
Love relentlessly. 持續地愛。
Love eternally. 永恆地愛。

BOOK 2・PART 1

Unit 7

Share blessings.
分享幸福。
Share wealth. 分享財富。
Share resources.
分享資源。

Share wisdom. 分享智慧。
Share knowledge.
分享知識。
Share dreams. 分享夢想。

Share joy. 分享喜悅。
Share happiness.
分享快樂。
Share love. 分享真愛。

Unit 8

Speak truthfully.
要說實話。
Speak honestly.
要誠實說。
Speak genuinely.
要真誠說。

Speak politely. 禮貌地說。
Speak courteously.
客氣地說。
Speak humbly. 謙卑地說。

Speak wisely. 智慧地說。
Speak gently. 溫和地說。
Speak thoughtfully.
體貼地說。

Unit 9

Work hard. 努力工作。
Work smart. 聰明工作。
Work intelligently.
明智工作。

Work diligently. 辛勤工作。
Work efficiently. 有效工作。
Work tirelessly. 不倦工作。

Work passionately.
熱情工作。
Work earnestly. 認真工作。
Work enthusiastically.
熱忱工作。

BOOK 2 / PART 2

Live a Good Life
過著美好的生活

PART 2・Unit 1~9
英文錄音QR碼

UNIT 1

Just Do It! 做就對了！

Do good.
做好事。

Do right.
做對事。

Do well.
做得好。

** good〔gʊd〕*adj.* 好的　*n.* 善；好事
　right〔raɪt〕*adj.* 正確的　*adv.* 對地；正確地
　well〔wɛl〕*adv.* 好地

Do it.

趕快做。

Do enough.

做得夠。

Do more.

做更多。

** **do it** 做吧

enough 〔 ə′nʌf, ɪ′nʌf 〕 *adv.* 足夠地；
充分地

more 〔 mɔr 〕 *adv.* 更多地

Do great.
做得好。

Do wonderfully.
做得棒。

Do magnificently.
做得讚。

** great〔gret〕*adv.* 很好地　*adj.* 很棒的；極好的
wonderfully〔ˈwʌndɚfəlɪ〕*adv.* 很棒地；極好地
magnificently〔mægˈnɪfəsn̩tlɪ〕*adv.* 壯麗地；
　華麗地；極好地

【Unit 1 背景説明】

Do good. 要做好事。(= *Do good deeds*.) 也可説成：***Do right***. (做正確的事。) Act morally. (行爲舉止要合乎道德。) Do things that are helpful. (要做有用的事。)

Do well. 要好好地做。(= *Do things well*.) 也可説成：Do a good job. (要做得好。)

Do it. (做吧。) 也可説成：Act. (要行動。) Take action. (採取行動。) Get it done. (要把事情完成。)

Do enough. (要做得充分。) 也可説成：Do what is necessary. (要做必須做的事。) Don't leave anything undone. (不要有任何事情沒做。)

Do more. (要多做一點。) 也可説成：Do more than expected. (要做得比預期的多。) Do more than necessary. (要做得比需要的多。)

Do great. (要做得很好。) 也可説成：***Do wonderfully***. (要做得很棒。) ***Do magnificently***. (要做得極好。) Do it very well. (要做得非常好。) Do a great job. (要做得很棒。)(= *Do an excellent job*. = *Do a splendid job*. = *Do a wonderful job*.) Be awesome. (要非常棒。) Be extraordinary. (要很傑出。)

UNIT 2

The Important Things
重要的事物

Have hope.

有希望。

Have faith.

有信心。

Have courage.

有勇氣。

** hope〔hop〕*n.* 希望
faith〔feθ〕*n.* 信念;信心
courage〔'kɜɪdʒ〕*n.* 勇氣

Have fun.

要開心。

Have joy.

要快樂。

Have peace.

要平靜。

** fun〔fʌn〕*n.* 快樂;樂趣
have fun 玩得愉快
peace〔pis〕*n.* 和平;平靜

Have love.

要有愛。

Have kindness.

要善良。

Have wisdom.

有智慧。

** love〔lʌv〕*n.* 愛
kindness〔ˈkaɪndnɪs〕*n.* 親切；仁慈；善意
wisdom〔ˈwɪzdəm〕*n.* 智慧

【Unit 2 背景説明】

Have hope.（要有希望。）也可説成：Be hopeful.
（要充滿希望。）Never give up hope.（絕不放棄
希望。）

Have faith.（要有信心。）也可説成：Be optimistic.
（要樂觀。）Believe it will happen.（要相信事情
會發生。）Believe you can do it.（要相信你能
做到。）

Have courage. 要有勇氣。(= *Be courageous*.)
也可説成：Be brave.（要勇敢。）Be fearless.
（要無所畏懼。）

Have fun. 要玩得愉快。(= *Have a good time*.
= *Enjoy yourself*.)

Have joy. 要快樂。(= *Be happy*.)

Have peace. 要平靜。(= *Be serene*. = *Be calm*.)
也可説成：Be relaxed.（要放鬆。）

Have love.（要有愛。）也可説成：Love others.
（要愛別人。）Be loved.（要受人喜愛。）

Have kindness. 要善良。(= *Be kind*.) 也可説成：
Be nice.（要親切。）

Have wisdom.（要有智慧。）也可説成：Be wise.
（要明智。）Be clever.（要聰明。）Be shrewd.
（要精明。）

UNIT 3

Never Stop 絕不停止

Keep trying.

繼續努力。

Keep working.

繼續加油。

Keep improving.

繼續改進。

** never〔'nɛvɚ〕*adv.* 絕不

love〔lʌv〕*n.* 愛　　***keep + V-ing*** 持續…

try〔traɪ〕*v.* 嘗試；努力

work〔wɝk〕*v.* 工作；努力

improve〔ɪm'pruv〕*v.* 改善；進步

Keep giving.

持續給與。

Keep sharing.

持續分享。

Keep loving.

持續去愛。

** ***keep + V-ing*** 持續⋯
give〔gɪv〕*v.* 給與;付出
share〔ʃɛr〕*v.* 分享
love〔lʌv〕*v.* 愛

Keep beaming.

笑口常開。

Keep laughing.

持續大笑。

Keep dreaming.

持續夢想。

** *keep* + *V-ing* 持續…
   beam〔bim〕*v.* 高興地微笑；眉開眼笑
   laugh〔læf〕*v.* 笑
   dream〔drim〕*v.* 做夢；夢想

【Unit 3 背景説明】

Keep trying.（要持續嘗試；要持續努力。）也可
說成：Keep going.（要持續努力。）Try again.
（再試一次。）

Keep working. 要持續工作；要持續努力。
（= *Keep going*.）也可說成：Don't give up.
（不要放棄。）

Keep improving.（要持續進步。）也可說成：
Continue to get better.（要持續變得更好。）

Keep giving.（要持續給與。）也可說成：Keep
providing.（要持續供給。）

Keep sharing. 要持續分享。（= *Continue
sharing*.）

Keep loving.（要持續愛人。）也可說成：
Continue to be affectionate.（要持續充滿愛。）
Continue to care.（要持續關心。）

Keep beaming.（要持續眉開眼笑。）也可說成：
Keep smiling.（要持續微笑。）Don't stop
smiling.（不要停止微笑。）Keep a smile on
your face.（你的臉上要保持微笑。）

Keep laughing.（要持續地笑。）也可說成：
Don't stop laughing.（要不停地笑。）

Keep dreaming. 要持續做夢；要持續夢想。
（= *Continue to dream*.）也可說成：Continue
to imagine.（要持續想像。）

BOOK 2・PART 2

UNIT 4

Take the Important Things in Life
要掌握人生中重要的事物

Take charge.

負責管理。

Take control.

掌控一切。

Take responsibility.

負起責任。

** charge〔tʃɑrdʒ〕n. 費用；指控；責任；義務
take charge 負責管理
control〔kən'trol〕n. 控制
take control 控制；掌控
responsibility〔rɪ,spɑnsə'bɪlətɪ〕n. 責任
take responsibility 負起責任；承擔責任

Take advice.

接受勸告。

Take action.

採取行動。

Take steps.

採取步驟。

** advice〔əd'vaɪs〕*n.* 勸告；建議
   take advice 聽從勸告
   action〔'ækʃən〕*n.* 行動
   take action 採取行動
   step〔stɛp〕*n.* 步驟
   take steps 採取步驟

Take care.
要小心。

Take heed.
要留意。

Take precautions.
要防護。

** *take care* 小心；保重
　heed〔hid〕*n.* 注意；留意
　take heed 注意；提防
　precaution〔prɪˋkɔʃən〕*n.* 小心；警惕；
　（*pl.*）預防措施
　take precautions 小心；謹慎；採取
　　預防措施

【Unit 4 背景説明】

Take charge.（要負責管理。）也可説成：***Take control***.（要掌控一切。）(= *Take the reins*.)

Take responsibility. 要負起責任。(= *Take accountability*.) 也可説成：Assume responsibility.（要承擔責任。）

Take advice.（要聽從勸告。）也可説成：Listen to others.（要聽別人的話。）Take others' suggestions.（要接受別人的建議。）

Take action.（要採取行動。）也可説成：Do something.（要做點事；行動吧。）Do it.（做吧。）

Take steps.（要採取步驟。）也可説成：Start.（開始吧。）(= *Begin*.) Take action.（要採取行動。）Take measures.（要採取措施。）Execute the plan.（要執行計劃。）(= *Carry out the plan*.)

Take care. 要小心。(= *Be careful*. = *Be cautious*.) 也可説成：Be mindful.（要留意。）Be wary.（要機警。）***Take heed***.（要注意。）***Take precautions***.（要小心謹慎。）

UNIT 5

Believe in Miracles 相信奇蹟

Miracles happen.

奇蹟必發生。

Miracles occur.

奇蹟必出現。

Miracles exist.

奇蹟必存在。

** ***believe in*** 相信；相信有
   miracle 〔'mɪrəkl̩〕 *n.* 奇蹟
   happen 〔'hæpən〕 *v.* 發生
   occur 〔ə'kɝ〕 *v.* 發生
   exist 〔ɪg'zɪst〕 *v.* 存在

Miracles shine.

奇蹟會閃耀。

Miracles spark.

奇蹟會發光。

Miracles illuminate.

奇蹟會照亮。

** miracle〔'mɪrəkḷ〕*n.* 奇蹟

　　shine〔ʃaɪn〕*v.* 照耀；發光；發亮

　　spark〔spɑrk〕*v.* 發出火花；閃耀；閃光

　　illuminate〔ɪ'lumə,net〕*v.* 照亮；啟發

Miracles inspire.

奇蹟鼓舞人心。

Miracles uplift.

奇蹟振奮人心。

Miracles rejuvenate.

奇蹟讓人重生。

** miracle〔'mɪrəkḷ〕*n.* 奇蹟

　inspire〔ɪn'spaɪr〕*v.* 激勵；給予靈感

　uplift〔'ʌp,lɪft〕*v.* 使上升；提高；振奮；
　　鼓舞

　rejuvenate〔rɪ'dʒuvə,net〕*v.* 使返老還童；
　　使恢復活力

【Unit 5 背景説明】

Miracles happen. 奇蹟會發生。(= *Miracles occur.*) 也可説成：*Miracles exist.* (奇蹟是存在的。) Believe in miracles. (要相信會有奇蹟。)

Miracles shine. (奇蹟會閃耀。) 也可説成：*Miracles spark.* (奇蹟會發光。) *Miracles illuminate.* (奇蹟會照亮。) Miracles are wonderful. (奇蹟很棒。) (= *Miracles are great.* = *Miracles are fantastic.* = *Miracles are amazing.* = *Miracles are spectacular.*)

Miracles inspire. (奇蹟激勵人心。) 也可説成：Wonders give people hope. (奇蹟給人希望。) Wonders give people encouragement. (奇蹟給人鼓勵。)

Miracles uplift. (奇蹟振奮人心。) 也可説成：Wonders make people feel better. (奇蹟使人感覺更好。)

Miracles rejuvenate. (奇蹟讓人恢復活力。) 也可説成：Wonders give new energy. (奇蹟能提供新的活力。)

BOOK 2 · PART 2

UNIT 6

Be the Best You 做最好的自己

Be wise.

要聰明。

Be creative.

要創意。

Be innovative.

要創新。

** wise 〔 waɪz 〕 *adj.* 明智的；聰明的
   creative 〔 krɪ'etɪv 〕 *adj.* 有創造力的；
      有創意的
   innovative 〔 'ɪnə,vetɪv 〕 *adj.* 創新的

Be flexible.

要有彈性。

Be adaptable.

要能適應。

Be resourceful.

要有機智。

** flexible〔ˈflɛksəbl̩〕*adj.* 有彈性的；
   可變通的
   adaptable〔əˈdæptəbl̩〕*adj.* 能適應的
   resourceful〔rɪˈsorsfəl, -ˈsɔrs-〕*adj.*
   機智的；足智多謀的；善於隨機應變的

Be careful.
要小心。

Be mindful.
要留心。

Be cautious.
要謹慎。

** careful〔ˈkɛrfəl〕 *adj.* 小心的

mindful〔ˈmaɪndfəl〕 *adj.* 注意的；留心的

（= *aware* = *attentive*）

cautious〔ˈkɔʃəs〕 *adj.* 謹慎的；小心的

【Unit 6 背景説明】

Be wise. 要聰明。(= *Be smart.*) 也可説成：
Be sensible. (要明智。) Be prudent. (要謹
慎。) Be shrewd. (要精明。)

Be creative. (要有創意。) 也可説成：Be
inventive. (要創造發明。) *Be innovative.*
(要創新。)

Be flexible. (要有彈性；要懂得變通。) 也可
説成：*Be adaptable.* (要能適應。) Be
accommodating. (要隨和。) Be open to
other ideas. (要能接受其他的想法。)

Be resourceful. (要足智多謀。) 也可説成：
Be ingenious. (要有獨創性。) Be capable.
(要有能力。) Be quick-witted. (要機智。)

Be careful. (要小心。) 也可説成：*Be
mindful.* (要留意。) *Be cautious.* (要謹
慎。) Be aware. (要注意。) Be wary. (要
機警。) (= *Be vigilant.*) Be thoughtful.
(要深思熟慮。)

UNIT 7

Make What You Do Count
讓自己做的事有價值

Make plans.
定計畫。

Make choices.
做選擇。

Make decisions.
做決定。

** make〔mek〕*v.* 使；做；制定
plan〔plæn〕*n.* 計劃
choice〔tʃɔɪs〕*n.* 選擇
decision〔dɪ'sɪʒən〕*n.* 決定

Make changes.
要改變。

Make progress.
要進步。

Make improvements.
要改進。

** change〔tʃendʒ〕*n.* 改變
make a change 做出改變
progress〔'prɑgrɛs〕*n.* 進步
make progress 進步
improvement〔ɪm'pruvmənt〕*n.* 改善；
　　改進

Make efforts.

付出努力。

Make sacrifices.

做出犧牲。

Make magic.

創造奇蹟。

** effort〔ˈɛfət〕*n.* 努力
make efforts 努力
sacrifice〔ˈsækrə,faɪs〕*n.* 犧牲
make sacrifices 做出犧牲
magic〔ˈmædʒɪk〕*n.* 魔法；魔力
make magic 使奇蹟發生

【**Unit 7 背景說明**】

Make plans.（要做計劃。）也可說成：Think about what you want to do.（要考慮你想要做什麼。）Know what you want to do.（要知道你想要做什麼。）Think about how you will do it.（要考慮你會怎麼做。）

Make choices.（要做選擇。）也可說成：Make a choice.（要做選擇。）Choose what you want.（選擇你想要的。）

Make decisions.（要做決定。）(= *Decide*.) 也可說成：Make a decision.（要做決定。）Decide what you want.（要決定你想要什麼。）Decide what you will do.（要決定你會做什麼。）

Make changes.（要做出改變。）也可說成：Change the way things are.（要改變事情的現狀。）Change yourself.（要改變你自己。）

Make progress. 要進步。(= *Advance*.) 也可
說成：Move ahead. (要向前進。) Move
toward your goal. (要朝著你的目標前進。)

Make improvements. (要改進。) 也可說成：
Make things better. (要使情況變得更好。)
(= *Improve things*.)

Make efforts. 要努力。(= *Make an effort*.
= *Try*. = *Try hard*. = *Work hard*.)

Make sacrifices. (要做出犧牲。) 也可說成：
Forgo something to get what you want.
(要放棄某樣東西以得到你想要的。) Give
something up. (要放棄某樣東西。)

Make magic. 要施魔法，引申為「要使奇蹟發
生。」也可說成：Work wonders. (要創造奇
蹟。) (= *Create miracles*. = *Create magic*.)
Do great things. (要做很棒的事。) (= *Do
wonderful things*. = *Do something wonderful*.
= *Do something amazing*.)

UNIT 8

Stay Who You Are 保持本性

Stay kind.

保持善良。

Stay loving.

保持愛心。

Stay friendly.

保持友善。

** stay〔ste〕*v.* 保持；維持
   who you are 真實的自己
   kind〔kaɪnd〕*adj.* 親切的；仁慈的；和善的
   loving〔ˈlʌvɪŋ〕*adj.* 充滿愛的
   friendly〔ˈfrɛndlɪ〕*adj.* 友善的

Stay generous.
保持慷慨。

Stay gracious.
保持親切。

Stay respectful.
保持恭敬。

** stay〔ste〕v. 保持；維持
generous〔'dʒɛnərəs〕adj. 慷慨的；大方的
gracious〔'greʃəs〕adj. 親切的
respectful〔rɪ'spɛktfəl〕adj. 尊敬的；
　　恭敬的；很有禮貌的；彬彬有禮的；
　　謙恭的

Stay true.

保持真實。

Stay calm.

保持冷靜。

Stay determined.

保持決心。

** stay〔ste〕*v.* 保持

true〔tru〕*adj.* 真實的；忠實的；忠誠的

calm〔kɑm〕*adj.* 冷靜的

determined〔dɪˈtɜmɪnd〕*adj.* 下定決心的；
　堅決的

【Unit 8 背景説明】

Stay kind. 保持善良。(= *Remain kind.*) 也可説成：Continue being kind. (要持續善良。) Remain nice. (要保持親切。) Remain compassionate. (要一直有同情心。)

Stay loving. 持續充滿愛。(= *Remain loving.* = *Continue being loving.* = *Remain affectionate.*)

Stay friendly. 保持友善。(= *Remain friendly.*) 也可説成：Continue being friendly. (要持續友善。) Remain pleasant. (要持續令人愉快。) Remain sociable. (要持續喜歡交際。) Remain amiable. (要一直和藹可親。)

Stay generous. (保持慷慨。) 也可説成：Continue being charitable. (要持續慈善。) Continue giving. (要持續付出。)

Stay gracious*.（要一直很親切。）也可說成：
Continue being tactful.（要持續圓融。）
Continue being cordial.（要持續親切。）

Stay respectful*.* 保持恭敬。(= *Continue being
respectful.*）也可說成：Continue being
polite.（要持續有禮貌。）(= *Continue being
courteous.*）Continue being civil.（要持續
彬彬有禮。）

Stay true*.*（保持真實；保持忠實。）也可說
成：Stay real.（保持真實。）Be genuine.
（要真實。）Stay faithful.（保持忠實。）
Stay loyal.（保持忠誠。）

Stay calm*.*（保持冷靜。）也可說成：Remain
composed.（保持鎮定。）Remain relaxed.
（保持放鬆。）

Stay determined*.* 保持堅決。(= *Remain
resolute.*）也可說成：Remain firm.
（保持堅定。）

BOOK 2・PART 2

UNIT 9

Eat Well 要吃得好

Eat fresh.

吃得新鮮。

Eat cleanly.

吃得乾淨。

Eat seasonally.

吃季節食。

** fresh〔frɛʃ〕*adj.* 新鮮的
cleanly〔ˈklinlɪ〕*adv.* 乾淨地
seasonally〔ˈsiznl̩ɪ〕*adv.* 季節性地

Eat nutritiously.

吃得營養。

Eat healthily.

吃得健康。

Eat wholesomely.

健康飲食。

** nutritiously〔nju'trɪʃəslɪ〕 *adv.* 有營養地
   healthily〔'hɛlθɪlɪ〕 *adv.* 健康地；有益健康地
   wholesomely〔'holsəmlɪ〕 *adv.* 有益健康地
   (= *healthily* = *healthfully*)

Eat happily.

快樂地吃。

Eat joyfully.

喜悅地吃。

Eat cheerfully.

愉快地吃。

** happily〔ˈhæpɪlɪ〕 *adv.* 快樂地
joyfully〔ˈdʒɔɪfəlɪ〕 *adv.* 高興地；喜悅地
cheerfully〔ˈtʃɪrfəlɪ〕 *adv.* 愉快地

【**Unit 9 背景説明**】

Eat fresh.（要吃得新鮮。）是慣用句。也可説成：Eat fresh food.（要吃新鮮的食物。）Avoid processed food.（要避免加工食品。）

Eat cleanly.（要吃得乾淨。）也可説成：Eat clean food.（要吃乾淨的食物。）

Eat seasonally.（要吃季節性的食物。）也可説成：Eat food that is in season.（要吃當季的食物。）Eat what is available now.（要吃現在買得到的食物。）

Eat nutritiously.（要吃得營養。）也可説成：Eat food that is high in nutrition.（要吃富含營養的食物。）

Eat healthily. 要吃得健康。(= *Eat healthfully*. = *Eat healthy*.）也可説成：*Eat wholesomely*.（要吃有益健康的食物。）Eat a healthy diet.（要有健康的飲食。）Eat food that is good for you.（要吃對你有益的食物。）

Eat happily. 要吃得快樂。(= *Eat joyfully*. = *Eat cheerfully*.）也可説成：Enjoy what you eat.（要喜歡你吃的東西。）Be happy to eat.（要快樂地吃。）Take pleasure in eating.（要以吃東西爲樂。）

PART 2 總整理

PART 2・Unit 1~9
中英文**錄音QR碼**

Unit 1

Do good. 做好事。
Do right. 做對事。
Do well. 做得好。

Do it. 趕快做。
Do enough. 做得夠。
Do more. 做更多。

Do great. 做得好。
Do wonderfully.
做得棒。
Do magnificently.
做得讚。

Unit 2

Have hope. 有希望。
Have faith. 有信心。
Have courage. 有勇氣。

Have fun. 要開心。
Have joy. 要快樂。
Have peace. 要平靜。

Have love. 要有愛。
Have kindness. 要善良。
Have wisdom. 有智慧。

Unit 3

Keep trying. 繼續努力。
Keep working. 繼續加油。
Keep improving.
繼續改進。

Keep giving. 持續給與。
Keep sharing. 持續分享。
Keep loving. 持續去愛。

Keep beaming. 笑口常開。
Keep laughing. 持續大笑。
Keep dreaming. 持續夢想。

Unit 4

Take charge. 負責管理。
Take control. 掌控一切。
Take responsibility.
負起責任。

Take advice.
接受勸告。
Take action.
採取行動。
Take steps. 採取步驟。

Take care. 要小心。
Take heed. 要留意。
Take precautions.
要防護。

Unit 5

Miracles happen.
奇蹟必發生。
Miracles occur.
奇蹟必出現。
Miracles exist.
奇蹟必存在。

Miracles shine.
奇蹟會閃耀。
Miracles spark.
奇蹟會發光。
Miracles illuminate.
奇蹟會照亮。

Miracles inspire.
奇蹟鼓舞人心。
Miracles uplift.
奇蹟振奮人心。
Miracles rejuvenate.
奇蹟讓人重生。

Unit 6

Be wise. 要聰明。
Be creative. 要創意。
Be innovative. 要創新。

Be flexible. 要有彈性。
Be adaptable. 要能適應。
Be resourceful. 要有機智。

Be careful. 要小心。
Be mindful. 要留心。
Be cautious. 要謹慎。

Unit 7

Make plans. 定計畫。
Make choices. 做選擇。
Make decisions. 做決定。

BOOK 2・PART 2

Make changes. 要改變。
Make progress.
要進步。
Make improvements.
要改進。

Make efforts.
付出努力。
Make sacrifices.
做出犧牲。
Make magic. 創造奇蹟。

Unit 8

Stay kind. 保持善良。
Stay loving.
保持愛心。
Stay friendly.
保持友善。

Stay generous.
保持慷慨。
Stay gracious.
保持親切。
Stay respectful.
保持恭敬。

Stay true. 保持真實。
Stay calm. 保持冷靜。
Stay determined.
保持決心。

Unit 9

Eat fresh. 吃得新鮮。
Eat cleanly.
吃得乾淨。
Eat seasonally.
吃季節食。

Eat nutritiously.
吃得營養。
Eat healthily.
吃得健康。
Eat wholesomely.
健康飲食。

Eat happily.
快樂地吃。
Eat joyfully.
喜悅地吃。
Eat cheerfully.
愉快地吃。

BOOK 2　PART 3

Wise Words for Personal Development
個人成長的智慧箴言

PART 3・Unit 1~9
英文錄音QR碼

UNIT 1

Being Kind Is Worth It
善良很值得

Kindness pays.
善良值得。

Kindness rewards.
善良有償。

Kindness returns.
善良回報。

** kind〔kaɪnd〕*adj.* 親切的;仁慈的;善良的
   worth it 值得的
   kindness〔'kaɪndnɪs〕*n.* 親切;仁慈;善意
   pay〔pe〕*v.* 值得;有益;划得來;能獲利
   reward〔rɪ'wɔrd〕*v.* 報答;獎賞
   return〔rɪ'tɜn〕*v.* 返回;報答;回報

Kindness shines.

善良發光。

Kindness radiates.

善良煥發。

Kindness enlightens.

善良啓發。

** kindness〔'kaındnıs〕*n.* 親切；仁慈；善意
shine〔∫aın〕*v.* 照耀；發光；發亮；出色；
　　出類拔萃
radiate〔'redı͵et〕*v.* 輻射；散發（光、熱等）
enlighten〔ın'laıtṇ〕*v.* 啓蒙；啓發；開導

Kindness empowers.

善良給人力量。

Kindness connects.

善良增加人脈。

Kindness unites.

善良促進團結。

** kindness〔'kaɪndnɪs〕*n.* 親切;仁慈;善意
empower〔ɪm'pauə〕*v.* 給與力量;授權
connect〔kə'nɛkt〕*v.* 連接;與…建立
良好關係
unite〔ju'naɪt〕*v.* 團結;使團結

【**Unit 1 背景説明**】

Kindness pays. (善良很值得。) 也可説成：
Kindness rewards. (善良會有報酬。)
(= *Kindness is rewarding*.) *Kindness returns*. (善良會有回報。) If you are kind, good things will happen to you. (如果你很善良，好事就會發生在你身上。) If you are kind, you will receive kindness in return. (如果你很善良，就會獲得善意的回報。)

Kindness shines. 善良會發光。(= *Kindness radiates*. = *Kindness glows*. = *Kindness is radiant*.) 也可説成：Kindness is amazing. (善良令人驚奇。) Compassion shines. (同情發光。) (= *Compassion radiates*.)

Kindness enlightens. (善良給人啓發。) 也可説成：Kindness informs. (善良給人資訊。) Kindness clarifies. (善良能使事情清晰。) (= *Kindness makes things clear*.) Compassion educates. (同情能教育大家。)

Compassion illuminates. (同情能照亮世界。)
Compassion inspires. (同情能激勵人心。)

Kindness empowers. 善良給人力量。
(= *Kindness gives people power.* = *Kindness
gives people strength.*) 也可説成：Being
kind gives you power. (善良能給你力量。)
(= *Being kind gives you strength.*) Kindness
makes people stronger. (善良使人更強大。)
Kindness gives people more opportunities.
(善良給人更多機會。)

Kindness connects. 善良使人建立關係。
(= *Kindness connects people.*) 也可説
成：Kindness helps you develop new
relationships. (善良能幫助你發展新的關
係。)

Kindness unites. 善良使人團結。(= *Kindness
brings people together.*)

UNIT 2

Be an Active Person 要主動積極

Get busy.

找事情做。

Get active.

要動起來。

Get involved.

參與其中。

** get〔gɛt〕*v.* 變得
busy〔'bɪzɪ〕*adj.* 忙碌的　***get busy*** 開始做
active〔'æktɪv〕*adj.* 活躍的；主動的；
　　忙於…的；參與…的
involve〔ɪn'vɑlv〕*v.* 使參與；牽涉
get involved 參與

Get well.

身體要好。

Get healthy.

變得健康。

Get outdoors.

走出戶外。

** get〔gɛt〕*v.* 變得
well〔wɛl〕*adj.* 健康的
healthy〔'hɛlθɪ〕*adj.* 健康的
outdoors〔'aut'dorz〕*adv.* 在戶外；到戶外
get outdoors 到戶外

Get inspired.

要受激勵。

Get motivated.

要受鼓舞。

Get determined.

要下決心。

** get〔gɛt〕*v.* 變得

inspired〔ɪn'spaɪrd〕*adj.* 受到激勵的；
　得到啓發的；有靈感的

motivated〔'motə,vetɪd〕*adj.* 有動機的；
　受到激勵的；充滿熱情的

determined〔dɪ'tɜmɪnd〕*adj.* 下定決心的；
　堅決的

【**Unit 2** 背景說明】

Get busy. 要變得忙碌，引申為「要找事情做；
要開始做。」(= *Get started.* = *Get to work.*)

Get active. (要動起來。) 也可說成：Do a
lot of things. (要做很多事。) Participate
in many things. (要參與很多事。)

Get involved. 要參與。(= *Participate.*)
Participate actively. (要積極參與。)
(= *Be an active participant.*) Join a lot
of activities. (要參加很多的活動。)

Get well. 要變得健康。(= ***Get healthy.***) 也
可說成：Improve your health. (要改善你
的健康。)

Get outdoors. (要到戶外。) 也可說成：Go
outside. (要去外面。) Spend time outside.
(要待在外面。) Spend time outdoors. (要待
在戶外。) Get out of the house. (要離開家。)
Get out of the office. (要離開辦公室。)

Get inspired. 要受到激勵。(= *Be inspired.*) 也可說成：Be enthused. (要充滿熱情。) Be energized. (要充滿活力。) Be excited. (要很興奮。) Find your inspiration. (要找到能激勵你的事物。) (= *Find your motivation.*)

Get motivated. (要有動機；要受到激勵。) (= *Get inspired.*) 也可說成：Be ambitious. (要有抱負。) Be enthusiastic. (要有熱忱。) Be keen. (要熱心。) Motivate yourself. (要激勵自己。)

Get determined. (要下定決心。) 也可說成：Be firm. (要堅定。) Be resolute. (要堅決。) Be resolved. (要下定決心。) Be unwavering. (要堅定不移。) Be determined to do it. (要堅決去做。) Set your mind on doing it. (要下定決心去做。)

determine 主動、被動意義相同。【詳見「文法寶典」p.388】

UNIT 3

Seek Out the Best Things in Life
找出人生中最棒的事物

Find love.
尋找真愛。

Find beauty.
尋找美好。

Find happiness.
尋找快樂。

```
** seek〔sik〕v. 尋求；尋找      seek out 找出
   find〔faɪnd〕v. 找到；發現
   love〔lʌv〕n. v. 愛
   beauty〔'bjutɪ〕n. 美；美麗
   happiness〔'hæpɪnɪs〕n. 快樂；幸福
```

Find passion.

尋找愛好。

Find purpose.

尋找目標。

Find direction.

尋找方向。

** find〔faɪnd〕v. 找到；發現
　passion〔'pæʃən〕n. 熱情；愛好
　purpose〔'pɝpəs〕n. 目的；目標
　direction〔də'rɛkʃən〕n. 方向

Find peace.
尋找和平。

Find harmony.
尋找和諧。

Find tranquility.
尋找寧靜。

** find〔faɪnd〕v. 找到；發現
peace〔pis〕n. 和平；平靜
harmony〔ˈhɑrmənɪ〕n. 和諧
tranquility〔trænˈkwɪlətɪ〕n. 平靜；寧靜；
　祥和；安靜

【**Unit 3 背景説明**】

Find love.（要找到愛。）也可説成：Find someone to love.（要找個人愛。）Find someone who loves you.（要找個愛你的人。）

Find beauty.（要找到美好。）也可説成：Discover marvels.（要發現令人驚奇的事物。）Find something you enjoy seeing.（要找到你喜歡看的事物。）

Find happiness.（要找到快樂。）也可説成：Find out what makes you happy.（要找出能使你快樂的事物。）Be happy.（要快樂。）

Find passion.（要找到愛好。）也可説成：Find out what you really want to do.（要找出你眞正想要做的事。）Find out what you really care about.（要找出你眞正在乎的東西。）Be enthusiastic.（要有熱忱。）Be inspired.（要受到激勵。）

Find purpose.　要找到目標。(= *Find a goal*. = *Discover your goal*.) 也可説成：Develop a goal.（要培養目標。）Develop an ambition.（要培養抱負。）

Find direction. （要找到方向。）也可說成：
Find a goal. （要找到目標。）Find an
ambition. （要找到抱負。）Discover what
you want to do. （要發現你想要做什麼。）
Find out how to do something. （要查明如
何做某事。）

Find peace. 要找到平靜。（= *Find calm*. ）也
可說成：Find what gives you peace. （要
找到能使你平靜的事物。）Discover what
helps you stay calm. （要發現能幫助你保持
冷靜的事物。）Find peace and quiet. （要找
到寧靜。）

Find harmony. （要找到和諧。）也可說成：
Find understanding. （要尋找理解。）Find
goodwill. （要尋找善意。）Reach an
agreement. （要達成協議。）

Find tranquility. （要找到寧靜。）也可說成：
Find peace. （要找到平靜。）Discover what
helps you find serenity. （要發現能幫助你找
到寧靜的事物。）

UNIT 4

Never Underestimate the Power of Money 絕不可低估金錢的力量

Money talks.
錢能說話。

Money speaks.
錢能發言。

Money matters.
金錢重要。

** underestimate〔͵ʌndɚˋɛstə͵met〕*v.* 低估
power〔ˋpaʊɚ〕*n.* 力量　money〔ˋmʌnɪ〕*n.* 錢
talk〔tɔk〕*v.* 說話　speak〔spik〕*v.* 說話
matter〔ˋmætɚ〕*v.* 重要（＝*count*）

Money rules.

金錢萬能。

Money leads.

金錢領導。

Money dominates.

金錢支配。

** money〔'mʌnɪ〕 *n.* 錢

rule〔rul〕 *v.* 統治

lead〔lid〕 *v.* 領導

dominate〔'dɑmə,net〕 *v.* 支配;統治

Money decides.

金錢決定。

Money manages.

金錢管理。

Money influences.

金錢影響。

** money〔ˈmʌnɪ〕 *n.* 錢
decide〔dɪˈsaɪd〕 *v.* 決定
manage〔ˈmænɪdʒ〕 *v.* 管理；處理
influence〔ˈɪnfluəns〕 *v. n.* 影響

【Unit 4 背景説明】

Money talks. 是一句諺語，錢會説話，引申爲
「金錢萬能。」(= ***Money speaks.***) 也可説成：
Money is influential. (金錢有影響力。)

Money matters. 錢很重要。(= *Money counts.*
= *Money is what matters.* = *Money is what
counts.* = *Money is important.*) 也可説成：
Money carries weight. (錢有很大的影響力。)

Money rules. (錢能統治；金錢萬能。) 也可説
成：***Money leads.*** (錢能領導。) ***Money
dominates.*** (錢能支配。) Money is the most
important thing. (錢是最重要的東西。)

Money decides. (錢能決定。) 也可説成：
Whoever has the money makes the
decisions. (有錢的人決定。)

Money manages. (錢能管理。) 也可説成：
Whoever has the money controls what
happens. (有錢的人能掌控發生的事。)

Money influences. (錢能影響。) 也可説成：
Whoever has the money has the most
influence. (有錢的人最有影響力。)
Whoever has the money has the most
power. (有錢的人最有力量。)

UNIT 5

What You Do Is Important
你的行爲很重要

Actions speak.

行爲說話。

Actions lead.

行爲領導。

Actions guide.

行爲引導。

** action〔ˈækʃən〕*n.* 行動；(*pl.*) 行爲
speak〔spik〕*v.* 說話
lead〔lid〕*v.* 領導
guide〔gaɪd〕*v.* 引導

Actions matter.

行為重要。

Actions count.

行為有價。

Actions inspire.

行為鼓舞。

** action〔'ækʃən〕 *n.* 行動;(*pl.*) 行為
　matter〔'mætɚ〕 *v.* 重要
　count〔kaʊnt〕 *v.* 數;計算;有價值;
　　很重要 (= *matter*)
　inspire〔ɪn'spaɪr〕 *v.* 激勵;給與靈感

Actions show.

行為展示。

Actions reveal.

行為透露。

Actions communicate.

行為傳達。

** action〔'ækʃən〕 *n.* 行動；(*pl.*) 行為
    show〔ʃo〕 *v.* 顯示
    reveal〔rɪ'vil〕 *v.* 透露
    communicate〔kə'mjunə‚ket〕 *v.* 溝通；
    傳達

【Unit 5 背景説明】

Actions speak.（行爲會說話。）也可説成：What you
do says a lot about you.（你的行爲透露出很多關於
你的事。）

Actions lead.（行爲會領導。）也可説成：*Actions
guide*.（行爲會引導。）You can lead others through
your actions.（你可以用你的行爲來領導別人。）
You can lead by example.（你可以以身作則。）

Actions matter.　行爲很重要。（= *Actions count*.）
也可説成：What you do is important.（你的行爲
很重要。）

Actions inspire.（行爲能激勵人心。）也可説成：
What you do can inspire others.（你的行爲能激勵
別人。）What you do can encourage others.（你
的行爲能鼓勵別人。）

Actions show.（行爲能顯示。）也可説成：*Actions
reveal*.（行爲能透露。）What you do says a lot
about you.（你的行爲透露很多關於你的事。）

Actions communicate.（行爲能傳達。）也可説成：
Actions send a message.（行爲能傳達訊息。）
Your actions tell people what you want to say.
（你的行爲告訴別人你想說的話。）Your actions
tell people who you are.（你的行爲告訴別人你是
什麼樣的人。）

BOOK 2 · PART 3

UNIT 6

Understand the Importance of Time 了解時間的重要

Time flies.
時間飛逝。

Time passes.
時間流逝。

Time vanishes.
時間消逝。

** importance〔ɪm'pɔrtn̩s〕*n.* 重要性
 time〔taɪm〕*n.* 時間
 fly〔flaɪ〕*v.* 飛；(光陰) 如箭般飛逝
 pass〔pæs〕*v.* 過去
 vanish〔'vænɪʃ〕*v.* 消失 (= *disappear*)

Time tells.
時間說明一切。

Time tests.
時間考驗一切。

Time heals.
時間治療一切。

** time〔taɪm〕*n.* 時間
  tell〔tɛl〕*v.* 告訴；說；顯示
  test〔tɛst〕*v.* 測驗；考驗
  heal〔hil〕*v.* 治癒

Time matters.

時間相當重要。

Time equalizes.

時間使人平等。

Time matures.

時間使人成熟。

** time〔taɪm〕*n.* 時間

matter〔'mætɚ〕*v.* 重要

equalize〔'ikwəlˌaɪz〕*v.* 使相等;使平等

mature〔mə'tʃʊr〕*v.* 使成熟 *adj.* 成熟的

【**Unit 6 背景説明**】

Time flies. (【諺】時光飛逝。) 也可説成：
Time goes by quickly. (時間很快就過去了。)

Time passes. (時間會過去。) 也可説成：*Time vanishes*. (時間會消失。) Time marches on. (時間會持續向前進。) Time doesn't stop. (時間不會停止。)

Time tells. 時間會說明一切。(= *Time tells all*.) 也可説成：The answer will be known eventually. (答案最終會被知道。) The truth will be known eventually. (眞相最終會被知道。)

Time tests. 時間考驗一切。(= *Time tests all*.) 也可説成：Time tries us. (時間考驗我們。)

Time heals. 時間會治療一切。(= *Time heals all*. = *Time cures all*.) 也可説成：With time, things get better. (隨著時間的過去，情況會變好。) (= *Things improve with the passage of time*.)

Time matters. 時間很重要。(= *Time counts*.
= *Time is important*.)

Time equalizes.（時間使一切平等。）也可説
成：Everything becomes equal with time.
（隨著時間的過去，一切都會變得平等。）
Everything will turn out to be the same in
the end.（到最後一切事物都會變成一樣。）
Time will cancel out any differences.（時間
會抵消任何的差異。）

Time matures.（時間使一切變成熟。）也可説
成：Everyone gets more mature with time.
（隨著時間的過去，每個人都會變得更成熟。）
Everything gets more mature with time.（隨
著時間的過去，一切事物都會變得更成熟。）
Everyone grows up with time.（每個人都會
隨著時間而長大。）Everything develops
with time.（一切事物都會隨著時間而發展。）

UNIT 7

Look to the Future 放眼未來

Look far.
要看得遠。

Look afar.
要看久遠。

Look ahead.
要向前看。

** look〔luk〕*v.* 看　　***look to*** 朝⋯看去
future〔'fjutʃɚ〕*n.* 未來
far〔fɑr〕*adv.* 向遠處；遠遠地
afar〔ə'fɑr〕*adv.* 遙遠地
ahead〔ə'hɛd〕*adv.* 向前方

Look wider.

眼界要寬。

Look broader.

眼界要廣。

Look further.

看得更遠。

** look 〔 lʊk 〕 *v.* 看

wide 〔 waɪd 〕 *adj.* 寬廣的　*adv.* 寬闊地

broad 〔 brɔd 〕 *adj.* 寬廣的

　adv. 寬闊地；廣闊地

further 〔 ˈfɝðɚ 〕 *adv.* 較遠；更遠；

　更進一步地

Look deeply.

深入地看。

Look beyond.

放眼未來。

Look overall.

綜觀全局。

** look〔luk〕*v.* 看
deeply〔'diplɪ〕*adv.* 深深地
beyond〔bɪ'jɑnd〕*adv.* 在遠處；更遠地
overall〔ˌovə'ɔl〕*adv.* 就整體來說；全面地

【**Unit 7 背景説明**】

Look far. 要看得遠。(= *Look afar*.) 也可説成：*Look ahead*. (要向前看。) Look to the future. (要放眼未來。)

Look wider. (眼界要寬一點。) 也可説成：*Look broader*. (要看得寬廣一點。) *Look further*. (要看得遠一點。) Look for more opportunities. (要尋找更多的機會。) Be open to all opportunities. (要樂於接受所有的機會。)

Look deeply. 要深入地看。(= *Look profoundly*.) 也可説成：Look seriously. (要認眞地看。) Consider deeply. (要深入地考慮)

Look beyond. 要看得更遠，引申爲「要放眼未來。」(= *Look to the future*.) 也可説成：Look forward. (要向前看；要放眼未來。) (= *Look ahead*. = *Look further*. = *Look past the current situation*.)

Look overall. (要看全面。) 也可説成：See the big picture. (要看到全局。) (= *Take in the big picture*.)

UNIT 8

Overcome Whatever Stands in Your Way 克服阻礙

Conquer fear.
克服恐懼。

Conquer hate.
克服仇恨。

Conquer doubt.
克服懷疑。

** overcome〔͵ovɚˋkʌm〕*v.* 克服
stand in *one's* ***way*** 阻礙某人
conquer〔ˋkɑŋkɚ〕*v.* 征服;克服
fear〔fɪr〕*n.* 害怕;恐懼
hate〔het〕*n.* 仇恨;憎恨
doubt〔daʊt〕*n.* 懷疑

Conquer adversity.

克服逆境。

Conquer hardships.

克服艱苦。

Conquer difficulties.

克服困難。

** conquer〔'kɑŋkɚ〕 *v.* 征服；克服
adversity〔əd'vɝsətɪ〕 *n.* 逆境
hardship〔'hɑrdʃɪp〕 *n.* 艱難；困苦
difficulty〔'dɪfəˌkʌltɪ〕 *n.* 困難

Conquer obstacles.

克服障礙。

Conquer challenges.

克服挑戰。

Conquer temptations.

克服誘惑。

** conquer〔ˋkɑŋkɚ〕v. 征服；克服
obstacle〔ˋɑbstək!〕n. 阻礙
challenge〔ˋtʃælɪndʒ〕n. 挑戰
temptation〔tɛmpˋteʃən〕n. 誘惑

BOOK 2 · PART 3

【**Unit 8 背景説明**】

Conquer fear.（要克服恐懼。）也可説成：
Defeat your fears.（要打敗你的恐懼。）
Don't let fear stop you.（不要讓恐懼阻止
你。）

Conquer hate.（要克服仇恨。）也可説成：
Defeat hate.（要打敗仇恨。）Eliminate hate.
（要消除仇恨。）Get rid of hate.（要擺脱仇
恨。）

Conquer doubt.（要克服懷疑。）也可説成：
Defeat your doubts.（要打敗你的懷疑。）
Overcome your doubts.（要克服你的懷疑。）
Don't let doubt stop you.（不要讓懷疑阻止
你。）

Conquer adversity.　要克服逆境。（ = *Overcome
adversity*. ）也可説成：*Conquer hardships*.
（要克服艱難困苦。）(= *Overcome hardships*.)
Conquer difficulties.（要克服困難。）
(= *Overcome difficulties*.) Overcome
problems.（要克服問題。）Overcome

setbacks. (要克服挫折。) Overcome trouble. (要克服麻煩。) Overcome misfortune. (要克服不幸。) Overcome obstacles. (要克服阻礙。) Overcome complications. (要克服麻煩的問題。)

Conquer obstacles. 要克服阻礙。(= *Overcome obstacles.*) 也可說成：*Conquer challenges.* (要克服挑戰。) (= *Overcome challenges.*) Overcome problems. (要克服問題。) Overcome setbacks. (要克服挫折。) Overcome hardships. (要克服艱難困苦。) Overcome difficulties. (要克服困難。) Overcome trouble. (要克服麻煩。) Overcome misfortunc. (要克服不幸。) Overcome complications. (要克服麻煩的問題。)

Conquer temptations. 要克服誘惑。 (= *Overcome temptations.*) 也可說成： Ignore temptations. (要忽視誘惑。) Don't be distracted by temptations. (不要因為誘惑而分心。)

UNIT 9

Don't Be Afraid of Change
不要怕改變

Expect change.
期待改變。

Create change.
創造改變。

Ignite change.
引發改變。

** afraid〔ə'fred〕*adj.* 害怕的
be afraid of 害怕
change〔tʃendʒ〕*n.* 改變
expect〔ɪk'spɛkt〕*v.* 預期;期待
create〔krɪ'et〕*v.* 創造
ignite〔ɪg'naɪt〕*v.* 點燃;引發;激起;激發

Promote change.

促進改變。

Advocate change.

提倡改變。

Propel change.

推動改變。

** promote〔prə'mot〕*v.* 提倡；促進
change〔tʃendʒ〕*n.* 改變
advocate〔'ædvə,ket〕*v.* 主張；擁護；提倡
propel〔prə'pɛl〕*v.* 推進；推動；
促使（= *push*）

Accept change.

接受改變。

Welcome change.

歡迎改變。

Weather change.

度過改變。

** accept〔əkˈsɛpt〕v. 接受

   change〔tʃendʒ〕n. 改變

   welcome〔ˈwɛlkəm〕v. 歡迎

   weather〔ˈwɛðɚ〕n. 天氣 v. 平安

    度過（困境）；經受住（= *withstand*）

【**Unit 9 背景說明**】

Expect change.（要期待改變。）也可說成：
Know that everything will change.（要知
道一切事物都會改變。）Know that things
always change.（要知道情況總是會改變。）
Don't be surprised by change.（不要對改變
感到驚訝。）

Create change.（要創造改變。）也可說成：
Ignite change.（要引發改變。）Instigate
change.（要使改變發生。）Be the one who
changes things.（要成爲改變情況的人。）

Promote change.（要促進改變。）也可說成：
Advocate change.（要提倡改變。）
Encourage change.（要鼓勵改變。）
Be in favor of change.（要贊成改變。）

Propel change.（要推動改變。）也可說成：
Foster change.（要促進改變。）Push
change.（要推動改變。）Make change
happen.（要讓改變發生。）

BOOK 2 · PART 3

Accept change.（要接受改變。）也可說成：
Welcome change.（要歡迎改變。）
Embrace change.（要擁抱改變。）Support
change.（要支持改變。）Adjust to change.
（要適應改變。）Adopt new things.（要採
用新事物。）Don't fight change.（不要對抗
改變。）

Weather change.（要度過改變。）也可說成：
Withstand change.（要經得起改變。）
Endure change.（要忍受改變。）Survive
change.（要安然度過改變。）When things
change, tough it out.（當情況改變時，要堅
強度過。）When things change, deal with
it.（當情況改變時，要好好應付。）

BOOK 2 · PART 3

PART 3 總整理

PART 3 · Unit 1~9
中英文錄音QR碼

Unit 1

Kindness pays. 善良值得。
Kindness rewards.
善良有償。
Kindness returns. 善良回報。

Kindness shines. 善良發光。
Kindness radiates.
善良煥發。
Kindness enlightens.
善良啟發。

Kindness empowers.
善良給人力量。
Kindness connects.
善良增加人脈。
Kindness unites.
善良促進團結。

Unit 2

Get busy. 找事情做。
Get active. 要動起來。
Get involved. 參與其中。

Get well. 身體要好。
Get healthy. 變得健康。
Get outdoors.
走出戶外。

Get inspired. 要受激勵。
Get motivated. 要受鼓舞。
Get determined.
要下決心。

Unit 3

Find love. 尋找真愛。
Find beauty. 尋找美好。
Find happiness.
尋找快樂。

Find passion. 尋找愛好。
Find purpose. 尋找目標。
Find direction. 尋找方向。

Find peace. 尋找和平。
Find harmony. 尋找和諧。
Find tranquility.
尋找寧靜。

Unit 4

Money talks. 錢能說話。
Money speaks. 錢能發言。
Money matters.
金錢重要。

Money rules. 金錢萬能。
Money leads. 金錢領導。
Money dominates.
金錢支配。

Money decides.
金錢決定。
Money manages.
金錢管理。
Money influences.
金錢影響。

Unit 5

Actions speak. 行為說話。
Actions lead. 行為領導。
Actions guide. 行為引導。

Actions matter. 行為重要。
Actions count. 行為有價。
Actions inspire.
行為鼓舞。

Actions show.
行為展示。
Actions reveal.
行為透露。
Actions communicate.
行為傳達。

Unit 6

Time flies. 時間飛逝。
Time passes. 時間流逝。
Time vanishes.
時間消逝。

Time tells.
時間說明一切。
Time tests.
時間考驗一切。
Time heals.
時間治療一切。

Time matters.
時間相當重要。
Time equalizes.
時間使人平等。
Time matures.
時間使人成熟。

Unit 7

Look far. 要看得遠。
Look afar. 要看久遠。
Look ahead. 要向前看。

Look wider. 眼界要寬。
Look broader. 眼界要廣。
Look further. 看得更遠。

Look deeply. 深入地看。
Look beyond. 放眼未來。
Look overall. 綜觀全局。

Unit 8

Conquer fear.
克服恐懼。
Conquer hate.
克服仇恨。
Conquer doubt.
克服懷疑。

Conquer adversity.
克服逆境。
Conquer hardships.
克服艱苦。
Conquer difficulties.
克服困難。

Conquer obstacles.
克服障礙。
Conquer challenges.
克服挑戰。
Conquer temptations.
克服誘惑。

Unit 9

Expect change.
期待改變。
Create change.
創造改變。
Ignite change.
引發改變。

Promote change.
促進改變。
Advocate change.
提倡改變。
Propel change.
推動改變。

Accept change.
接受改變。
Welcome change.
歡迎改變。
Weather change.
度過改變。

BOOK 3 / **PART 1**

Wise Words
智慧箴言

PART 1・Unit 1~9
英文錄音QR碼

BOOK 3・PART 1

BOOK 3・PART 1

UNIT 1

Seek Out What Matters
找出重要的事物

Seek joy.
尋找歡樂。

Seek happiness.
尋找快樂。

Seek opportunities.
尋找機會。

** seek〔sik〕*v.* 尋求;尋找
seek out 找出　　matter〔'mætə〕*v.* 重要
joy〔dʒɔɪ〕*n.* 喜悅;高興;快樂
happiness〔'hæpɪnɪs〕*n.* 快樂;幸福
opportunity〔ˌɑpə'tjunətɪ〕*n.* 機會

Seek growth.

尋求成長。

Seek progress.

尋求進步。

Seek blessings.

尋找幸福。

** seek〔sik〕*v.* 尋求；尋找
　growth〔groθ〕*n.* 成長
　progress〔'prɑgrɛs〕*n.* 進步
　blessing〔'blɛsɪŋ〕*n.* 幸福；幸運的事

BOOK 3．PART 1

Seek friendships.

尋找友誼。

Seek connections.

尋找人脈。

Seek solace.

尋找慰藉。

** seek〔sik〕v. 尋求；尋找
   friendship〔'frɛndʃɪp〕n. 友誼
   connection〔kə'nɛkʃən〕n. 連接；關係；
     關聯；(pl.) 人脈
   solace〔'salɪs〕n. 安慰；慰藉 (= comfort)

【Unit 1 背景説明】

Seek joy. 要尋找歡樂。(= *Find joy.* = *Look for joy.* = *Search for joy.*) 也可説成：Look for happiness. (要尋找快樂。) Enjoy yourself. (要過得愉快。)

Seek happiness. 要尋找快樂。(= *Find happiness.* = *Look for happiness.* = *Search for happiness.*)

Seek opportunities. 要尋找機會。(= *Find opportunities.* = *Look for chances.* = *Search for chances.*) 也可説成：Look for chances to advance. (要尋找機會進步。) Look for chances to improve yourself. (要尋找機會讓自己更好。)

Seek growth. 要尋求成長。(= *Find growth.* = *Look for growth.* = *Search for growth.*) 也可説成：Look for ways to develop. (要尋找方法發展。) Look for ways to advance. (要尋找方法進步。) (= *Look for ways to progress.*)

BOOK 3 · PART 1

Seek progress. 要尋求進步。(= *Find progress.*
= *Look for advancement.* = *Search for*
improvement.)

Seek blessings. 要尋找幸福。(= *Find*
blessings.) 也可説成：Look for good
fortune. (要尋找好運。) (= *Search for*
good luck.)

Seek friendships. 要尋找友誼。(= *Find*
friendships. = *Look for companionship.*)
也可説成：Find friends. (要尋找朋友。)
(= *Look for friends.* = *Search for friends.*)

Seek connections. 要尋找人脈。(= *Find*
connections.) 也可説成：Look for contacts.
(要尋找人脈。) (= *Search for networks.*)
Develop relationships. (要培養人際關係。)
(= *Develop ties.*)

Seek solace. 要尋求慰藉。(= *Find comfort.*)
也可説成：Look for comfort. (要尋找安
慰。) (= *Search for consolation.*)

UNIT 2

Make Good Choices
做出好的選擇

Choose kindness.
選擇善良。

Choose integrity.
選擇正直。

Choose forgiveness.
選擇寬恕。

** choice〔tʃɔɪs〕n. 選擇　　*make a choice* 做選擇
choose〔tʃuz〕v. 選擇
kindness〔'kaɪndnɪs〕n. 親切；仁慈；善意
integrity〔ɪn'tɛgrətɪ〕n. 正直
forgiveness〔fə'gɪvnɪs〕n. 原諒；寬恕

Choose loyalty.

選擇忠誠。

Choose peace.

選擇和平。

Choose moderation.

選擇中庸。

** choose〔tʃuz〕v. 選擇
　　loyalty〔'lɔɪəltɪ〕n. 忠誠；忠心
　　peace〔pis〕n. 和平；平靜
　　moderation〔͵madə'reʃən〕n. 適度；適中

Choose freedom.

選擇自由。

Choose simplicity.

選擇簡單。

Choose advancement.

選擇進步。

** choose 〔 tʃuz 〕 *v.* 選擇

freedom 〔 'fridəm 〕 *n.* 自由

simplicity 〔 sɪm'plɪsətɪ 〕 *n.* 簡單

advancement 〔 əd'vænsmənt 〕 *n.* 進步

【**Unit 2 背景説明**】

Choose kindness. 選擇善良。(= *Choose to be kind*. = *Opt for kindness*. = *Opt to be kind*.) 也可説成：Always make the kind choice. (一定要做出善良的選擇。)

Choose integrity. (選擇正直。) 也可説成： Be honorable. (要品德高尚；要值得尊敬。) Be honest. (要誠實。) Be reliable. (要可靠。)

Choose forgiveness. 選擇原諒。(= *Decide to forgive*.) 也可説成：Decide to be forgiving. (選擇寬容。) Always be forgiving. (一定要寬容。)

Choose loyalty. (選擇忠誠。) 也可説成： Always be loyal. (一定要忠誠。) Always choose to support your friends. (一定要選擇支持你的朋友。) Don't be disloyal. (不要不忠誠。)(= *Don't be faithless*.)

Choose peace. (= *Opt for peace*.) 有兩個意思：① 「選擇和平。」也可説成：Choose

not to fight. (選擇不要打架。) Choose not
to argue. (選擇不要爭吵。) Decide to
reconcile. (選擇和解。) ②「要選擇平靜。」
也可說成：Make the choice that will lead to
peace. (要做能使你平靜的選擇。)(= *Make
the choice that will give you peace.*)

Choose moderation. (選擇中庸。) 也可說成：
Don't do anything to excess. (做任何事都不
要過度。) Be moderate in everything you
do. (做任何事都要適度。)

Choose freedom. 選擇自由。(= *Choose to
be free.* = *Decide to be free.*) 也可說成：
Make the choice that gives you freedom.
(要做能給你自由的選擇。)

Choose simplicity. (選擇簡單。) 也可說成：
Choose a simple life. (選擇簡單的生活。)
Don't be extravagant. (不要太奢侈。)

Choose advancement. 選擇進步。(= *Choose
progress.* = *Choose to advance.* = *Decide to
move forward.*)

UNIT 3

Embrace Good Qualities
欣然接受好的特質

Embrace learning.
擁抱學習。

Embrace laughter.
擁抱笑聲。

Embrace discipline.
擁抱自律。

** embrace〔ɪmˋbres〕*v.* 擁抱；欣然接受；樂意
　　利用；體會　　quality〔ˋkwɑlətɪ〕*n.* 特質
　　learning〔ˋlɝnɪŋ〕*n.* 學習
　　laughter〔ˋlæftɚ〕*n.* 笑；笑聲
　　discipline〔ˋdɪsəplɪn〕*n.* 紀律；約束；自制力

Embrace courage.
擁抱勇氣。

Embrace contentment.
擁抱滿足。

Embrace compassion.
擁抱同情。

** embrace〔 ɪmˋbres 〕v. 擁抱；欣然接受；
　樂意利用；體會
　courage〔ˋkɝɪdʒ 〕n. 勇氣
　contentment〔 kənˋtɛntmənt 〕n. 滿足
　compassion〔 kəmˋpæʃən 〕n. 同情

Embrace generosity.

擁抱慷慨。

Embrace creativity.

擁抱創意。

Embrace authenticity.

擁抱眞實。

** embrace〔 ɪm'bres 〕*v.* 擁抱；欣然接受；
　　樂意利用；體會
　　generosity〔ˌdʒɛnə'rɑsətɪ〕*n.* 慷慨；大方
　　creativity〔ˌkrie'tɪvətɪ〕*n.* 創造力；獨創力
　　authenticity〔ˌɔθɛn'tɪsətɪ〕*n.* 眞實；誠實；
　　可靠性；確實性

【**Unit 3 背景説明**】

記憶技巧：<u>l</u>earning 和 <u>l</u>aughter 都是 l 開頭。

Embrace learning.（擁抱學習。）也可説成：
Want to learn.（要想學習。）Be willing to
learn.（要願意學習。）Welcome the chance
to learn.（要樂於接受能學習的機會。）
Appreciate the opportunity to learn.（重視
學習的機會。）

Embrace laughter.（擁抱歡笑。）也可説成：
Appreciate laughter.（重視歡笑。）
Appreciate happiness.（重視快樂。）

Embrace discipline. 擁抱紀律。（= *Accept
discipline.* = *Welcome discipline.*）也可説
成：Practice self-control.（要自制。）
（= *Practice self-restraint.*）

記憶技巧：<u>co</u>urage，<u>co</u>ntentment，
<u>co</u>mpassion 都是 co 開頭。

Embrace courage.（擁抱勇氣。）也可説成：
Be courageous.（要有勇氣。）Be brave.
（要勇敢。）Accept courage.（接受勇氣。）
Welcome bravery.（樂於接受勇敢。）

Embrace contentment.（擁抱滿足。）也可說
成：Be content.（要滿足。）Be satisfied
with what you have.（要對你所擁有的感到
滿足。）

Embrace compassion.（擁抱同情。）也可說
成：Be compassionate.（要有同情心。）
Accept kindness.（接受善意。）Welcome
sympathy.（樂於接受同情。）

記憶技巧：generos<u>ity</u>，creativ<u>ity</u>，
authentic<u>ity</u> 都是 ity 結尾。

Embrace generosity.（擁抱慷慨。）也可說
成：Appreciate generosity.（重視慷慨。）
Welcome giving.（樂於接受給與。）

Embrace creativity.（擁抱創意。）也可說
成：Appreciate creativity.（重視創意。）
Welcome inventiveness.（樂於接受發明
才能。）

Embrace authenticity.（擁抱真實。）也可說
成：Appreciate genuineness.（重視真實。）
Welcome sincerity.（樂於接受真誠。）

UNIT 4

Be a Traveler 去旅行

Travel light.
輕裝旅行。

Travel far.
遠程旅行。

Travel abroad.
出國旅行。

** traveler〔'trævḷɚ〕*n.* 旅行者；遊客
　travel〔'trævḷ〕*v.* 旅行
　light〔laɪt〕*adv.* 輕地；輕裝地
　travel light 輕裝旅行
　far〔fɑr〕*adv.* 遙遠地；到很遠的距離
　abroad〔ə'brɔd〕*adv.* 到國外

Travel happily.

快樂旅行。

Travel joyfully.

歡樂旅行。

Travel freely.

自由旅行。

** travel〔ˋtrævḷ〕 *v.* 旅行
　　happily〔ˋhæpɪlɪ〕 *adv.* 快樂地
　　joyfully〔ˋdʒɔɪfəlɪ〕 *adv.* 喜悅地；高興地
　　freely〔ˋfrilɪ〕 *adv.* 自由地；無拘無束地

Travel safely.

安全旅行。

Travel sensibly.

明智旅行。

Travel purposefully.

目標旅行。

** travel〔'trævḷ〕 *v.* 旅行

　safely〔'seflɪ〕 *adv.* 安全地

　sensibly〔'sɛnsəblɪ〕 *adv.* 明智地

　purposefully〔'pɝpəsfəlɪ〕 *adv.* 有目的地

【**Unit 4 背景説明**】

Travel light.（輕裝旅行。）也可説成：
Don't take too many things when you
travel.（當你旅行時，不要帶太多東西。）
Don't overpack.（不要打包太多東西。）

Travel far. 去遙遠的地方旅行。(= *Travel
to far-flung places*.) 也可説成：Go to
faraway places.（要去遙遠的地方。）

Travel abroad.（出國旅行。）也可説成：
Travel to other countries.（要去其他的國
旅家行。）Visit other countries.（要去其
他的國家。）(= *Go to other countries*.)

Travel happily. 快樂地旅行。(= *Travel
joyfully*.) 也可説成：Enjoy traveling.
（要喜歡旅行。）Be happy to travel.（要
樂於旅行。）Be excited about traveling.
（要對旅行感到興奮。）

Travel freely.（自由地旅行。）也可説成：
Travel without restrictions.（要毫無限制
地旅行。）Don't restrict yourself when
you travel.（當你旅行時，不要限制自己。）

Travel safely. 安全地旅行。(= *Be safe when
you travel.*) 也可説成：Don't do anything
risky when you travel.（當你旅行時，不要
做任何危險的事。）

Travel sensibly.（明智地旅行。）也可説成：
Travel wisely.（聰明地旅行。）Travel
carefully.（小心地旅行。）

Travel purposefully. 要有目的地旅行。
(= *Travel with purpose.* = *Travel with
intention.*) 也可説成：Travel consciously.
（要有意識地旅行；要知道旅行的目的。）
(= *Travel mindfully.* = *Travel thoughtfully.*)

UNIT 5

Adapt to New Things 適應新事物

Adapt cheerfully.

愉快地適應。

Adapt confidently.

自信地適應。

Adapt courageously.

勇敢地適應。

** adapt〔ə'dæpt〕*v.* 適應 < *to* >
  cheerfully〔'tʃɪrfəlɪ〕*adv.* 愉快地
  confidently〔'kɑnfədəntlɪ〕*adv.* 有信心地；
    充滿自信地
  courageously〔kə'redʒəslɪ〕*adv.* 勇敢地

Adapt quickly.

快速地適應。

Adapt graciously.

親切地適應。

Adapt gracefully.

優雅地適應。

** adapt〔 ə'dæpt 〕*v.* 適應
quickly〔'kwɪklɪ 〕*adv.* 快地
graciously〔'greʃəslɪ 〕*adv.* 親切地
gracefully〔'gresfəlɪ 〕*adv.* 優雅地

Adapt positively.

樂觀地適應。

Adapt persistently.

持續地適應。

Adapt passionately.

熱情地適應。

** adapt〔ə'dæpt〕*v.* 適應

positively〔'pɑzətɪvlɪ〕*adv.* 積極地；樂觀地

persistently〔pə'sɪstəntlɪ〕*adv.* 持續地

passionately〔'pæʃənɪtlɪ〕*adv.* 熱情地

【Unit 5 背景說明】

記憶技巧：<u>c</u>heerfully，<u>c</u>onfidently，<u>c</u>ourageously 都是 c 開頭。

Adapt cheerfully. 要愉快地適應。(＝*Adjust happily.*) 也可說成：Adapt willingly. (要願意適應。) (＝*Adjust willingly.*) Change willingly. (要願意改變。) Be happy to adapt. (要樂於適應。) (＝*Be happy to adjust.*) Be happy to change. (要樂於改變。)

Adapt confidently. 要有信心地適應。(＝*Adjust with confidence.*) 也可說成：Don't be afraid of change. (不要害怕改變。) Know that you can adapt. (要知道你能適應。) Believe that you can adapt. (要相信你能適應。)

Adapt courageously. 要勇敢地適應。(＝*Adjust bravely.*) 也可說成：Adjust without fear. (要毫不畏懼地適應。)

記憶技巧：<u>grac</u>iously，<u>grac</u>efully 都是 grac 開頭。

Adapt quickly. 要很快地適應。(＝*Adjust fast.*) 也可說成：Adjust without delay. (要立刻適應。)

Adapt graciously. 要親切地適應。(= *Adjust amiably*.) 也可說成：Adjust without complaint.（要毫無怨言地適應。）

Adapt gracefully.（要優雅地適應。）也可說成：Adjust with poise.（要泰然自若地適應。）Don't resist change.（不要抗拒改變。）(= *Don't fight change*.) Adjust to new things without complaint.（要毫無怨言地適應新事物。）

記憶技巧：positively，persistently，passionately 都是 p 開頭。

Adapt positively. 要樂觀地適應。(= *Adjust optimistically*.) 也可說成：Adjust without complaint.（要毫無怨言地適應。）Adjust without reluctance.（要毫不勉強地適應。）

Adapt persistently.（要持續地適應。）也可說成：Keep trying to adapt.（要持續努力地適應。）(= *Keep trying to adjust*.)

Adapt passionately. 要熱情地適應。(= *Adjust enthusiastically*.) 也可說成：Adjust confidently.（要充滿自信地適應。）

UNIT 6

Be Mindful 凡事要留意

Speak mindfully.

謹慎發言。

Act mindfully.

謹慎行動。

Interact mindfully.

謹慎互動。

BOOK 3 · PART 1

** mindful〔'maɪndfəl〕*adj.* 留心的；注意的
mindfully〔'maɪndfəlɪ〕*adv.* 謹慎地；注意地；
   留意地；用心地　　speak〔spik〕*v.* 說話
act〔ækt〕*v.* 行動；做事；舉止；表現
interact〔ˌɪntə'ækt〕*v.* 互動

Love mindfully.

用心愛。

Learn mindfully.

用心學。

Listen mindfully.

用心聽。

** love〔lʌv〕 *v.* 愛

mindfully〔'maɪndfəlɪ〕 *adv.* 謹慎地；

注意地；留意地；用心地

listen〔'lɪsn̩〕 *v.* 聽；傾聽

Walk mindfully.

小心地走。

Work mindfully.

用心工作。

Eat mindfully.

注意飲食。

** walk〔wɔk〕*v.* 走；散步

   mindfully〔'maɪndfəlɪ〕*adv.* 謹慎地；

     注意地；留意地；用心地

   work〔wɜk〕*v.* 工作

   eat〔it〕*v.* 吃東西

【Unit 6 背景説明】

Speak mindfully. 要謹慎地說話。(= *Speak carefully.*) 也可說成：Speak with intention. (要有意圖地說話。)

Act mindfully. 行為要謹慎。(= *Act carefully.*) 也可說成：Be aware of what you are doing. (要知道自己在做什麼。)

Interact mindfully. (要謹慎地互動。) 也可說成：Interact carefully. (要小心地互動。) Engage with others in a thoughtful way. (以深思熟慮的方式與他人互動。)

記憶技巧：Love，Learn，Listen 都是 L 開頭。

Love mindfully. 要謹慎地愛。(= *Love carefully.* = *Love cautiously.*) 也可說成：Love sensibly. (要明智地愛。) Love attentively. (要專注地愛。)

Learn mindfully. 要謹慎地學習。(= *Learn carefully.* = *Learn cautiously.*) 也可說成：Learn sensibly. (要明智地學習。) Learn attentively. (要專注地學習。)

Listen mindfully. 要注意聽。(= *Listen attentively*.) 也可説成：Listen carefully. (要小心地聽。)(= *Listen cautiously*.) Listen sensibly. (要明智地聽。)

記憶技巧：<u>W</u>alk 和 <u>W</u>ork 都是 W 開頭。

Walk mindfully. 要謹慎地走路。(= *Walk carefully*. = *Walk thoughtfully*.) 也可説成： Walk with attention. (走路要注意。) Be aware of where you are walking. (要知道自己要走去哪裡。) Be aware of where you are going. (要知道自己要去哪裡。)

Work mindfully. (要用心地工作。) 也可説成：Work attentively. (要專注地工作。) (= *Work with attention*.) Work carefully. (要小心地工作。) Work thoughtfully. (要深思熟慮地工作。)

Eat mindfully. 要謹慎地吃東西。(= *Eat carefully*. = *Eat thoughtfully*.) 也可説成：Eat attentively. (吃東西要注意。) (= *Eat with attention*. = *Pay attention to what you eat*.)

UNIT 7

Appreciate Good Music
欣賞美好的音樂

Nice voice.
美好聲音。

Beautiful tones.
美麗音調。

Lovely vocals.
美妙嗓音。

** appreciate〔əˈpriʃɪ͵et〕*v.* 欣賞
nice〔naɪs〕*adj.* 好的　　voice〔vɔɪs〕*n.* 聲音
beautiful〔ˈbjutəfəl〕*adj.* 美麗的；美好的
tone〔ton〕*n.* 音調；音色
lovely〔ˈlʌvlɪ〕*adj.* 可愛的；令人舒服的；極好的
vocal〔ˈvokl̩〕*n.* （流行歌曲的）歌唱部分
　adj. 嗓音的；歌唱的

Radiant sound.

宏亮之音。

Harmonious melody.

和諧旋律。

Enchanting symphony.

迷人之樂。

** radiant〔'redɪənt〕*adj.* 發光的;發熱的;開心的;
美麗的;容光煥發的;光芒四射的;幸福洋溢的

sound〔saʊnd〕*n.* 聲音

harmonious〔hɑr'monɪəs〕*adj.* 和諧的

melody〔'mɛlədɪ〕*n.* 旋律

enchanting〔ɪn'tʃæntɪŋ〕*adj.* 迷人的

symphony〔'sɪmfənɪ〕*n.* 交響樂

Sweet pitch.

甜美音調。

Heavenly intonation.

天籟之音。

Soulful resonance.

心靈共鳴。

** sweet〔swit〕*adj.* 甜美的；聲音悅耳的

pitch〔pɪtʃ〕*n.* (聲音的)高低度；音調；(棒球的)投；擲；扔　*v.* 投；擲；扔；拋

heavenly〔ˈhɛvənlɪ〕*adj.* 天堂似的；來自天上的；絕妙的；極好的

intonation〔ˌɪntoˈneʃən〕*n.* 音調；語調

soulful〔ˈsolfəl〕*adj.* 心靈上的；充滿感情的

resonance〔ˈrɛznəns〕*n.* 反響；回響；共鳴

【Unit 7 背景說明】

Nice voice.（好聽的聲音。）也可說成：
Beautiful tones.（優美的音調。）You have
a nice voice.（你有很好的聲音。）(= *You
have a good voice. =* Y*ou have a beautiful
voice. = You have a wonderful voice.*)

Lovely vocals.（美妙的歌聲。）也可說成：
The singing is wonderful.（唱得很棒。）
You sing very well.（你唱歌唱得很好。）
You have a good voice.（你有很好的聲
音。）

Radiant sound.（亮麗的聲音。）也可說成：
Beautiful sound.（優美的聲音。）Wonderful
sound.（很棒的聲音。）(= *Amazing sound.
= Fantastic sound.*)

Harmonious melody.　和諧的旋律。
(= *Balanced melody.*) 也可說成：Pleasant
melody.（令人愉快的旋律。）Pleasant tune.
（令人愉快的曲調。）A harmonious piece of

music.（一首和諧的樂曲。）A pleasant song.
（令人愉快的歌曲。）

Enchanting symphony. 迷人的交響樂。
（*= Fascinating symphony. = Charming
symphony.*）也可說成：Fascinating music.
（迷人的音樂。）A charming piece of music.
（一首迷人的樂曲。）

Sweet pitch.（甜美的音調。）也可說成：
Delightful pitch.（令人愉快的音調。）
（*= Delightful tone.*）Delightful quality of
music.（令人愉快的音質。）

Heavenly intonation. 絕妙的音調；天籟之音。
（*= Divine tone.*）也可說成：Delightful
singing.（令人愉快的歌唱。）

Soulful resonance.（充滿感情的共鳴。）也可
說成：Emotional tone.（充滿感情的音調。）
Expressive tone.（生動的音調。）

UNIT 8

Respond to Criticism 回應評論

Cool comment.
超酷評論。

Fantastic feedback.
絕妙意見。

Incredible input.
極佳意見。

** respond〔rɪ'spɑnd〕*v.* 回應 < *to* >
criticism〔'krɪtə,sɪzəm〕*n.* 批評;評論
cool〔kul〕*adj.* 酷的;很棒的
comment〔'kɑmɛnt〕*n.* 評論
fantastic〔fæn'tæstɪk〕*adj.* 極好的;很棒的
feedback〔'fid,bæk〕*n.* 反饋;意見反應
incredible〔ɪn'krɛdəbḷ〕*adj.* 令人難以置信的;
   了不起的;絕妙的 input〔'ɪn,pʊt〕*n.*(想法
   的)投入;輸入;意見;想法

BOOK 3・PART 1

Impressive insight.

卓越見解。

Outstanding observation.

傑出觀點。

Perfect perspective.

完美看法。

** impressive〔ɪm'prɛsɪv〕*adj.* 令人印象深刻的；
令人佩服的

insight〔'ɪn,saɪt〕*n.* 洞察力；深刻的見解

outstanding〔'aʊt'stændɪŋ〕*adj.* 傑出的

observation〔,ɑbzɚ'veʃən〕*n.* 觀察；觀點

perfect〔'pɝfɪkt〕*adj.* 完美的

perspective〔pɚ'spɛktɪv〕*n.* 看法；觀點

Remarkable remark.

出色評論。

Super statement.

絕佳敘述。

Terrific thought.

超棒想法。

** remarkable〔rɪ'mɑrkəbḷ〕*adj.* 引人注目的；
出色的

remark〔rɪ'mɑrk〕*n.* 評論

super〔'supɚ〕*adj.* 超級的；極好的

statement〔'stetmənt〕*n.* 敘述

terrific〔tə'rɪfɪk〕*adj.* 非常好的；很棒的

thought〔θɔt〕*n.* 想法

BOOK 3 · PART 1

【Unit 8 背景説明】

記憶技巧：<u>Co</u>ol <u>co</u>mment. 都是 co 開頭；
<u>F</u>antastic <u>f</u>eedback. 都是 f 開頭；
<u>In</u>credible <u>in</u>put. 都是 in 開頭。

Cool comment.（很酷的評論。）也可説成：
Bold remark.（大膽的評論。）Excellent
remark.（優秀的評論。）Good remark.
（很好的評論。）

Fantastic feedback.（很棒的意見。）也可説
成：Great response.（很棒的回應。）Clever
reaction.（很聰明的反應。）Ingenious
advice.（很聰明的建議。）

Incredible input. 很棒的意見。(= *Great
input.*）也可説成：Wonderful advice.（很棒
的建議。）Marvelous observation.（很棒的
觀點。）Terrific comment.（很棒的評論。）

記憶技巧：<u>I</u>mpressive <u>i</u>nsight. 都是 i 開頭；
<u>O</u>utstanding <u>o</u>bservation. 都是 o 開頭；
<u>P</u>erfect <u>p</u>erspective. 都是 p 開頭。

Impressive insight.（令人佩服的見解。）也可
說成：Splendid idea.（很棒的想法。）
Splendid perspective.（很棒的看法。）

Outstanding observation.（傑出的觀點。）也
可說成：Remarkable comment.（出色的評
論。）Superb opinion.（超棒的意見。）
Excellent statement.（極佳的敘述。）

Perfect perspective.（完美的看法。）也可說
成：Flawless perception.（完美無暇的看法。）

記憶技巧：Remarkable remark. 都有
remark；Super statement. 字首都是 s；
Terrific thought. 字首都是 t。

Remarkable remark. 出色的評論。
（＝*Extraordinary remark.* ＝*Outstanding*
comment. ＝*Incredible comment.* ）

Super statement.（超好的敘述。）也可說成：
Great observation.（很棒的觀點。）Great
comment.（很棒的評論。）（＝*Great remark.* ）

Terrific thought. 很棒的想法。（＝*Great idea.* ）
也可說成：Great insight.（很棒的見解。）

UNIT 9

Give Thanks 表達感謝

Endless thanks.

無盡感謝。

Limitless thanks.

無限感謝。

Abundant thanks.

萬分感謝。

** thanks〔θæŋks〕*n. pl.* 感謝

give thanks 致謝；感謝

endless〔'ɛndlɪs〕*adj.* 無止盡的；無窮盡的

limitless〔'lɪmɪtlɪs〕*adj.* 無限的；無限度的

abundant〔ə'bʌndənt〕*adj.* 豐富的；大量的

True thanks.

真心感謝。

Genuine thanks.

真誠感謝。

Sincere thanks.

由衷感謝。

** true〔tru〕*adj.* 真的；真正的；真誠的
thanks〔θæŋks〕*n. pl.* 感謝
genuine〔'dʒɛnjuɪn〕*adj.* 真的；真誠的
sincere〔sɪn'sɪr〕*adj.* 真心的；由衷的

Lifelong thanks.

終生感謝。

Eternal thanks.

永遠感謝。

Everlasting thanks.

永久感謝。

** lifelong〔ˈlaɪfˌlɔŋ〕adj. 終生的

thanks〔θæŋks〕n. pl. 感謝

eternal〔ɪˈtɜnḷ〕adj. 永恆的；永久的；永遠的

everlasting〔ˌɛvɚˈlæstɪŋ〕adj. 永遠的；
永久的；持久的；永恆的（= eternal）

【Unit 9 背景説明】

Endless thanks. 感激不盡。(= *Limitless thanks.*) 也可説成：*Abundant thanks.* (非常感謝。) I'm eternally grateful. (我永遠感激。) I'll be forever grateful. (我會永遠心存感激。)

True thanks. 眞心感謝。(= *Genuine thanks.* = *Sincere thanks.*) 也可説成：I'm truly thankful. (我眞的很感謝。) (= *I'm genuinely thankful.* = *I'm sincerely thankful.*)

Lifelong thanks. (終生感謝。) 也可説成：*Eternal thanks.* (永遠感謝。) *Everlasting thanks.* (永久感謝。) You have my eternal gratitude. (我會永遠感激你。) I'll never forget this. (我絕不會忘記這件事。) I can't thank you enough. (我再怎麼感謝你都不爲過。)

PART 1　總整理

Unit 1

Seek joy.　尋找歡樂。
Seek happiness.　尋找快樂。
Seek opportunities.
尋找機會。

Seek growth.　尋求成長。
Seek progress.　尋求進步。
Seek blessings.　尋找幸福。

Seek friendships.
尋找友誼。
Seek connections.
尋找人脈。
Seek solace.　尋找慰藉。

Unit 2

Choose kindness.　選擇善良。
Choose integrity.　選擇正直。
Choose forgiveness.
選擇寬恕。

Choose loyalty.　選擇忠誠。
Choose peace.　選擇和平。
Choose moderation.
選擇中庸。

Choose freedom.　選擇自由。
Choose simplicity.
選擇簡單。
Choose advancement.
選擇進步。

Unit 3

Embrace learning.
擁抱學習。
Embrace laughter.
擁抱笑聲。
Embrace discipline.
擁抱自律。

Embrace courage.
擁抱勇氣。
Embrace contentment.
擁抱滿足。
Embrace compassion.
擁抱同情。

Embrace generosity.
擁抱慷慨。
Embrace creativity.
擁抱創意。
Embrace authenticity.
擁抱真實。

Unit 4

Travel light. 輕裝旅行。
Travel far. 遠程旅行。
Travel abroad. 出國旅行。

Travel happily. 快樂旅行。
Travel joyfully. 歡樂旅行。
Travel freely. 自由旅行。

Travel safely. 安全旅行。
Travel sensibly. 明智旅行。
Travel purposefully.
目標旅行。

Unit 5

Adapt cheerfully.
愉快地適應。
Adapt confidently.
自信地適應。
Adapt courageously.
勇敢地適應。

Adapt quickly. 快速地適應。
Adapt graciously.
親切地適應。
Adapt gracefully.
優雅地適應。

Adapt positively.
樂觀地適應。
Adapt persistently.
持續地適應。
Adapt passionately.
熱情地適應。

Unit 6

Speak mindfully.
謹慎發言。
Act mindfully.
謹慎行動。
Interact mindfully.
謹慎互動。

Love mindfully.
用心愛。
Learn mindfully.
用心學。
Listen mindfully.
用心聽。

Walk mindfully.
小心地走。
Work mindfully.
用心工作。
Eat mindfully. 注意飲食。

BOOK 3 · PART 1

Unit 7

Nice voice. 美好聲音。
Beautiful tones.
美麗音調。
Lovely vocals. 美妙嗓音。

Radiant sound.
宏亮之音。
Harmonious melody.
和諧旋律。
Enchanting symphony.
迷人之樂。

Sweet pitch. 甜美音調。
Heavenly intonation.
天籟之音。
Soulful resonance.
心靈共鳴。

Unit 8

Cool comment.
超酷評論。
Fantastic feedback.
絕妙意見。
Incredible input.
極佳意見。

Impressive insight.
卓越見解。
Outstanding observation.
傑出觀點。
Perfect perspective.
完美看法。

Remarkable remark.
出色評論。
Super statement. 絕佳敘述。
Terrific thought. 超棒想法。

Unit 9

Endless thanks. 無盡感謝。
Limitless thanks.
無限感謝。
Abundant thanks.
萬分感謝。

True thanks. 真心感謝。
Genuine thanks. 真誠感謝。
Sincere thanks. 由衷感謝。

Lifelong thanks. 終生感謝。
Eternal thanks. 永遠感謝。
Everlasting thanks.
永久感謝。

BOOK 3 PART 2

Habits to Quit and Habits to Keep
應戒除及該維持的習慣

PART 2・Unit 1~9
英文錄音QR碼

UNIT 1

Stop Bad Habits 戒除壞習慣

Stop worrying.
不要擔心。

Stop fearing.
不要害怕。

Stop doubting.
不要懷疑。

** habit〔'hæbɪt〕*n.* 習慣
　　stop〔stɑp〕*v.* 停止　　***stop + V-ing*** 停止…
　　worry〔'wɝɪ〕*v.* 擔心
　　fear〔fɪr〕*v.* 害怕
　　doubt〔daʊt〕*v.* 懷疑

Stop hesitating.
不要猶豫。

Stop delaying.
不要拖延。

Stop procrastinating.
不要拖拉。

** stop〔stɑp〕*v.* 停止
stop + *V-ing* 停止…
hesitate〔ˈhɛzə͵tet〕*v.* 猶豫
delay〔dɪˈle〕*v.* 拖延
procrastinate〔proˈkræstə͵net〕*v.* 拖延
　(= *delay*)

Stop arguing.

不要爭論。

Stop yelling.

不要大叫。

Stop complaining.

不要抱怨。

** stop〔stɑp〕*v.* 停止

stop + *V-ing* 停止…

argue〔'ɑrgjʊ〕*v.* 爭論

yell〔jɛl〕*v.* 大叫

complain〔kəm'plen〕*v.* 抱怨

【Unit 1 背景説明】

Stop worrying. 停止擔心。(= *Quit fretting.*) 也可説成：Quit agonizing. (停止煩惱。)

Stop fearing. 停止害怕。(= *Quit being afraid.* = *Quit being scared.* = *Quit being frightened.*) 也可説成：Quit being anxious. (停止焦慮。)

Stop doubting. 停止懷疑。(= *Quit being doubtful.* = *Quit being suspicious.*) 也可説成：Quit being distrustful. (停止不信任。)

Stop hesitating. 停止猶豫。(= *Quit being hesitant.*)

Stop delaying. 停止拖延。(= ***Stop procrastinating***. = *Stop postponing.* = *Stop stalling.* = *Stop putting things off.*) 也可説成：Stop dragging your feet. (不要再拖拖拉拉。)

Stop arguing. (停止爭論。) 也可説成：Quit quarreling. (停止爭吵。)

Stop yelling. (停止大叫。) 也可説成：Quit shouting. (停止吼叫。)

Stop complaining. 停止抱怨。(= *Stop whining.*)

UNIT 2

Avoid Bad Behavior

避免不良的行為

Never brag.

絕不吹牛。

Never boast.

絕不誇耀。

Never exaggerate.

絕不誇大。

** avoid〔ə'vɔɪd〕v. 避免

behavior〔bɪ'hevjɚ〕n. 行為

never〔'nɛvɚ〕*adv.* 絕不　　brag〔bræg〕v. 吹牛

boast〔bost〕v. 自誇；誇耀；自吹自播

exaggerate〔ɪg'zædʒə,ret〕v. 誇大

Never lie.

絕不說謊。

Never deceive.

絕不欺騙。

Never backstab.

絕不背叛。

** never〔ˈnɛvɚ〕*adv.* 絕不
lie〔laɪ〕*v.* 說謊　*n.* 謊言
deceive〔dɪˈsiv〕*v.* 欺騙
backstab〔ˈbækˌstæb〕*v.* 背後中傷；暗箭傷人；
以卑鄙的手段害（人）
【stab〔stæb〕*v.* 刺；戳；捅】

backstab

Never overact.

絕不做得過分。

Never overwork.

絕不工作過度。

Never overeat.

絕不吃得過多。

** never〔'nɛvɚ〕*adv.* 絕不
  overact〔͵ovɚ'ækt〕*v.* 表演過火；做得過分；
    反應過度
  overwork〔͵ovɚ'wɝk〕*v.* 工作過度
  overeat〔͵ovɚ'it〕*v.* 吃得太多

【Unit 2 背景説明】

Never brag.（絕對不要吹牛。）也可説成：
Never boast.（絕對不要自誇。）Don't show
off.（不要炫耀。）Don't crow.（不要誇耀。）
Don't gloat.（不要洋洋得意。）

Never exaggerate.（絕對不要誇大。）也可説
成：Don't overstate things.（不要誇張。）
Don't stretch the truth.（不要誇大事實。）
Don't brag.（不要吹牛。）Don't boast.（不
要自誇。）

Never lie. 絕對不要説謊。(= *Never tell lies.*)
也可説成：Never misrepresent the truth.
（絕對不要曲解事實。）Never misinform
anyone.（絕不給人錯誤的消息。）

Never deceive.（絕對不要欺騙。）也可説成：
Never lie.（絕對不要説謊。）Never trick
anyone.（絕對不要欺騙任何人。）(= *Never
cheat anyone.*)

Never backstab. 絕不暗箭傷人。(= *Never stab anyone in the back*.) 也可說成：Never betray anyone. (絕不出賣任何人。) (= *Never sell anyone out*. = *Never double-cross anyone*.) Never be disloyal. (絕對不要不忠誠。)

Never overact. (絕對不要做得太過分；絕對不要反應過度。) 也可說成：Don't exaggerate. (不要誇張。) Don't be so dramatic. (不要這麼戲劇化。) Don't cross the line. (不要越過界限。)

Never overwork. 絕對不要工作過度。(= *Don't work to excess*.) 也可說成：Don't work too hard. (不要太努力工作。) Under no circumstances do too much work. (絕對不要做太多工作。)

Never overeat. 絕對不要吃得過多。(= *Don't eat too much*.) 也可說成：Don't eat more than you should. (不要吃超過你應該吃的。)

UNIT 3

Take It Easy　放輕鬆

Don't hurry.

不要匆忙。

Don't rush.

不要著急。

Don't dash.

不要急忙。

** ***take it easy***　放輕鬆
　　hurry〔'hɝ ɪ〕*v.* 匆忙
　　rush〔rʌʃ〕*v.* 匆忙
　　dash〔dæʃ〕*v.* 猛衝；匆忙完成

Don't panic.
不要恐慌。

Don't freak.
不要抓狂。

Don't stress.
不要緊張。

** panic〔ˋpænɪk〕*v.* 恐慌
freak〔frik〕*v.* 極度激動；抓狂　*n.* 怪人
stress〔strɛs〕*v.* 緊張；焦慮；擔心；強調
　n. 壓力

Don't despair.

不要絕望。

Don't fret.

不要煩惱。

Don't succumb.

不要屈服。

** despair〔dɪ'spɛr〕*v.* 絕望；失去希望　*n.* 絕望

fret〔frɛt〕*v.* 煩惱；焦慮；發愁

(= *worry about something continuously*)

succumb〔sə'kʌm〕*v.* 屈服；放棄抵抗；

承認失敗

【Unit 3 背景説明】

Don't hurry. 不要太匆忙。(= *Don't rush*.) 也可説成:*Don't dash*. (不要匆忙完成。) Don't do it too quickly. (不要做得太快。) Take your time. (慢慢來。) Relax. (放輕鬆。)

Don't panic. 不要恐慌。(= *Don't be alarmed*.) 也可説成:Don't overreact. (不要反應過度。) Don't be hysterical. (不要歇斯底里。) Don't get worked up. (不要激動。)

Don't freak. (不要抓狂。) 也可説成:Don't lose it. (不要失去理智。) Don't go crazy. (不要發瘋。) Don't lose your cool. (不要失去冷靜。)

Don't stress. (不要緊張。) 也可説成:Don't worry. (不要擔心。) Don't torture yourself. (不要折磨你自己。)

Don't despair. (不要絕望。) 也可説成:Don't lose hope. (不要失去希望。)

Don't fret. (不要煩惱。) 也可説成:Don't worry. (不要擔心。)

Don't succumb. 不要屈服。(= *Don't give in*.) 也可説成:Don't surrender. (不要投降。)

UNIT 4

Pursue Good Things

追求美好的事物

Chase goals.

追求目標。

Chase desires.

追求願望。

Chase ambitions.

追求抱負。

** pursue〔pɚˋsu〕*v.* 追求
chase〔tʃes〕*v.* 追求　　goal〔gol〕*n.* 目標
desire〔dɪˋzaɪr〕*n.* 渴望；慾望；願望
ambition〔æmˋbɪʃən〕*n.* 抱負

Chase success.

追求成功。

Chase greatness.

追求偉大。

Chase excellence.

追求卓越。

** chase〔tʃes〕 v. 追求
success〔sək'sɛs〕 n. 成功
greatness〔'gretnɪs〕 n. 偉大；崇高
excellence〔'ɛksḷəns〕 n. 優秀；卓越

Chase fortune.

追求財富。

Chase love.

追求眞愛。

Chase teamwork.

追求合作。

** chase〔tʃes〕*v.* 追求
   fortune〔'fɔrtʃən〕*n.* 財富
   love〔lʌv〕*n.* 愛；愛情
   teamwork〔'tim,wɝk〕*n.* 團隊合作

【Unit 4 背景説明】

Chase goals. (追求目標。) 也可説成 :
Pursue your goals. (追求你的目標。)
(= *Go after your goals*.)

Chase desires. (追求願望。) 也可説成 :
Pursue what you want. (追求你想要的。)
(= *Go after what you want*.) Pursue your
dreams. (追求你的夢想。) (= *Go after your
dreams*.)

Chase ambitions. (追求抱負。) 也可説成 :
Pursue your ambitions. (追求你的抱負。)
(= *Go after your ambitions*.) Pursue your
goals. (追求你的目標。)

Chase success. 追求成功。(= *Go after
success*. = *Pursue success*.) 也可説成 :
Try to succeed. (努力追求成功。)

Chase greatness. 追求偉大。(= *Pursue
greatness*.) 也可説成 : Strive to be the
best. (努力成為最好的。)

Chase excellence. 追求卓越。(*Pursue excellence. = Go after excellence.*) 也可説成：Try to be excellent. (努力變得優秀。) Try to be the best. (努力成爲最好的。) Do your best. (要盡全力。)

Chase fortune. (追求財富。) 也可説成：Strive to be rich. (努力致富。) Try to increase your wealth. (努力增加你的財富。)

Chase love. 追求眞愛。(= *Go after love. = Pursue love.*) 也可説成：Pursue the one you love. (追求你愛的人。)

Chase teamwork. 追求團隊合作。(= *Pursue teamwork.*) 也可説成：Develop teamwork. (培養團隊合作。) Create a team. (創造一個團隊。)

UNIT 5

Share Positive Things
分享正能量

Spread cheer.
散播愉快。

Spread laughter.
散播歡笑。

Spread positivity.
傳正能量。

** share〔ʃɛr〕*v.* 分享
  positive〔'pɑzətɪv〕*adj.* 正面的；積極的；樂觀的
  spread〔sprɛd〕*v.* 散播　　cheer〔tʃɪr〕*n.* 歡樂
  laughter〔'læftɚ〕*n.* 笑；笑聲
  positivity〔,pɑzə'tɪvətɪ〕*n.* 正面；積極；樂觀

Spread goodness.

散播善意。

Spread friendship.

散播友誼。

Spread information.

散播資訊。

** spread〔sprɛd〕v. 散播
goodness〔'gʊdnɪs〕n. 善良；仁慈；美德
friendship〔'frɛndʃɪp〕n. 友誼
information〔,ɪnfɚ'meʃən〕n. 資訊

Spread unity.

傳播團結。

Spread cooperation.

傳播合作。

Spread consensus.

傳播共識。

** spread〔sprɛd〕*v.* 散播
unity〔'junətɪ〕*n.* 團結
cooperation〔koˌɑpə'reʃən〕*n.* 合作
consensus〔kən'sɛnsəs〕*n.* 共識

【**Unit 5 背景説明**】

Spread cheer. (散播歡樂。) 也可説成：
Spread laughter. (散播歡笑。)
Make others laugh. (要讓別人笑。)

Spread positivity. (要散播樂觀；要散播正能
量。) 也可説成：Share your positivity.
(要分享你的樂觀；要分享你的正能量。)
(= *Share your optimism*.)

Spread goodness. 散播善意。(= *Spread
kindness*. = *Spread goodwill*.) 也可説成：
Spread generosity. (散播慷慨。) Spread
compassion. (散播同情。) Spread
warmth. (散播溫暖。)

Spread friendship. (散播友誼。) 也可説
成：Be a good friend. (成為好的朋友。)
Be friendly. (要友善。) Make new friends.
(結交新的朋友。)

Spread information.（散播資訊。）也可説
成：Tell people what you know.（把你知
道的告訴別人。）(= *Tell others what you
know.*) Inform others.（通知別人。）

Spread unity.（散播團結。）也可説成：
Unite people.（使大家團結。）Encourage
teamwork.（要促進團隊合作。）

Spread cooperation.（散播合作。）也可説
成：Encourage cooperation.（促進合作。）
(= *Encourage collaboration.*) Be
cooperative.（要樂意合作。）

Spread consensus.（散播共識。）也可説
成：Encourage consensus.（促進共識。）
(= *Encourage agreement.*) Encourage
compromise.（鼓勵妥協。）

UNIT 6

Value the Best Things in Life
重視人生中最美好的事物

Cherish time.
珍惜時間。

Cherish health.
珍惜健康。

Cherish freedom.
珍惜自由。

** value〔'vælju〕*v.* 重視
cherish〔'tʃɛrɪʃ〕*v.* 珍惜
health〔hɛlθ〕*n.* 健康
freedom〔'fridəm〕*n.* 自由

Cherish friends.

珍惜朋友。

Cherish harmony.

珍惜和諧。

Cherish beauty.

珍惜美好。

** cherish〔ˈtʃɛrɪʃ〕 v. 珍惜
  harmony〔ˈhɑrmənɪ〕 n. 和諧
  beauty〔ˈbjutɪ〕 n. 美；美麗；美麗的事物或
    景色；美人

Cherish hope.

珍惜希望。

Cherish dreams.

珍惜夢想。

Cherish compassion.

珍惜關愛。

** cherish〔'tʃɛrɪʃ〕*v.* 珍惜

hope〔hop〕*n.* 希望

dream〔drim〕*n.* 夢；夢想

compassion〔kəm'pæʃən〕*n.* ①憐憫（= *pity*）
②同情（= *sympathy*）③仁愛（= *benevolence*）
④關愛（= *caring*）⑤仁慈（= *kindness*）⑥慈悲
（= *mercy*）⑦心懷慈悲（= *tenderheartedness*）
⑧同理心（= *empathy*）⑨溫暖（= *warmth*）

【**Unit 6 背景説明**】

Cherish time.（珍惜時間。）也可説成：
Value time.（重視時間。）Recognize the
importance of time.（認清時間的重要。）
Don't waste time.（不要浪費時間。）

Cherish health.（珍惜健康。）也可説成：
Value good health.（重視良好的健康。）
(= *Appreciate good health.*) Recognize
the importance of good health.（要認清
良好健康的重要。）

Cherish freedom.（珍惜自由。）也可説成：
Value freedom.（重視自由。）(= *Appreciate
freedom.*) Recognize the importance of
freedom.（認清自由的重要。）

Cherish friends.（珍惜朋友。）也可説成：
Value your friends.（重視你的朋友。）
Recognize the importance of friends.（認
清朋友的重要。）Recognize the importance
of your friends.（認清你的朋友的重要。）

Cherish harmony.（珍惜和諧。）也可說成：
Value harmony.（重視和諧。）Recognize
the importance of harmony.（認清和諧的
重要。）

Cherish beauty.（要珍惜美。）也可說成：
Value beauty.（要重視美。）(= *Appreciate
beauty*.) Recognize the importance of
beauty.（要認清美的重要。）

Cherish hope.（珍惜希望。）也可說成：
Value hope.（重視希望。）Recognize the
importance of hope.（認清希望的重要。）

Cherish dreams.（珍惜夢想。）也可說成：
Value dreams.（重視夢想。）Value your
dreams.（重視你的夢想。）Recognize the
importance of dreams.（認清夢想的重要。）
Recognize the importance of your dreams.
（認清你的夢想的重要。）

Cherish compassion.（珍惜同情。）也可
說成：Value kindness.（重視善良。）
Recognize the importance of kindness.
（認清善良的重要。）

BOOK 3・PART 2

UNIT 7

Express Positivity 展現積極態度

Show approval.
表示贊同。

Show recognition.
表示認同。

Show agreement.
表示同意。

** express〔ɪk'sprɛs〕v. 表達
positivity〔͵pɑzə'tɪvətɪ〕n. 正面；積極；樂觀
show〔ʃo〕v. 展現；表示
approval〔ə'pruvḷ〕n. 贊成；批准；認可
recognition〔͵rɛkəg'nɪʃən〕n. 認出；認可；表揚
agreement〔ə'grimənt〕n. 同意

Show passion.

展現熱情。

Show enthusiasm.

展現熱心。

Show appreciation.

展現讚賞。

** show〔ʃo〕*v.* 展現；表示
  passion〔'pæʃən〕*n.* 熱情
  enthusiasm〔ɪn'θjuzɪ͵æzəm〕*n.* 熱忱
  appreciation〔ə͵priʃɪ'eʃən〕*n.* 欣賞；感激；
    重視

Show support.

表示支持。

Show encouragement.

表示鼓勵。

Show endorsement.

表示認可。

** show〔 ʃo 〕*v.* 展現；表示
support〔 sə'port 〕*n.* 支持
encouragement〔 ɪn'kɝɪdʒmənt 〕*n.* 鼓勵
endorsement〔 ɪn'dɔrsmənt 〕*n.* 認可；支持
【endorse〔 ɪn'dɔrs 〕*v.* 背書；認可；贊同；支持】

【**Unit 7 背景説明**】

Show approval.（表示贊成。）也可説成：
Express your approval.（表達你的贊成。）
Express your consent.（表達你的同意。）

Show recognition.（表示認同。）也可説成：
Recognize what others do.（認同別人做的事。）Acknowledge what others say.（認可別人說的話。）

Show agreement.（表示同意。）也可説成：Express your agreement.（表達你的同意。）Show that you agree.（表示你同意。）Let others know you agree.（讓別人知道你同意。）

Show passion.（展現熱情。）也可説成：
Show your passion.（展現你的熱情。）
Show your enthusiasm.（展現你的熱忱。）

Show enthusiasm.（展現熱忱。）也可説成：
Show your enthusiasm.（展現你的熱忱。）
Express your enthusiasm.（表達你的熱忱。）

Show appreciation. 有兩個意思：①「表
示欣賞。」也可說成：Express your
admiration.（表達你的讚賞。）Express
your enjoyment.（表達你的喜歡。）
②「表示感激。」也可說成：Show your
gratitude.（表示你的感激。）Express
your gratitude.（表達你的感激。）

Show support.（表示支持。）也可說成：
Express your willingness to help.（表示
你願意幫忙。）(= *Express your willingness
to assist.*）

Show encouragement.（表示鼓勵。）也可
說成：Encourage others.（鼓勵別人。）
Be encouraging.（令人鼓舞。）

Show endorsement.（表示認可。）也可說
成：Show your endorsement.（表達你的
認可。）Express your endorsement.（表
達你的認同；表達你的支持。）

UNIT 8

Don't Delay 不要拖延

No waiting.
絕不等待。

No hesitation.
絕不猶豫。

No indecision.
絕不遲疑。

** delay〔dɪˋle〕*v.* 拖延

| *no* + *V-ing*/*N*. 禁止；不許；絕不 |

wait〔wet〕*v.* 等待
hesitation〔ˌhɛzəˋteʃən〕*n.* 猶豫
indecision〔ˌɪndɪˋsɪʒən〕*n.* 猶豫不決

No quitting.

絕不停止。

No retreat.

絕不退縮。

No surrender.

絕不投降。

** no〔no〕*adv.* 禁止；不許；不可以
   quit〔kwɪt〕*v.* 停止；放棄
   retreat〔rɪ'trit〕*n. v.* 退縮；撤退
   surrender〔sə'rɛndə〕*n. v.* 投降

No fear.

絕不害怕。

No doubts.

絕不懷疑。

No regrets.

絕不後悔。

** no〔no〕*adv.* 禁止；不許；不可以
　　fear〔fɪr〕*n. v.* 害怕；恐懼
　　doubt〔daʊt〕*n. v.* 懷疑
　　regret〔rɪˈgrɛt〕*n. v.* 後悔

【**Unit 8 背景説明**】

No waiting. 不要等待。(= *Don't wait.*) 也可説成：*No hesitation*.(不要猶豫。)(= *Don't hesitate.*) Take action.(要採取行動。)

No indecision.(不要猶豫不決。)也可説成：Don't hesitate.(不要猶豫。) Be decisive.(要果斷。)

No quitting. ①不要停止。(= *Don't quit.* = *Don't stop.*) ②不要放棄。(= *Don't quit.* = *Don't give up.*)

No retreat. 不要退縮。(= *Don't back off.*)也可説成：*No surrender*.(不要投降。)(= *Don't surrender.*) Don't give up.(不要放棄。)

No fear. 不要害怕。(= *Don't be afraid.*)

No doubts.(不要懷疑。)也可説成：Don't hesitate.(不要猶豫。) Be confident.(要有信心。) Be decisive.(要果斷。)

No regrets.(不要後悔。)也可説成：Don't regret what you do.(不要後悔你做的事。) Don't have second thoughts.(不要重新考慮。)

UNIT 9

Make the Most of What You've Got 善用你所擁有的

Seize chances.

抓住機會。

Seize opportunities.

把握機會。

Seize challenges.

接受挑戰。

** *make the most of* 善加利用
　have got 有（= *have*）
　seize〔siz〕*v.* 抓住；控制；支配
　chance〔tʃæns〕*n.* 機會
　opportunity〔͵ɑpə'tjunətɪ〕*n.* 機會
　challenge〔'tʃælɪndʒ〕*n.* 挑戰

Seize love.

把握真愛。

Seize kindness.

接受善意。

Seize gratitude.

接受感激。

** seize〔siz〕v. 抓住;控制;支配

love〔lʌv〕n. 愛

kindness〔'kaɪndnɪs〕n. 親切;仁慈;善意

gratitude〔'grætə,tjud〕n. 感激

Seize growth.

追求成長。

Seize connections.

抓住人脈。

Seize happiness.

抓住快樂。

** seize 〔 siz 〕 *v.* 抓住;控制;支配
　growth 〔 groθ 〕 *n.* 成長
　connections 〔 kəˈnɛkʃənz 〕 *n. pl.* 關係;人脈
　happiness 〔ˈhæpɪnɪs 〕 *n.* 快樂;幸福

【Unit 9 背景說明】

Seize chances. 要抓住機會。(= *Seize opportunities.*) 也可説成：Take the opportunity. (要把握機會。) Take advantage of opportunities. (要利用機會。)

Seize challenges. (要抓住挑戰。) 也可説：成 Take on challenges. (要接受挑戰。) Be eager to accept challenges. (要渴望接受挑戰。) Don't be afraid of challenges. (不要害怕挑戰。)

Seize love. 要抓住愛。(= *Hold on to love.*) 也可説成：Go after love. (要追求愛。)

Seize kindness. 要抓住善意。(= *Hold on to kindness.*) 也可説成：Accept kindness. (要接受善意。) Be kind. (要善良。)

Seize gratitude. 要抓住感激。(= *Hold on to gratitude.*) 也可説成：Accept gratitude.

（要接受感激。）Be thankful.（要充滿感謝。）Be grateful.（要充滿感激。）

Seize growth.（要抓住成長。）也可說成：Pursue growth.（要追求成長。）Pursue advancement.（要追求進步。）Pursue development.（要追求發展。）

Seize connections. 要抓住人脈。(*= Hold on to connections. = Hold on to relationships.*)也可說成：Pursue connections.（要追求人脈。）Take advantage of connections.（要利用人脈。）

Seize happiness. 要抓住快樂。(*= Hold on to happiness. = Hold on to joy.*)

PART 2 總整理

Unit 1

Stop worrying.
不要擔心。
Stop fearing. 不要害怕。
Stop doubting. 不要懷疑。

Stop hesitating.
不要猶豫。
Stop delaying. 不要拖延。
Stop procrastinating.
不要拖拉。

Stop arguing. 不要爭論。
Stop yelling. 不要大叫。
Stop complaining.
不要抱怨。

Unit 2

Never brag. 絕不吹牛。
Never boast. 絕不誇耀。
Never exaggerate.
絕不誇大。

Never lie. 絕不說謊。
Never deceive. 絕不欺騙。
Never backstab. 絕不背叛。

Never overact.
絕不做得過分。
Never overwork.
絕不工作過度。
Never overeat.
絕不吃得過多。

Unit 3

Don't hurry. 不要匆忙。
Don't rush. 不要著急。
Don't dash. 不要急忙。

Don't panic. 不要恐慌。
Don't freak. 不要抓狂。
Don't stress. 不要緊張。

Don't despair. 不要絕望。
Don't fret. 不要煩惱。
Don't succumb. 不要屈服。

Unit 4

Chase goals. 追求目標。
Chase desires. 追求願望。
Chase ambitions.
追求抱負。

Chase success.
追求成功。
Chase greatness.
追求偉大。
Chase excellence.
追求卓越。

Chase fortune.
追求財富。
Chase love. 追求真愛。
Chase teamwork.
追求合作。

Unit 5

Spread cheer. 散播愉快。
Spread laughter.
散播歡笑。
Spread positivity.
傳正能量。

Spread goodness. 散播善意。
Spread friendship.
散播友誼。
Spread information.
散播資訊。

Spread unity. 傳播團結。
Spread cooperation.
傳播合作。
Spread consensus.
傳播共識。

Unit 6

Cherish time. 珍惜時間。
Cherish health. 珍惜健康。
Cherish freedom. 珍惜自由。

Cherish friends. 珍惜朋友。
Cherish harmony.
珍惜和諧。
Cherish beauty. 珍惜美好。

Cherish hope. 珍惜希望。
Cherish dreams. 珍惜夢想。
Cherish compassion.
珍惜關愛。

BOOK 3．PART 2

BOOK 3 • PART 2

Unit 7

Show approval. 表示贊同。
Show recognition.
表示認同。
Show agreement.
表示同意。

Show passion. 展現熱情。
Show enthusiasm.
展現熱心。
Show appreciation.
展現讚賞。

Show support. 表示支持。
Show encouragement.
表示鼓勵。
Show endorsement.
表示認可。

Unit 8

No waiting. 絕不等待。
No hesitation. 絕不猶豫。
No indecision.
絕不遲疑。

No quitting. 絕不停止。
No retreat. 絕不退縮。
No surrender. 絕不投降。

No fear. 絕不害怕。
No doubts. 絕不懷疑。
No regrets. 絕不後悔。

Unit 9

Seize chances. 抓住機會。
Seize opportunities.
把握機會。
Seize challenges.
接受挑戰。

Seize love. 把握真愛。
Seize kindness. 接受善意。
Seize gratitude.
接受感激。

Seize growth. 追求成長。
Seize connections.
抓住人脈。
Seize happiness.
抓住快樂。

BOOK 3 / **PART 3**

Show Your Best Qualities
展現你最好的特質

PART 3・Unit 1~9
英文錄音QR碼

UNIT 1

Let Your Light Shine
讓你的光芒閃耀

Shine bright.
發光發亮。

Shine brightly.
閃閃發光。

Shine brilliantly.
閃耀發光。

** light〔laɪt〕*n.* 光　shine〔ʃaɪn〕*v.* 閃耀；
　照耀；發光；發亮；表現突出；出眾
bright〔braɪt〕*adj.* 明亮的　*adv.* 明亮地
shine bright 燦爛（= *shine brightly*）
brightly〔'braɪtlɪ〕*adv.* 明亮地
brilliantly〔'brɪljəntlɪ〕*adv.* 明亮地；鮮豔地

Shine beautifully.
亮麗發光。

Shine gloriously.
耀眼發光。

Shine radiantly.
光芒四射。

** shine〔ʃaɪn〕*v.* 閃耀；照耀；發光；
　　發亮；表現突出；出眾
　beautifully〔'bjutəfəlɪ〕*adv.* 漂亮地
　gloriously〔'glorɪəslɪ〕*adv.* 輝煌地；
　　壯麗地；光榮地
　radiantly〔'redɪəntlɪ〕*adv.* 輝煌地；
　　光芒四射地

Shine magically.

神奇發光。

Shine marvelously.

奇妙發光。

Shine magnificently.

壯麗發光。

** shine〔ʃaɪn〕v. 照耀；閃耀；發光；發亮；
　　表現突出；出衆

magically〔'mædʒɪklɪ〕adv. 神奇地

marvelously〔'mɑrvḷəslɪ〕adv. 奇妙地；
　　絕妙地；不可思議地；極好地

magnificently〔mæg'nɪfəsṇtlɪ〕adv. 極好地；
　　壯麗地

【Unit 1 背景説明】

記憶技巧：<u>b</u>right-<u>b</u>rightly-<u>b</u>rilliantly 都是 b 開頭。

Shine bright. 要光輝燦爛。(= ***Shine brightly***. = ***Shine brilliantly***.) 也可説成：Be radiant. (要光芒四射。) Be brilliant. (要光輝燦爛。) Show your talents. (要展現你的才能。)

Shine beautifully. (要散發美麗的光芒。) 也可説成：***Shine gloriously***. (要發出耀眼的光芒。) ***Shine radiantly***. (要光芒四射。) Shine magnificently. (要散發亮麗的光芒。)

記憶技巧：<u>m</u>agically-<u>m</u>arvelously-<u>m</u>agnificently 都是 m 開頭。

Shine magically. 要神奇地發光發亮。(= ***Shine marvelously***. = *Shine wonderfully*.) 也可説成：***Shine magnificently***. (要壯麗地發光發亮。) Shine beautifully. (要散發美麗的光芒。) Shine exquisitely. (要散發精緻的光芒。) Shine gloriously. (要光耀燦爛。)

UNIT 2

Let Yourself Glow 要讓自己發光

Radiate joy.
散發歡樂。

Radiate happiness.
散發快樂。

Radiate kindness.
散發善意。

** glow〔glo〕*v.* 發光

radiate〔'redɪˌet〕*v.* 輻射；散發

joy〔dʒɔɪ〕*n.* 愉快；高興；快樂

happiness〔'hæpɪnɪs〕*n.* 快樂

kindness〔'kaɪndnɪs〕*n.* 親切；仁慈；善意

Radiate love.

散發真愛。

Radiate warmth.

散發溫暖。

Radiate benevolence.

散發大愛。

** radiate〔'redɪˌet〕 *v.* 輻射；散發

love〔lʌv〕 *n.* 愛

warmth〔wɔrmθ〕 *n.* 溫暖

benevolence〔bə'nɛvələns〕 *n.* 慈悲心；
博愛；慈善

Radiate positivity.

散播正向。

Radiate optimism.

散播樂觀。

Radiate authenticity.

散播眞實。

```
** radiate ('redɪ‚et ) v. 輻射；散發
   positivity (‚pɑzə'tɪvətɪ ) n. 正面；
      積極；樂觀
   optimism ('ɑptə‚mɪzəm ) n. 樂觀
   authenticity (‚ɔθɛn'tɪsətɪ ) n. 眞實
```

【**Unit 2 背景説明**】

Radiate joy. 散發快樂。(= ***Radiate
happiness****.*) 也可説成：Express joy.（表達
快樂。）(= *Express happiness.*) Let your
joy show.（讓你的快樂展現出來。）(= *Let
your happiness show.*)

Radiate kindness.（散發善意。）也可説
成：Express kindness.（表達善意。）
(= *Express goodwill.*) Express your
compassion.（表達你的同情。）Let your
kindness show.（讓你的善意表現出來。）
(= *Let your goodwill show.*) Let your
generosity show.（讓你的慷慨表現出來。）

Radiate love.（散發愛意。）也可説成：
Express your love.（表達你的愛。）Show
your love.（展現你的愛。）Let your love
show.（讓你的愛展現出來。）

Radiate warmth.（散發溫暖。）也可説成：
Express warmth.（表達溫暖。）Show your

warmth.（展現你的溫暖。）Let your warmth show.（讓你的溫暖展現出來。）Show your compassion.（展現你的同情。）Let your compassion show.（讓你的同情展現出來。）

Radiate benevolence.（散發慈悲。）也可説成：Radiate goodwill.（散發善意。）Express kindness.（表示善意。）Express generosity.（表示慷慨。）

Radiate positivity.（散發正能量。）也可説成：*Radiate optimism*.（散發樂觀。）Express optimism.（表達樂觀）Express confidence.（表達信心。）Express enthusiasm.（表達熱忱。）Express idealism.（表達理想主義。）

Radiate authenticity.（散發真實。）也可説成：Show your authenticity.（展現你的真實。）（= *Show your genuineness*.）Let your authenticity show.（讓你的真實展現出來。）Express sincerity.（表達真誠。）Show your sincerity.（展現你的真誠。）

UNIT 3

Delight in Laughter 以笑爲樂

Laugh often.
笑口常開。

Laugh daily.
天天都笑。

Laugh freely.
盡情地笑。

** delight〔dɪ'laɪt〕*v.* 感到高興
   delight in 以…爲樂
   laughter〔'læftɚ〕*n.* 笑；笑聲
   laugh〔læf〕*v.* 笑   often〔'ɔfən〕*adv.* 常常
   daily〔'delɪ〕*adv.* 每天
   freely〔'frilɪ〕*adv.* 自由地；不受限制地；
      慷慨大方地；坦率地

Laugh abundantly.

大笑盈盈。

Laugh brightly.

笑得燦爛。

Laugh cheerfully.

笑得開心。

** laugh〔læf〕*v.* 笑

abundantly〔ə'bʌndəntlɪ〕*adv.* 豐富地；
　大量地

brightly〔'braɪtlɪ〕*adv.* 明亮地；快樂地

cheerfully〔'tʃɪrfəlɪ〕*adv.* 愉快地

Laugh graciously.

親切地笑。

Laugh gracefully.

優雅地笑。

Laugh genuinely.

眞正地笑。

** laugh〔læf〕*v.* 笑
graciously〔'greʃəslɪ〕*adv.* 親切地
gracefully〔'gresfəlɪ〕*adv.* 優雅地
genuinely〔'dʒɛnjʊɪnlɪ〕*adv.* 眞正地;
眞誠地

【**Unit 3 背景説明**】

Laugh often. 要常常笑。(= *Laugh frequently.*
= *Laugh regularly.*)

Laugh daily. 要每天笑。(= *Laugh every day.*)

Laugh freely. (要自由地笑。) 也可説成：Don't
suppress your laughter. (不要壓抑你的笑。)
Don't be afraid to laugh. (不要害怕笑。) Don't
hold back your laughter. (不要克制你的笑。)

Laugh abundantly. 要大量地笑；要常常笑。
(= *Laugh a lot.*)

Laugh brightly. 要快樂地笑。(= ***Laugh
cheerfully***. = *Laugh merrily.* = *Laugh joyfully.*
= *Laugh happily.*)

記憶技巧：graciously-gracefully-genuinely 都是
g 開頭的字。

Laugh graciously. 要親切地笑。(= *Laugh kindly.*)
也可説成：Laugh politely. (要有禮貌地笑。)
(= *Laugh courteously.*)

Laugh gracefully. (要優雅地笑。) 也可説成：
Laugh delicately. (要文雅地笑。) Laugh
charmingly. (要迷人地笑。) Laugh courteously.
(要有禮貌地笑。) Laugh kindly. (要親切地笑。)

Laugh genuinely. 要眞誠地笑。(= *Laugh
sincerely*.) 也可説成：Laugh wholeheartedly.
(要全心全意地笑。) Laugh naturally. (要自然
地笑。)

UNIT 4

Offer What You Can
盡量提供

Offer help.

提供幫助。

Offer support.

提供支持。

Offer assistance.

提供協助。

** offer〔'ɔfə〕*v.* 提供；給與；願意
   help〔hɛlp〕*n.* 幫助
   support〔sə'port〕*n.* 支持
   assistance〔ə'sɪstəns〕*n.* 協助

Offer inspiration.

給人激勵。

Offer motivation.

給人動力。

Offer encouragement.

給人鼓勵。

** offer〔'ɔfɚ〕*v.* 提供；給與；願意
inspiration〔,ɪnspə'reʃən〕*n.* 激勵
motivation〔,motə'veʃən,〕*n.* 激勵
encouragement〔ɪn'kɝɪdʒmənt〕*n.* 鼓勵

Offer love.

給人眞愛。

Offer kindness.

給人善意。

Offer sympathy.

給人同情。

** offer〔ˈɔfɚ〕*v.* 提供;給與;願意

love〔lʌv〕*n.* 愛

kindness〔ˈkaɪndnɪs〕*n.* 親切;仁慈;
  善意

sympathy〔ˈsɪmpəθɪ〕*n.* 同情

【**Unit 4 背景説明**】

Offer help.（提供幫助。）也可説成：*Offer support*.
（提供支持。）*Offer assistance*.（提供協助。）
Express a willingness to help.（表示願意幫忙。）
Express a willingness to assist.（表示願意協
助。）Express a willingness to support others.
（表示願意支持別人。）Express a willingness to
aid others.（表示願意幫助別人。）

Offer inspiration.　給人激勵。（= *Offer motivation*.）
也可説成：*Offer encouragement*.（給人鼓勵。）
Give others hope.（給人希望。）Give others
confidence.（給人信心。）Give others inspiration.
（給人激勵。）（= *Give others motivation*.）Give
others encouragement.（給人鼓勵。）

Offer love.（要給人愛。）也可説成：Express love.
（要表達愛。）Be loving.（要充滿愛。）

Offer kindness.（給人善意。）也可説成：Be kind.
（要善良。）Be kindhearted.（要心地善良。）

Offer sympathy.（給人同情。）也可説成：Be
sympathetic.（有同情心。）Be understanding.
（要能體諒。）

UNIT 5

Savor the Good Things in Life
品味生活中美好的事物

Savor life.
品味人生。

Savor love.
體會眞愛。

Savor laughter.
感受歡笑。

** savor〔'sevɚ〕*v.* 品嚐；品味；體會
   life〔laɪf〕*n.* 生活；生命；人生
   love〔lʌv〕*n.* 愛
   laughter〔'læftɚ〕*n.* 笑；笑聲

Savor joy.

品味快樂。

Savor beauty.

品味美麗。

Savor blessings.

品味幸福。

** savor〔ˈsevə〕v. 品嚐；品味；體會
joy〔dʒɔɪ〕n. 愉快；高興；快樂
beauty〔ˈbjutɪ〕n. 美；美麗的事物；美人
blessing〔ˈblɛsɪŋ〕n. 幸福；幸運的事

Savor friendships.

品味友誼。

Savor relationships.

品味關係。

Savor connections.

品味人脈。

** savor〔'sevɚ〕*v.* 品嚐；品味；體會

　friendship〔'frɛndʃɪp〕*n.* 友誼

　relationship〔rɪ'leʃənˌʃɪp〕*n.* 關係

　connections〔kə'nɛkʃənz〕*n. pl.* 關係；人脈

【Unit 5 背景説明】

記憶技巧：<u>l</u>ife-<u>l</u>ove-<u>l</u>aughter 字首都是 l 開頭。

***Savor life*.** 品味生活。(= *Relish life.*) 也可説
成：Enjoy life. (享受生活。) Appreciate
life. (重視生活。) 句中的 life 也可用 your
life 代替。

***Savor love*.** 要品味愛。(= *Relish love.*) 也可説
成：Enjoy love. (要享受愛。) Appreciate
love. (要重視愛。) Treasure love. (要珍惜愛。)

***Savor laughter*.** 要品味笑。(= *Relish laughter.*)
也可説成：Enjoy laughter. (要享受笑。)
Appreciate laughter. (要重視笑。)

***Savor joy*.** 品味快樂。(= *Relish joy.*) 也可説
成：Enjoy happiness. (享受快樂。)
Appreciate happiness. (重視快樂。)

***Savor beauty*.** 要品味美。(= *Relish beauty.*)
也可説成：Appreciate beauty. (要重視美。)
Enjoy lovely things. (要享受可愛的事物。)

Savor blessings. 品味幸福。(= *Relish blessings.*) 也可說成：Enjoy good fortune. (享受好運。) Appreciate good fortune. (重視好運。)

Savor friendships. 品味友誼。(= *Relish friendships.*) 也可說成：Appreciate your friends. (重視你的朋友。)

Savor relationships. (品味關係。) 也可說成：Enjoy your relationships with others. (享受你和別人的關係。) Appreciate your relationships with others. (重視你和別人的關係。)

Savor connections. (品味人脈。) 也可說成：Enjoy connections. (享受人脈。) (= *Enjoy relationships.*) Appreciate connections. (重視人脈。) (= *Appreciate relationships.*) Treasure connections. (珍惜人脈。) (= *Cherish relationships.*)

UNIT 6

Know What to Avoid
要知道該避免什麼

Avoid extremes.
避免極端行為。

Avoid overspending.
避免過度花費。

Avoid overreacting.
避免反應過度。

** avoid〔ə'vɔɪd〕*v.* 避免
avoid + N./V-ing 避免…
extreme〔ɪk'strim〕*n.* 極端
overspend〔,ovə'spɛnd〕*v.* 花錢過多；超支
overreact〔,ovərɪ'ækt〕*v.* 反應過度

Avoid hurry.

避免匆忙。

Avoid haste.

避免急促。

Avoid rushing.

避免倉促。

** avoid〔ə'vɔɪd〕*v.* 避免
　hurry〔'hɜɪ〕*n.* 匆忙
　haste〔hest〕*n.* 匆忙
　rush〔rʌʃ〕*v.* 衝；趕緊；倉促行動
　　n. 衝；匆忙

Avoid despair.

避免絕望。

Avoid pessimism.

避免悲觀。

Avoid negativity.

避免負面。

** avoid〔əˋvɔɪd〕*v.* 避免
despair〔dɪˋspɛr〕*n. v.* 絕望
pessimism〔ˋpɛsəˌmɪzəm〕*n.* 悲觀
negativity〔ˌnɛgəˋtɪvətɪ〕*n.* 負面；
　否定；消極

【**Unit 6 背景説明**】

Avoid extremes.（避免極端。）也可説成：

Don't go to extremes.（不要走極端。）

Do things in moderation.（做事要中庸。）

Avoid overspending.（避免過度花費。）也可説

成：Don't spend too much.（不要花太多錢。）

Don't spend more than you should.（不要花

超過你應該花的錢。）Don't spend more than

you intend.（不要花超過你打算花的錢。）

Avoid overreacting.（避免反應過度。）也可説

成：Don't overreact.（不要反應過度。）

Don't be dramatic.（不要戲劇化。）Don't

exaggerate.（不要誇張。）Don't make a

big deal out of it.（不要小題大作。）

Avoid hurry.（避免匆忙。）也可説成：Don't

be in a hurry.（不要匆匆忙忙。）

Avoid haste.（避免匆忙。）也可説成：Don't

be hasty.（不要匆忙。）Don't hurry.（不要

匆忙。）（= *Don't rush.*）

Avoid rushing. 避免匆忙。(= *Avoid hurry.*
= *Avoid haste.*) 也可說成：Don't hurry. (不
要匆忙。) (= *Don't rush.*) Don't be in a
rush. (不要匆匆忙忙。) Take your time. (慢
慢來。) Give yourself enough time. (給你
自己足夠的時間。)

Avoid despair. (避免絕望。) 也可說成：Don't
despair. (不要絕望。) Don't lose hope. (不
要失去希望。) Don't give up. (不要放棄。)

Avoid pessimism. (避免悲觀。) 也可說成：
Don't be pessimistic. (不要悲觀。)
(= *Don't be gloomy*.) Don't be negative.
(不要有負面的想法。)

Avoid negativity. (避免負面的想法。) 也可說
成：Don't be negative. (不要有負面情緒。)
Don't be pessimistic. (不要悲觀。) Avoid
negative people. (避開有負面情緒的人。)

UNIT 7

Accept What You Can't Change
接受你無法改變的事

Accept loss.
接受失去。

Accept setbacks.
接受挫折。

Accept defeat.
接受落敗。

** accept〔əkˈsɛpt〕*v.* 接受
change〔tʃendʒ〕*v.* 改變
loss〔lɔs〕*n.* 喪失；損失；失敗
setback〔ˈsɛtˌbæk〕*n.* 挫折
defeat〔dɪˈfit〕*n.* 失敗；戰敗；落敗 *v.* 打敗

Accept failure.

接受失敗。

Accept downturns.

接受衰敗。

Accept downfalls.

接受垮台。

** accept〔əkˈsɛpt〕v. 接受
failure〔ˈfeljɚ〕n. 失敗
downturn〔ˈdaʊnˌtɝn〕n. 衰退;下滑
downfall〔ˈdaʊnˌfɔl〕n. 垮台;失敗

BOOK 3・PART 3

Accept misfortune.

接受不幸。

Accept fiascos.

接受慘敗。

Accept tragedy.

接受悲劇。

** accept〔ək'sɛpt〕*v.* 接受

misfortune〔mɪs'fɔrtʃən〕*n.* 不幸

fiasco〔fɪ'æsko〕*n.* 慘敗；完全失敗；
 尷尬的結局

tragedy〔'trædʒədɪ〕*n.* 悲劇；災難；不幸

【Unit 7 背景説明】

Accept loss. 要接受失敗。(= *Accept failure.*)
也可説成：Bear loss. (要忍受失敗。)
Admit loss. (要承認失敗。) (= *Acknowledge
loss.*) Accept responsibility for loss. (要接
受失敗的責任。)

Accept setbacks. (要接受挫折。) 也可説成：
Tolerate setbacks. (要忍受挫折。)
(= *Endure setbacks.*) Bear disappointment.
(要忍受失望。)

Accept defeat. 要接受落敗。(= *Accept
failure.*) 也可説成：Admit defeat. (要
承認失敗。) (= *Acknowledge defeat.*)
Accept responsibility for defeat. (要
接受失敗的責任。)

Accept failure. (要接受失敗。) 也可説成：
Admit failure. (要承認失敗。) Endure
failure. (要忍受失敗。) Accept
responsibility for failure. (要接受失敗的
責任。)

Accept downturns. (要接受衰退。) 也可説
成：Admit downturns. (要承認衰退。)

Tolerate downturns.（要忍受衰退。）
Bear setbacks.（要忍受挫折。）(= *Endure*
reversals.) Accept responsibility for
downturns.（要接受衰退的責任。）

Accept downfalls. 要接受垮台；要接受失敗。
(= *Accept failure*.) 也可說成：Admit
downfalls.（要承認失敗。）Bear downfalls.
（要忍受失敗。）Accept responsibility for
downfalls.（要接受失敗的責任。）

Accept misfortune. 要接受不幸。(= *Accept*
bad luck. = *Accept hard luck*.) 也可說成：
Endure misfortune.（要忍受不幸。）
Tolerate adversity.（要忍受逆境。）

Accept fiascos.（要接受慘敗。）也可說成：
Accept failures.（要接受失敗。）Tolerate
disasters.（要忍受災難。）Admit fiascos.
（要承認慘敗。）Take responsibility for
fiascos.（要承擔慘敗的責任。）

Accept tragedy. 要接受悲劇；要接受不幸。
(= *Accept misfortunes*. = *Accept disasters*.
= *Accept catastrophes*.)

UNIT 8

Keep Striving 持續努力

Strive consistently.

持續努力。

Strive relentlessly.

不斷努力。

Strive tirelessly.

不倦努力。

** ***keep + V-ing*** 持續… strive〔straɪv〕*v.* 努力
consistently〔kən'sɪstəntlɪ〕*adv.* 堅持地；不斷
地；始終如一地
relentlessly〔rɪ'lɛntlɪslɪ〕*adv.* 不斷地；持續地
tirelessly〔'taɪrlɪslɪ〕*adv.* 不知疲倦地；不覺疲勞地

Strive earnestly.

認眞努力。

Strive devotedly.

全心投入。

Strive wholeheartedly.

全心努力。

** strive〔straɪv〕*v.* 努力
earnestly〔'ɜnɪstlɪ〕*adv.* 認眞地
devotedly〔dɪ'votɪdlɪ〕*adv.* 忠實地；
　　專注地；一心一意地；全心全意地
wholeheartedly〔ˌhol'hɑrtɪdlɪ〕*adv.*
　　全心全意地

Strive steadfastly.

堅定努力。

Strive resolutely.

堅決努力。

Strive tenaciously.

堅持努力。

** strive〔 straɪv 〕*v.* 努力
steadfastly〔'stɛd,fæstlɪ 〕*adv.* 堅定地；堅決地
resolutely〔'rɛzə,lutlɪ 〕*adv.* 堅決地；毅然地
tenaciously〔 tɪ'neʃəslɪ 〕*adv.* 堅持地；堅韌地；
　頑強地；持久地

BOOK 3・PART 3

【**Unit 8 背景說明**】

Strive consistently. 要持續努力。(= *Make an effort continually.* = *Try continually.* = *Work continually.*)

Strive relentlessly. 要不斷努力。(= *Try ceaselessly.* = *Make an effort without stopping.* = *Work continually.*)

Strive tirelessly. (要不知疲倦地努力。) 也可說成：Try firmly. (要堅定地努力。) Work resolutely. (要堅決地努力。) (= *Make an effort determinedly.* = *Make an effort steadfastly.*)

Strive earnestly. 要認真努力。(= *Make an effort seriously.*) 也可說成：Try eagerly. (要熱切地努力。) Work passionately. (要充滿熱情地努力。)

Strive devotedly. (要專注地努力。) 也可說成：Make an effort resolutely. (要堅決地

努力。）Devote yourself to the attempt.
（要盡力嘗試。）

Strive wholeheartedly.（要全心全意地努力。）
也可說成：Make an effort without
reservation.（要毫不保留地努力。）（= *Try
unreservedly.*）Try as hard as you can.
（要盡量努力。）

Strive steadfastly.（要堅定地努力。）也可說
成：Make an effort persistently.（要持續地
努力。）Try unwaveringly.（要堅定不移地
努力。）Work doggedly.（要頑強地努力。）

Strive resolutely. 要堅決地努力。（= *Make an
effort determinedly.*）也可說成：Try firmly.
（要堅定地努力。）Work intensely.（要認眞
地努力。）

Strive tenaciously.（要堅持努力。）也可說成：
Make an effort unwaveringly.（要毫不動搖
地努力。）Work determinedly.（要堅決地努
力。）（= *Try resolutely.*）

UNIT 9

Be Tenacious 堅定不移

Pursue tenaciously.

堅持追求。

Learn tenaciously.

堅持學習。

Work tenaciously.

堅定工作。

** tenacious〔tɪ'neʃəs〕*adj.* 頑強的;堅持的;
 不屈不撓的 pursue〔pə'su〕*v.* 追求
 tenaciously〔tɪ'neʃəslɪ〕*adv.* 堅持地;
 堅韌地;頑強地;持久地
 learn〔lɜn〕*v.* 學習 work〔wɜk〕*v.* 工作

Fight tenaciously.

堅持奮鬥。

Advance tenaciously.

堅持前進。

Overcome tenaciously.

堅持克服。

** fight 〔 faɪt 〕 *v.* 打架；奮鬥；搏鬥
    tenaciously 〔 tɪˈneʃəslɪ 〕 *adv.* 堅持地；
        堅韌地；頑強地；持久地
    advance 〔 ədˈvæns 〕 *v.* 前進；進步
    overcome 〔ˌovɚˈkʌm 〕 *v.* 克服

Hope tenaciously.

要堅持希望。

Believe tenaciously.

要堅定信仰。

Dream tenaciously.

要堅持夢想。

** hope〔hop〕*v.* 希望；期待
　　tenaciously〔tɪ'neʃəslɪ〕*adv.* 堅持地；
　　　堅韌地；頑強地；持久地
　　believe〔bɪ'liv〕*v.* 相信；信任；信仰
　　dream〔drim〕*v.* 做夢；夢想

【**Unit 9 背景説明**】

Pursue tenaciously. 要堅定地追求。(= *Search firmly*.) 也可説成：Search resolutely. (要堅決地追求。) (= *Search determinedly*.)

Learn tenaciously. 要堅定地學習。(= *Learn steadfastly*.) 也可説成：Learn persistently. (要持續學習。) Learn doggedly. (要頑強地學習。)

Work tenaciously. (要堅定地工作。) 也可説成：Work determinedly. (要堅決地工作。) Work unwaveringly. (要毫不動搖地工作。) Work doggedly. (要頑強地工作。)

Fight tenaciously. (要堅定地奮鬥。) 也可説成：Strive resolutely. (要堅決地努力。) (= *Strive determinedly*.) Work hard. (要努力。) (= *Try hard*.)

Advance tenaciously. (要堅定地向前進。) 也可説成：Progress. (要向前進。) (= *Proceed*.) Proceed with determination. (要堅決地向前進。) Proceed persistently. (要持續向前進。)

Overcome tenaciously. (要堅定地克服。)
也可說成：Triumph determinedly. (要
堅決地獲勝。) (= *Win resolutely*.) Win
unwaveringly. (要堅定不移地獲勝。)

Hope tenaciously. (要堅持希望。) 也可說
成：Aspire resolutely. (要堅決地渴望。)
(= *Aspire determinedly*.)

Believe tenaciously. 要堅定地相信。(= *Be
tenacious in your beliefs*.) 也可說成：Trust
firmly. (要堅定地信任。) Be persistent in
your beliefs. (要堅持你的信念。) (= *Hold
on to your beliefs*.) Accept steadfastly. (要
堅定地接受。)

Dream tenaciously. (要堅持夢想。) 也可說
成：Imagine unwaveringly. (要堅定不移地
想像。) Visualize determinedly. (要堅決地
想像。)

PART 3　總整理

Unit 1

Shine bright.　發光發亮。
Shine brightly.　閃閃發光。
Shine brilliantly.　閃耀發光。

Shine beautifully.　亮麗發光。
Shine gloriously.　耀眼發光。
Shine radiantly.　光芒四射。

Shine magically.　神奇發光。
Shine marvelously.
奇妙發光。
Shine magnificently.
壯麗發光。

Unit 2

Radiate joy.　散發歡樂。
Radiate happiness.　散發快樂。
Radiate kindness.　散發善意。

Radiate love.　散發眞愛。
Radiate warmth.　散發溫暖。
Radiate benevolence.
散發大愛。

Radiate positivity.
散播正向。
Radiate optimism.
散播樂觀。
Radiate authenticity.
散播眞實。

Unit 3

Laugh often.　笑口常開。
Laugh daily.　天天都笑。
Laugh freely.　盡情地笑。

Laugh abundantly.
大笑盈盈。
Laugh brightly.　笑得燦爛。
Laugh cheerfully.
笑得開心。

Laugh graciously.
親切地笑。
Laugh gracefully.
優雅地笑。
Laugh genuinely.
眞正地笑。

Unit 4

Offer help.　提供幫助。
Offer support.　提供支持。
Offer assistance.
提供協助。

Offer inspiration.
給人激勵。
Offer motivation.
給人動力。
Offer encouragement.
給人鼓勵。

Offer love.　給人真愛。
Offer kindness.
給人善意。
Offer sympathy.
給人同情。

Unit 5

Savor life.　品味人生。
Savor love.　體會真愛。
Savor laughter.　感受歡笑。

Savor joy.　品味快樂。
Savor beauty.　品味美麗。
Savor blessings.　品味幸福。

Savor friendships.
品味友誼。
Savor relationships.
品味關係。
Savor connections.
品味人脈。

Unit 6

Avoid extremes.
避免極端行為。
Avoid overspending.
避免過度花費。
Avoid overreacting.
避免反應過度。

Avoid hurry.　避免匆忙。
Avoid haste.　避免急促。
Avoid rushing.
避免倉促。

Avoid despair.
避免絕望。
Avoid pessimism.
避免悲觀。
Avoid negativity.
避免負面。

Unit 7

Accept loss. 接受失去。
Accept setbacks. 接受挫折。
Accept defeat. 接受落敗。

Accept failure. 接受失敗。
Accept downturns.
接受衰敗。
Accept downfalls.
接受垮台。

Accept misfortune.
接受不幸。
Accept fiascos. 接受慘敗。
Accept tragedy. 接受悲劇。

Unit 8

Strive consistently.
持續努力。
Strive relentlessly.
不斷努力。
Strive tirelessly. 不倦努力。

Strive earnestly. 認真努力。
Strive devotedly. 全心投入。
Strive wholeheartedly.
全心努力。

Strive steadfastly.
堅定努力。
Strive resolutely.
堅決努力。
Strive tenaciously.
堅持努力。

Unit 9

Pursue tenaciously.
堅持追求。
Learn tenaciously.
堅持學習。
Work tenaciously.
堅定工作。

Fight tenaciously.
堅持奮鬥。
Advance tenaciously.
堅持前進。
Overcome tenaciously.
堅持克服。

Hope tenaciously.
要堅持希望。
Believe tenaciously.
要堅定信仰。
Dream tenaciously.
要堅持夢想。

BOOK 4   PART 1

Good Traits
良好的特質

PART 1・Unit 1~9
英文錄音QR碼

UNIT 1

The Wonders of Happiness
快樂的奇蹟

Happiness shines.
快樂發光。

Happiness radiates.
快樂發熱。

Happiness illuminates.
快樂發亮。

** wonder〔ˈwʌndə〕*n.* 奇蹟
happiness〔ˈhæpɪnɪs〕*n.* 快樂；幸福
shine〔ʃaɪn〕*v.* 照耀；發光；發亮；
　表現突出；出眾
radiate〔ˈredɪˌet〕*v.* 輻射；散發（光、熱）
illuminate〔ɪˈluməˌnet〕*v.* 照亮

Happiness charms.

快樂有魅力。

Happiness fascinates.

快樂吸引人。

Happiness captivates.

快樂迷死人。

** happiness〔'hæpɪnɪs〕*n.* 快樂；幸福
　　charm〔tʃɑrm〕*v.* 吸引人；有魅力
　　fascinate〔'fæsn̩‚et〕*v.* 使著迷
　　captivate〔'kæptə‚vet〕*v.* 使著迷

Happiness uplifts.
快樂振奮人心。

Happiness energizes.
快樂給人能量。

Happiness empowers.
快樂給人力量。

** happiness〔'hæpɪnɪs〕*n.* 快樂；幸福
uplift〔ʌp'lɪft〕*v.* 振奮；鼓舞；振作
energize〔'ɛnɚˌdʒaɪz〕*v.* 使精力充沛；
　　使有活力
empower〔ɪm'pauɚ〕*v.* 給與力量；
　　授權；使有權力

【**Unit 1 背景説明**】

Happiness shines. 快樂會發光。(= *Happiness glows*.) 也可説成：*Happiness radiates*. (快樂會散發光和熱。) Happiness light up the world. (快樂照亮全世界。)

Happiness illuminates. (快樂能照亮。) 也可説成：Happiness lights things up. (快樂照亮萬物。) Happiness lights people up. (快樂給人光明。) Happiness shows the way. (快樂指引道路。)

Happiness charms. (快樂有魅力。) 也可説成：Happiness charms people. (快樂使人著迷。) (= *Happiness enchants people*.) Happiness delights others. (快樂使人高興。) (= *Happiness pleases others*.)

Happiness fascinates. 快樂使人著迷。(= *Happiness fascinates people*. = *Happiness enthralls others*.) 也可説成：Happiness interests others. (快樂使人感興趣。)

Happiness captivates. 快樂令人著迷。
（ = *Happiness captivates people.*
= *Happiness fascinates people.* = *Happiness
enchants people.* ）也可說成：Happiness
entertains others.（快樂使人開心。）

Happiness uplifts.（快樂振奮人心。）也可說
成：Happiness inspires.（快樂激勵人心。）
Happiness strengthens.（快樂使人堅強。）

Happiness energizes. 快樂使人有活力。
（ = *Happiness invigorates.* = *Happiness
rejuvenates.* = *Happiness energizes people.*
= *Happiness invigorates people.* = *Happiness
gives people energy.* ）

Happiness empowers.（快樂使人有力量。）也
可說成：Happiness encourages.（快樂給人
鼓勵。）Happiness emboldens.（快樂使人有
膽量。）

UNIT 2

Create Great Things
創造很棒的事物

Create magic.

創造魔法。

Create miracles.

創造奇蹟。

Create wonders.

創造驚奇。

** create〔krɪˋet〕*v.* 創造
    great〔gret〕*adj.* 極好的；很棒的
    magic〔ˋmædʒɪk〕*n.* 魔法；魔術
    miracle〔ˋmɪrək!〕*n.* 奇蹟
    wonder〔ˋwʌndɚ〕*n.* 驚奇；奇蹟；奇觀

Create dreams.

創造夢想。

Create beauty.

創造美好。

Create happiness.

創造快樂。

** create〔krɪ'et〕v. 創造
dream〔drim〕n. 夢；夢想
beauty〔'bjutɪ〕n. 美
happiness〔'hæpɪnɪs〕n. 快樂；幸福

Create opportunities.

創造機會。

Create connections.

創造人脈。

Create success.

創造成功。

** create 〔 krɪ'et 〕 *v.* 創造

opportunity 〔 ,ɑpə'tjunətɪ 〕 *n.* 機會

connection 〔 kə'nɛkʃən 〕 *n.* 連接;連結;

   關連;關係;(*pl.*) 人脈

success 〔 sək'sɛs 〕 *n.* 成功

【Unit 2 背景説明】

Create magic.（要創造魔法。）也可説成：*Create miracles*.（要創造奇蹟。）(= *Create wonders*.) Do something wonderful.（要做很棒的事。）(= *Do something great*.) Do something remarkable.（要做很出色的事。）(= *Do something magnificent*.) Do something unexpected.（要做出人意料的事。）

Create dreams.（要創造夢想。）也可説成：Make your dreams come true.（要實現你的夢想。）(= *Realize your dreams*.)

Create beauty.（要創造美好。）也可説成：Make something beautiful.（要使某樣事物變得美麗。）

Create happiness.（要創造快樂。）也可説成：Make someone happy.（要使人快樂。）

Create opportunities.（要創造機會。）也可説成：Create your own chances.（要創造你自己的機會。）Create your own good luck.（要創造你自己的幸運。）

Create connections. 要創造人脈。(= *Make connections*.)也可説成：Network.（要建立人脈。）

Create success.（要創造成功。）也可説成：Make your own success.（要創造自己的成功。）Be successful.（要成功。）

UNIT 3

Don't Delay 不要拖延

Start now.

現在開始。

Start off.

開始動手。

Get started.

開始做吧。

** delay〔dɪ'le〕*v.* 拖延

start〔stɑrt〕*v.* 開始

now〔naʊ〕*adv.* 現在；立刻；馬上

start off 開始；出發

get started 開始；起動

Get going.

馬上開始。

Get moving.

馬上行動。

Get cracking.

快點開始。

** ***get going*** 出發；實行
move〔muv〕*v.* 移動
get moving 迅速開始
crack〔kræk〕*v.* 裂開
get cracking 開始

Begin now.

現在開始。

Begin immediately.

立刻開始。

Begin straightaway.

馬上開始。

** begin 〔 bɪˋgɪn 〕 v. 開始

now 〔 naʊ 〕 adv. 現在；立刻；馬上

immediately 〔 ɪˋmidɪɪtlɪ 〕 adv. 立刻

straightaway 〔ˋstretəˌwe 〕 adv. 立刻；馬上

　(= *straight away*)

【Unit 3 背景説明】

Start now. 現在就開始。(= *Begin now*.)

Start off. 開始。(= *Get started*. = *Begin*. = *Get going*.)

Get going. (開始。) 也可説成：*Get moving*. (迅速開始。) *Get cracking*. (開始。) (= *Get started*.) Hurry up. (趕快。)

Begin now. 現在就開始。(= *Start now*.) 也可説成：Get started. (開始。)

Begin immediately. 立刻開始。(= *Begin right away*. = *Begin at once*.)

Begin straightaway. 立刻開始。(= *Begin straight away*. = *Begin right away*.)

UNIT 4

Persevere 堅持到底

Go on.

加油。

Carry on.

繼續加油。

Continue on.

持續加油。

** persevere〔ˌpɝsəˈvɪr〕*v.* 堅忍;不屈不撓

go on 繼續;繼續做

carry on 繼續;繼續下去

continue〔kəˈtɪnju〕*v.* 繼續

continue on 繼續

Push on.
繼續向前。

Power on.
加足馬力。

Press on.
堅持下去。

** push〔puʃ〕*v.* 推
push on 繼續向前；堅決進行下去
power〔'pauɚ〕*n.* 力量　*v.* 給…提供動力
power on 通電；接通電源
press〔prɛs〕*v.* 壓
press on 堅持下去

Go forward.

持續前進。

Move forward.

向前邁進。

Press forward.

奮勇前進。

** forward〔'fɔrwəd〕*adv.* 向前

　go forward 前進

　move〔muv〕*v.* 移動

　move forward 前進；進步

　press〔prɛs〕*v.* 壓

　press forward 向前推進；奮勇前進

【Unit 4 背景説明】

Go on.（繼續。）也可説成：*Carry on*.
（繼續下去。）*Continue on*.（繼續。）
Keep going.（持續前進。）Proceed.
（要向前進。）

Push on.（繼續前進。）也可説成：*Power on*.（要接通電源；力量加持；加足馬力。）
Press on.（要堅持下去。）Keep going.
（要持續前進。）Persevere.（要堅忍不拔。）

Go forward.　要向前進。(= *Move forward*.)
也可説成：*Press forward*.（奮勇前進。）
Advance.（要向前進。）(= *Progress*.)
Keep going.（持續前進。）

UNIT 5

Be an Explorer 做一個探險家

Explore unknowns.

探索未知。

Explore wonders.

探索奇蹟。

Explore mysteries.

探索奧祕。

**explorer〔ɪkˋsplorə〕 *n.* 探險家

　explore〔ɪkˋsplor〕 *v.* 探險；探索

　unknown〔ʌnˋnon〕 *n.* 不了解的事物　*adj.* 未

　　知的　　wonder〔ˋwʌndə〕 *n.* 奇蹟；奇觀

　mystery〔ˋmɪstrɪ〕 *n.* 奧祕；謎

Explore nature.

探索大自然。

Explore possibilities.

探索可能性。

Explore opportunities.

探索好機會。

** explore〔ɪk'splor〕v. 探險;探索
  nature〔'netʃɚ〕n. 大自然
  possibility〔ˌpɑsə'bɪlətɪ〕n. 可能性
  opportunity〔ˌɑpɚ'tjunətɪ〕n. 機會

Explore boldly.

大膽探索。

Explore fearlessly.

無畏探索。

Explore courageously.

勇於探索。

** explore 〔 ɪk'splor 〕 *v.* 探險；探索
   boldly 〔 'boldlɪ 〕 *adv.* 大膽地；勇敢地
   fearlessly 〔 'fɪrlɪslɪ 〕 *adv.* 無所畏懼地
   courageously 〔 kə'redʒəslɪ 〕 *adv.* 勇敢地

【Unit 5 背景說明】

Explore unknowns.（探索未知的事物。）也可說成：Investigate what you don't know.（調查你不知道的事物。）Investigate new things.（調查新的事物。）

Explore wonders.（探索奇蹟。）也可說成：Explore amazing things.（探索神奇的事物。）Discover amazing things.（發現神奇的事物。）Study amazing things.（研究神奇的事物。）

Explore mysteries.（探索奧祕。）也可說成：Study what you don't know.（研究你不知道的事物。）Investigate the unknown.（調查未知的事物。）

Explore nature.（探索大自然。）也可說成：Investigate nature.（調查大自然。）Study the natural world.（研究自然界。）

Explore possibilities.（探索可能性。）也可説
成：*Explore opportunities*.（探索各種機會。）
Investigate your options.（調查你有什麼選
擇。）Study your options.（研究你有什麼選
擇。）

Explore boldly.（要大膽地探索。）也可説成：
Investigate boldly.（要大膽地調查。）Don't
be afraid to explore.（不要害怕探索。）

Explore fearlessly.（要毫不畏懼地探索。）也
可説成：Investigate fearlessly.（要毫不畏懼
地調查。）

Explore courageously.　要勇敢地探索。
（＝*Explore bravely*.）也可説成：Investigate
courageously.（要勇敢地調查。）Be
courageous enoug to explore.（要有足夠的
勇氣去探索。）

UNIT 6

Realize Your Dreams 實現你的夢想

Fulfill goals.

實現目標。

Fulfill targets.

實現目的。

Fulfill desires.

實現願望。

** realize〔'riə‚laɪz〕*v.* 實現
dream〔drim〕*n.* 夢;夢想
fulfill〔fʊl'fɪl〕*v.* 履行;實行;達成;實現;
　滿足　　goal〔gol〕*n.* 目標
target〔'tɑrgɪt〕*n.* 目標;標靶
desire〔dɪ'zaɪr〕*n.* 渴望;願望

Fulfill aims.

達成目標。

Fulfill plans.

實現計劃。

Fulfill objectives.

達成目的。

** fulfill〔fʊlˋfɪl〕*v.* 履行；實行；達成；
實現；滿足

aim〔em〕*n.* 目標；目的

plan〔plæn〕*n.* 計劃；規劃

objective〔əbˋdʒɛktɪv〕*n.* 目標；目的
adj. 客觀的

Fulfill intentions.

實現意圖。

Fulfill ambitions.

實現抱負。

Fulfill missions.

達成任務。

** fulfill〔fʊlˈfɪl〕v. 履行；實行；達成；
　　實現；滿足

intention〔ɪnˈtɛnʃən〕n. 意圖；目的

ambition〔æmˈbɪʃən〕n. 抱負；雄心；
　　野心；目標

mission〔ˈmɪʃən〕n. 任務；使命

【Unit 6 背景説明】

Fulfill goals. 要實現目標。(= *Fulfill targets*.)
也可説成：Achieve aims. (要達成目標。)
(= *Achieve objectives*.) Achieve ambitions.
(要實現抱負。) Achieve intentions. (要達
成目的。)

Fulfill desires. 要實現願望。(= *Fulfill
aspirations*.) 也可説成：Achieve your
desires. (要達成你的願望。) Get what
you want. (要得到你想要的。)

Fulfill aims. 要實現目標。(= *Fulfill goals*.)
也可説成：Achieve your goals. (要達成你
的目標。)

Fulfill plans. 要實現計劃。(= *Achieve plans*.)
也可説成：Fulfill your plans. (要實現你的
計劃。)

Fulfill objectives. 要達成目標。(= *Achieve
objectives*. = *Achieve goals*. = *Achieve*

targets.) 也可說成：Achieve intentions.
（要達成目的。） Achieve aspirations.
（要達成願望。）(= *Achieve desires.*)

Fulfill intentions. （要達到目的。）也可說成：
Fulfill aims. （要實現目標。）(= *Fulfill*
objectives.) Achieve your goals. （要達成你
的目標。）

Fulfill ambitions. （要實現抱負。）也可說
成：Fulfill aspirations. （要實現願望。）
(= *Fulfill desires.*) Achieve goals. （要
達到目標。）

Fulfill missions. （要達成任務。）也可說成：
Achieve your missions. （要達成你的任務。）
Achieve your objectives. （要達到你的目
標。）Complete tasks. （要完成任務。）

UNIT 7

Make Good Qualities a Habit
把良好的特質變成習慣

Practice kindness.
要善良。

Practice forgiveness.
要原諒。

Practice mindfulness.
要謹慎。

** make〔mek〕v. 使成為　quality〔'kwɑlətɪ〕n.
品質；特質　habit〔'hæbɪt〕n. 習慣
practice〔'præktɪs〕v. 練習；實行；實踐
kindness〔'kaɪndnɪs〕n. 仁慈；善意
forgiveness〔fə'gɪvnɪs〕n. 原諒；寬恕
mindfulness〔'maɪndfəlnɪs〕n. 謹慎

BOOK 4・PART 1

Practice patience.

要有耐心。

Practice resilience.

要有韌性。

Practice persistence.

要能堅持。

** practice〔'præktɪs〕v. 練習；實行；實踐
patience〔'peʃəns〕n. 耐心
resilience〔rɪ'zɪlɪəns〕n. 韌性
persistence〔pə'sɪstəns〕n. 堅持；堅持不懈

Practice honesty.

要誠實。

Practice integrity.

要正直。

Practice humility.

要謙虛。

BOOK 4 • PART 1

** practice〔'præktɪs〕*v.* 練習；實行；實踐
    honesty〔'ɑnɪstɪ〕*n.* 誠實
    integrity〔ɪn'tɛgrətɪ〕*n.* 正直
    humility〔hju'mɪlətɪ〕*n.* 謙虛 (= *modesty*)

【Unit 7 背景說明】

Practice kindness. 要善良。(= *Be kind.*)

> practice + 名詞 / 動名詞
> ①練習… ②實行…；要…【可用來加強語氣】

Practice forgiveness. 要原諒。(= *Be forgiving.*)
也可說成：Pardon others. (要原諒別人。)

Practice mindfulness. (要謹慎。) 也可說成：
Be aware. (要注意。)

Practice patience. 要有耐心。(= *Be patient.*)
也可說成：Be easy-going. (要悠哉。)

Practice resilience. 要有韌性。(= *Be resilient.*)
也可說成：Be strong. (要堅強。) Be tough.
(要強悍。)

Practice persistence. 要堅持。(= *Be persistent.*)
也可說成：Be determined. (要堅決。)

Practice honesty. 要誠實。(= *Be honest.*) 也可
說成：Be sincere. (要真誠。)

Practice integrity. 要正直。(= *Have integrity.*)
也可說成：Have honor. (要有高尚的品德。)

Practice humility. 要謙虛。(= *Be humble.* = *Be modest.* = *Be unassuming.* = *Have humility.*
= *Have modesty.*)

UNIT 8

Encourage Good Qualities
培養良好的特質

Foster love.
培養愛心。

Foster trust.
培養信任。

Foster support.
培養支持。

** encourage〔ɪnˈkɝɪdʒ〕v. 鼓勵；促進；助長；激發
  foster〔ˈfɔstɚ, ˈfɑstɚ〕v. 培養；助長；心懷（希
  望等）   love〔lʌv〕n. 愛
  trust〔trʌst〕n. 信任
  support〔səˈport〕n. 支持

Foster teamwork.

培養團隊。

Foster cooperation.

培養合作。

Foster collaboration.

培養團結。

** foster〔ˈfɔstɚ, ˈfɑstɚ〕v. 培養；助長；心懷
（希望等）

teamwork〔ˈtimˌwɜk〕n. 團隊合作

cooperation〔koˌɑpəˈreʃən〕n. 合作

collaboration〔kəˌlæbəˈreʃən〕n. 合作
（= *cooperation*）

Foster positivity.

培養樂觀。

Foster generosity.

培養慷慨。

Foster curiosity.

培養好奇。

** foster〔ˈfɔstɚ, ˈfɑstɚ〕v. 培養；助長；心懷
（希望等）

positivity〔ˌpɑzəˈtɪvətɪ〕n. 正面；積極；樂觀

generosity〔ˌdʒɛnəˈrɑsətɪ〕n. 慷慨；大方

curiosity〔ˌkjʊrɪˈɑsətɪ〕n. 好奇心

BOOK 4・PART 1

【Unit 8 背景説明】

Foster love.（要培養愛。）也可説成：Be
loving.（要充滿愛。）

Foster trust.（培養信任。）也可説成：
Promote trust.（促進信任。）

Foster support.（培養支持。）也可説成：
Be supportive.（給予支持。）

Foster teamwork.（培養團隊合作。）也可説
成：Promote teamwork.（促進團隊合作。）

Foster cooperation.（培養合作。）（= *Foster
collaboration.*）也可説成：Promote
cooperation.（促進合作。）（= *Promote
collaboration.*）

Foster positivity.（培養樂觀。）也可説成：
Have a positive attitude.（要有樂觀的態度。）

Foster generosity.（培養慷慨。）也可説成：
Be generous.（要慷慨。）（= *Be giving.*）

Foster curiosity.（培養好奇心。）也可説成：
Encourage curiosity.（鼓勵好奇心。）
Encourage questions.（鼓勵問問題。）Be
curious.（要有好奇心。）（= *Be inquisitive.*）

UNIT 9

Be Agreeable 要欣然同意

Agree happily.
高高興興同意。

Agree joyfully.
快快樂樂同意。

Agree cheerfully.
愉愉快快同意。

** agreeable〔əˈgriəbḷ〕*adj.* 令人愉快的；欣然
    同意的   agree〔əˈgri〕*v.* 同意
  happily〔ˈhæpɪlɪ〕*adv.* 高興地
  joyfully〔ˈdʒɔɪfəlɪ〕*adv.* 高興地；快樂地
  cheerfully〔ˈtʃɪrfəlɪ〕*adv.* 愉快地

Agree gladly.

欣喜同意。

Agree willingly.

樂於同意。

Agree genuinely.

眞誠同意。

** agree 〔 ə'gri 〕 *v.* 同意

　gladly 〔'glædlɪ 〕 *adv.* 高興地；愉快地

　willingly 〔'wɪlɪŋlɪ 〕 *adv.* 願意地；樂意地；
　　心甘情願地

　genuinely 〔'dʒɛnjʊɪnlɪ 〕 *adv.* 眞正地；
　　眞實地；眞誠地

Agree graciously.

親切地同意。

Agree amiably.

和藹地同意。

Agree warmly.

熱心地同意。

** agree〔ə'gri〕*v.* 同意

　　graciously〔'greʃəslı〕*adv.* 親切地

　　amiably〔'emıəblı〕*adv.* 和藹可親地；

　　　親切友好地

　　warmly〔'wɔrmlı〕*adv.* 溫暖地；親切地；

　　　熱心地

BOOK 4 · PART 1

【**Unit 9** 背景説明】

Agree happily. 要快樂地同意。(= *Agree joyfully*. = *Agree cheerfully*.) 也可説成：Be happy to concur. (要高興地同意。) Agree willingly. (要心甘情願地同意。)

Agree gladly. 要高興地同意。(= *Agree happily*. = *Agree joyfully*. = *Agree cheerfully*.) 也可説成：*Agree willingly*. (要心甘情願地同意。)

Agree genuinely. 要真心地同意。(= *Agree sincerely*. = *Say yes sincerely*.)

Agree graciously. 要親切地同意。(= *Agree amiably*.) 也可説成：Agree civilly. (要有禮貌地同意。) Say yes in a friendly way. (要親切地同意。) (= *Say yes kindly*.)

Agree warmly. 要熱心地同意。(= *Agree cordially*.) 也可説成：Agree tenderly. (要温柔地同意。) Agree sincerely. (要真心地同意。)

PART 1 總整理

Unit 1

Happiness shines.
快樂發光。
Happiness radiates.
快樂發熱。
Happiness illuminates.
快樂發亮。

Happiness charms.
快樂有魅力。
Happiness fascinates.
快樂吸引人。
Happiness captivates.
快樂迷死人。

Happiness uplifts.
快樂振奮人心。
Happiness energizes.
快樂給人能量。
Happiness empowers.
快樂給人力量。

Unit 2

Create magic.　創造魔法。
Create miracles.　創造奇蹟。
Create wonders.　創造驚奇。

Create dreams.　創造夢想。
Create beauty.　創造美好。
Create happiness.
創造快樂。

Create opportunities.
創造機會。
Create connections.
創造人脈。
Create success.
創造成功。

Unit 3

Start now.　現在開始。
Start off.　開始動手。
Get started.　開始做吧。

Get going.　馬上開始。
Get moving.　馬上行動。
Get cracking.　快點開始。

Begin now.　現在開始。
Begin immediately.
立刻開始。
Begin straightaway.
馬上開始。

BOOK 4 · PART 1

Unit 4

Go on. 加油。
Carry on. 繼續加油。
Continue on. 持續加油。

Push on. 繼續向前。
Power on. 加足馬力。
Press on. 堅持下去。

Go forward. 持續前進。
Move forward. 向前邁進。
Press forward. 奮勇前進。

Unit 5

Explore unknowns.
探索未知。
Explore wonders.
探索奇蹟。
Explore mysteries.
探索奧祕。

Explore nature.
探索大自然。
Explore possibilities.
探索可能性。
Explore opportunities.
探索好機會。

Explore boldly.
大膽探索。
Explore fearlessly.
無畏探索。
Explore courageously.
勇於探索。

Unit 6

Fulfill goals. 實現目標。
Fulfill targets.
實現目的。
Fulfill desires.
實現願望。

Fulfill aims.
達成目標。
Fulfill plans.
實現計劃。
Fulfill objectives.
達成目的。

Fulfill intentions.
實現意圖。
Fulfill ambitions.
實現抱負。
Fulfill missions.
達成任務。

Unit 7

Practice kindness.　要善良。
Practice forgiveness.
要原諒。
Practice mindfulness.
要謹慎。

Practice patience.　要有耐心。
Practice resilience.
要有韌性。
Practice persistence.
要能堅持。

Practice honesty.　要誠實。
Practice integrity.　要正直。
Practice humility.　要謙虛。

Unit 8

Foster love.　培養愛心。
Foster trust.　培養信任。
Foster support.　培養支持。

Foster teamwork.　培養團隊。
Foster cooperation.
培養合作。
Foster collaboration.
培養團結。

Foster positivity.
培養樂觀。
Foster generosity.
培養慷慨。
Foster curiosity.
培養好奇。

Unit 9

Agree happily.
高高興興同意。
Agree joyfully.
快快樂樂同意。
Agree cheerfully.
愉愉快快同意。

Agree gladly.　欣喜同意。
Agree willingly.
樂於同意。
Agree genuinely.
真誠同意。

Agree graciously.
親切地同意。
Agree amiably.
和藹地同意。
Agree warmly.
熱心地同意。

BOOK 4・PART 1

BOOK 4 / PART 2

Words Worth Remembering
值得記住的話

PART 2・Unit 1~9
英文錄音QR碼

UNIT 1

Be a Builder　做一個建造者

Build trust.
建立信任。

Build consensus.
建立共識。

Build connections.
建立人脈。

** builder〔ˈbɪldɚ〕 *n.* 建造者
　build〔bɪld〕 *v.* 建造；建立
　trust〔trʌst〕 *n.* 信任
　consensus〔kənˈsɛnsəs〕 *n.* 共識
　connection〔kəˈnɛkʃən〕 *n.* 關連；關係；
　　（*pl.*）人脈

Build teamwork.

建立合作。

Build relationships.

建立關係。

Build fellowship.

建立交情。

** build〔bɪld〕*v.* 建造；建立
   teamwork〔'tim‚wɜk〕*n.* 團隊合作
   relationship〔rɪ'leʃən‚ʃɪp〕*n.* 關係
   fellowship〔'fɛlo‚ʃɪp〕*n.* 夥伴關係；
      友情；交情

Build dreams.

建造夢想。

Build knowledge.

累積知識。

Build confidence.

建立自信。

** build〔bɪld〕*v.* 建造；建立；發展；
　　累積；加強
　　dream〔drim〕*n.* 夢；夢想
　　knowledge〔'nɑlɪdʒ〕*n.* 知識
　　confidence〔'kɑnfədəns〕*n.* 信心；自信

【Unit 1 背景說明】

Build trust.（建立信任。）也可說成：
Create trust.（創造信任。）Develop trust.
（培養信任。）Develop confidence.（培
養信心。）

Build consensus.（建立共識。）也可說成：
Create consensus.（創造共識。）Create
agreement.（達成協議。）(= *Create
compromise*.) Develop harmony.（培養
和諧。）

Build connections.（建立人脈。）也可說成：
Create connections.（創造人脈。）Develop
networks.（培養人脈。）(– *Develop ties*.)

Build teamwork.（建立團隊合作。）也可說
成：Create teamwork.（創造團隊合作。）
Develop teamwork.（培養團隊合作。）
Create cooperation.（創造合作。）
(= *Develop collaboration*.) Create
solidarity.（創造團結。）

Build relationships. (建立關係。) 也可說
成：Create relationships. (創造關係。)
Develop relationships. (培養關係。)
Develop contacts. (培養人脈。)

Build fellowship. (建立交情。) 也可說成：
Create fellowship. (創造交情。) Develop
fellowship. (培養交情。) (= *Nurture*
fellowship.)

Build dreams. (打造夢想。) 也可說成：
Create dreams. (創造夢想。) Develop
goals. (培養目標。) Pursue your dreams.
(追求你的夢想。)

Build knowledge. (累積知識。) 也可說成：
Become knowledgeable. (要變得知識豐
富。) Develop your knowledge. (要拓展
你的知識。) Learn more. (要多學習。)

Build confidence. (建立信心。) 也可說成：
Create confidence. (創造信心。) Develop
self-confidence. (培養自信。) (= *Nurture*
self-assurance. = *Develop assertiveness.*)

UNIT 2

You're Awesome　你很棒

You shine.

你發光。

You glow.

你發亮。

You radiate.

你發熱。

** awesome〔ˋɔsəm〕*adj.* 很棒的
　shine〔ʃaɪn〕*v.* 照耀；發光；發亮；出眾；出色
　glow〔glo〕*v.* 發光
　radiate〔ˋredɪ͵et〕*v.* 輻射；散發（光、熱等）

You rock.

你很棒。

You matter.

你重要。

You excel.

你卓越。

** rock〔rɑk〕 *v.* 輕輕搖晃；演奏搖滾樂；
　　眞棒；極具震撼力
　　matter〔'mætɚ〕 *v.* 重要
　　excel〔ɪk'sɛl〕 *v.* 擅長；突出；勝過別人

You prosper.

你發了。

You thrive.

你茁壯。

You succeed.

你成功。

** prosper〔'praspɚ〕v. 繁榮;興盛;成功
thrive〔θraɪv〕v. 繁榮;興盛;成功
　(= prosper = flourish)
succeed〔səkˈsid〕v. 成功

【Unit 2 背景説明】

You shine. 你會發光發亮。(= *You glow.*) 也可
説成：*You radiate.* (你會散發光和熱。) You
sparkle. (你閃閃發亮。) You emanate love.
(你散發出愛。) You emanate positivity.
(你散發正能量。) You emanate kindness.
(你散發出善意。)

You rock. (你很棒。) 也可説成：You rule.
(你真的很棒。) You're impressive. (你令
人印象深刻。) You're great at that. (你很
擅長那個。) Nicely done. (做得好。)
(= *Well done.*)

You matter. 你很重要。(= *You count.* = *You're
important.*)

You excel. (你勝過別人。) 也可説成：You
stand out. (你很傑出。) You shine. (你發光
發亮。) You're the best. (你是最棒的。)

You prosper. 你很成功。(= *You thrive.* = *You
flourish.*)

You succeed. 你很成功。(= *You're successful.*)

UNIT 3

You're a Great Role Model
你是很好的榜樣

You inspire.
你激發靈感。

You motivate.
你激勵他人。

You encourage.
你鼓勵大家。

** great〔gret〕*adj.* 極好的；很棒的
　　role〔rol〕*n.* 角色
　　model〔'madl̩〕*n.* 榜樣；典範
　　role model 模範；榜樣
　　inspire〔ɪn'spaɪr〕*v.* 激勵；給予靈感
　　motivate〔'motə,vet〕*v.* 激勵
　　encourage〔ɪn'kɝɪdʒ〕*v.* 鼓勵

You charm.

你有魅力。

You dazzle.

耀眼奪目。

You captivate.

魅不可擋。

** charm〔tʃɑrm〕v. 吸引人；有魅力
dazzle〔ˈdæzl̩〕v. 使目眩；使迷惑；
  使傾倒；使讚嘆
captivate〔ˈkæptə͵vet〕v. 使著迷

BOOK 4・PART 2

You win.

你會贏的。

You prevail.

你會勝利。

You triumph.

勝券在握。

** win〔wɪn〕*v.* 贏；獲勝
prevail〔prɪˋvel〕*v.* 佔優勢；戰勝；優勝
triumph〔ˋtraɪəmf〕*v.* 勝利；取得巨大成功

【Unit 3 背景説明】

You inspire. 你激勵人心。(= *You inspire people*.) 也可説成：*You motivate*. (你激勵人心。) (= *You motivate people*.) *You encourage*. (你鼓勵大家。) (= *You encourage people*.) You enthuse. (你使大家充滿熱情。)

You charm. 你很迷人。(= *You're charming*.) 也可説成：*You captivate*. (你令人著迷。) (= *You're captivating*.) You fascinate. (你使人著迷。) You enchant. (你很有魅力。) (= *You entrance*. = *You enthrall*.)

You dazzle. 你非常亮麗。(= *You're dazzling*.) 也可説成：You amaze. (你令人驚嘆。) (= *You astonish*. = *You awe*.) You impress. (你令人印象深刻。)

You win. (你會贏。) 也可説成：*You prevail*. (你會獲勝。) *You triumph*. (你會勝利。) (= *You are victorious*.) You succeed. (你會成功。)

UNIT 4

We're Better Together
我們在一起更好

We learn.
我們學習。

We grow.
我們成長。

We progress.
我們進步。

** together〔təˋgɛðə〕*adv.* 一起
learn〔lɝn〕*v.* 學習　　grow〔gro〕*v.* 成長
progress〔prəˋgrɛs〕*v.* 進步

We persist.

我們堅持。

We endure.

我們忍耐。

We persevere.

我們堅忍。

** persist〔pə'sɪst〕v. 堅持
　 endure〔ɪn'djʊr〕v. 忍耐
　 persevere〔ˏpɝsə'vɪr〕v. 堅忍

We unite.

團結一致。

We collaborate.

合作無間。

We conquer.

征服困難。

** unite〔ju'naɪt〕v. 團結
  collaborate〔kə'læbə,ret〕v. 合作
    (= *cooperate*)
  conquer〔'kɑŋkɚ〕v. 征服

【Unit 4 背景説明】

We learn. (我們學習。) 也可説成：We gain knowledge. (我們獲得知識。)

We grow. (我們成長。) 也可説成：We mature. (我們變成熟。) We develop. (我們不斷在發展。)

We progress. (我們進步。) 也可説成：We advance. (我們在進步。) We move forward. (我們向前進。)

We persist. (我們堅持。) 也可説成：*We endure*. (我們忍耐。) *We persevere*. (我們堅忍。) We continue. (我們繼續。) We proceed. (我們向前進。) We keep going. (我們持續前進。)

We unite. (我們團結。) 也可説成：We join together. (我們結合在一起。) We come together. (我們團結在一起。)

We collaborate. 我們合作。(= *We work together*. = *We cooperate*.)

We conquer. (我們征服。) 也可説成：We win. (我們獲勝。)(= *We triumph*. = *We prevail*.)

UNIT 5

Try Your Best 要盡力而為

Try it.
嘗試看看。

Try hard.
盡力一試。

Try again.
再試一下。

** try〔traɪ〕v. 嘗試;努力
   try* one's *best 盡力 (= *do one's best*)
   hard〔hɑrd〕*adv.* 拼命地;努力地
   try hard 努力;盡力而為
   again〔ə'gɛn〕*adv.* 再一次

Try boldly.

大膽嘗試。

Try bravely.

勇敢嘗試。

Try fearlessly.

無懼嘗試。

** try〔traɪ〕*v.* 嘗試；努力
　　boldly〔'boldlɪ〕*adv.* 大膽地
　　bravely〔'brevlɪ〕*adv.* 勇敢地
　　fearlessly〔'fɪrlɪslɪ〕*adv.* 無所畏懼地

Try passionately.

熱於嘗試。

Try diligently.

勤於嘗試。

Try relentlessly.

不斷嘗試。

** try〔traɪ〕v. 嘗試；努力
passionately〔'pæʃənɪtlɪ〕adv. 熱情地
diligently〔'dɪlədʒəntlɪ〕adv. 勤勉地
relentlessly〔rɪ'lɛntlɪslɪ〕adv. 不斷地

【**Unit 5** 背景說明】

Try it. 試試看。(= *Give it a try*.) 也可說成：
Make an attempt. (要盡力。)

Try hard. (要努力。) 也可說成：Do your
best. (要盡力。)

Try again. (再試一次。) 也可說成：Give it
another try. (再試試看。) Don't give up.
(不要放棄。)

Try boldly. (大膽地嘗試。) 也可說成：*Try
bravely*. (勇敢地嘗試。) *Try fearlessly*. (無
所畏懼地嘗試。) Try courageously. (勇敢地
嘗試。) Try confidently. (有信心地嘗試。)

Try passionately. 熱情地嘗試。(= *Try
enthusiastically*. = *Try it enthusiastically*.)

Try diligently. (勤奮地嘗試。) 也可說成：
Try hard. (努力嘗試。) Keep trying. (持續
嘗試。)

Try relentlessly. (不斷嘗試。) 也可說成：
Keep trying. (持續嘗試。) Don't give up.
(不要放棄。)

UNIT 6

Keep in Touch 要保持連絡

Text me.
給我簡訊。

Message me.
給我留言。

Write me.
給我寫信。

** touch〔tʌtʃ〕*n.* 碰觸；連絡
    keep in touch 保持連絡
    text〔tɛkst〕*v.* 傳簡訊給（某人）   *n.* 簡訊
    （ *= text message* ）
    message〔'mɛsɪdʒ〕*v.* 傳訊息給（某人）
    n. 訊息；留言
    write〔raɪt〕*v.* 寫；寫信給（某人）

Follow me.

關注我。

Call me.

打給我。

Join me.

加入我。

** follow〔ˈfalo〕*v.* 跟隨;追蹤;關注
　 call〔kɔl〕*v.* 打電話給(某人)
　 join〔dʒɔɪn〕*v.* 加入;和(某人)一起
　　 做同樣的事

Persuade me.
說服我。

Convince me.
勸服我。

Teach me.
教導我。

** persuade〔pɚ'swed〕v. 說服
convince〔kən'vɪns〕v. 使相信；說服
teach〔titʃ〕v. 教導

【**Unit 6 背景説明**】

Text me.　傳簡訊給我。(= *Send me a text*.)

Message me.　傳訊息給我。(= *Send me a message*.)

Write me. (寫信給我。) 也可説成：Send me a letter. (寄信給我。) Send me an e-mail. (傳電子郵件給我。) Send me a text. (傳簡訊給我。) Send me a message. (傳訊息給我。)

Follow me. (關注我；追踪我。) 也可説成：Keep up with me on my socials. (在我的社群媒體上關注我的最新動態。) Become one of my followers. (成爲我的粉絲。)

Call me.　打電話給我。(= *Phone me*. = *Give me a call*.)

Join me. (加入我。) 也可説成：Come with me. (和我一起來。) Support me. (支持我。)

Persuade me. 説服我。(= *Convince me*. = *Talk me into it*.) 也可説成：Change my mind. (改變我的想法。)

Teach me. (教導我。) 也可説成：Tell me how to do it. (告訴我該怎麼做。) (= *Show me how to do it*.)

UNIT 7

Expressions of Surprise 表示驚訝

My God!
我的天！

My goodness!
蒼天啊！

Jesus Christ!
老天啊！

** expression〔ɪk'sprɛʃən〕*n.* 表達

surprise〔sə'praɪz〕*n.* 驚訝

God〔gɑd〕*n.* 上帝

goodness〔'gʊdnɪs〕*n.* 善良；仁慈；美德

　　interj. （表示驚訝、驚慌等）天啊；啊呀

Jesus Christ〔'dʒizəs 'kraɪst〕*n.* 耶穌基督

Oh, my!

喔，哇！

Oh, boy!

喔，哎！

Oh, man!

喔，啊！

** oh〔o〕*interj.* 喔；哦

my〔maɪ〕*adj.* 我的 *interj.* 哎呀；啊；
哇；咦

boy〔bɔɪ〕*n.* 男孩 *interj.* 哇；咦

man〔mæn〕*n.* 男人 *interj.*（用於表示
強烈的情感）啊；呀；哈；嘿

Oh, dear!

喔，哎呀！

Oh, wow!

喔，哇啊！

Oh, heavens!

喔，上天！

** oh〔o〕*interj.* 喔

    dear〔dɪr〕*adj.* 親愛的　*interj.* 哎呀

    wow〔waʊ〕*interj.* 哇

    heaven〔ˈhɛvən〕*n.* 天堂；(*pl.*) 天國；上帝

【Unit 7 背景説明】

My God! 我的天啊！（＝*My goodness!*
＝*Jesus Christ!*）也可說成：Gosh!（天
啊！）Gee!（天啊！）Wow!（哇！）
Gracious!（天哪！）

Oh, my! 喔，啊！（＝*Oh, boy!* ＝ *Oh, man!*）
也可說成：Holy cow!（天啊！）（＝*Holy
smokes!* ＝ *Good gracious!*）

Oh, dear! 喔，哎呀！（＝*Dear me!* ＝*Dear
Lord!*）也可說成：Oh, no!（喔，不！）Uh
oh!（呃哦！）Good grief!（哎呀！；天啊！）

Oh, wow!（喔，哇！）也可說成：Wow,
really?（哇，真的嗎？）My goodness!（我
的天啊！）Good God!（天啊！）Oh, my!
（喔，啊！）

Oh, heavens!（喔，天啊！）也可說成：
Heavens no!（天啊，不會吧！）Heavens
above!（老天啊！）

UNIT 8

I Was Wrong 我錯了

My bad.

我的錯。

My fault.

我錯了。

My mistake.

是我錯。

** wrong〔rɔŋ〕*adj.* 錯誤的

bad〔bæd〕*n.* 壞的事物

my bad 是我不好；是我的錯（= *my fault*）

fault〔fɔlt〕*n.* 過錯

mistake〔mə'stek〕*n.* 錯誤

Excuse me.

對不起。

Pardon me.

寬恕我。

Forgive me.

原諒我。

** excuse〔ɪkˈskjuz〕*v.* 原諒
   pardon〔ˈpɑrdn̩〕*v.* 原諒；寬恕；赦免
   forgive〔fɚˈgɪv〕*v.* 原諒

BOOK 4・PART 2

Silly me.

我真傻。

Foolish me.

我真笨。

Stupid me.

我真蠢。

** silly〔ˈsɪlɪ〕*adj.* 愚蠢的；傻的

foolish〔ˈfulɪʃ〕*adj.* 愚蠢的

stupid〔ˈstjupɪd〕*adj.* 愚蠢的；笨的

【Unit 8 背景説明】

My bad. 我的錯。(= *My fault.* = *My mistake.*)
也可説成：It's my fault. (是我的錯。)
(= *It's my mistake.*) I was wrong. (我錯
了。) I take the blame. (我要承擔責任。)

Excuse me. (原諒我。) 也可説成：*Pardon
me.* (寬恕我。) *Forgive me.* (原諒我。) 還
可再説：I'm sorry. (我很抱歉。) It won't
happen again. (這種事不會再發生。)

Silly me. 我眞傻。(= *I was silly.*) 也可説成：
Oops. (哎呀。)

Foolish me. 我眞笨。(= *I was foolish.*) 也可
説成：I was a fool. (我是個傻瓜。)

Stupid me. 我眞蠢。(= *I was stupid.*) 也可説
成：That was dumb of me. (我眞的很愚
蠢。)

UNIT 9

You Can Do It 你能做到

Cheer up.
要振作。

Lighten up.
要放鬆。

Brighten up.
要開朗。

** cheer〔tʃɪr〕v. 歡呼

　　cheer up 振作起來；高興起來

　　lighten〔'laɪtn̩〕v. 變成明亮；發亮；(心情)變

　　　輕鬆　　***lighten up*** 放鬆；緩和

　　brighten〔'braɪtn̩〕v. 變亮；放晴；(心情)愉快；

　　　快活起來　　***brighten up*** 高興起來

Chin up.

抬起頭。

Perk up.

要振作。

Fire up.

要熱情。

** chin〔tʃɪn〕*n.* 下巴　*v.* 在單槓上作引體向上
的動作

chin up 振作起來；打起精神；別氣餒；別灰
心；加油

perk〔pɝk〕*v.* 振作；活躍起來

perk up 快活起來；振作起來；活潑起來

fire〔faɪr〕*v.* 激發（熱情）

fire up 充滿熱情

Man up.

像個男人。

Toughen up.

變得堅強。

Shape up.

變得更好。

** man〔mæn〕*n.* 男人　*v.* 使增強勇氣
man up 拿出點男子氣慨；要像個男人
【用於鼓勵他人勇敢面對】
toughen〔'tʌfn̩〕*v.* 要堅韌；變強壯
toughen up 變強悍；變得堅強
shape〔ʃep〕*v.* 成形；成長；發展
shape up 取得長足進步；表現良好

【Unit 9 背景説明】

Cheer up. 振作起來；高興起來。(= *Buck up*.) 也可説成：*Lighten up*. (放輕鬆。) *Brighten up*. (要心情愉快。) Be optimistic. (要樂觀。) (= *Be positive*.)

Chin up. (打起精神；別氣餒。) 也可説成：Keep your chin up. (別灰心。) Don't be discouraged. (別氣餒。) Be brave. (要勇敢。)

Perk up. (振作起來。) 也可説成：Revive. (要恢復精神。) (= *Recover*. = *Rally*.)

Fire up. 要充滿熱情。(= *Get fired up*.) 也可説成：Get excited. (要振奮。) Get inspired. (要激勵自己。)

Man up. (拿出男子氣慨。) 也可説成：Accept responsibility. (承擔責任。) Face the music. (承擔後果。) Face the facts. (面對事實。) Grin and bear it. (逆來順受。) Bite the bullet. (忍辱負重。) Deal with it. (要好好處理。) Put up with it. (要忍受。)

Toughen up. (變得堅強。) 也可説成：Hang tough. (堅持到底。) (= *Tough it out*.) Be stronger. (要更強大。)

Shape up. 要改善。(= *Improve*.) 也可説成：Get better. (要變得更好。)

PART 2 總整理

Unit 1

Build trust.
建立信任。
Build consensus.
建立共識。
Build connections.
建立人脈。

Build teamwork.
建立合作。
Build relationships.
建立關係。
Build fellowship.
建立交情。

Build dreams.
建造夢想。
Build knowledge.
累積知識。
Build confidence.
建立自信。

Unit 2

You shine. 你發光。
You glow. 你發亮。
You radiate. 你發熱。

You rock. 你很棒。
You matter. 你重要。
You excel. 你卓越。

You prosper. 你發了。
You thrive. 你茁壯。
You succeed. 你成功。

Unit 3

You inspire.
你激發靈感。
You motivate.
你激勵他人。
You encourage.
你鼓勵大家。

You charm. 你有魅力。
You dazzle. 耀眼奪目。
You captivate.
魅不可擋。

You win. 你會贏的。
You prevail. 你會勝利。
You triumph. 勝券在握。

Unit 4

We learn. 我們學習。
We grow. 我們成長。
We progress. 我們進步。

We persist. 我們堅持。
We endure. 我們忍耐。
We persevere.
我們堅忍。

We unite. 團結一致。
We collaborate.
合作無間。
We conquer.
征服困難。

Unit 5

Try it. 嘗試看看。
Try hard. 盡力一試。
Try again. 再試一下。

Try boldly. 大膽嘗試。
Try bravely. 勇敢嘗試。
Try fearlessly. 無懼嘗試。

Try passionately.
熱於嘗試。
Try diligently. 勤於嘗試。
Try relentlessly.
不斷嘗試。

Unit 6

Text me. 給我簡訊。
Message me. 給我留言。
Write me. 給我寫信。

Follow me. 關注我。
Call me. 打給我。
Join me. 加入我。

Persuade me. 說服我。
Convince me. 勸服我。
Teach me. 教導我。

Unit 7

My God! 我的天！
My goodness! 蒼天啊！
Jesus Christ! 老天啊！

Oh, my! 喔，哇！
Oh, boy! 喔，哎！
Oh, man! 喔，啊！

Oh, dear! 喔，哎呀！
Oh, wow! 喔，哇啊！
Oh, heavens!
喔，上天！

Unit 8

My bad. 我的錯。
My fault. 我錯了。
My mistake.
是我錯。

Excuse me. 對不起。
Pardon me. 寬恕我。
Forgive me. 原諒我。

Silly me. 我真傻。
Foolish me. 我真笨。
Stupid me. 我真蠢。

Unit 9

Cheer up. 要振作。
Lighten up. 要放鬆。
Brighten up.
要開朗。

Chin up. 抬起頭。
Perk up. 要振作。
Fire up. 要熱情。

Man up.
像個男人。
Toughen up.
變得堅強。
Shape up.
變得更好。

BOOK 4　PART 3

Brief Comments
簡短的評論

PART 3 · Unit 1~9
英文錄音QR碼

UNIT 1

Say Hello 打招呼

Hi, there!

嗨，你好！

Hey, there!

嘿，你好！

Hello, there!

哈囉，你好！

** hello〔həˋlo〕*interj.* 哈囉

　　say hello 說「哈囉」；打招呼

　　hi〔haɪ〕*interj.* 嗨　　*hi, there* 嗨，你好

　　hey〔he〕*interj.* 嘿　　*hey, there* 嘿，你好

　　hello, there 哈囉，你好

What's up?

有何新鮮事？

What's new?

有何新消息？

What's happening?

發生了何事？

** ***What's up?*** 有什麼事？

   (= *What's going on?*)

new〔nju〕*adj.* 新的；新鮮的；不一樣的

happen〔'hæpən〕*v.* 發生

How's life?
生活如何？

How're things?
情況如何？

Going well?
一切安好？

** life〔laɪf〕*n.* 生活

   things〔θɪŋz〕*n. pl.* 事情；情況

   go〔go〕*v.* 進展

   well〔wɛl〕*adv.* 良好地

【 Unit 1 背景説明 】

Hi, there!（嗨，你好！）也可説成：*Hey, there!*（嘿，你好！）*Hello, there!*（哈囉，你好！）Hi!（嗨！）Greetings!（你好！）Good morning!（早安！）Good afternoon!（午安！）Good evening!（晚安！）

What's up?（有什麼事？；你好嗎？）*What's new?*（有什麼新鮮事？；你好嗎？）*What's happening?*（發生了什麼事？；你好嗎？）（= *What's going on?*）這三句話意思相同，都是打招呼用語，不是真正在問「發生了什麼事？」只是在問候，相當於 How are you?（你好嗎？）也可説成：How have you been?（你好嗎？）可以回答：Nothing much.（沒什麼事。）

How's life?（生活過得如何？）也可説成：*How're things?*（情況如何？）（= *How's everything?*）How's it going?（情況如何？）How are you?（你好嗎？）

Going well? 進展得順利嗎？（= *Are things going well?*）也可説成：Is everything fine?（一切都好嗎？）

UNIT 2

Be Nice 要和善

Don't judge.
不要評判。

Don't criticize.
不要批評。

Go easy.
對人溫和。

** nice〔naɪs〕*adj.* 好的；親切的
judge〔dʒʌdʒ〕*v.* 判斷；批評；指責
criticize〔'krɪtə,saɪz〕*v.* 批評
go〔go〕*v.* 變得；成為
easy〔'izɪ〕*adj.* 容易的；輕鬆的；不嚴的；寬大的
go easy 溫和寬容地對待

Show mercy.

展現慈悲。

Show compassion.

有同情心。

Display empathy.

有同理心。

** show〔ʃo〕*v.* 表現；表示
  mercy〔'mɝsɪ〕*n.* 慈悲
  compassion〔kəm'pæʃən〕*n.* 同情
  display〔dɪ'sple〕*v.* 展示；表現
  empathy〔'ɛmpəθɪ〕*n.* 同感；共鳴；同理心

Be understanding.

要體諒。

Be sympathetic.

要同情。

Be lenient.

要寬大。

** understanding〔ˌʌndɚˈstændɪŋ〕*adj.* 明白事理的；能體諒別人的

sympathetic〔ˌsɪmpəˈθɛtɪk〕*adj.* 有同情心的

lenient〔ˈlinjənt〕*adj.* 寬大的（*= tolerant = forgiving*）；仁慈的（*= benevolent*）；溫和的（*= soft*）

【**Unit 2 背景說明**】

Don't judge.（不要批評；不要指責。）也可說成：Don't be judgmental.（不要做主觀判斷；不要愛批評人。）Don't be critical.（不要批評。）Don't be negative.（不要負面思考。）

Don't criticize. 不要批評。(= *Don't be critical.*)

Go easy. 溫和寬容地對待別人。(= *Be tolerant.* = *Be lenient.*)也可說成：Don't be too strict.（不要太嚴格。）

Show mercy.（展現慈悲。）也可說成：*Show compassion.*（展現同情。）Be merciful.（要慈悲。）Be compassionate.（要有同情心。）Be understanding.（要體諒別人。）Be lenient.（要寬大。）

Display empathy.（展現同理心。）也可說成：Be empathetic.（要有同理心。）Show understanding.（要表示體諒。）

Be understanding.（要能體諒別人。）也可說成：*Be sympathetic.*（要有同情心。）(= *Be compassionate.*)

Be lenient.（要寬大。）也可說成：Be compassionate.（要有同情心。）Be merciful.（要慈悲。）

UNIT 3

Forgive and Forget 既往不咎

It's OK.

沒有關係。

It happens.

常會發生。

Never mind.

別太介意。

** forgive ﹝ fɚˋgɪv ﹞ v. 原諒　forget ﹝ fɚˋgɛt ﹞ v.

忘記　*forgive and forget* 既往不咎

OK ﹝ˋoˋke﹞ adj. 好的；沒問題的 (= ok = okay)

happen ﹝ˋhæpən﹞ v. 發生

never ﹝ˋnɛvɚ﹞ adv. 絕不　mind ﹝ maɪnd ﹞ v. 介意

Totally fine.
沒有問題。

Totally understood.
全然理解。

Forget it.
就算了吧。

** totally〔'totḷɪ〕*adv.* 完全地
fine〔faɪn〕*adj.* 好的
understand〔ˌʌndɚ'stænd〕*v.* 了解
forget〔fɚ'gɛt〕*v.* 忘記
forget it 算了吧

All's forgiven.

全都原諒。

Absolutely forgiven.

完全原諒。

Apology accepted.

接受道歉。

** forgive 〔 fə'gɪv 〕 *v.* 原諒

absolutely 〔'æbsə,lutlɪ 〕 *adv.* 絕對地；
完全地

apology 〔 ə'pɑlədʒɪ 〕 *n.* 道歉

accept 〔 ək'sɛpt 〕 *v.* 接受

【Unit 3 背景説明】

It's OK. 沒關係。(= *It's all right.* = *It's fine.*)
也可説成：Don't worry about it. (不用擔
心；沒關係。)

It happens. (有時候會這樣的；總會有這樣
的事情發生。) 也可説成：It couldn't be
helped. (這是無法避免的。) It's common.
(這很常見。) You didn't mean it. (你不
是有意的。)

Never mind. (不用介意；別擔心；沒關係。)
也可説成：Don't worry about it. (不用擔
心；沒關係。) Don't give it a second
thought. (不要再去想它；沒關係。)

Totally fine. 完全沒事。(= *It's totally fine.*
= *It's all good.*) 也可説成：It's fine. (沒
關係。)(= *It's OK.*) It's not a problem.
(那不是問題。)

Totally understood. 完全了解。(= *It's totally understood*.) 也可說成：I understand completely. (我完全了解。)

Forget it. (算了；別再提了；沒關係。) 也可說成：Don't worry about it. (不用擔心；沒關係。) Don't give it a second thought. (不要再去想它；沒關係。)

All's forgiven. 全都被原諒。(= *All is forgiven*.) 也可說成：I forgive you. (我原諒你。) You're forgiven. (你被原諒了。)

Absolutely forgiven. 完全被原諒。(= *All is absolutely forgiven*. = *Completely forgiven*.)

Apology accepted. (道歉已經被接受。) (= *Your apology is accepted*.) Don't give it another thought. (別再想它了；沒關係。)

BOOK 4 · PART 3

UNIT 4

Let's Eat 我們吃飯吧

I'm hungry.

我好餓喔。

I'm starving.

我餓死了。

I'm starved.

我餓極了。

** eat〔it〕*v.* 吃；吃飯
hungry〔'hʌŋgrɪ〕*adj.* 飢餓的
starve〔starv〕*v.*（使）挨餓；（使）餓死
starving〔'starvɪŋ〕*adj.* 快餓死的；十分飢餓的；
　餓得要命的
starved〔starvd〕*adj.* 十分飢餓的；餓得要命的

Let's indulge!
我們放縱一下！

Pig out!
我們大吃一頓！

Chow down!
我們大快朵頤！

** indulge〔ɪnˈdʌldʒ〕v. 沈迷；放縱自己

pig〔pɪg〕n. 豬；貪吃的人　v. 舉動像豬；

　行為像豬；貪吃

pig out 大吃大喝；狼吞虎嚥

chow〔tʃaʊ〕v. 吃；喝

chow down 大口吃；大快朵頤；狼吞虎嚥

I'm full.

我吃飽了。

I'm stuffed.

吃得很飽。

I'm satisfied.

我很滿足。

** full〔fʊl〕*adj.* 滿的；吃飽的

stuff〔stʌf〕*v.* 填塞

stuffed〔stʌft〕*adj.* 塞滿的；吃飽的；吃撐的

satisfy〔'sætɪs,faɪ〕*v.* 使滿足

satisfied〔'sætɪs,faɪd〕*adj.* 感到滿意的；
滿足的

【Unit 4 背景説明】

I'm hungry. （我餓了。）也可說成：I'm really hungry. （我真的很餓。）

I'm starving. （我快餓死了。）也可說成：*I'm starved*. （我餓得要命。）I'm famished. （我非常餓。）

Let's indulge! （我們放縱一下！）也可說成：Let's treat ourselves! （我們好好享受一下！）

Pig out! （大吃一頓！）也可說成：Let's pig out! （我們大吃一頓！）Let's stuff ourselves! （我們好好吃一頓吧！）

Chow down! （大快朵頤！）也可說成：Let's chow down! （我們大快朵頤！）Let's eat! （我們吃吧！）

I'm full. （我吃飽了。）也可說成：*I'm stuffed*. （我吃得很飽。）I couldn't eat another bite. （我再也吃不下了。）

I'm satisfied. （我很滿足。）也可說成：I've had enough. （我已經吃飽了。）

UNIT 5

Accept Thanks　接受道謝

You're welcome.
不用客氣。

My pleasure.
我的榮幸。

You bet.
樂意之至。

** accept〔əkˋsɛpt〕*v.* 接受

thanks〔θæŋks〕*n. pl.* 感謝

welcome〔ˋwɛlkəm〕*v.* 歡迎　*adj.* 受歡迎的

pleasure〔ˋplɛʒɚ〕*n.* 愉快；樂趣；快樂的事；

　榮幸　*my pleasure* 我的榮幸

bet〔bɛt〕*v.* 打賭　*you bet* 當然

No problem.

沒有問題。

No trouble.

毫不麻煩。

No sweat.

輕鬆搞定。

** problem〔'prabləm〕 *n.* 問題
no problem 沒問題
trouble〔'trʌbḷ〕 *n.* 麻煩
no trouble 不麻煩；沒問題；不客氣
sweat〔swɛt〕 *v.* 流汗　*n.* 汗
no sweat 毫不費力；不麻煩；沒問題

Of course.

由衷樂意。

Sure thing.

當然樂意。

No worries.

沒有關係。

** *of course* 當然

　sure〔ʃʊr〕*adj.* 確定的

　sure thing 當然；沒問題

　worry〔ˈwɝɪ〕*v.* 擔心　*n.* 擔心；煩惱的事

　no worries 不用擔心

【Unit 5 背景説明】

You're welcome. 不客氣。(= *Don't mention it.* = *Anytime.*)

My pleasure. 這是我的榮幸。(= *It's my pleasure.* = *The pleasure is all mine.*)

You bet. (表示強調) 的確；當然；(回應對方的感謝時) 不用謝；不客氣。(= *Of course.* = *No problem.* = *No worries.*)

No problem. 沒問題；(用於回答對方的感謝) 沒什麼；不客氣。(= ***No trouble.***) 也可説成：***No sweat.*** (一點也不困難；毫不費力；沒問題；不用擔心；沒關係；不客氣。) (= *No worries.* = *You're welcome.*)

Of course. (當然；不客氣。) 也可説成：***Sure thing.*** (當然；不客氣。)

No worries. 不用擔心；不客氣。(= *Don't worry about it.* = *No problem.*) 也可説成：Don't mention it. (不客氣。) (= *Anytime.* = *You're welcome.*)

UNIT 6

Get in Shape 鍛鍊身體

Try exercise.

嘗試運動。

Get fit.

變得健康。

Get strong.

變得強壯。

** shape〔ʃep〕*n.* 形狀;(健康等的)狀況

get in shape 健身;鍛鍊身體

try〔traɪ〕*v.* 嘗試

exercise〔'ɛksə͵saɪz〕*n.* 運動

get〔gɛt〕*v.* 變得　　fit〔fɪt〕*adj.* 健康的

strong〔strɔŋ〕*adj.* 強壯的

Go jogging.

要去慢跑。

Pump iron.

舉重運動。

Lift weights.

要做舉重。

** ***go + V-ing*** 去…　　jog〔dʒɑg〕v. 慢跑
pump〔pʌmp〕v. 用幫浦抽（水）；給…打氣
iron〔'aɪən〕n. 鐵；鐵製品；（舉重槓鈴的）鐵片
pump iron 舉重；用啞鈴健身
lift〔lɪft〕v. 舉起；抬起
weight〔wet〕n. 重量；重物
lift weights 舉重

Sweat daily.

每天流汗。

Detox daily.

每日排毒。

Eliminate waste.

清除廢物。

** sweat〔swɛt〕*v. n.* 流汗

daily〔'delɪ〕*adv.* 每天（*= every day*）

detox〔'ditɑks〕*v.* 排毒

eliminate〔ɪ'lɪmə,net〕*v.* 除去

waste〔west〕*n.* 廢物；廢棄物

【**Unit 6 背景説明**】

Try exercise. 嘗試運動。(= *Give exercise a try.* = *Give working out a try.*) 也可説成： Get some exercise. (要做些運動。)

Get fit. 變得健康。(= *Get healthy.*) 也可説成： Improve your health. (改善你的健康。)

Get strong. (要變強壯。) 也可説成： Increase your strength. (增加你的體力。)

Go jogging. (去慢跑。) 也可説成：Go for a run. (去跑步。)

Pump iron. 要舉重。(= *Lift weights*.) 也可説成： Do some weight training. (要做一些重訓。)

Sweat daily. 每天流汗。(= *Work up a sweat every day.*)

Detox daily. (每天排毒。) 也可説成：Do something to eliminate toxins every day. (每天都要做點事來消除毒素。) Drink a detox drink every day. (每天喝一杯排毒的飲料。)

Eliminate waste. 除去廢物。(= *Get rid of waste*.)

BOOK 4 • PART 3

UNIT 7

Stay on Top of Things 掌控局勢

Be alert.
要警覺。

Be aware.
要留神。

Pay attention.
要注意。

** stay〔ste〕*v.* 保持　***on top of*** 控制著…
stay on top of things 控制事情的發展
alert〔ə'lɜt〕*adj.* 警覺的；留神的
aware〔ə'wɛr〕*adj.* 知道的；察覺到的
attention〔ə'tɛnʃən〕*n.* 注意；注意力
pay attention 注意

Be committed.

要投入。

Be devoted.

要專心。

Be dedicated.

要專注。

** commit〔kə'mɪt〕 *v.* 使致力於；投入（時間或金錢）
committed〔kə'mɪtɪd〕 *adj.* 盡心盡力的
devote〔dɪ'vot〕 *v.* 奉獻；使致力於
devoted〔dɪ'votɪd〕 *adj.* 獻身的；專心於⋯的
dedicate〔'dɛdə‚ket〕 *v.* 奉獻（全部精力、時間等）
dedicated〔'dɛdə‚ketɪd〕 *adj.* 一心一意的；熱誠的

Work harder.

更加努力。

Get tougher.

更加堅強。

Give everything.

全力以赴。

** hard〔hɑrd〕*adv.* 努力地

　work hard 努力工作；努力

　get〔gɛt〕*v.* 變得

　tough〔tʌf〕*adj.* 堅強的；強硬的；強悍的

　give〔gɪv〕*v.* 給與；付出

　give everything 付出一切；竭盡所能；

　　全力以赴

【Unit 7 背景說明】

Be alert. 要警覺。(= *Be vigilant.*)

Be aware. (要察覺到;要留神。) 也可說成:
Be prepared. (要做好準備。) Know what's
going on. (要知道發生了什麼事。)

Pay attention. 要注意。(= *Be attentive.*)

Be committed. (要盡心盡力。) 也可說成:
Be devoted. (要投入。) *Be dedicated*. (要
有熱誠。) Be steadfast. (要堅定。) Be
zealous. (要有熱誠。) Be true. (要忠實。)
(= *Be faithful.*)

Work harder. (要更努力。) 也可說成:Do
more. (要多做一點。) Give it some more
effort. (要更加努力。)

Get tougher. 要變得更堅強。(= *Be stronger.*)
也可說成:Be uncompromising. (要不妥
協。) Be resilient. (要有韌性。)

Give everything. 要付出一切;要全力以赴。
(= *Give it your all.*) 也可說成:Hold
nothing back. (要毫無保留。)

UNIT 8

Don't Waste Time 不要浪費時間

Hurry up!
快點！

Speed up!
加速！

Make haste!
趕快！

** waste〔west〕*v.* 浪費
hurry〔ˈhɝɪ〕*v.* 趕快；急忙　***hurry up*** 趕快
speed〔spid〕*n.* 速度　*v.* 快速前進；加速
speed up 加速　haste〔hest〕*n.* 匆忙；急忙
make haste 趕快

Go faster!

走快一點！

Move faster!

快一點走！

Move quickly!

快速行動！

** go〔go〕v. 去；移動；前進
fast〔fæst〕adv. 快速地
move〔muv〕v. 移動；前進；行進
quickly〔ˈkwɪklɪ〕adv. 快速地

Go quickly!

走快點！

Rush ahead!

向前衝！

Time's ticking!

沒時間了！

** go〔go〕*v.* 去；移動；前進

quickly〔'kwɪklɪ〕*adv.* 快速地

rush〔rʌʃ〕*v.* 衝；倉促行動

ahead〔ə'hɛd〕*adv.* 向前

rush ahead 向前衝

tick〔tɪk〕*v.*（鐘錶）滴答響；發出滴答聲

【Unit 8 背景説明】

Hurry up!（趕快！）也可説成：*Speed up!*（加速！）*Make haste!*（趕快！）Step on it!（快點！）Pick up the pace!（加快腳步！）Get a move on!（快點動起來！）

Go faster!（走快一點！）也可説成：*Move faster!*（動作快一點！）*Move quickly!*（要快速行動！）Step on it!（趕快！）Pick up the pace!（加快腳步！）

Go quickly!　走快點！（= *Go fast!* = *Go faster!*）

Rush ahead!（向前衝！）也可説成：Full speed ahead!（全速前進！）Go on!（繼續進行！）

Time's ticking! 時間正在滴答響，也就是「時間在走；時間在流逝！」（= *The clock is ticking!* = *Time is passing!*）用來催促別人動作快一點，快要沒有時間了。

UNIT 9

Take a Break 休息一下

I'm beat.
我累死了。

I'm bushed.
我累垮了。

I'm exhausted.
我筋疲力盡。

** break〔brek〕*n.* 休息　　***take a break*** 休息一下
beat〔bit〕*v.* 打；擊敗；使疲倦不堪　*adj.* 疲乏的
bush〔buʃ〕*n.* 灌木叢　*v.* 使筋疲力盡
bushed〔buʃt〕*adj.* 疲憊不堪的；筋疲力盡的
exhausted〔ɪgˈzɔstɪd〕*adj.* 筋疲力盡的

I'm spent.

我很疲倦。

I'm drained.

我累斃了。

I'm wiped.

我累掛了。

** spend〔spɛnd〕*v.* 花費;耗盡(精力)

spent〔spɛnt〕*adj.* 筋疲力盡的;疲憊的

drain〔dren〕*v.* 排(水);使逐漸消耗;
使(體力)衰弱

drained〔drend〕*adj.* 疲憊不堪的;累極了

wipe〔waɪp〕*v.* 擦;擦去;消滅;使消失;
揍;打

wiped〔waɪpt〕*adj.* 疲倦的;筋疲力盡的
(= *wiped out*)

I'm run-down.

我疲憊不堪。

I'm worn-down.

我非常疲乏。

Dead tired.

快要累死了。

** run-down〔ˋrʌnˋdaʊn〕*adj.* ①破舊的 ②（尤指
因為工作過度而）筋疲力盡的；疲憊不堪的；
衰弱的【*run down* 由於過度勞累而疲憊】

worn-down〔ˋwɔrnˋdaʊn〕*adj.* 磨損不堪的；
疲乏不堪的

dead〔dɛd〕*adj.* 死的；筋疲力盡的 *adv.* 完全
地；極為 tired〔taɪrd〕*adj.* 疲倦的；累的

dead tired 累得要命；筋疲力盡

【**Unit 9 背景說明**】

I'm beat. 我被打敗了，引申爲「我累死了。」
（ = *I'm very tired.* ）也可說成：I'm weary.
（我很疲倦。）

I'm bushed. 句中的 bush 是指「灌木叢」，一
直躲在灌木叢中，非常累，引申爲「我疲憊
不堪。」（ = *I'm dog-tired.* ）

I'm exhausted. 我筋疲力盡。（ = *I'm fatigued.*
= *I'm knackered.* = *I'm dead.* = *I'm done in.* ）

I'm spent. （我很疲倦。）也可說成：***I'm
drained***. （我非常累。）***I'm wiped***. （我筋
疲力盡。）I'm very tired. （我非常累。）
（ = *I'm dog-tired.* ）I'm exhausted. （我筋
疲力盡。）

I'm run-down. （我筋疲力盡。）也可說成：
I'm worn-down. （我非常疲乏。）（ = *I'm
worn out.* ）***Dead tired***. （快要累死了。）
（ = *I'm dead tired.* = *I'm dog-tired.* = *I'm
very tired.* ）

BOOK 4・PART 3

PART 3　總整理

Unit 1

Hi, there!　嗨，你好！
Hey, there!　嘿，你好！
Hello, there!　哈囉，你好！

What's up?　有何新鮮事？
What's new?　有何新消息？
What's happening?
發生了何事？

How's life?　生活如何？
How're things?　情況如何？
Going well?　一切安好？

Unit 2

Don't judge.　不要評判。
Don't criticize.　不要批評。
Go easy.　對人溫和。

Show mercy.　展現慈悲。
Show compassion.
有同情心。
Display empathy.
有同理心。

Be understanding.
要體諒。
Be sympathetic.
要同情。
Be lenient.　要寬大。

Unit 3

It's OK.　沒有關係。
It happens.　常會發生。
Never mind.
別太介意。

Totally fine.
沒有問題。
Totally understood.
全然理解。
Forget it.　就算了吧。

All's forgiven.
全都原諒。
Absolutely forgiven.
完全原諒。
Apology accepted.
接受道歉。

Unit 4

I'm hungry. 我好餓喔。
I'm starving. 我餓死了。
I'm starved. 我餓極了。

Let's indulge!
我們放縱一下！
Pig out!
我們大吃一頓！
Chow down!
我們大快朵頤！

I'm full.
我吃飽了。
I'm stuffed.
吃得很飽。
I'm satisfied.
我很滿足。

Unit 5

You're welcome.
不用客氣。
My pleasure.
我的榮幸。
You bet.
樂意之至。

No problem. 沒有問題。
No trouble. 毫不麻煩。
No sweat. 輕鬆搞定。

Of course. 由衷樂意。
Sure thing. 當然樂意。
No worries. 沒有關係。

Unit 6

Try exercise.
嘗試運動。
Get fit.
變得健康。
Get strong.
變得強壯。

Go jogging. 要去慢跑。
Pump iron. 舉重運動。
Lift weights. 要做舉重。

Sweat daily.
每天流汗。
Detox daily.
每日排毒。
Eliminate waste.
清除廢物。

Unit 7

Be alert. 要警覺。
Be aware. 要留神。
Pay attention. 要注意。

Be committed. 要投入。
Be devoted. 要專心。
Be dedicated. 要專注。

Work harder. 更加努力。
Get tougher. 更加堅強。
Give everything.
全力以赴。

Unit 8

Hurry up! 快點！
Speed up! 加速！
Make haste! 趕快！

Go faster!
走快一點！
Move faster!
快一點走！
Move quickly!
快速行動！

Go quickly!
走快點！
Rush ahead!
向前衝！
Time's ticking!
沒時間了！

Unit 9

I'm beat. 我累死了。
I'm bushed. 我累垮了。
I'm exhausted.
我筋疲力盡。

I'm spent.
我很疲倦。
I'm drained.
我累斃了。
I'm wiped. 我累掛了。

I'm run-down.
我疲憊不堪。
I'm worn-down.
我非常疲乏。
Dead tired.
快要累死了。

「英文二字經」是個藝術品

有一次清華大學「高階主管研習班」結業典禮時，校長説，你們三個月所學的領導、統御、管理，歸根結底，只有一個字，那就是「愛」(love)。

Love wins. 愛能勝出。
Love conquers. 愛能征服。
Love prevails. 愛能戰勝。

每天背「英文二字經」，心中有愛，做事情就能成功。

Love achieves. 愛能達成。
Love overcomes. 愛能克服。
Love succeeds. 愛能成功。

所有大企業家，共同的特色，就是全身充滿著愛，愛家人、愛同事、愛朋友、愛客戶、愛國家，愛所有的人。愛人者，人恆愛之，自己最受益。

快樂很重要，不快樂就是在浪費時間。我們説：
Happiness is important. 不如説：

Happiness first. 快樂第一。
Stay joyful. 保持快樂。
Remain cheerful. 保持愉快。

每句話兩個字，説出來更有力量。這樣的三句話，一説出來，就會讓人震撼。出口成章，句句金句，成爲一個藝術品，人人聽到，都會佩服得五體投地，而你會越説越好，越説越有成就感，不斷在進步中。

劉毅

BOOK 5　PART 1

How to Express Feelings
如何表達感受

PART 1・Unit 1~9
英文錄音QR碼

UNIT 1

I Feel Great! 我覺得很棒！

I'm happy.

我很快樂。

I'm glad.

我很開心。

I'm pleased.

我很高興。

** great〔gret〕*adj.* 很棒的；極好的

happy〔ˋhæpɪ〕*adj.* 快樂的；高興的

glad〔glæd〕*adj.* 高興的；歡喜的

pleased〔plizd〕*adj.* 高興的

I'm elated.

我很高興。

I'm delighted.

我很愉快。

I'm overjoyed.

欣喜若狂。

** elated〔ɪ'letɪd〕*adj.* 很得意的;興高采烈的
delighted〔dɪ'laɪtɪd〕*adj.* 高興的;快樂的
overjoyed〔ˌovɚ'dʒɔɪd〕*adj.* 狂喜的;
非常高興的

I'm joyful.
我很高興。

I'm cheerful.
我很愉快。

I'm gleeful.
我很開心。

** joyful〔ˈdʒɔɪfəl〕 *adj.* 高興的;快樂的;歡喜的
cheerful〔ˈtʃɪrfəl〕 *adj.* 愉快的;高興的;快樂的
gleeful〔ˈglifəl〕 *adj.* 歡天喜地的;興高采烈的;
快樂的;開心的

【Unit 1 背景説明】

I'm happy.（我很快樂。）也可説成：*I'm glad*.（我很高興。）*I'm pleased*.（我很高興。）I'm on top of the world.（我非常幸福。）

I'm elated.（我很高興。）也可説成：*I'm delighted*.（我很愉快。）*I'm overjoyed*.（我欣喜若狂。）（= *I'm ecstatic*.）I'm on cloud nine.（我非常幸福。）I'm in seventh heaven.（我非常快樂。）I'm walking on air.（我非常高興。）

I'm joyful.（我很高興。）也可説成：*I'm cheerful*.（我很愉快。）*I'm gleeful*.（我很開心。）I'm over the moon.（我非常快樂。）

UNIT 2

I Feel Aggravated 我覺得火大

I'm angry.

我很生氣。

I'm upset.

我很不爽。

I'm mad.

我發火了。

** aggravated〔'ægrə,vetɪd〕*adj.* 憤怒的
angry〔'æŋgrɪ〕*adj.* 生氣的；憤怒的
upset〔ʌp'sɛt〕*adj.* 不高興的
mad〔mæd〕*adj.* 發瘋的；憤怒的；生氣的

I'm annoyed.

我很惱怒。

I'm furious.

我很憤怒。

I'm infuriated.

火冒三丈。

** annoyed〔əˈnɔɪd〕*adj.* 惱怒的；心煩的；
    生氣的
    furious〔ˈfjʊrɪəs〕*adj.* 狂怒的
    infuriated〔ɪnˈfjʊrɪ͵etɪd〕*adj.* 憤怒的；
    火冒三丈的

I'm boiling.

我抓狂了。

I'm fuming.

我發怒了。

I'm steaming.

我極憤怒。

** boil〔bɔɪl〕*v.* 沸騰；暴怒

　　fume〔fjum〕*v.* 冒煙；發怒；生氣

　　steam〔stim〕*v.* 冒蒸氣；生氣；發火

【Unit 2 背景説明】

I'm angry.（我很生氣。）也可説成：*I'm upset*.（我很不高興。）*I'm mad*.（我非常生氣。）也可説成：I'm unhappy.（我不高興。）I'm displeased.（我很不高興。）I'm offended.（我很生氣。）

I'm annoyed.（我很惱怒。）也可説成：*I'm furious*.（我很憤怒。）*I'm infuriated*.（我火冒三丈。）I'm enraged.（我很生氣。）I'm indignant.（我很氣憤。）

I'm boiling. 我正在沸騰，引申爲「我非常生氣。」也可説成：*I'm fuming*. 我正在冒煙，引申爲「我很生氣。」*I'm steaming*. 我正在冒蒸氣，也表示「我非常生氣。」I'm extremely upset.（我非常不高興。）

UNIT 3

I Feel Amazed 我覺得驚訝

I'm surprised.

我很驚訝。

I'm shocked.

我很震驚。

I'm stunned.

目瞪口呆。

** amazed〔ə'mezd〕*adj.* 十分驚奇的；
深感驚訝的
surprised〔sə'praɪzd〕*adj.* 驚訝的
shocked〔ʃɑkt〕*adj.* 震驚的
stunned〔stʌnd〕*adj.* 目瞪口呆的

I'm amazed.

我很驚奇。

I'm astonished.

我很驚訝。

I'm astounded.

大吃一驚。

** amazed〔ə'mezd〕*adj.* 十分驚奇的；
  深感驚訝的
astonished〔ə'stɑnɪʃt〕*adj.* 感到驚訝的
astounded〔ə'staʊndɪd〕*adj.* 感到震驚的；
  大吃一驚的

I'm thunderstruck.
我非常震撼。

I'm dumbstruck.
我吃驚無語。

I'm flabbergasted.
我大吃一驚。

** thunderstruck〔ˈθʌndɚˌstrʌk〕adj. 極其震
驚的；目瞪口呆的

dumbstruck〔ˈdʌmˌstrʌk〕adj. 震驚得說
不出話的；驚呆的

flabbergasted〔ˈflæbɚˌɡæstɪd〕adj. 目瞪
口呆的；大吃一驚的

【Unit 3 背景說明】

I'm surprised.（我很驚訝。）也可說成：*I'm
shocked.*（我很震驚。）*I'm stunned.*（我目
瞪口呆。）I'm startled.（我嚇了一跳。）
I'm paralyzed.（我驚呆了。）

I'm amazed.（我很驚奇。）也可說成：*I'm
astonished.*（我很驚訝。）*I'm astounded.*
（我大吃一驚。）I'm staggered.（我嚇了一
跳。）

I'm thunderstruck. 字面的意思是「我被雷打
到」，引申為「我非常震驚。」也可說成：
I'm dumbstruck.（我驚訝得說不出話來。）
（= *I'm dumbfounded.*）【dumb〔dʌm〕*adj.*
啞的】*I'm flabbergasted.*（我大吃一驚。）
I'm speechless.（我說不出話來。）

BOOK 5・PART 1

UNIT 4

I Feel Inspired 我感到振奮

I'm excited.
我很興奮。

I'm thrilled.
我很激動。

I'm psyched.
我很雀躍。

** inspire〔ɪn'spaɪr〕*v.* 激勵;給予靈感
excited〔ɪk'saɪtɪd〕*adj.* 興奮的
thrilled〔θrɪld〕*adj.* 興奮的;激動的
psyched〔saɪkt〕*adj.* 激動的;興奮的

I'm hyped.

我非常興奮。

I'm enthusiastic.

我興奮不已。

I'm exhilarated.

我興高采烈。

** hyped〔haɪpt〕*adj.* 興奮的（＝ *hyped up*）
   enthusiastic〔ɪn͵θjuzɪˈæstɪk〕*adj.* 狂熱的；
      熱中的
   exhilarated〔ɪgˈzɪlə͵retɪd〕*adj.* 興奮的；
      高興的

I'm pumped.

我很興奮。

I'm jazzed.

我很熱衷。

I'm buzzing.

我很陶醉。

** pumped〔pʌmpt〕*adj.* 熱情高漲的；高度興奮的
（ = *hyped up*）【pump *v.* (用幫浦) 抽水；打 (氣)】

jazzed〔dʒæzd〕*adj.* 興奮的（ = *jazzed up*）

【jazz〔dʒæz〕*n.* 爵士樂】

buzz〔bʌz〕*v.* 發出嗡嗡聲；(因喝酒等而) 陶醉；
興奮

【**Unit 4 背景説明**】

I'm excited. 我很興奮。(= *I'm thrilled.* = *I'm psyched.*) 也可説成：I'm motivated. (我受到激勵。) I'm delighted. (我很高興。) I'm fired up. (我很興奮。)

I'm hyped. (我很興奮。) 也可説成：*I'm enthusiastic.* (我充滿熱忱。) (= *I'm enthused.*) *I'm exhilarated.* (我很興奮。) I'm keen. (我很渴望。) I'm overjoyed. (我欣喜若狂。) (= *I'm ecstatic.*)

I'm pumped. 我被打氣了，引申爲「我很興奮。」也可説成：*I'm jazzed.* 我受到爵士樂的影響，引申爲「我很興奮。」*I'm buzzing.* 我正發出嗡嗡聲，也引申爲「我很興奮。」(= *I'm excited.* = *I'm thrilled.*)

UNIT 5

I Feel Bewildered 我覺得困惑

I'm confused.
我很困惑。

I'm puzzled.
我很迷茫。

I'm perplexed.
我很迷惑。

** bewildered〔bɪˋwɪldəd〕*adj.* 困惑的
confused〔kənˋfjuzd〕*adj.* 困惑的
puzzled〔ˋpʌzḷd〕*adj.* 困惑的；搞糊塗的；茫然的
perplexed〔pəˋplɛkst〕*adj.* 困惑的；茫然不知
　所措的

I'm unsure.

我不確定。

I'm uncertain.

我很徬徨。

I'm lost.

我迷失了。

** unsure〔ʌnˈʃʊr〕*adj.* 不確定的；沒把握的

　 uncertain〔ʌnˈsɝtn̩〕*adj.* 不確定的

　 lost〔lɔst〕*adj.* 迷失的；迷惑的；困惑的

I'm troubled.

我很苦惱。

I'm disoriented.

失去方向。

I'm mixed-up.

我很糊塗。

** troubled〔ˈtrʌbḷd〕*adj.* 苦惱的；煩惱的；
　　困惑的
　　disoriented〔dɪsˈorɪˌɛntɪd〕*adj.* 迷失方向的；
　　迷惘的；失去判斷力的
　　mixed-up〔ˈmɪkstˌʌp〕*adj.* 頭腦混亂的；
　　迷惑的；糊塗的

【Unit 5 背景説明】

I'm confused. 我很困惑。(= *I'm puzzled.* = *I'm perplexed.* = *I'm bewildered.* = *I'm baffled.*)

I'm unsure. 我不確定。(= *I'm uncertain.*) 也可説成：I'm doubtful.（我很懷疑。） I'm hesitant.（我很猶豫。）

I'm lost. 我很迷惑；我很困惑。(= *I'm confused.* = *I'm puzzled.*)

I'm troubled.（我很苦惱。）也可説成： I'm worried.（我很擔心。）I'm anxious. （我很焦慮。）(= *I'm apprehensive.*) I'm disturbed.（我很不安。）

I'm disoriented. 我迷失方向。(= *I'm lost.*)

I'm mixed-up.（我很糊塗。）也可説成：I'm confused.（我很困惑。）(= *I'm bewildered.*)

UNIT 6

I Feel Miserable 我覺得悲慘

I'm sad.
我很悲傷。

I'm unhappy.
我不快樂。

I'm discouraged.
我很洩氣。

** miserable〔ˈmɪzərəbḷ〕 *adj.* 悲慘的
sad〔sæd〕 *adj.* 悲傷的；難過的
unhappy〔ʌnˈhæpɪ〕 *adj.* 不快樂的；不高興的
discouraged〔dɪsˈkɝɪdʒd〕 *adj.* 氣餒的；洩氣的

I'm low.

我很消沈。

I'm down.

我很低落。

I'm blue.

我很憂鬱。

** low〔lo〕*adj.* 情緒低落的；消沈的；憂鬱的
down〔daun〕*adj.* 沮喪的；不高興的；情緒
  低落的；提不起精神的
blue〔blu〕*adj.* 憂鬱的；悲傷的；沮喪的

I'm depressed.
我很沮喪。

I'm distressed.
我很苦惱。

I'm dejected.
情緒低落。。

** depressed〔dɪ'prɛst〕*adj.* 沮喪的；消沈的
distressed〔dɪ'strɛst〕*adj.* 痛苦的；苦惱的
dejected〔dɪ'dʒɛktɪd〕*adj.* 沮喪的；垂頭
喪氣的；情緒低落的

【Unit 6 背景說明】

I'm sad.（我很悲傷。）也可説成：*I'm unhappy.*（我不快樂。）*I'm discouraged.*（我很氣餒。）I'm dispirited.（我很沮喪。）

I'm low. 我情緒低落。（＝ *I'm in low spirits.* ＝ *I'm depressed.*）

I'm down. 我心情不好。（＝ *I'm downhearted.*）也可説成：I'm down in the dumps.（我的心情很沮喪。）

I'm blue. 我很憂鬱。（＝ *I'm melancholy.*）也可説成：I'm miserable.（我很悲慘。）

I'm depressed.（我很沮喪。）也可説成：I'm disheartened.（我很灰心。）

I'm distressed. 我很苦惱。（＝ *I'm troubled.*）也可説成：I'm worried.（我很擔心。）I'm anxious.（我很焦慮。）

I'm dejected. 我很沮喪。（＝ *I'm depressed.*）

UNIT 7

I Feel You're Out of Control
我覺得你失控了

Calm down.

冷靜下來。

Settle down.

平靜下來。

Pipe down.

安靜下來。

** control〔kən'trol〕*n.* 控制
out of control 失去控制
calm〔kɑm〕*adj.* 平靜的;鎮定的 *v.* 鎮定(下
　來);安靜(下來) *calm down* 冷靜下來
settle〔'sɛtl̩〕*v.* 安頓下來;定居;安靜下來;
　平靜下來 *settle down* 安頓下來;安靜下來
pipe〔paɪp〕*v.* 吹笛子;高聲說
pipe down 安靜下來

Cool it.

冷靜一點。

Stay cool.

保持鎮定。

Chill out.

冷靜下來。

BOOK 5・PART 1

** cool〔kul〕v. 使冷卻；使平息

　adj. 涼爽的；冷靜的

cool it 冷靜點；沈住氣；息怒

stay〔ste〕v. 保持

chill〔tʃɪl〕v. 變冷；冷卻　adj. 冷靜的

chill out 徹底放鬆；冷靜；鎮靜

Stay serene.

保持平靜。

Stay mellow.

保持放鬆。

Stay peaceful.

保持平和。

** stay〔 ste 〕*v.* 保持

serene〔 sə'rin 〕*adj.* 平靜的；安詳的

mellow〔'mɛlo 〕*adj.* 成熟的；柔和的；

放鬆的

peaceful〔'pisfəl 〕*adj.* 和平的；平靜的；

寧靜的；安詳的

【**Unit 7 背景説明**】

Calm down. (冷靜下來。) 也可説成：***Settle down.*** (平靜下來。) ***Pipe down.*** (安靜下來。) (= *Be quiet.*) Relax. (放輕鬆。)

Cool it. (冷靜一點。) 也可説成：Cool your jets. (冷靜下來。) Control yourself. (要控制自己。)

Stay cool. 保持冷靜。(= *Keep your cool.*) 也可説成：Never lose your cool. (絕不要失去冷靜。) Don't lose your head. (不要慌張。)

Chill out. (冷靜下來。) 也可説成：Chill. (冷靜。) Chillax. (冷靜一點，放輕鬆。) Take a chill pill. (冷靜下來。)

Stay serene. (保持平靜。) 也可説成：Be tranquil. (要平靜。)

Stay mellow. 保持放鬆。(= *Stay relaxed.*) 也可説成：Stay calm. (保持冷靜。) Don't get tense. (不要緊張。)

Stay peaceful. (保持平靜。) 也可説成：Remain calm. (要保持冷靜。) Don't lose your cool. (不要失去冷靜。)

UNIT **8**

I Feel So Thankful
我覺得非常感謝

I'm touched.
我感動了。

I'm moved.
我很感動。

I'm affected.
我被感動。

** so〔so〕*adv.* 很；非常
thankful〔'θæŋkfəl〕*adj.* 感謝的
touched〔tʌtʃt〕*adj.* 感動的
moved〔muvd〕*adj.* 感動的
affected〔ə'fɛktɪd〕*adj.* 受到影響的；被感動的

How wonderful!

眞是太棒！

Truly fantastic!

眞的極好！

It's uplifting!

令人振奮！

** how〔haʊ〕*adv.* 多麼地

wonderful〔'wʌndɚfəl〕*adj.* 很棒的；極好的

truly〔'trulɪ〕*adv.* 眞地

fantastic〔fæn'tæstɪk〕*adj.* 極好的；很棒的

uplifting〔ʌp'lɪftɪŋ〕*adj.* 鼓舞的；令人振奮的

Simply amazing!
簡直驚人！

Totally awesome!
令人讚嘆！

Definitely splendid!
太了不起！

** simply〔ˋsɪmplɪ〕*adv.* 真正地；的確；實際上
　amazing〔əˋmezɪŋ〕*adj.* 驚人的；令人驚奇的；
　　很棒的
　totally〔ˋtotḷɪ〕*adv.* 徹底地；完全地；全然
　awesome〔ˋɔsəm〕*adj.* 令人驚嘆的；很好的；
　　了不起的；很棒的
　definitely〔ˋdɛfənɪtlɪ〕*adv.* 的確；一定
　splendid〔ˋsplɛndɪd〕*adj.* 極好的；了不起的；
　　華麗的；壯麗的；輝煌的

【Unit 8 背景説明】

I'm touched. 我很感動。(= *I'm moved*. = *I'm affected*.) 也可説成：You've warmed my heart. (你温暖了我的心。) I'm impressed. (我印象深刻。)

How wonderful! 真棒！(= *That's wonderful!*) 也可説成：*Truly fantastic!* (真的很棒！) (= *That's fantastic!*) That's great! (那真的很棒！)

It's uplifting! (真是令人振奮！) 也可説成：It's inspiring! (真是激勵人心！) (= *It's inspirational!*) It's touching! (真令人感動！) (= *It's moving!*)

Simply amazing! (真是太棒了！) 也可説成：*Totally awesome!* (真的很棒！) (= *That's awesome!*)

Definitely splendid! (非常了不起！) 也可説成：That's remarkable! (真的很出色！) That's breathtaking! (真是令人驚艷！) That's incredible! (真是令人無法置信！)

UNIT 9

I Feel Sure 我覺得很確定

I promise.
我保證。

I swear.
我發誓。

It's guaranteed.
我擔保。

** sure〔ʃʊr〕*adj.* 確定的
promise〔'prɑmɪs〕*v.* 承諾；答應；保證
swear〔swɛr〕*v.* 發誓
guarantee〔ˌgærən'ti〕*v.* 保證

Trust me.

信任我。

Believe me.

相信我。

I'll deliver.

我兌現。

** trust〔trʌst〕*v.* 信任；相信
　believe〔bɪˈliv〕*v.* 相信
　deliver〔dɪˈlɪvə〕*v.* 遞送；實現；
　　兌現（諾言）

Without fail.

一定做到。

No doubt.

不要懷疑。

Rest assured.

請你放心。

** fail〔fel〕*v.* 失敗

without fail 一定；必定

doubt〔daʊt〕*n.* 懷疑

no doubt 無疑地；必定地

rest〔rɛst〕*v.* 休息；放心

assure〔ə'ʃʊr〕*v.* 向…保證；使安心

rest assured 放心

【Unit 9 背景説明】

I promise. (我保證。) 也可説成：*I swear*. (我發誓。)

It's guaranteed. (我保證。) 不可説成：*I guarantee*. 【誤】要説成：I guarantee it. (我保證。)

Trust me. (信任我。) 也可説成：*Believe me*. (相信我。) I give you my word. (我向你保證。)

I'll deliver. 字面的意思是「我會遞送。」在此引申爲「我會兌現；我會兌現承諾。」也可説成：I'll do it. (我會做到。) I'll finish it. (我會把它完成。)

Without fail. 一定；必定；毫無例外。(= *It's certain*. = *It's definite*.) 句中的 fail 是動詞，故須將 Without fail. 視爲慣用句，不可説成：*Without failing*. (誤) 或 *Without failure*. (誤)

No doubt. 毫無疑問。(= *Without doubt*. = *Undoubtedly*.)

Rest assured. (放心。) 也可説成：You can rest assured. (你可以放心。) You can count on it. (你儘管放心。)

PART 1 · Unit 1~9
中英文錄音QR碼

PART 1 總整理

Unit 1

I'm happy. 我很快樂。
I'm glad. 我很開心。
I'm pleased. 我很高興。

I'm elated. 我很高興。
I'm delighted.
我很愉快。
I'm overjoyed.
欣喜若狂。

I'm joyful. 我很高興。
I'm cheerful. 我很愉快。
I'm gleeful. 我很開心。

Unit 2

I'm angry. 我很生氣。
I'm upset. 我很不爽。
I'm mad. 我發火了。

I'm annoyed. 我很惱怒。
I'm furious. 我很憤怒。
I'm infuriated. 火冒三丈。

I'm boiling. 我抓狂了。
I'm fuming. 我發怒了。
I'm steaming. 我極憤怒。

Unit 3

I'm surprised.
我很驚訝。
I'm shocked.
我很震驚。
I'm stunned.
目瞪口呆。

I'm amazed. 我很驚奇。
I'm astonished.
我很驚訝。
I'm astounded.
大吃一驚。

I'm thunderstruck.
我非常震撼。
I'm dumbstruck.
我吃驚無語。
I'm flabbergasted.
我大吃一驚。

Unit 4

I'm excited. 我很興奮。
I'm thrilled. 我很激動。
I'm psyched. 我很雀躍。

I'm hyped.
我非常興奮。
I'm enthusiastic.
我興奮不已。
I'm exhilarated.
我興高采烈。

I'm pumped. 我很興奮。
I'm jazzed. 我很熱衷。
I'm buzzing. 我很陶醉。

Unit 5

I'm confused. 我很困惑。
I'm puzzled. 我很迷茫。
I'm perplexed. 我很迷惑。

I'm unsure. 我不確定。
I'm uncertain.
我很徬徨。
I'm lost. 我迷失了。

I'm troubled.
我很苦惱。
I'm disoriented.
失去方向。
I'm mixed-up.
我很糊塗。

Unit 6

I'm sad.
我很悲傷。
I'm unhappy.
我不快樂。
I'm discouraged.
我很洩氣。

I'm low. 我很消沈。
I'm down. 我很低落。
I'm blue. 我很憂鬱。

I'm depressed.
我很沮喪。
I'm distressed.
我很苦惱。
I'm dejected.
情緒低落。

BOOK 5・PART 1

Unit 7

Calm down. 冷靜下來。
Settle down. 平靜下來。
Pipe down. 安靜下來。

Cool it. 冷靜一點。
Stay cool. 保持鎮定。
Chill out. 冷靜下來。

Stay serene. 保持平靜。
Stay mellow. 保持放鬆。
Stay peaceful. 保持平和。

Unit 8

I'm touched. 我感動了。
I'm moved. 我很感動。
I'm affected. 我被感動。

How wonderful!
真是太棒！
Truly fantastic!
真的極好！
It's uplifting!
令人振奮！

Simply amazing!
簡直驚人！
Totally awesome!
令人讚嘆！
Definitely splendid!
太了不起！

Unit 9

I promise.
我保證。
I swear. 我發誓。
It's guaranteed.
我擔保。

Trust me. 信任我。
Believe me. 相信我。
I'll deliver. 我兌現。

Without fail.
一定做到。
No doubt.
不要懷疑。
Rest assured.
請你放心。

BOOK 5　PART 2

Know What to Say
要知道該說什麼

PART 2・Unit 1~9
英文錄音QR碼

UNIT 1

When You're Enthusiastic
當你充滿熱忱時

I'm impressed.
你打動了我。

I'm energized.
我充滿能量。

I'm uplifted.
我振奮不已。

** enthusiastic〔ɪn͵θjuzɪ'æstɪk〕*adj.* 熱心的；
熱情的；極感興趣的
impress〔ɪm'prɛs〕*v.* 使印象深刻；使佩服
energize〔'ɛnɚ͵dʒaɪz〕*v.* 使精力充沛；使充
滿活力　　uplift〔ʌp'lɪft〕*v.* 鼓舞；振作

I'm inspired.

我受到激勵。

I'm motivated.

我充滿動力。

I'm encouraged.

我受到鼓勵。

** inspire〔ɪn'spaɪr〕*v.* 激勵；給予靈感
motivate〔'motə,vet〕*v.* 激勵
encourage〔ɪn'kɝɪdʒ〕*v.* 鼓勵

BOOK 5・PART 2

I'm enchanted.
真令我著迷。

I'm fascinated.
真讓我著迷。

I'm captivated.
我被吸引了。

** enchant〔ɪn'tʃænt〕v. 使陶醉；使入迷

enchanted〔ɪn'tʃæntɪd〕adj. 被施了魔法的；
入迷的

fascinate〔'fæsn̩ˌet〕v. 使著迷

fascinated〔'fæsn̩ˌetɪd〕adj. 入迷的；極感
興趣的

captivate〔'kæptəˌvet〕v. 使著迷；迷住；吸引

【Unit 1 背景説明】

I'm impressed.（我印象深刻；我非常佩服。）
也可説成：I'm astounded.（我非常驚訝。）
（= *I'm stunned.* = *I'm amazed.*）I'm touched.
（我很感動。）（= *I'm moved.*）I'm fascinated.
（我十分著迷。）I'm interested.（我很感興趣。）

I'm energized.（我充滿活力。）也可説成：I'm
excited.（我很興奮。）I'm ready to go.（我
已經準備好了。）

I'm uplifted. 我受到鼓舞。（= *I'm cheered.*）
也可説成：I'm delighted.（我很高興。）
（= *I'm happy.*）

I'm inspired. 我受到激勵。（= *I'm motivated.*）
也可説成：*I'm encouraged.*（我受到鼓勵。）
I'm enthused.（我充滿熱忱。）（= *I'm
enthusiastic.* = *I'm keen.* = *I'm eager.*）I'm
excited.（我很興奮。）（= *I'm exhilarated.*）

I'm enchanted. 我非常著迷。（= *I'm fascinated.*
= *I'm captivated.* = *I'm charmed.* = *I'm
mesmerized.* = *I'm entranced.* = *I'm
enthralled.* = *I'm spellbound.*）也可説成：
I'm overjoyed.（我非常高興。）

BOOK 5・PART 2

UNIT 2

Know What's Going On
要知道發生什麼事

Have insight.
要有洞察力。

Have information.
要消息靈通。

Have imagination.
要有想像力。

** ***go on*** 發生
insight〔'ɪn,saɪt〕 *n.* 洞察力;深入的見解
information〔,ɪnfə'meʃən〕 *n.* 資訊
imagination〔ɪ,mædʒə'neʃən〕 *n.* 想像力

Have compassion.
有同情心。

Have sympathy.
有憐憫心。

Have empathy.
有同理心。

** compassion〔kəm'pæʃən〕*n.* 同情；
　同理心
　sympathy〔'sɪmpəθɪ〕*n.* 同情；憐憫
　empathy〔'ɛmpəθɪ〕*n.* 同感；共鳴；
　同理心

Have patience.

要有耐心。

Have discipline.

要能自律。

Have determination.

要有決心。

** patience〔ˈpeʃəns〕n. 耐心
discipline〔ˈdɪsəplɪn〕n. 紀律；自制力
determination〔dɪ͵tɝməˈneʃən〕n. 決心

【**Unit 2 背景說明**】

背誦技巧：<u>i</u>nsight-<u>i</u>nformation-<u>i</u>magination
字首都是 i。

Have insight.（要有洞察力。）也可說成：Be
perceptive.（要觀察敏銳。）Be aware.（要
警覺。）Be discerning.（要有辨別力。）

Have information.（要有資訊。）也可說成：
Be knowledgeable.（要知識淵博。）Be
well-informed.（要消息靈通。）

Have imagination. 要有想像力。(= *Be
imaginative.*) 也可說成：Be creative.（要有
創造力。）Be inventive.（要有發明才能。）
Be innovative.（要創新。）Be original.（要
有創意。）

Have compassion. 要有同情心。(= *Be
compassionate.*) 也可說成：Be kind.
（要善良。）

Have sympathy. 要有同情心。(= *Have
compassion.* = *Be sympathetic.* = *Be
compassionate.*)

Have empathy. 要有同理心。(= *Be empathetic.*) 也可說成：Be understanding. (要能體諒別人。) Be aware of other people's feelings. (要知道別人的感受。)

com + pass + ion	sym + pathy	em + pathy
| | |	| |	| |
together + suffer + n.	*same + feeling*	*in + feeling*
(一起受苦)	(相同的感情)	(感情移入)

Have patience. 要有耐心。(= *Be patient.*) 也可說成：Be tolerant. (要寬容。) Be uncomplaining. (要沒有怨言。) Be easygoing. (要隨和。)

Have discipline. 要有紀律；要能自律。(= *Be disciplined. = Be self-controlled.*) 也可說成：Be organized. (要有條理。) Be efficient. (要有效率。)

Have determination. 要有決心。(= *Be determined. = Be resolute.*) 也可說成：Be committed. (要盡心盡力。)

UNIT 3

Don't Be Defeated 不要被打敗

Defeat failure.

戰勝失敗。

Defeat despair.

戰勝絕望。

Defeat setbacks.

戰勝挫折。

** defeat〔dɪˈfit〕*v.* 打敗；戰勝
failure〔ˈfeljɚ〕*n.* 失敗
despair〔dɪˈspɛr〕*n.* 絕望
setback〔ˈsɛt,bæk〕*n.* 挫折

Defeat distraction.

不要分心。

Defeat hesitation.

不要猶豫。

Defeat procrastination.

不要拖延。

** defeat〔dɪ'fit〕 *v.* 打敗；戰勝

distraction〔dɪ'strækʃən〕 *n.* 分心；令人分心
　的事物

hesitation〔͵hɛzə'teʃən〕 *n.* 猶豫

procrastination〔pro͵kræstə'neʃən〕 *n.* 拖延
　(= *delay*)

Defeat negativity.
擊敗負面。

Defeat mediocrity.
擊敗平庸。

Defeat impossibility.
擊敗無望。

** defeat〔dɪˋfit〕v. 打敗；戰勝
　negativity〔͵nɛgəˋtɪvətɪ〕n. 否定；消極的
　　態度；負面的看法
　mediocrity〔͵midɪˋɑkrətɪ〕n. 平庸
　impossibility〔ɪm͵pɑsəˋbɪlətɪ〕n. 不可能

【Unit 3 背景説明】

Defeat failure. 戰勝失敗。(= *Overcome failure*. = *Overcome defeats*. = *Overcome loss*.) 也可説成：Overcome frustration. (克服沮喪。)

Defeat despair. 戰勝絕望。(= *Overcome despair*. = *Overcome hopelessness*.) 也可説成：Overcome melancholy. (要克服憂鬱。)

Defeat setbacks. 戰勝挫折。(= *Overcome setbacks*.) 也可説成：Overcome obstacles. (克服阻礙。) Overcome misfortune. (克服不幸。) Overcome problems. (克服問題。) Overcome challenges. (克服挑戰。)

中外文化不同，外國人認爲「分心即是失敗。」(Distraction is defeat.) 我們能夠説出 Defeat distraction. 就是高檔英文。

Defeat distraction. 戰勝分心；不要分心。(= *Overcome distraction*.) 也可説成：Overcome interference. (克服干擾。) Ignore interruption. (忽視打擾。) Ignore distractions. (忽視令人分心的事物。)

Defeat hesitation. 克服猶豫。(= *Overcome hesitation.*) 也可說成：Overcome doubt.
（克服懷疑。）

Defeat procrastination. 克服拖延。(= *Overcome procrastination.* = *Overcome delay.*) 也可說成：Don't procrastinate. （不要拖延。）
(= *Don't delay.* = *Don't postpone things.*)

背誦技巧：negativ<u>ity</u>-mediocr<u>ity</u>-impossibil<u>ity</u> 字尾都是 **ity**。

Defeat negativity. 戰勝負面情緒。(= *Overcome negativity.*) 也可說成：Overcome pessimism.
（克服悲觀。）Overcome cynicism.（克服憤世嫉俗的態度。）

Defeat mediocrity. 戰勝平庸。(= *Overcome mediocrity.*) 也可說成：Don't be ordinary.
（不要普普通通。）(= *Don't be commonplace.* = *Don't be average.*)

Defeat impossibility.（戰勝不可能。）也可說成：Make the impossible possible.（要使不可能的事成為可能。）Do the impossible.
（要做不可能的事。）

BOOK 5・PART 2

UNIT 4

Know Who You Are 了解你自己

Be humble.

要謙虛。

Be honorable.

被敬佩。

Be hospitable.

要好客。

** humble〔ˈhʌmbḷ〕*adj.* 謙虛的
　　honorable〔ˈɑnərəbḷ〕*adj.* 光榮的；品德
　　　高尚的；值得尊敬的
　　hospitable〔ˈhɑspɪtəbḷ〕*adj.* 好客的

Be invaluable.

要寶貴無價。

Be indispensable.

要不可或缺。

Be impressive.

要令人佩服。

** invaluable〔ɪn'væljəbl̩〕 *adj.* 珍貴的；無價的
indispensable〔͵ɪndɪ'spɛnsəbl̩〕 *adj.* 不可或缺的
impressive〔ɪm'prɛsɪv〕 *adj.* 令人印象深刻的；
　感人的；令人欽佩的

Be solid.

要紮紮實實。

Be stable.

要穩如泰山。

Be straightforward.

要直接了當。

** solid〔'sɑlɪd〕*adj.* 堅固的；實心的；
　　紮實的；可靠的
　stable〔'steblֽ〕*adj.* 穩定的
　straightforward〔ˌstret'fɔrwəd〕*adj.*
　　直率的；直接了當的

【Unit 4 背景説明】

背誦技巧：<u>h</u>umble-<u>h</u>onorable-<u>h</u>ospitable 字首都是 h。

Be humble. 要謙虛。(= *Be modest.* = *Be unassuming.*)

Be honorable.（要值得尊敬；要品德高尚。）也可説成：Be honest.（要誠實。）Be ethical.（要合乎道德。）Be virtuous.（要有美德。）

Be hospitable.（要好客。）也可説成：Be welcoming.（要熱情友好；要好客。）Be sociable.（要善於交際。）Be neighborly.（要和睦友善。）

背誦技巧：<u>i</u>nvaluable-<u>i</u>ndispensable-<u>i</u>mpressive 字首都是 i。

Be invaluable.（要很珍貴。）也可説成：*Be indispensable*.（要不可或缺。）Make yourself necessary.（要讓自己不可或缺。）

Make yourself essential. (要使自己非常重要。)

Be impressive. (要令人印象深刻。) 也可說成：Be outstanding. (要很傑出。)

背誦技巧：**s**olid-**s**table-**s**traightforward 字首都是 s。

Be solid. 要可靠。(= *Be dependable.* = *Be reliable.*) 也可說成：Be trustworthy. (要值得信任。)

Be stable. (要穩定。) 也可說成：Be steadfast. (要堅定。) Be level-headed. (頭腦要冷靜。) Be even-tempered. (要性情平和。) Be self-controlled. (要能自制。)

Be straightforward. (要直率。) 也可說成：Be direct. (要直接。) Be honest. (要誠實。)

UNIT 5

Foster Positive Things
培養好的特質

Promote kindness.
提倡善良。

Promote compassion.
提倡同情。

Promote positivity.
提倡正面。

** foster〔ˈfɔstɚ, ˈfɑstɚ〕v. 培養；促進；鼓勵
positive〔ˈpɑzətɪv〕adj. 正面的；積極的
promote〔prəˈmot〕v. 提倡；鼓勵；促進
kindness〔ˈkaɪndnɪs〕n. 仁慈；善意；善良
compassion〔kəmˈpæʃən〕n. 同情
positivity〔͵pɑzəˈtɪvətɪ〕n. 正面；積極；樂觀

BOOK 5・PART 2

Promote growth.

鼓勵成長。

Promote innovation.

鼓勵創新。

Promote creativity.

鼓勵創意。

** promote〔prə'mot〕v. 提倡；鼓勵；促進
　　growth〔groθ〕n. 成長
　　innovation〔͵ɪnə'veʃən〕n. 創新
　　creativity〔͵krie'tɪvətɪ〕n. 創造力

Promote unity.

促進團結。

Promote harmony.

促進和諧。

Promote cooperation.

促進合作。

** promote〔prə'mot〕*v.* 提倡；鼓勵；促進
　　unity〔'junətɪ〕*n.* 團結
　　harmony〔'hɑrmənɪ〕*n.* 和諧
　　cooperation〔ko͵apə'reʃən〕*n.* 合作
　　　（ = *collaboration* ）

【Unit 5 背景説明】

Promote kindness. 要鼓勵善良。(= *Encourage kindness*.)

Promote compassion. 要鼓勵同情。
(= *Encourage compassion*.) 也可説成：
Encourage understanding. (要鼓勵體諒別人。)

Promote positivity. 要鼓勵樂觀。(= *Encourage positivity*. = *Encourage optimism*.) 也可説成：Encourage a positive attitude. (要鼓勵樂觀的態度。)

Promote growth. (要促進成長。) 也可説成：
Encourage growth. (要鼓勵成長。)
Encourage development. (要鼓勵發展。)

Promote innovation. 要鼓勵創新。
(= *Encourage innovation*.) 也可説成：
Encourage progress. (要鼓勵進步。)

Promote creativity. 要鼓勵創意。(= *Encourage creativity.* = *Encourage originality.* = *Encourage ingenuity.*) 也可説成： Encourage imagination. (要鼓勵想像力。)

Promote unity. 要促進團結。(= *Encourage solidarity.*) 也可説成： Encourage teamwork. (要鼓勵團隊合作。)

Promote harmony. 要促進和諧。(= *Encourage harmony.*) 也可説成： Encourage agreement. (要鼓勵意見一致。) Encourage consensus. (要鼓勵達成共識。)

Promote cooperation. 要促進合作。 (= *Encourage cooperation.*) 也可説成： Encourage collaboration. (要鼓勵合作。) Encourage coordination. (要鼓勵協調。) Encourage unity. (要鼓勵團結。)

UNIT 6

Make the World a Better Place
讓世界變得更好

Advocate prosperity.
提倡富強。

Advocate democracy.
提倡民主。

Advocate dedication.
提倡敬業。

** make〔mek〕*v.* 使成為
advocate〔'ædvə,ket〕*v.* 提倡；擁護；主張
prosperity〔pras'pɛrətɪ〕*n.* 繁榮
democracy〔də'makrəsɪ〕*n.* 民主
dedication〔,dɛdə'keʃən〕*n.* 奉獻；專心致力；敬業

Advocate integrity.

提倡誠信。

Advocate civility.

提倡文明。

Advocate equality.

提倡平等。

** advocate〔'ædvəˌket〕*v.* 提倡；擁護；主張
   integrity〔ɪn'tɛgrətɪ〕*n.* 正直；誠信
   civility〔sɪ'vɪlətɪ〕*n.* 禮貌；客氣；端莊；文明
   equality〔ɪ'kwɑlətɪ〕*n.* 平等

Advocate freedom.

提倡自由。

Advocate justice.

提倡公正。

Advocate patriotism.

提倡愛國。

** advocate〔ˈædvəˌket〕*v.* 擁護；提倡；主張
freedom〔ˈfridəm〕*n.* 自由
justice〔ˈdʒʌstɪs〕*n.* 正義；公正
patriotism〔ˈpetrɪəˌtɪzəm〕*n.* 愛國心；
　　愛國主義

【Unit 6 背景説明】

Advocate prosperity.（提倡繁榮。）也可説成：
Encourage success.（鼓勵成功。）Support
financial well-being.（支持經濟狀況良好。）

Advocate democracy.（提倡民主。）也可説
成：Encourage democracy.（鼓勵民主。）
Support democracy.（支持民主。）

Advocate dedication. 提倡全心投入。
(= *Promote commitment.*) 也可説成：
Encourage commitment.（鼓勵全心全意。）
Support commitment.（支持盡心盡力。）
Encourage loyalty.（鼓勵忠誠。）

Advocate integrity.（提倡正直。）也可説成：
Encourage honor.（鼓勵品德高尚。）Support
honor.（支持品德高尚。）Promote good
character.（提倡良好的性格。）Encourage
virtue.（鼓勵美德。）Promote honesty.（提
倡誠實。）Support decency.（支持正直。）

Advocate civility.（提倡禮貌。）也可説成：
Encourage respect.（鼓勵尊重。）

Encourage politeness.（鼓勵禮貌。）
(= *Encourage courtesy*.)

Advocate equality.（提倡平等。）也可說成：
Encourage fairness.（鼓勵公平。）
Support fairness.（支持公平。）

Advocate freedom.（提倡自由。）也可說成：
Encourage liberty.（鼓勵自由。）
Encourage free will.（鼓勵自由意志。）
Support liberty.（支持自由。）Support
free will.（支持自由意志。）

Advocate justice.（提倡公平正義。）也可說成：
Encourage fairness.（鼓勵公平。）Support
fairness.（支持公平。）Promote fairness.
（提倡公平。）

Advocate patriotism.（提倡愛國主義。）也可
說成：Encourage nationalism.（鼓勵國家
主義。）Support nationalism.（支持國家主
義。）Promote loyalty to one's country.
（提倡對自己的國家忠誠。）Encourage love
of country.（鼓勵愛國。）

UNIT 7

Know When to Say You're Sorry
要知道何時說抱歉

I'm sorry.

我很抱歉。

I apologize.

我要道歉。

I'm regretful.

我很後悔。

** sorry〔ˈsɑrɪ〕*adj.* 抱歉的；難過的
apologize〔əˈpɑlə͵dʒaɪz〕*v.* 道歉
regretful〔rɪˈgrɛtfəl〕*adj.* 後悔的

Truly sorry.

眞的抱歉。

Terribly sorry.

非常抱歉。

Wholeheartedly sorry.

由衷抱歉。

** truly〔'trulɪ〕 adv. 眞地

　　sorry〔'sɑrɪ〕 adj. 抱歉的；難過的

　　terribly〔'tɛrəblɪ〕 adv. 非常地

　　wholeheartedly〔ˌhol'hɑrtɪdlɪ〕 adv.

　　　　全心全意地

I'm downhearted.

我沮喪。

I'm brokenhearted.

我傷心。

I'm heartbroken.

我心碎。

** downhearted〔ˋdaʊnˋhɑrtɪd〕*adj.* 灰心喪氣的；
　沮喪的；悶悶不樂的
brokenhearted〔͵brokənˋhɑrtɪd〕*adj.* 心碎的；
　傷心欲絕的
heartbroken〔ˋhɑrt͵brokən〕*adj.* 心碎的；
　極為傷心的

【Unit 7 背景說明】

I'm sorry.（我很抱歉。）也可說成：Pardon me.（原諒我。）I beg your pardon.（請原諒我。）

I apologize.（我道歉。）也可說成：My apologies.（我道歉。）

I'm regretful.　我很後悔。(= *I regret it*.) 也可說成：I want to express my regret.（我想要表達我很後悔。）

Truly sorry.（真的很抱歉。）也可說成：*Terribly sorry*.（非常抱歉。）*Wholeheartedly sorry*.（真心感到抱歉。）I am very sorry.（我非常抱歉。）(= *I am extremely sorry*.)

I'm downhearted.　我很沮喪。(= *I'm dejected*.) 也可說成：I'm down.（我情緒低落。）(= *I'm in low spirits*.) I'm discouraged.（我很氣餒。）

I'm brokenhearted.（我傷心。）也可說成：*I'm heartbroken*.（我心碎。）I'm sad.（我很悲傷。）I'm blue.（我很憂鬱。）I'm feeling low.（我覺得意志消沈。）I'm unhappy.（我不快樂。）

UNIT 8

Recognize Others 認可別人

Great job!
做得好！

Good job!
幹得好！

Nice job!
做得棒！

** recognize〔'rɛkəg,naɪz〕*v.* 承認；認可
　 great〔gret〕*adj.* 很棒的；極好的
　 job〔dʒɑb〕*n.* 工作　　***good job*** 做得好
　 nice〔naɪs〕*adj.* 好的

Super job!
做得超棒！

Superb job!
做得太好！

Splendid job!
做得太棒！

** super〔ˋsupɚ〕adj. 超級的；極佳的
job〔dʒɑb〕n. 工作
superb〔suˋpɝb〕adj. 極好的；一流的
splendid〔ˋsplɛndɪd〕adj. 燦爛的；壯麗的；
極好的；了不起的

Marvelous job!

表現很棒！

Remarkable job!

表現出色！

Magnificent job!

表現卓越！

** marvelous（'mɑrvḷəs）*adj.* 令人驚嘆的；
很棒的

job（dʒɑb）*n.* 工作

remarkable（rɪ'mɑrkəbḷ）*adj.* 出色的；
引人注目的

magnificent（mæg'nɪfəsṇt）*adj.* 壯麗的；
很棒的

【Unit 8 背景説明】

Great job! 做得很好！(＝ *You did a great job!*) 也可説成：You did an awesome job!（你做得很棒！）

Good job! 做得好！(＝ *You did a good job!*) 也可説成：You did an amazing job!（你做得很棒！）

Nice job! 做得好！(＝ *You did a nice job!*) 也可説成：You did a fantastic job!（你做得很棒！）

背誦技巧：**S**uper-**S**uperb-**S**plendid 字首都是 S。

Super job! 做得超棒！(＝ *You did a super job!*) 也可説成：You did a fabulous job!（你做得很棒！）

Superb job! 做得太好！(＝ *You did a superb job!*) 也可説成：You did a spectacular job!（你做得很出色！）

Splendid job! 做得太棒！(= *You did a splendid job!*) 也可說成：You did a wonderful job! (你做得很棒！)

背誦技巧：<u>M</u>arvelous-Re<u>m</u>arkable-<u>M</u>agnificent 三個字都有 **m**。

Marvelous job! 表現很棒！(= *You did a marvelous job!*) 也可說成：You did an incredible job! (你做得很棒！)

Remarkable job! 表現出色！(= *You did a remarkable job!*) 也可說成：You did an excellent job! (你做得非常好！) You did an outstanding job! (你做得很傑出！)

Magnificent job! 表現卓越！(= *You did a magnificent job!*) 也可說成：You did a tremendous job! (你做得很棒！) (= *You did a phenomenal job!*)

UNIT 9

Recognize the Contributions of Others 認可別人的貢獻

Fine work!
精湛表現！

Excellent work!
最佳表現！

Exceptional work!
出色表現！

** recognize（'rɛkəg,naɪz）*v.* 承認；認可
contribution（,kɑntrə'bjuʃən）*n.* 貢獻
fine（faɪn）*adj.* 好的　　work（wɜk）*n.* 工作
excellent（'ɛksḷənt）*adj.* 優秀的
exceptional（ɪk'sɛpʃənḷ）*adj.* 卓越的；
　傑出的；不同凡響的

Terrific work!

極好表現！

Spectacular work!

驚人表現！

First-rate work!

一流表現！

** terrific〔təˈrɪfɪk〕*adj.* 令人讚嘆的；極好的；
絕妙的；很棒的

work〔wɜk〕*n.* 工作

spectacular〔spɛkˈtækjələ〕*adj.* 壯觀的；
令人驚嘆的

first-rate〔ˌfɜstˈret〕*adj.* 一流的；最佳的；極好
的；很棒的【rate〔ret〕*n.* 等級（= *grade*）】

Top-class work!

頂尖表現！

Top-notch work!

高端表現！

Top-drawer work!

頂級表現！

** top-class〔'tɑp͵klæs〕*adj.* 第一流的；頂級的
　　【top〔tɑp〕*adj.* 頂端的　　class〔klæs〕*n.* 等級】
work〔wɜk〕*n.* 工作
top-notch〔'tɑp'nɑtʃ〕*adj.* 頂呱呱的；第一流的
　　【notch〔nɑtʃ〕*n.* (V 字形的) 刻痕】
top-drawer〔'tɑp͵drɔr〕*adj.* 最高級的；
　　最重要的【drawer〔drɔr〕*n.* 抽屜】

【Unit 9 背景説明】

Fine work!（表現得很好！）也可説成：You
　did a good job!（你做得很好！）

Excellent work!（表現得很棒！）也可説成：
　You did an excellent job!（你做得很棒！）

Exceptional work!（表現得很出色！）也可説
　成：You did an exceptional job!（你做得很
　傑出！）You did a wonderful job!（你做得
　很棒！）You did a remarkable job!（你做得
　很出色！）

Terrific work!　表現得很棒！（＝*Awesome
　work! ＝ Fantastic work!*）也可説成：You
　did a terrific job!（你做得很棒！）

Spectacular work!（驚人的表現！）也可説成：
　You did a spectacular job!（你做得很棒！）
　（＝*You did an amazing job! ＝ You did a
　fantastic job!*）

BOOK 5・PART 2

First-rate work!（一流表現！）也可說成：
　Unparalleled work!（無與倫比的表現！）
　Outstanding work!（傑出的表現！）
　(= *Exceptional work! = Superior work!*)
　Excellent work!（優秀的表現！）(= *Quality work!*)

Top-class work!（頂級的表現！）也可說成：
　Top-notch work!（一流的表現！）【top notch
　用來比喻某事物的「最高點」】You did a good
　job!（你做得很好！）

Top-drawer work!（最好的表現！）【top drawer
是指「（社會地位的）最上層；最高層；精華」
(= *somebody or something of the highest social
class or of the highest quality*)，源自維多利亞時
代的貴族，通常會將自己的貴重物品，如金銀珠
寶等，放置於臥室抽屜櫃最上層的抽屜中】也可
說成：You did a remarkable job!（你做得很
出色！）

PART 2 總整理

Unit 1

I'm impressed. 你打動了我。
I'm energized. 我充滿能量。
I'm uplifted. 我振奮不已。

I'm inspired. 我受到激勵。
I'm motivated.
我充滿動力。
I'm encouraged.
我受到鼓勵。

I'm enchanted.
真令我著迷。
I'm fascinated.
真讓我著迷。
I'm captivated.
我被吸引了。

Unit 2

Have insight. 要有洞察力。
Have information.
要消息靈通。
Have imagination.
要有想像力。

Have compassion.
有同情心。
Have sympathy.
有憐憫心。
Have empathy. 有同理心。

Have patience.
要有耐心。
Have discipline.
要能自律。
Have determination.
要有決心。

Unit 3

Defeat failure. 戰勝失敗。
Defeat despair. 戰勝絕望。
Defeat setbacks.
戰勝挫折。

Defeat distraction.
不要分心。
Defeat hesitation.
不要猶豫。
Defeat procrastination.
不要拖延。

BOOK 5・PART 2

Defeat negativity. 擊敗負面。
Defeat mediocrity.
擊敗平庸。
Defeat impossibility.
擊敗無望。

Unit 4

Be humble. 要謙虛。
Be honorable. 被敬佩。
Be hospitable. 要好客。

Be invaluable. 要寶貴無價。
Be indispensable.
要不可或缺。
Be impressive. 要令人佩服。

Be solid. 要紮紮實實。
Be stable. 要穩如泰山。
Be straightforward.
要直接了當。

Unit 5

Promote kindness. 提倡善良。
Promote compassion.
提倡同情。
Promote positivity.
提倡正面。

Promote growth.
鼓勵成長。
Promote innovation.
鼓勵創新。
Promote creativity.
鼓勵創意。

Promote unity.
促進團結。
Promote harmony.
促進和諧。
Promote cooperation.
促進合作。

Unit 6

Advocate prosperity.
提倡富強。
Advocate democracy.
提倡民主。
Advocate dedication.
提倡敬業。

Advocate integrity.
提倡誠信。
Advocate civility.
提倡文明。
Advocate equality.
提倡平等。

Advocate freedom.
提倡自由。
Advocate justice.
提倡公正。
Advocate patriotism.
提倡愛國。

Unit 7

I'm sorry.　我很抱歉。
I apologize.　我要道歉。
I'm regretful.　我很後悔。

Truly sorry.　真的抱歉。
Terribly sorry.　非常抱歉。
Wholeheartedly sorry.
由衷抱歉。

I'm downhearted.
我沮喪。
I'm brokenhearted.
我傷心。
I'm heartbroken.　我心碎。

Unit 8

Great job!　做得好！
Good job!　幹得好！
Nice job!　做得棒！

Super job!　做得超棒！
Superb job!　做得太好！
Splendid job!　做得太棒！

Marvelous job!　表現很棒！
Remarkable job!
表現出色！
Magnificent job!
表現卓越！

Unit 9

Fine work!　精湛表現！
Excellent work!
最佳表現！
Exceptional work!
出色表現！

Terrific work!　極好表現！
Spectacular work!
驚人表現！
First-rate work!　一流表現！

Top-class work!
頂尖表現！
Top-notch work!
高端表現！
Top-drawer work!
頂級表現！

BOOK 5 · PART 2

BOOK 5 PART 3

Short Phrases for a Good Life
幸福人生的簡短語錄

PART 3・Unit 1~9
英文錄音QR碼

UNIT 1

The Best Personality (I)
最好的個性 **(I)**

Be honest.
要誠實。

Be humorous.
要幽默。

Be generous.
要慷慨。。

** personality〔͵pɝsn̩ˋælətɪ〕*n.* 個性
honest〔ˋɑnɪst〕*adj.* 誠實的
humorous〔ˋhjumərəs〕*adj.* 幽默的
generous〔ˋdʒɛnərəs〕*adj.* 慷慨的；大方的

Be easy.

要輕鬆。

Be energetic.

有活力。

Be cheerful.

要開朗。

** easy〔'izɪ〕*adj.* 容易的；輕鬆的；自在的
   energetic〔,ɛnɚ'dʒɛtɪk〕*adj.* 充滿活力的
   cheerful〔'tʃɪrfəl〕*adj.* 高興的；愉快的

Be diligent.

要勤奮。

Be intelligent.

要聰明。

Be trustworthy.

被信任。

** diligent (ˈdɪlədʒənt) *adj.* 勤勉的
   intelligent (ɪnˈtɛlədʒənt) *adj.* 聰明的
   trustworthy (ˈtrʌst͵wɝðɪ) *adj.* 值得信任的

【Unit 1 背景説明】

這三個是擁有幸福人生最重要的個性。要誠實
才可靠；要幽默，別人才願意跟你在一起；
要慷慨，才交得到朋友。

Be honest.（要誠實。）也可説成：Be
truthful.（要說實話。）Don't tell lies.（不要
說謊。）

Be humorous.（要幽默。）也可説成：Be
funny.（要好笑。）Be witty.（要詼諧。）Be
amusing.（要有趣。）(= *Be entertaining.*）

Be generous.（要慷慨。）也可説成：Be
giving.（要慷慨大方。）Be charitable.（要慈
善。）(= *Be benevolent.*）Be kind.（要善良。）

人一定要有輕鬆的個性，不要緊張；要心胸寬
大、精力充沛，每天高高興興的，個性開朗，
才能讓人喜歡。

Be easy.　要輕鬆。(= *Be relaxed.*）也可説成：
Be carefree.（要無憂無慮。）Be friendly.
（要友善。）Be peaceful.（要平靜。）

BOOK 5・PART 3

Be energetic.（要充滿活力。）也可說成：Be lively.（要活潑。）Be enthusiastic.（要充滿熱忱。）Be spirited.（要有精神。）

Be cheerful.　要愉快。（＝ *Be happy.* ＝ *Be merry.* ＝ *Be jolly.*）也可說成：Be upbeat.（要樂觀。）

勤奮、聰明、而且值得別人信任，就會無往不利。

Be diligent.　要勤勉。（＝ *Be industrious.*）也可說成：Be dedicated.（要盡心盡力。）Be painstaking.（要辛勤。）Be conscientious.（要負責盡職。）

Be intelligent.　要聰明。（＝ *Be smart.* ＝ *Be clever.* ＝ *Be brilliant.* ＝ *Be bright.*）

Be trustworthy.（要值得信任。）也可說成：Be reliable.（要可靠。）（＝ *Be dependable.*）Be honorable.（要值得敬佩。）Be ethical.（要有道德。）Be responsible.（要負責任。）

UNIT 2

The Best Personality (II)
最好的個性 **(II)**

Be friendly.
要友善。

Be funny.
要有趣。

Be active.
要活躍。

** personality〔͵pɝsṇˋælətɪ〕*n.* 個性
friendly〔ˋfrɛndlɪ〕*adj.* 友善的
funny〔ˋfʌnɪ〕*adj.* 風趣的；好笑的
active〔ˋæktɪv〕*adj.* 活躍的；主動的；積極的

Be moral.

有道德。

Be modest.

要謙虛。

Be polite.

有禮貌。

** moral〔'mɔrəl〕*adj.* 道德的;有道德的;
品性端正的

modest〔'mɑdɪst〕*adj.* 謙虛的

polite〔pə'laɪt〕*adj.* 有禮貌的

Be true.

要眞實。

Be sensitive.

要體貼。

Be compassionate.

要同情。

** true〔tru〕*adj.* 眞的；眞實的；忠實的
sensitive〔'sɛnsətɪv〕*adj.* 敏感的；體貼的
compassionate〔kəm'pæʃənɪt〕*adj.*
　有同情心的

【**Unit 2 背景説明**】

對人要友善，要好笑、風趣，而且活躍；誰都
不願意跟一個整天垮著臉的人在一起。

Be friendly.（要友善。）也可説成：Be
amiable.（要和藹可親。）Be cordial.（要熱
心。）(= *Be warm.*)

Be funny.（要風趣。）也可説成：Be amusing.
（要有趣。）Be humorous.（要幽默。）

Be active.（要活躍。）也可説成：Be
energetic.（要充滿活力。）Be lively.（要活
潑。）Be spirited.（要有精神。）

有道德、品性端正、謙虛，而且有禮貌，這些
都是很好的個性。

Be moral.（要有道德。）也可説成：Be good.
（要做個好人。）Be honest.（要誠實。）Be
righteous.（要正直。）Be honorable.（要令
人敬佩。）Be principled.（要有原則。）

Be modest. 要謙虛。(= *Be humble.* = *Be unassuming.*) 也可說成：Be unpretentious. (要樸實無華。)

Be polite. 要有禮貌。(= *Be courteous.* = *Be gracious.* = *Be civil.*) 也可說成：Be respectful. (要恭敬。)

要做一個真實、體貼，富有同情心的人；不要做一個虛假無情的人。

Be true. 要真實。(= *Be genuine.* = *Be real.*) 也可說成：Be sincere. (要真誠。) Be loyal. (要忠誠。) Be faithful. (要忠實。) Be reliable. (要可靠。)

Be sensitive. 要敏感；要體貼。(= *Be thoughtful.* = *Be considerate.*) 也可說成：Be understanding. (要能體諒別人。)

Be compassionate. 要有同情心。(= *Be sympathetic.*) 也可說成：Be kind. (要善良。) Be understanding. (要體諒別人。) Be caring. (要關心別人。) (= *Be concerned.*)

UNIT 3

Don't Show Weakness
不要示弱

Be tough.
要耐操。

Be strong.
要強大。

Be durable.
有耐力。

** show〔ʃo〕*v.* 顯示
weakness〔'wiknɪs〕*n.* 虛弱;軟弱
tough〔tʌf〕*adj.* 堅強的;堅定的;強硬的
strong〔strɔŋ〕*adj.* 強壯的;意志堅定的
durable〔'djʊrəbḷ〕*adj.* 持久的;耐久的;耐用的

Be dogged.

要執著。

Be rugged.

要堅韌。

Be resilient.

有韌性。

** dogged〔'dɔgɪd〕*adj.* 頑強的；執著的
rugged〔'rʌgɪd〕*adj.* 崎嶇不平的；強健的；
　　能吃苦耐勞的
resilient〔rɪ'zɪlɪənt〕*adj.* 適應力強的；
　　有韌性的

Be firm.

要堅定。

Be resolute.

要堅決。

Be determined.

有決心。

** firm〔fɜm〕*adj.* 堅定的；堅決的

　　resolute〔'rɛzə,lut〕*adj.* 堅決的

　　determined〔dɪ'tɜmɪnd〕*adj.* 堅決的；

　　　　下定決心的

【Unit 3 背景説明】

Be tough.（要強悍；要耐操。）也可説成：Be hardy.（要能吃苦耐勞。）Be resilient.（要有韌性。）Be unyielding.（絕不屈服。）

Be strong.（要強壯；要堅強。）也可説成：Be fit.（要健康。）Be forceful.（要有力量。）Be firm.（要堅定。）Be determined.（要堅決。）

Be durable.（要有耐力。）也可説成：Be reliable.（要可靠。）Be sound.（要健全。）Be indestructible.（要堅不可摧。）Be true.（要忠實。）(= *Be faithful*.）

Be dogged.（要執著。）也可説成：Be committed.（要全心投入。）Be dedicated.（要盡心盡力。）Be unyielding.（絕不屈服。）Be unrelenting.（絕不鬆懈。）

Be rugged. 要強健；要能吃苦耐勞。(= *Be sturdy*.）也可説成：Be tough.（要強悍；

要耐操。) Be robust. (要健壯。) Be solid.
(要結實。)

Be resilient. (要有韌性。) 也可說成：Be
tough. (要強悍；要耐操。) Be hardy. (要
能吃苦耐勞。) Be headstrong. (要頑強。)

Be firm. 要堅定。(= *Be steadfast.*)

Be resolute. 要堅決。(= *Be resolved.*) 也可
說成：Be inflexible. (要不屈不撓。)

Be determined. 要堅決；要
下定決心。(= *Be resolute.*)
也可說成：Get determined.
(要下定決心。)【參照 p.233】

UNIT 4

Treasure Good Traits
珍惜好的特質

Appreciate friendship.
重視友誼。

Appreciate support.
重視支持。

Appreciate teamwork.
重視團隊。

** treasure〔ˋtrɛʒɚ〕 *v.* 珍惜　　trait〔tret〕 *n.* 特質
appreciate〔əˋpriʃɪˌet〕 *v.* 重視；欣賞；感激
friendship〔ˋfrɛndʃɪp〕 *n.* 友誼
support〔səˋport〕 *n.* 支持
teamwork〔ˋtimˌwɝk〕 *n.* 團隊合作

BOOK 5 · PART 3

Value loyalty.

重視忠誠。

Value simplicity.

重視簡樸。

Value generosity.

重視慷慨。

** value〔'væljʊ〕*v.* 重視
loyalty〔'lɔɪəltɪ〕*n.* 忠誠
simplicity〔sɪm'plɪsətɪ〕*n.* 簡單；
　樸素；單純
generosity〔ˌdʒɛnə'rɑsətɪ〕*n.*
　慷慨；大方

Value moderation.

重視中庸。

Value innovation.

重視創新。

Value collaboration.

重視合作。

** value 〔'væljʊ〕 v. 重視
moderation 〔ˌmɑdə'reʃən〕 n. 適度；適中
innovation 〔ˌɪnə'veʃən〕 n. 創新
collaboration 〔kəˌlæbə'reʃən〕 n. 合作
(= cooperation)

【Unit 4 背景説明】

Appreciate friendship. 重視友誼。(= *Value friendship*.) 也可説成：Be grateful for your friends.（要因為你的朋友而心存感激。）

Appreciate support. 重視支持。(= *Value support*.) 也可説成：Value assistance.（重視協助。）Value encouragement.（重視鼓勵。）

Appreciate teamwork. 重視團隊合作。(= *Value teamwork*.)

背誦技巧：loyal<u>ty</u>-simplici<u>ty</u>-generosi<u>ty</u> 字尾都是 ty。

Value loyalty. 重視忠誠。(= *Value fidelity*.) 也可説成：Treasure loyalty.（珍惜忠誠。）Recognize the importance of loyalty.（要知道忠誠的重要。）

Value simplicity.（重視簡單。）也可説成：Treasure minimalism.（珍惜極簡。）Recognize the importance of unpretentiousness.（要知道樸實無華的重要。）

Value generosity.（重視慷慨。）也可說成：
Value charity.（重視慈善。）Treasure
benevolence.（珍惜慈善。）Recognize the
importance of kindness.（要知道善良的重
要。）

背誦技巧：moder**ation**-innov**ation**-
collabor**ation** 字尾都是 **ation**。

Value moderation.（重視中庸。）也可說成：
Treasure balance.（珍惜均衡。）Recognize
the importance of restraint.（要知道節制的
重要。）

Value innovation.（重視創新。）也可說成：
Treasure creativity.（珍惜創意。）Recognize
the importance of originality.（要知道創意的
重要。）

Value collaboration.（重視合作。）也可說
成：Treasure cooperation.（珍惜合作。）
Recognize the importance of teamwork.
（要知道團隊合作的重要。）

UNIT 5

Compliment Good Work
讚美良好表現

Well said.
說得出色。

Well put.
言之有物。

Well spoken.
說得精彩。

** compliment〔ˈkɑmpləˌmɛnt〕*v.* 稱讚
　　這三句話句首都省略了 That was。
　　well〔wɛl〕*adv.* 良好地　　say〔se〕*v.* 說
　　put〔pʊt〕*v.* 放；說　　speak〔spik〕*v.* 說

Well written.

寫得眞好。

Well stated.

陳述得好。

Well composed.

寫得很好。

** 這三句話句首都省略了 That was。

well〔wɛl〕*adv.* 良好地

write〔raɪt〕*v.* 寫

state〔stet〕*v.* 敘述

compose〔kəm'poz〕*v.* 組成；作（文）；

作（曲）

Achieved well.

成功達成。

Accomplished well.

圓滿完成。

Completed well.

順利完成。

** 這三句話句首都省略了 That was。

achieve〔əˈtʃiv〕*v.* 達成

well〔wɛl〕*adv.* 良好地

accomplish〔əˈkɑmplɪʃ〕*v.* 完成

complete〔kəmˈplit〕*v.* 完成

【**Unit 5 背景說明**】

Well said. 說得好。(= *That was well said.*)
也可說成：You're very articulate. (你很
會說話。)

Well put. 說得好。(= *That was well put.*) 也
可說成：You're very expressive. (你很會
表達。)

Well spoken. 說得好。(= *That was well
spoken.*) 也可說成：You're well-spoken.
(你很會說話。) You're eloquent. (你的
口才很好。)

Well written. 寫得很好。(= *That was well
written.*) 也可說成：The writing is
excellent. (寫得很好。) (= *That is an
excellent piece of writing.*)

Well stated. 敘述得很好。(= *That was well
stated.*)

Well composed. 文章寫得很好。(= *That was well composed.*) 也可說成：That was composed in a very eloquent way. (文章寫得非常動人。) That was composed in a very polished way. (文章寫得非常優美。)

Achieved well. 成功達成。(= *That was achieved well.*) 也可說成：Well done. (做得好。)

Accomplished well. 圓滿完成。(= *That was accomplished well.*)

Completed well. 順利完成。(= *That was completed well.*) 也可說成：That was very well done. (做得非常好。)

UNIT 6

Guard Your Health
守護你的健康

Value health.
重視健康。

Embrace health.
擁抱健康。

Treasure health.
珍惜健康。

** guard〔gɑrd〕v. 看守;守護
health〔hɛlθ〕n. 健康　　value〔'væljʊ〕v. 重視
embrace〔ɪm'bres〕v. 擁抱;欣然接受;利用
treasure〔'trɛʒɚ〕v. 珍惜;珍愛;珍藏　　n. 寶藏

Foster health.

促進健康。

Sustain health.

保持健康。

Prioritize health.

健康第一。

** foster〔'fɔstə, 'fɑstə〕*v.* 培養；促進
health〔hɛlθ〕*n.* 健康
sustain〔sə'sten〕*v.* 維持
prioritize〔praɪ'ɔrə,taɪz〕*v.* 給予…優先權；
　優先考慮

Health counts.
健康重要。

Health empowers.
健康給力。

Health rejuvenates.
返老還童。

** health〔hɛlθ〕*n.* 健康

count〔kaʊnt〕*v.* 重要（= *matter*）

empower〔ɪmˈpaʊɚ〕*v.* 給與力量；授權

rejuvenate〔rɪˈdʒuvəˌnet〕*v.* 使恢復活力；
使返老還童

【**Unit 6 背景説明**】

Value health.（重視健康。）也可説成：Value your health.（重視你的健康。）Take care of your health.（照顧你的健康。）

Embrace health. 擁抱健康；利用你的健康。（= *Take advantage of your good health*.）也可説成：Live a healthy lifestyle.（要有健康的生活方式。）

Treasure health. 珍惜健康。（= *Cherish health*.）也可説成：Treasure your health.（珍惜你的健康。）（= *Cherish your health*.）Appreciate good health.（要重視良好的健康。）Don't take your health for granted.（不要把你的健康視爲理所當然。）

Foster health. 促進健康。（= *Promote health*.）也可説成：Nurture your health.（促進你的健康。）Improve your health.（改善你的健康。）（= *Build up your health*.）Live a healthy lifestyle.（要有健康的生活方式。）

Sustain health.（維持健康。）也可説成：Stay in good health.（保持良好的健康。）Support

good health. （維護健康。） Take care of
your health. （照顧你的健康。）

Prioritize health. （優先考慮健康。）也可説
成：Make health a priority. （要把健康放在第
一位。） Make health important. （要重視健
康。） Focus on your health. （要專注於你的
健康。）（ = *Concentrate on your health.* ）

Health counts. 健康重要。（ = *Health matters.* ）
也可説成：Good health is important. （良好
的健康很重要。）

Health empowers. （健康給人力量。）也可説
成：Health enables you to do what you want.
（健康使你能做你想做的事。） Good health
gives you the ability to do what you want.
（良好的健康使你有能力去做你想做的事。）

Health rejuvenates. （健康使人恢復活力。）也
可説成：Good health gives you energy. （良
好的健康使人有活力。）（ = *Good health will
energize you.* ） Good health will perk you up.
（良好的健康能使你振作精神。）
（ = *Good health will give you a boost.* ）

UNIT 7

Celebrate Others 讚頌別人

Truly awesome!
真是太棒！

Simply awesome!
簡直太棒！

Incredibly awesome!
難得的棒！

** celebrate〔ˈsɛləˌbret〕*v.* 慶祝；讚頌

truly〔ˈtrulɪ〕*adv.* 真地

awesome〔ˈɔsəm〕*adj.* 令人驚嘆的；很棒的
(= *wonderful*)

simply〔ˈsɪmplɪ〕*adv.* 完全地；非常；實在；的確

incredibly〔ɪnˈkrɛdəblɪ〕*adv.* 難以置信地；很；
極度；極其

Awesome friendship!

很棒的友誼！

Awesome connection!

很棒的人脈！

Awesome harmony!

很棒的和諧！

** awesome〔ˋɔsəm〕*adj.* 令人驚嘆的；很棒的
friendship〔ˋfrɛndʃɪp〕*n.* 友誼
connection〔kəˋnɛkʃən〕*n.* 關連；關係
harmony〔ˋhɑrmənɪ〕*n.* 和諧

Awesome surprise!
很棒的驚喜！

Awesome moment!
很棒的時刻！

Awesome achievement!
很棒的成就！

** awesome〔ˈɔsəm〕*adj.* 令人驚嘆的；很棒的
   surprise〔səˈpraɪz〕*n.* 驚訝；令人驚訝的事
   moment〔ˈmomənt〕*n.* 時刻
   achievement〔əˈtʃivmənt〕*n.* 成就

【**Unit 7 背景說明**】

Truly awesome! （眞的很棒！）也可說成：
  Really magnificent! （非常出色！）
  Truly tremendous! （眞了不起！）

Simply awesome! （實在很棒！）也可說成：
  So outstanding! （非常傑出！）

Incredibly awesome! （難得的棒！）也可說
  成：Just incredible! （眞是令人難以置信！）
  Simply amazing! （眞是太棒了！）

Awesome friendship! 很棒的友誼！
  （= *Fantastic friendship!* ）也可說成：
  What a great friendship! （多麼棒的友誼！）

Awesome connection! 很棒的關係！（= *What
  a great contact!* = *What a great relationship!* ）

Awesome harmony! 很棒的和諧！（= *What
  wonderful harmony!* ）

Awesome surprise! 很棒的驚喜！（ = *Terrific surprise!*）也可說成：That was a great surprise!（那是很棒的驚喜！）

Awesome moment!（很棒的時刻！）也可說成：That was a wonderful time!（那真是很棒的時刻！）What a wonderful occasion!（多麼棒的場合！）（ = *What a wonderful event!*）What a wonderful opportunity!（多麼棒的機會！）

Awesome achievement! 很棒的成就！（ = *Amazing achievement!*）也可說成：What a great achievement!（多麼偉大的成就！）Remarkable feat!（出色的豐功偉業！）Remarkable job!（做得很出色！）

UNIT 8

Kindness Matters 善良重要

Embrace kindness.

擁抱善良。

Cherish kindness.

珍惜善良。

Value kindness.

重視善良。

** kindness〔'kaɪndnɪs〕*n.* 仁慈；善良；善意；
好意　　matter〔'mætɚ〕*v.* 重要
embrace〔ɪm'bres〕*v.* 擁抱；欣然接受
cherish〔'tʃɛrɪʃ〕*v.* 珍惜
value〔'væljʊ〕*v.* 重視

Create kindness.

創造善良。

Foster kindness.

培養善良。

Show kindness.

展現善良。

** create〔krɪˋet〕v. 創造

kindness〔ˋkaɪndnɪs〕n. 仁慈；
善良；善意；好意

foster〔ˋfɔstɚ, ˋfastɚ〕v. 培養

show〔ʃo〕v. 展現；表現

Give kindness.

給與善意。

Share kindness.

分享善意。

Spread kindness.

傳播善意。

** give〔gɪv〕v. 給與；付出

kindness〔'kaɪndnɪs〕n. 仁慈；善良；
　善意；好意

share〔ʃɛr〕v. 分享

spread〔sprɛd〕v. 散播

【**Unit 8 背景説明**】

Embrace kindness. 擁抱善良；欣然接受善意。
（＝*Accept kindness.*）也可説成：Recognize
the importance of kindness.（知道善良的重
要。）

Cherish kindness. 珍惜善良。（＝*Treasure
kindness.*）也可説成：*Value kindness.*（重
視善良。）（＝*Appreciate kindness.*）

Create kindness.（創造善良。）也可説成：
Promote kindness.（鼓勵善良。）

Foster kindness. 培養善良。（＝*Nurture
kindness.*）也可説成：Encourage kindness.
（鼓勵善良。）Support kindness.（支持善良。）

Show kindness. 展現善良。（＝*Exhibit
kindness.* ＝*Display kindness.* ＝*Demonstrate
kindness.*）

Give kindness.（付出善意。）也可説成：*Share
kindness.*（分享善意。）Be kind.（要善良。）

Spread kindness.（散播善意。）也可説成：
Encourage kindness.（鼓勵善良。）

BOOK 5・PART 3

UNIT 9

Develop Good Qualities

培養良好的特質

Have soul.

要有靈魂。

Have strength.

要有力量。

Have substance.

要有內涵。

** develop〔dɪˋvɛləp〕*v.* 培養

quality〔ˋkwɑlətɪ〕*n.* 特質　　soul〔sol〕*n.* 靈魂

strength〔strɛŋθ〕*n.* 力量

substance〔ˋsʌbstəns〕*n.* 物質；實質；內容

Have passion.

要有熱情。

Have vision.

要有遠見。

Have persistence.

要能堅持。

** passion〔'pæʃən〕*n.* 熱情；愛好
vision〔'vɪʒən〕*n.* 眼光；遠見；眼力
persistence〔pə'sɪstəns〕*n.* 堅持

Have gratitude.
要能感恩。

Have laughter.
要有笑容。

Have acceptance.
要能包容。

** gratitude〔'grætə͵tjud〕*n.* 感激
laughter〔'læftɚ〕*n.* 笑；笑聲
acceptance〔ək'sɛptəns〕*n.* 接受；接納

【Unit 9 背景説明】

Have soul.（要有靈魂。）也可説成：Have spirit.（要有精神。）（= *Be spirited.*）

Have strength.（要有力量。）也可説成：Be strong.（要強壯。）Be determined.（要有決心。）（= *Be resolute.*）

Have substance.（要有實質的內容；要有料；要有實質的內涵。）也可説成：Be honest.（要誠實。）Be intelligent.（要聰明。）Have integrity.（要正直。）Be a person of good character.（要有好的性格。）

Have passion.（要有熱情。）也可説成：Have enthusiasm.（要有熱忱。）（= *Be enthusiastic.*）

Have vision. 要有遠見。（= *Have foresight.*）也可説成：Have a dream.（要有夢想。）Be creative.（要有創造力。）（= *Be inventive.* = *Be original.*）Be imaginative.（要有想像力。）

Have persistence. 要能堅持。(= *Be persistent.*) 也可說成：Be determined. (要下定決心。) Don't give up. (不要放棄。)

Have gratitude. (要能感恩。) 也可說成：Be grateful. (要感激。) Be thankful. (要感謝。)

Have laughter. (要有笑容。) 也可說成：Be joyful. (要快樂。) Have a good sense of humor. (要有良好的幽默感。)

Have acceptance. (要能接納；要有包容心。) 也可說成：Be accepting. (要能包容。) Be tolerant. (要寬容。)

PART 3 總整理

Unit 1

Be honest. 要誠實。
Be humorous. 要幽默。
Be generous. 要慷慨。

Be easy. 要輕鬆。
Be energetic. 有活力。
Be cheerful. 要開朗。

Be diligent. 要勤奮。
Be intelligent. 要聰明。
Be trustworthy. 被信任。

Unit 2

Be friendly. 要友善。
Be funny. 要有趣。
Be active. 要活躍。

Be moral. 有道德。
Be modest. 要謙虛。
Be polite. 有禮貌。

Be true. 要真實。
Be sensitive. 要體貼。
Be compassionate. 要同情。

Unit 3

Be tough. 要耐操。
Be strong. 要強大。
Be durable.
有耐力。

Be dogged. 要執著。
Be rugged. 要堅韌。
Bc resilient.
有韌性。

Be firm. 要堅定。
Be resolute. 要堅決。
Be determined.
有決心。

Unit 4

Appreciate friendship.
重視友誼。
Appreciate support.
重視支持。
Appreciate teamwork.
重視團隊。

BOOK 5・PART 3

Value loyalty. 重視忠誠。
Value simplicity.
重視簡樸。
Value generosity.
重視慷慨。

Value moderation.
重視中庸。
Value innovation.
重視創新。
Value collaboration.
重視合作。

Unit 5

Well said. 說得出色。
Well put. 言之有物。
Well spoken. 說得精彩。

Well written. 寫得真好。
Well stated. 陳述得好。
Well composed. 寫得很好。

Achieved well. 成功達成。
Accomplished well.
圓滿完成。
Completed well.
順利完成。

Unit 6

Value health. 重視健康。
Embrace health.
擁抱健康。
Treasure health.
珍惜健康。

Foster health. 促進健康。
Sustain health. 保持健康。
Prioritize health.
健康第一。

Health counts.
健康重要。
Health empowers.
健康給力。
Health rejuvenates.
返老還童。

Unit 7

Truly awesome!
真是太棒！
Simply awesome!
簡直太棒！
Incredibly awesome!
難得的棒！

Awesome friendship!
很棒的友誼！
Awesome connection!
很棒的人脈！
Awesome harmony!
很棒的和諧！

Awesome surprise!
很棒的驚喜！
Awesome moment!
很棒的時刻！
Awesome achievement!
很棒的成就！

Unit 8

Embrace kindness.
擁抱善良。
Cherish kindness.
珍惜善良。
Value kindness.
重視善良。

Create kindness.
創造善良。
Foster kindness.
培養善良。
Show kindness.
展現善良。

Give kindness.
給與善意。
Share kindness.
分享善意。
Spread kindness.
傳播善意。

Unit 9

Have soul.　要有靈魂。
Have strength.
要有力量。
Have substance.
要有內涵。

Have passion.
要有熱情。
Have vision.
要有遠見。
Have persistence.
要能堅持。

Have gratitude.
要能感恩。
Have laughter.
要有笑容。
Have acceptance.
要能包容。

附　錄 ▶▶

劉毅老師回覆粉絲留言，運用「完美英語」回答，學了要使用才不會忘記

【用「完美英語」寫文章①】

You're too good to be true. Unbeatable!
Unstoppable! Victorious! You're so kind.
Kindness empowers. Kindness is powerful. Be
kind to everyone, even to rotten people. Kill them
with kindness and silence. Your success is the best
revenge. You are our sunshine. Spread sunshine
everywhere. Spread kindness everywhere.
Remember. Don't forget. Kindness pays.
Kindness pays off. Kindness rewards. Kindness
is rewarding. Kindness returns. If you're kind,
you'll receive kindness in return. Your kindness
shines. Your kindness radiates. Your kindness
enlightens. Show kindness daily. Show kindness
freely. Practice kindness sincerely. Kindness
costs nothing, but means everything. Let your
light shine. Your light inspires others. Shine like

a star. Shine through life's storms. Shine through every challenge. You make me very proud. Stay firm. Stay strong. Stay the course. Keep sharing your kindness, love, and light with the world. Keep interacting with me. Let's connect. Let's build up our English network. Let's strengthen our language family.

　　你太好了，不像是眞的。所向無敵！無人可擋！獲得勝利！你人眞好。善良給人力量。善良很有力量。要對每個人好，甚至也對壞人好。用善良和沈默征服他們。你的成功就是最好的報復。你是我們的陽光。要到處散播陽光。要到處散播善意。要記得。不要忘記。善良很值得。善良划得來。善良會有報酬。善良有收穫。善良有回報。如果你善良，就會獲得善良作爲回報。你的善良會發光發亮。你的善良會散發光芒。你的善良能給人啓發。每天都要展現善良。要慷慨地展現善良。要眞的很善良。善良不花一毛錢，但卻意義重大。讓你的光芒閃耀。你的光能激勵別人。要像星星一樣閃亮。要閃耀度過人生的風雨。要閃耀度過每個挑戰。你讓我非常驕傲。保持堅定。保持堅強。堅持到底。持續和全世界分享你的善良、眞愛，和光芒。要持續和我互動。讓我們建立良好的關係。讓我們建立我們的英語網路。讓我們強化我們的語言家族。

【用「完美英語」寫文章②】

Let's speak English. Speak English like crazy. Write English like hell. Interact with us in English like there's no tomorrow. Learn by using English. Writing comments is cool. It's heart-to-heart communication. It's truly "give and take." Show up on our site. Be sure to check in. Be there or be square. Keep writing and interacting. Be diligent and follow me. With hard work and our methods, you'll win. You're not just learning English. You can also meet like-minded people. Make new friends every day. You'll be addicted to writing English comments. Day by day, you improve. Week after week, you progress. Before you know it, your English is great. Besides, Rambo's Champion English site can be your spiritual home. We're a global network. We have friends from the four corners of the world. Keep good company. Hang around with quality people. Have good friendships. Have meaningful relationships. With so many like-minded friends, you will never be

lonely. Friends are invaluable. Friends over wealth.
Friends make life more beautiful. Let's love life.
Enjoy life. Cherish life. Embrace life. Savor
every moment. Live fully. Live passionately.
Live wholeheartedly.

　　我們說英文吧。要拼命地說英文。要拼命地寫英
文。要拼命地用英文和我們互動。藉由使用英文來學
習。寫留言很酷。那是心對心的溝通。那真的是「思想
交流」。要在我們的網站上出現。一定要來報到。我們
不見不散。要持續留言和互動。要勤勉並跟隨我的腳
步。只要努力並使用我們的方法，你就會成功。你不只
是在學習英文。你也可以認識志同道合的人。每天結交
新朋友。你會對用英文留言上癮。你會一天一天地進
步。你會一週一週地進步。很快地，你的英文就會變得
很好。此外，Rambo 的「冠軍英語」網站，能夠成為你
心靈的歸宿。我們是個全球網路。我們有來自世界各地
的朋友。要結交益友。要和優質的人來往。要有好的友
誼。要有有意義的關係。有這麼多志同道合的朋友，你
絕不會寂寞。朋友非常珍貴。朋友重於財富。朋友使人
生更美好。我們要熱愛生活。享受生活。珍惜生活。擁
抱生活。品味每個時刻。要充實地生活。要熱情地生活。
要全心全意地過生活。

【用「完美英語」寫文章③】

You're a true talent. You're a genuine genius. I can't praise you enough. You're awesome. You're my pride and joy. I couldn't be more proud of you. Endless thanks. Limitless thanks. Abundant thanks. Let's seek joy. Seek growth. Seek blessings. Let's choose love. Choose kindness. Choose peace. Take life easy. Keep it simple. Don't overthink it. Life is good. Life is awesome. Love your life. Sing out loud. Smell the roses. Laugh to exhaustion. Laugh out loud. Laughter is medicine. You'll live longer. You're stunning both inside and out. You're both diligent and intelligent. You're a person of action. You act swiftly and kindly. You dream boldly, daringly, and fearlessly. You learn actively, proactively, and quickly. I thank God. I praise the Lord. We are so fortunate to have you as a friend. You're a godsend. You made a big difference. You really helped so much. It's all thanks to you. You have what it takes.

I believe in you. Win! Be the winner. Come out
on top! Make it big! Hit it big! Make big bucks.
Let's make a move. Make history. Make life
amazing!

　　你真的很有才華。你真的是個天才。我再怎麼稱讚
你都不夠。你很棒。你是我的驕傲和快樂。我非常以你
為榮。無盡感謝。無限感謝。萬分感謝。我們要追求快
樂。追求成長。追求幸福。我們要選擇愛。選擇善良。
選擇和平。輕鬆過生活。保持簡單。勿想太多。人生很
好。人生很棒。要愛你的生活。要大聲歌唱。要享受人
生。要笑至疲憊。要放聲大笑。笑是良藥。你會活得更
久。你內外都很棒。你既勤勉又聰明。你是行動家。你
動作快，而且舉止善良。你會大膽、勇敢，毫無畏懼地
做夢。你會積極、主動，而且快速地學習。我感謝上帝。
我讚美主。我們非常幸運，能有你這位朋友。你是天賜
之物。你產生巨大的影響。你真的幫忙很多。這一切全
都要歸功於你。你擁有必須具備的能力。我相信你。一
定要贏！要成為贏家。要出人頭地！要飛黃騰達！要一
炮而紅！要賺大錢。我們開始行動吧。要創造歷史。精
彩人生！

【用「完美英語」寫文章④】

Dream big. Dream bigger. Have a big dream. Do your best. Become the best. Be the best you can be. Improve! Advance! Onward and upward. Dream big dreams. Reach for the stars. The sky is your limit. I'm glad you found your purpose. Dream with a goal. Spread your wings. Chase your dreams wholeheartedly. Remember and never forget. Failure is inevitable. Expect to fail. Be willing to fail. Fail fast. Fail often. Fail forward. Failure isn't fatal. Failure breeds success. Enjoy the process. Enjoy every step. Process over outcome. You're moving up. You have a bright future. Big things will happen. You're on the way. You're going to be amazing. You light up my life. You energize me. You complete me. With you, life is more beautiful and meaningful. I'm forever grateful. You're much appreciated.

　　夢想要大。夢要很大。要有遠大的夢想。要盡全力。成為最好的。成為最好的自己。要改進！要進步！要向上提升。要有遠大的夢想。要設定不易達成的目標。你的潛力無限大。我很高興你找到你的目標。要和目標同做夢。展翅高飛。全心全意追求你的夢想。要記得，絕對不要忘記。失敗是無可避免的。要期待失敗。要願意失敗。快點失敗。常常失敗。失敗為前進之母。失敗不會死。失敗能造就成功。要享受過程。享受每一步。過程比結果重要。你正在向上提升。你有光明的未來。有大事會發生。你正在途中。你會變得很棒。你照亮我的人生。你使我充滿活力。你使我的生命更完整。有了你，人生更美好，而且更有意義。我永遠感激。非常感激你。

【用「完美英語」寫文章⑤】

Life is short. Time flies fast. Life is too short to waste. You only live once. Let's enjoy life. Savor life. Cherish life. Make every day count. Do as much as you can. Live gracefully. Live generously. Live wholeheartedly. Be kind daily. Be kind always. Help others out. Share your abundance. Share your blessings. Assist with generosity. Offer kind words. Make kind gestures. Ignore the insults. Don't take action. Turn the other cheek. Kill them with kindness. Spread good vibes. Kindness wins. Kindness conquers all.

Then, take a trip. Take a journey. Travel somewhere new. Join a tour. Explore other cultures. See unusual places. Open your mind. Expand your worldview. Create priceless memories. Find beauty everywhere. Enjoy good things. Most importantly, remember to relax. Recharge your batteries. Reset your mind. Health comes first.

Health over wealth. Don't burn the candle at both
ends. Don't stay up late. Don't burn the midnight
oil. Early to bed and early to rise makes a man
healthy, wealthy, and wise. Fingers crossed. Have
a great day. Break a leg!

　　人生很短暫。時光飛逝。生命太短，不能浪費。人
只能活一次。我們要享受人生。品味人生。珍惜生命。
要讓每一天都有價值。儘量多做一點。要優雅生活。要
慷慨生活。要全心全意地活。天天善良。時時善良。幫
助別人。分享你的財富。分享你的幸福。慷慨助他人。
要說好話。做善意舉動。別理會侮辱。不要採取行動。
不要還手。要好得讓他們受不了。散播正能量。善良獲
勝。善良征服一切。

　　然後，要出去旅行。展開旅程。去沒去過的地方。
參加旅行團。探索其他的文化。去看不尋常的地方。打
開眼界。拓展你的世界觀。創造無價的回憶。到處尋找
美好的事物。享受美好的的事物。最重要的是，要記得
放鬆。讓自己充電。重置思維。健康第一。健康勝過財
富。不要過分透支體力。不要熬夜到很晚。不要開夜車。
早睡早起使人健康，有錢，又聰明。祝你幸運。祝你有
美好的一天。祝你好運！

【用「完美英語」寫文章⑥】

　　Dear fans, followers, and friends. Good evening!
I have great advice. Don't fear change. Change is
progress. Make a change. Change your attitude. Change
your mindset. Change your outlook. Change your
routine. Spread your wings. Pursue your happiness.
Pursue your passion. Pursue your ambitions boldly.
Change! Change yourself. Change for the better.
Change to succeed. Change to achieve. Change to better
your life. Change from bad to best. Change from all
right to awesome. Change, change, change, or you will
fail, fail, fail. Please sound off after me. Change
happens. Change improves. Change empowers. Change
inspires. Change motivates. Change rejuvenates.
Embrace change. Embrace progress. Embrace
innovation. Change is the name of the game.

　　親愛的粉絲、關注者，以及朋友們。晚安！我有很棒的
建議。不要害怕改變。改變是進步。要做出改變。改變你的
態度。改變你的心態。改變你的看法。改變你的慣例。展翅
高飛。追求你的幸福。追求你的愛好。大膽追求你的抱負。
要改變！改變自己。要變得更好。改變才會成功。改變才能
達成目標。改變才能改善你的生活。要從不好變成最好。要
從還好變成很棒。變、變、變，否則你就會失敗、失敗、失
敗。請和我一起呼口號。改變會發生。改變能進步。改變給
人力量。改變激勵人心。改變鼓舞人心。改變能恢復活力。
擁抱改變。擁抱進步。擁抱創新。改變非常重要。

【用「完美英語」寫文章⑦】

Face adversity with a smile. Weather the storms with a smile. Show resilience with a smile. Seek sunshine on cloudy days. Look for rainbows after rain. Focus on the sunny side. Smile through storms. Smile through challenges. Embrace the sun. See light ahead. See rainbows after. Hope illuminates shadows. Choose joy daily. Choose optimism daily. Positive vibes prevail. Challenge is everywhere. Opportunity is everywhere. Embrace the challenges. Look far. Look ahead. Look to the future. Conquer hardships. Conquer difficulties. Conquer doubt. Time tells. Time tests. You're a winner. The world needs your light. Keep shining bright. You're the one and only. Let's get busy. Let's get involved. Get determined. The tide will turn. Your day will come. You'll see the light at the end of the tunnel! Success will follow you.

笑對逆境。笑對風雨。笑展現韌性。陰天尋找陽光。雨後尋找彩虹。要專注於光明面。微笑面對風雨。微笑面對挑戰。要擁抱太陽。看見前方光明。看見雨後彩虹。希望照亮黑暗。每天選擇快樂。每天選擇樂觀。正能量獲勝。挑戰到處都有。機會到處都有。要樂於接受挑戰。要看得遠。要向前看。要放眼未來。克服艱辛。克服困難。克服懷疑。時間說明一切。時間考驗一切。你是贏家。這個世界需要你的光。要持續光輝燦爛。你是獨一無二。我們開始做吧。我們要積極參與。要有決心。形勢會轉變。你會飛黃騰達。你會看到光明的未來！成功將會跟隨著你。

【用「完美英語」寫文章⑧】

　　Good morning, everybody! Seeing you here is like a breath of fresh air. You make me feel like a million bucks. You're my light. You're my sunshine. You're my life. You light me up. You inspire me. You motivate me. You mean the world to me. With you, life is more amazing, awesome, and beautiful. I'm now offering help, support, knowledge, guidance, experience, expertise, and love. I'm willing to sacrifice. I enjoy being taken advantage of. To give is to receive. Pay more, get more. Pay less, get less. You get what you pay for. Remember and never forget. Give with joy. Give with love. Give with kindness. Give without counting. Give without remembering. Give without demand. Giving is profitable. Sharing is beneficial. Charity pays off. Generosity pays off. Unselfishness pays off. Love conquers all. Kindness pays. Kindness rewards. Kindness empowers. Kindness shines. Kindness radiates. Kindness helps. Kindness connects. Kindness unites. Let's unite. Let's cooperate. Let's all work together as one. United we stand, divided we fall.

　　大家早安！看到你們在這裡，就像是呼吸了一口新鮮的空氣。你們使我感覺很好。你們是我的光。你們是我的陽光。你們是我的生命。你們照亮了我，你們激勵了我。你們鼓舞了我。你們對我而言非常重要。有了你們，人生更精采、更棒，而且更美好。我現在願意提供幫助、支持、知識、指導、經驗、專業知識，以及真愛。我願意犧牲。我喜歡吃虧。有捨才有得。付出多，就得到多。付出少，就得到少。種瓜得瓜。要記得，絕對不要忘記。要高興地給。要充滿愛意地給。要充滿善意地給。付出不計。付出勿念。付出不求。付出有利。分享有益。慈善值得。慷慨值得。無私值得。愛能征服一切。善良回報。善良有償。善良有報。善良給人力量。善良發光。善良發亮。善良有幫助。善良增加人脈。善良促進團結。我們要團結。我們要合作。我們大家要團結一致。團結則立，分散則倒。

【用「完美英語」寫文章⑨】

Here's my advice. Make speaking Perfect English your #1 priority. Once you start speaking, the rest will be easy. Speak and write like crazy. Interact on this site like hell. Enjoy talking all day every day like there's no tomorrow. Your English will take off in no time. Besides, you're not just learning English. You're using English. You're spreading love, kindness, happiness, and positivity everywhere. You benefit most. You become a better you. You become beautiful, gorgeous, stunning—both inside and out. You shine like a star. You meet many wonderful people. Make true-blue friends. People are a good investment. Friendships bring happiness. Connections make you happy, healthy, wealthy, and wise. Your life is sweet, awesome, and precious. Your light shines brilliantly, gloriously, magically, marvelously, and magnificently. With liked-minded friends, you live passionately, gracefully, gratefully, and generously.

Let's embrace life.　Cherish every minute.　Savor every second.　Grasp every opportunity.　Relax and enjoy.　Throw a party.　Toast to happiness.

　　以下是我的建議。要把說「完美英語」列為第一優先。一旦你開始說，其他的就容易了。要拼命地說和寫。要拼命地在這個網站上互動。要喜歡每天拼命地說一整天。很快地，你的英文就會突飛猛進。此外，你不只是在學英文。你是在使用英文。你是在到處散播愛、善意、快樂，和正能量。你獲益最多。你會變得更好。你會變得內外皆美，非常漂亮，而且很迷人。你會像星星一樣閃耀。你會認識許多很棒的人。要結交忠實的朋友。人是一項很好的投資。友誼帶來快樂。人脈會使你快樂、健康、有錢，又聰明。你的人生很甜美、很棒，而且又珍貴。你會閃閃發光、耀眼發光、神奇發光、奇妙發光，並且壯麗發光。有了志同道合的朋友，你會熱情地活、優雅地活、感激地活，以及慷慨地活。我們要擁抱生命。珍惜每一分。品味每一秒。抓住每個機會。放鬆並享受。要舉辦派對。要為快樂而乾杯。

，

句子索引

A

B

C

句子索引

G

I

句子索引

句子索引

J

K

句子索引

句子索引

句子索引

關鍵字索引

關鍵字索引

關鍵字索引

關鍵字索引

關鍵字索引

英文二字經
Two-Word English Wisdom

附錄音 QR 碼 售價：990 元

主　　　編／劉　毅

發　行　所／學習出版有限公司
　　　　　　TEL (02) 2704-5525

郵　撥　帳　號／05127272 學習出版社帳戶

登　記　證／局版台業 2179 號

印　刷　所／裕強彩色印刷有限公司

台　北　門　市／台北市許昌街 17 號 6F
　　　　　　TEL (02) 2331-4060

台灣總經銷／紅螞蟻圖書有限公司
　　　　　　TEL (02) 2795-3656

本公司網址／www.learnbook.com.tw

電　子　郵　件／learnbook0928@gmail.com

2024 年 3 月 1 日初版

ISBN 978-986-231-496-8

啞巴英語造成許多人傷害！

你的發音真差！

　　太多社會精英，我苦說、勸說，就是不敢再碰英語！我的同學因為老師的一句話—「你的發音太差！」，終生失去信心。

　　「完美英語」讓你中英雙語，出口成章，句句金句。此時，你可以勸他們：

> *Be determined.* 你要有決心。
> *The tide will turn.* 情勢會轉變。
> *Your day will come.* 會飛黃騰達。

這樣三句，無與倫比，中英雙語，口吐蓮花，人人愛你。可以再接再勵說：

> *Win!* 必須要贏！
> *Be the winner.* 成為贏家。
> *Come out on top.* 出人頭地。

　　英文要使用才不會忘記。把這些金句印在杯子上，看到等於「使用」，我每天備課，都讓我心中澎湃不已。I'm a lucky dog. 我太幸福了。「董事長班」從一個開始教起，同學愈來愈多！

有同學問我如何賺錢？

太容易了！要賣「獨一無二」的產品。
以「完美英語神杯」為例：

1. 獨特產品：全世界沒有可以喝水，學英文，又轉遞正能量
   的杯子。我現在每天使用，我進步極大，心平氣和，每天快
   快樂樂，沒有煩惱。

2. 物超所值：我希望讓同學發大財！在台灣，頂級馬克杯，出
   廠價500元新台幣，但我們賣給「董事長班」同學，每個僅
   100元新台幣，或20元人民幣，讓同學轉賣，把「完美英
   語」廣為流傳下去。我們如何做到？經由百萬粉絲協助，找
   到大陸著名的工廠合作，以量取勝。

3. 「完美英語神杯」有靈魂，每次我用它喝水，像是上帝在跟
   我說：Be good.（做好人。）Do good.（做好事。）Say good.
   （說好話。）

   全班50位同學，每人有不同的馬克杯，不知不覺，大家都
變成好朋友，好人，有禮貌，體貼，每位同學都會「中英雙語，
出口成章，句句金句」！

   由台灣出發，擴散至全球，大家喜歡說「完美英語」，家
家無爭吵，世界沒戰爭，這是我一生的願望。

> ***Change the world.*** 改變世界。
> ***Make a difference.*** 產生影響。
> ***Make it a better place.*** 讓世界更好。

說「完美英語」像是喝咖啡

　　我今天偶遇一位自稱華裔美國人，天生雙語。我問他「立德，立功，立言」怎麼說？「做好人，做好事，說好話」怎麼說？他說了半天，我說：Be good. Do good. Say good. 一般人只會說：Be a good person. Do good things. Say good words. 所以，「完美英語」所向無敵！

　　我現在提倡「中英文雙語，出口成章，句句金句」，一旦習慣說，便會上癮！像我就已經著迷，編輯「完美英語」著迷、說和教「完美英語」，像是喝了咖啡，非常有精神！例如，和別人道謝，只說Thanks. 和Thank you! 不夠熱情，不如說：

> ***Many thanks.*** 多謝多謝。
> ***I appreciate it.*** 我很感激。
> ***I owe you big.*** 欠你很多。

　　自己愈說，愈進步，自己受益最大！我們將陸續製作「完美英語神杯」，大家自然而然喜歡說「完美英語＋完美中文」，每天口吐金句，財源滾滾，財富自來，健康痛快過一生！

我到80歲才學會

「劉毅董事長英語班」同學餐費，由200元新台幣，提高至1,500元。「劉毅英文」員工午餐餐費，由200元增加到400元，每週一1,000元。「師訓」餐費由200元提高至1,500元，熱情款待每個人。

我受到「英文三字經」潛移默化的影響。

> *Generosity changes life.*
> 慷慨改變人生。
> *Generosity inspires generosity.*
> 慷慨激發慷慨。
> *Generosity promotes unity.*
> 慷慨促進團結。

對人慷慨，自己最受益，員工上班更努力，朋友、學生愈來愈多！

> *Generosity pays off.*
> 慷慨會得到回報。
> *Selflessness pays off.*
> 無私會得到回報。
> *Kindness is always worth it.*
> 善良一定划得來。

一般人喜歡佔小便宜，人人離開他，結果終生窮困潦倒！我絕對不會讓我身旁的人吃虧！吃虧就是佔便宜。（The best gain is to lose.）我喜歡幫人成功。（Help others succeed.）

魚翅大王吳昌林，在我們一樓開私廚料理，我租給別人29萬台幣，只租他23萬，而且我已經花費100多萬元餐費。他也投桃報李，400元員工餐吃到1,000元，1,500元吃到價值4,500元大套餐，這樣人生不是很美嗎？

我以前年輕不懂事，歡迎所有的老員工回家一敘，讓我有機會補償一下！